PRAISE FOR HOMELESS

"*My Heart Belongs in an Empty Big Mac Container Buried Beneath the Ocean Floor* is a miserere of grease-soaked depression 2,100 fathoms deep. Surreal and achingly vulnerable. Anyone who has sat paralyzed in the darkest fathoms of human emotion will find this book unsettlingly relatable, and maybe even a little hopeful. Homeless took the kind of desperation that leads you to the point of no return and created something beautiful."

—ALAN TEN-HOEVE, AUTHOR OF *NOTES FROM A WOOD-PANELED BASEMENT*

"*My Heart Belongs in an Empty Big Mac Container Buried Beneath the Ocean Floor* is a wildly fantastical coming-of-late-age nautical romp by a mysterious New York-based weirdo named Homeless, who I've championed for years, and he's at the top of his literary powers here, picking up where subversive authors like Donald Barthelme, James Purdy and Mark Leyner have gloriously treaded before, adding a dripping slice of post-Millennial anxiety into a touching and humorous examination of a not-so-random American life riddled in classic existential turmoil—a triumph of the sub-human soul."

—BRIAN ALAN ELLIS, AUTHOR OF *HOBBIES YOU ENJOY*

MY HEART BELONGS IN AN EMPTY BIG MAC CONTAINER BURIED BENEATH THE OCEAN FLOOR

Cover by Matthew Revert

ISBN: 9781960988379

CLASH Books

Troy, NY

clashbooks.com

For everyone
everywhere
seeing the sad-looking blue whales...

MY HEART BELONGS IN AN EMPTY BIG MAC CONTAINER BURIED BENEATH THE OCEAN FLOOR

A NOVEL BY

HOMELESS

PART 1

"DANIEL, *it's me. Please call me back as soon as you get this, okay? It's an emergency and I really need to talk to you. Please. Call me...*"

GREASY, CARDBOARD HEART-COFFIN

A SMALL, bright-orange boat floats in the ocean, bobbing up and down like a Cheez-It in the deep end of God's swimming pool.

A young man, Daniel—thirty-one-years-old, buzzed head, eyes like boarded up windows, and a beard longer and more disgruntled than a Civil War general's—sits at one end of the motorless boat. A six-foot-tall blue whale wearing a fanny pack who looks like he's just finished watching *Titanic* sits at the other.

"I'm never going to see Laura again," Daniel says out of nowhere, his tone of voice sounding the way the sad-looking blue whale looks.

"I'm never going to finish my novel," the sad-looking blue whale says, his tone of voice also sounding the way he looks.

"You're writing a novel?"

The sad-looking blue whale nods. Even his nod is sad-looking and looks like it just finished watching *Titanic.*

"What's it about?" Daniel asks.

"It's so hot," the sad-looking blue whale says as he looks up at the sun and wipes sweat from his forehead. "Sorry. What'd you say?"

"Your novel," Daniel says. "What's it about?"

"Oh..." the sad-looking blue whale says, then pauses and thinks, or pauses and pretends to think, Daniel isn't sure.

"I dunno. It's about nothing, really," the sad-looking blue whale says, intentionally staring down at the boat's floor as if trying to punctuate the end of this novel-geared conversation by purposefully severing eye contact with Daniel, leaving Daniel to momentarily feel bad, as if he embarrassed the sad-looking blue whale by asking him about his novel.

"Sorry," Daniel says. "I hate when people ask me what my novel's about. Ya know... whenever I let it slip I'm working on one."

"It's okay," the sad-looking blue whale says. And then, after a little while, "The frailty of life... If I had to say my novel was about something, I guess I'd say it's about that."

"Hmm..." Daniel says. "When I was eleven, I wrote a novel—the only one I ever finished—and the protagonist was a fart contemplating its brief mortality. It was over eight-hundred pages long."

"*Passing Gas,*" Daniel adds. "That was the title of it... *Passing Gas.*"

"Our books sound very different," the sad-looking blue whale says.

Daniel nods even though he disagrees with the sad-looking blue whale.

To Daniel, it sounds like their novels could be brothers.

"Are you sure you don't know how to swim?" Daniel asks the sad-looking blue whale as he looks over the ocean, examining the water that's beginning to take on a mesmerizing, Lindy-Hopping quality.

"I'm a sad-looking blue whale," the sad-looking blue whale says. "None of us know how to swim.

Daniel vaguely nods.

"Too sad to have ever learned," the sad-looking blue whale elaborates.

"Too busy watching *Titanic,*" the sad-looking blue whale elaborates even further.

"I liked the part where she showed her breasts," Daniel says hypnotically, now staring out across the ocean as if trying to transform the water into something more exciting to look at, like an entire ocean made out of Kate Winslet breasts bobbing up and down, jiggling, all of her breasts—thousands upon thousands of them—singing with soft, soothing, fluent motions, harmonizing with one another, lulling Daniel and the sad-looking blue whale to sleep with their song of the ocean as the sun tucks them in with its unending, pile-driving heat.

"I liked all the sad parts. Her breasts were nice and all I guess, but they just weren't sad-looking enough for my taste," the sad-looking blue whale says as he wipes more sweat from his glossy head. "Maybe if they looked more like that one shot where the elderly husband and wife were lying in bed and holding each other as water flooded into their room. Then I probably would've enjoyed looking at her breasts more."

"Breast stroke..." Daniel accidentally mutters out loud, imagining himself swimming in an ocean of Kate Winslet-breasts.

"What?" the sad-looking blue whale asks.

"I think the heat's starting to get to me," Daniel says as he furrows his brow, really feeling the sunburn on his forehead for the first time.

Sunburn... says Daniel's brain.

Kate Winslet's breasts...

Kate Winslet's sunburned breasts...

Laura's sunburned breasts...

Rubbing aloe on Laura's big, natural, sunburned breasts...

Applying aloe softly, lovingly...

Rubbing it all over...

Rubbing it underneath her breasts "just to be thorough..."

"Thank you, bay-bee. You're such a good man..."

Putting the cap back on the aloe and staring at Laura's sunburned breasts...

Like two flaming zeppelins slowly going down, screaming, milky and beautiful...

KA-BOOM!

KA-BOOM!

"You okay?" the sad-looking blue whale asks, his question extinguishing the flaming carcasses of Laura's zeppelin-breasts in Daniel's head.

"Yeah," Daniel answers, unsure of how long he's been spaced out. "Why?"

The sad-looking blue whale shrugs.

"You just looked different all of a sudden."

"Different?"

"Yeah," the sad-looking blue whale says, then squints, peering further into Daniel's eyes. "Like you had two charred Hindenburgs in your head or something."

Embarrassed, Daniel looks away. The sad-looking blue whale turns his attention to the empty Big Mac container on the boat's floor, sitting in-between him and Daniel like a small and unusual campfire just beginning to smolder.

"He still not talking to you?" the sad-looking blue whale asks.

Daniel looks down at the empty Big Mac container and shakes his head.

"You'll hear him when he does. And see it too. His lid flaps up and down. Like this."

Daniel puts his elbows together and makes his arms flap up and down, imitating the empty Big Mac container's lid whenever it talks to him. Not knowing what to say, or having nothing to say, the sad-looking blue whale kind of nods.

"What? You don't believe me?" Daniel says, his tone of voice suddenly becoming mildly aggressive and threatening, like a maliciously pointed spork.

"I never said that," the sad-looking blue whale says.

"I'm not crazy. He's just pissed at me right now so he's not talking to me. And I can't really blame him either."

As if having nothing more to say on the matter, the sad-looking blue whale fixes his attention on the horizon. Daniel sighs. He leans over and presses the play button on the small round boombox beside him but, as expected, it makes the same, dull, lifeless click as the last time he pressed it. Daniel leans back in his seat, sighs again.

"You should've double checked," the sad-looking blue whale says. "Made sure the batteries were still good."

"You were the one who brought the boombox," Daniel says, bludgeoning the sad-looking blue whale over the head with a dull and pained look of utter incredulousness.

"Oh… Yeah…" the sad-looking blue whale says.

"You still think they'll be able to find us anyway? Ya know, without the song playing?"

"Maybe."

"Really?"

"But probably not," the sad-looking blue whale admits.

Feeling defeated, Daniel holds his face in his hands and rests his elbows on his knees. The sun screams at the back of his neck like Robert Plant if Robert Plant had vocal cords made of plasma.

"I'm sorry I got you into this," Daniel says through his hands. "I dunno… Maybe this was all just one big mistake."

The sad-looking blue whale doesn't respond, and when Daniel looks up at him something about the sad-looking blue whale seems to flicker and shake, like the screen of a paused VHS tape trying to hold a frame in place.

Like the screen of a paused Titanic *VHS tape trying to hold a frame in place...* says Daniel's brain.

Titanic...

Titanic *on VHS...*

Kate Winslet...

Kate Winslet's breasts on VHS...

Laura's breasts on VHS...

Laura's breasts on VHS are even better than Kate Winslet's breasts in HD...

Laura...

Laura, Laura, Laura...

Say her name three times out loud and maybe she'll appear like Beetlejuice...

"I need to tell you something. Something I should've told you before we left. But, I dunno... I just wasn't sure how to tell you," the sad-looking blue whale says.

"Okay..."

"Your heart... you want to bury it, right?"

Daniel nods.

"Beneath the ocean floor?"

Daniel nods again.

"Okay. And I'm going to help you do that. Well, I mean we. *We're* going to help you do that. Me and the sad-looking blue whales back home."

"Back home?"

"Yeah. In our underwater kingdom. It's like a big snow globe on the ocean floor. But minus the water and snow. And with a lot more *Titanic* statues and monuments."

Too fried from the unrelenting, bully-like sun to begin to understand what the sad-looking blue whale is trying to say to him, Daniel stares down at the empty Big Mac container, focusing on the grease spot on its top.

It's shaped like Sweden... says Daniel's brain even though Daniel's brain has no idea what Sweden is shaped like, nor could it find Sweden on a map in under fifteen seconds if someone held a gun to his head.

Sweden... says Daniel's brain.

Sweden, Sweden, Sweden...

Say the country's name three times out loud and maybe you'll appear there...

"You're The Chosen One," the sad-looking blue whale says to Daniel. "I guess that's what I'm trying to get at."

The Chosen One... Daniel's brain echoes with a delirious pride, momentarily making him feel special and unique, reminding him of a time back in fifth grade when his teacher, Mrs. Burke, read a short story Daniel wrote for English class and then told him, "You have a very special creative talent you're going to do great things with someday." The next day, truly inspired for, perhaps, the first time in his short life, Daniel wrote the first twenty pages of his epic tome, *"Passing Gas."*

"Laura, Laura, Laura..." Daniel says under his breath, but to his disappointment, although not his surprise, Laura doesn't appear, and the bright-orange boat just continues apolitically bobbing up and down in the water, leaving Daniel and the sad-looking blue whale to do nothing but, most likely, wait for a slow-roasting, pointless death.

IT'S A HORRIBLE LIFE

AFTER LAURA, the days were long and filled with even more sad-looking blue whales than usual. The rooms of Daniel's house became packed like subway cars during rush hour, often leaving him warm, uncomfortable and unable to move, not to mention so crowded with sadness he could barely even lift his hand up high enough to scratch his nose. And every time Daniel looked out a window, regardless of the time of day, the sky was always wet-looking and gray and, or so Daniel thought at least, seemed gradually approaching, like it was calculatedly moving in on him—an insanely focused assassin coming to smother him with its grayness until he suffocated. And rather than do anything about all this (*What* is *there to do?* was the question Daniel's brain kept rhetorically asking), Daniel just accepted his current situation. He knew he could only wait it out and hope for the assassin-sky to either change its mind or grow lazy and apathetic over killing him because, seeing him helplessly pinned down by sad-looking blue whales, there would be no sport or challenge in removing the speck that was Daniel from this world, and so, instead, it would just leave him be. Then Daniel, with nothing else to do, would do all he could do—wait for some of the sad-looking blue whales to eventually wander out of his house on their own, as if bored or suddenly remembering they wanted to watch *Titanic* again.

And so the days passed like gravestones made of mud slowly toppling into each other, forcing Daniel to eventually call out of work one morning about three and a half months after he and Laura had broken up. Even though they were no longer together, Daniel could still hear Laura getting mad at him. "You really think you can afford to call out of work? What? You want to be *homeless* someday?" Which always left Daniel feeling guilty (although over what exactly he didn't know), as well as incapable of taking care of himself, of being an adult and forcing himself to do things he didn't want to do.

Daniel did what he always did whenever he had a day off—he drove to his Graceland, his fast-food office, his Golden Arched home away from home.

Daniel drove to McDonald's.

Or *his* McDonald's, as he often referred to it.

Christian rock was playing from the speakers hidden in the ceiling when Daniel walked inside (for whatever reason this was the radio station management had decided to tune into for the past month). The nice Spanish lady working the register who knew Daniel by name already had his order punched in before he reached the counter. Daniel smiled, said thank you, paid for his iced coffee with exact change, feeling embarrassed as he did so, feeling poor as he did so—even though Daniel was poor, more so just feeling ashamed of it, really—and then grabbed his usual seat in the far back corner of the restaurant as far away from the gossipy elder patrons who frequented the restaurant as well.

Daniel took his notebook out of his messenger bag and opened to a blank page. Daniel was a writer who did the vast majority of his writing in McDonald's because McDonald's was the one place in the entire world where sad-looking blue whales didn't stalk him. Any McDonald's. The location never mattered. For whatever reason, the sad-looking blue whales refused to follow him inside. Instead, they'd stand by the front door and patiently wait for Daniel to return. And when it was time for Daniel to leave, the sad-looking blue whales picked up where they left off. They'd trail Daniel back to his car, ride shotgun, or sometimes, and which Daniel found even more humiliating and degrading, the sad-looking blue whales would sit in the back and Daniel would chauffeur them around. They controlled Daniel, the sad-looking blue whales, and as much as it killed him to admit it, although over the years he had gotten used to doing so (not that that made it sting any less), the sad-looking blue whales dictated almost everything he did.

Sometimes it was simply their laid back yet imposing presence that made Daniel do certain things, or feel certain things, or think certain things. Other times just a meager look from their lifeless black eyes, eyes like pieces of coal dropped in a murky street puddle. But most of the time, and which Daniel found to be the absolute worst, the sad-looking blue whales controlled him by crying.

"Oooooh, oooh, ooh!"

Although Daniel had heard hundreds of thousands of sad-looking blue whale cries throughout his life, it was something he'd never gotten used to, and now, at this point—thirty-one-years-old and not getting any younger—he knew he never would. Daniel didn't understand their crying, especially considering there never seemed to be any rhyme or reason to it. At least not that Daniel was ever able to figure out.

A lot of the time the crying felt random, but also directed at other sad-looking blue whales even if there weren't any present. And during these frequent impromptu studio sessions of their own sad, sappy music, mainly consisting of just one sad-looking blue whale but it also not being impossible during the really bad days for there to be almost an entire choir of them, it became impossible for Daniel to feel content in his own skin. Something about their cries brought to the surface the quiet, subterranean knowledge of how innately alone Daniel was, of how alone all humans were, of the underlying facts that most people who weren't stalked by sad-looking blue whales were usually able to forget about or just completely ignore—that each of us comes into this world alone and that each of us leaves it alone, that each of us is trapped inside one human body with one conscious mind that no other person will ever be able to physically step inside of and, therefore, fully understand. And that, Daniel understood, was true loneliness—your weak and lame human brain being unable to perfectly articulate what it thinks, your mind being unable to form something vague and sharp inside of you into words for the world to comprehend. But the sad-looking blue whales had found words for it. Or maybe not words, but sounds. Sounds that said more about sadness and loneliness than any human language ever would.

"Oooooh, ooooh, ooh!"

Daniel had no idea what the sad-looking blue whales were saying exactly when they cried to each other, but his mind always translated it into "I'm alone! I'm alone! I'm alone!" And when it was late at night and Daniel was lying in bed with his cats and listening to the sad-looking blue whales cry outside his window like lonely wolves howling at a moon that had forgotten all about them, Daniel would always call back to them in his head, softly, mournfully, *Me too… Me too… Me too…*

Daniel took his pen out of his pocket, his favorite pen—a Simpsons pen Laura had bought him, momentarily making him ache for her like his heart had blue balls. He stared down at the blank pages of his notebook, at the cruel, goring whiteness of them, but nothing remotely creative came to mind. Ever since Laura left, Daniel's brain had become immobile, like a dead car with its license plates ripped off, left on the street for the city to tow. He couldn't write, he couldn't draw, and these two things he once looked forward to doing now just seemed to scare and intimidate him because, being unable to do both, these activities only made him feel worse about himself, which, therefore, only summoned even more sad-looking blue whales.

Daniel gave up on the idea of writing for the moment, took his headphones out of his messenger bag and plugged them into his iPhone. Daniel played the song "Careless Soul" by Daniel Johnston and put it on repeat. It was a live track and sounded like it was recorded in a coffee shop or bookstore. A girl could be heard coughing at one point and Daniel Johnston broke into tears twice during the track. There were no instruments. Just Daniel Johnston singing about being called to meet your God.

Daniel Johnston is Christian rock… Daniel's brain said.

Daniel non-Johnson laughed at himself. He felt sick and hated himself. He still loved Daniel Johnston, though. Daniel Johnston was certifiable but brilliant. Daniel Johnston loved Mountain Dew and McDonald's. Daniel Johnston even worked in a McDonald's. Daniel non-Johnston never worked in a McDonald's. He'd worked at a golf course, the video department of his college, a Michael's Arts & Crafts, a Home Depot, two doggie daycares and three animal hospitals. Now, Daniel non-Johnston worked in the stock room of a PR agency that represented beauty products. The stock room was warm, cramped, had no windows and was filled with sad-looking blue whales that were extra sad-looking and invasive. But since only Daniel could see the sad-looking blue whales, it was as if they didn't exist to the rest of the world. So, bitterly, as well as half-heartedly, Daniel was forced to go through day after day as if nothing were wrong, as if he were completely and totally healthy, all the while still being foolishly expected to travel the same speed as everyone else in the normal world even though he was carrying an extra couple hundred tons of sad-looking blue whale dead weight.

This is bullshit… Daniel's mind would often complain to itself throughout the course of his day at his dead end job, and then allow itself to feel momentarily good, justified in its own righteousness, knowing that, yes, this indeed was bullshit, a mass amount of it, ripe, stinking and unfair, but then the same recollection would always inevitably creep back in shortly thereafter. That life wasn't supposed to be fair, that everyone had their own metaphorical crosses to bear, and that this one, enormous and heavier than most with a sad-looking blue whale nailed to it who cried *"Oooh, ooh, oooh!"* was unwaveringly his. And there was no trading it for another. There was no putting this cross down and resting, and Daniel's mind, happy just seconds ago in the brief victory of knowing that it was right, that this curse of his was, again, in fact, bullshit, Daniel's mind would then return to its usual damp and sullen state. He would drag himself through the day as best he could, often too frustrated and tired to care how well he was doing, just wanting nothing more than to make it to the finish line where, at the very end of the day, a box of wine was chilling in the fridge at home, waiting for him.

Knock, knock, knock...

Daniel took his headphones off and looked behind him. Uncharacteristically, a sad-looking blue whale was at the back door of McDonald's, pointing down at the handle as if asking Daniel to open it even though the door wasn't locked.

Daniel hesitated. Not because he was actually contemplating letting the sad-looking blue whale inside, but rather because he had never seen their kind exhibit this unusually nosy behavior outside of a McDonald's before.

Daniel turned away. He picked up his Simpsons pen and stared down at his notebook, ready to work.

The sad-looking blue whale could go fuck itself.

BAYYYBEE!!!

LAURA AND DANIEL'S first date was at Laura's house. Laura wore a navy-blue dress with sunflowers on it and went barefoot. She decanted red wine. On his way over, Daniel picked up a large pizza but, because of first date nerves, neither of them ended up having more than a slice. Laura seemed especially nervous and acted slightly erratic, or manic, Daniel thought, like at one point during the beginning of the date when she said, "Wait, hold on," then grabbed some Visine off her glass coffee table and lay down on her bed in the middle of her living room.

"My bed frame wouldn't fit upstairs," she explained as she put eye drops in.

Laura remained on her bed, letting the drops do their work, her hands folded over her stomach like a corpse at a wake. Daniel sat on the couch and sipped wine just to have something to do while this pretty girl stared up at the ceiling with her eyes bugged open, occasionally blinking in a Morse code type of pattern, as if communicating to another girl on a faraway planet who was doing the exact same thing.

When Laura sat back down beside Daniel she apologized. She admitted she was nervous and that she'd smoked a little weed before Daniel came over to calm her nerves. She said she hoped he didn't mind. Daniel laughed and told her he didn't. Then Laura said, "Candles... We need to light more candles."

Laura stood up, stormed off and found her lighter and some more candles. As she walked around the open-spaced bottom floor of her house, lighting candles and talking vaguely about the candles she was lighting, almost like some weird candle salesperson you end up buying candles from not because she's a good salesman but because you enjoy her frantic charm, Daniel didn't feel awkward anymore.

Who the fuck does this? his brain kept repeating as he watched Laura move around, possessed by some kind of self-taught frenzied magic. She made Daniel excited, like she could make him see things he'd never seen before. Even something as simple as a girl running off in the middle of conversation, lying on her bed and putting Visine in her eyes. It didn't matter to Daniel, really. He just wanted his eyes opened to things no one had ever seen before, or things rarely seen. Daniel wasn't good at seeing things like this himself. He needed help, and Laura, he thought, could very well potentially be that help—beautiful, blonde-haired help with big breasts and cute feet and lazily brushed messy hair that was trying it's best not to look messy.

Daniel and Laura spent the majority of the night talking and drinking wine. Then Laura played some music and they got closer together on the couch.

"You don't mind me sitting close?" Daniel asked with a smile, knowing Laura didn't mind at all.

"You can't rape the willing," Laura replied with a smile and drained the rest of her wine.

The night ended with Daniel and Laura semi-drunkenly crawling into bed together. Daniel performed horribly and couldn't make her cum, leaving himself to feel ashamed and disappointed. It wasn't until the next morning when they had sex again that Daniel made Laura cum for the first time. Her "O face" made Daniel think of a bug zapper that a bluebird had accidentally flown into, which, oddly enough, turned him on. So much so, Daniel quickly pulled out and came all over Laura's pubic hair and stomach, the small spurts of liquid machine gunfire making Laura smile. Daniel collapsed onto the bed and Laura nestled herself into his arm without cleaning herself off.

"I liked the dress you wore last night," Daniel said to Laura after a while, which he did, even though there was nothing particularly special about it. He just liked the dress so much because she'd been in it.

"Yeah?" Laura said. "I went crazy trying to figure out what to wear. God, girls are so stupid like that. Do you smoke?"

Daniel shook his head.

"Do you mind if I do?"

Daniel shook his head again.

"Good. I love a smoke after good sex."

Laura grabbed a light blue pack of American Spirits off her night table. She and Daniel put on clothes, grabbed their coats and went and sat on the front steps of her house. It was chilly out and the sky looked bi-polar, like it couldn't tell if it wanted to be gray or blue, like it couldn't decide if it wanted to hate itself or love itself.

"I love smoking but I don't want the stink in my house," Laura said. "You want one?"

Daniel hesitated, then said, "Sure."

"You don't have to."

"I know."

Daniel and Laura both lit their cigarettes. Daniel coughed after his first drag and Laura laughed at him.

"Stupid, healthy pink lungs," she said.

Daniel laughed and coughed at the same time. Laura inched closer to him and Daniel felt excited over her increased proximity.

"You're the first non-smoker guy I've dated who's hasn't been all like, 'You should quit.'"

"You really should, though."

Laura blew a huge plume of smoke.

"I know. Maybe you can help. Like if you see me smoking or hear me say I want to smoke I give you permission to punch me in the face."

"Hm… How about in the tit instead?"

"Haha, okay. Deal."

"Let's make a contract, though. To protect me from a lawsuit and possible jail time for when I inevitably punch you square in the tit."

"Alright," Laura said. "One sec."

Laura went inside. Left alone, Daniel tried taking another drag. He failed and began coughing uncontrollably. Just as he finished clearing his throat, Laura came back with a pen and yellow legal pad that she handed to Daniel. Daniel put the legal pad down on the top step and began writing.

"Oh my god. Your handwriting is so neat. You write like a fucking girl.

"Fuck off," Daniel said. "And stop looking."

Laura looked away and took another drag. A few seconds later, Daniel finished writing the contract and handed it to Laura for her to read.

I, Laura, hereby give my permission to Daniel, who will henceforth be referred to as Studly McRamrod, to punch me square in the tit, either left or right, as to be decided by Mr. McRamrod at the time of said tit punching, if he ever catches me smoking or so much as hears me talking about smoking. A-tit-punch, babyyy!

"Studly McRamrod?" Laura said after she finished reading.

Daniel raised his eyebrows up and down like Groucho Marx.

"I heard the last sentence in the voice of Fred Schneider from the B-52's," Laura said.

"Haha, yes. Exactly."

"Really?"

"Yeah. Alright, now we both just need to sign."

Daniel handed Laura the pen and she signed her name. Daniel signed it Studly McRamrod and then signed his real name underneath in parentheses.

"We need to put this someplace where I'll see it a lot," Laura said.

"Tape it above the door knob of your front door. So every time you leave your house you're reminded your tits are in danger if I catch you smoking."

"Okay," Laura said and flicked her cigarette into the gravel of her driveway. "Come on."

Daniel did the same and followed Laura inside. Laura got some Scotch tape and taped their contract on the front door. Then they both stood back and looked at it.

"I feel good about this," Laura said.

"Yeah," Daniel said, smiling. "Me too."

GREASY, CARDBOARD HEART-COFFIN

WITH WAVES ROCKING the bright-orange boat as gently as a lite FM radio station, the sad-looking blue whale, lulled by their smooth and lush hits of today (brought to him commercial free by that big saline body of water they call the ocean), is busy trying his best not to fall asleep sitting up. Daniel, however, despite being sun bleached of nearly all his energy, is wide awake.

The Chosen One... Daniel's mind utters as he stares trance-like at the empty Big Mac container.

Daniel's eyes are so honed in on the empty Big Mac container he looks like he's trying to communicate telepathically with the soon-to-be greasy, cardboard heart-coffin, as if he's asking its thoughts on all of this "Chosen One" business and expecting an answer. But if the empty Big Mac container is giving Daniel the silent treatment verbally, which it very well seems to be, then it's giving him the silent treatment telepathically as well. The empty Big Mac container returns absolutely no thoughts to Daniel. Not even a mundane one it just so happens to be casually mumbling to itself like, *"Holy shit, it's hot out here even for a small, cardboard box,"* forcing Daniel to give up, forcing him to look at the sad-looking blue whale just in time to see his head droop forward then quickly snap back up in an attempt to stay awake.

"Hey," Daniel says.

The sad-looking blue whale throws Daniel a bland, rice cake-expression of attention with his eyes.

"I've never been a Chosen One before. What does that entail exactly?"

The sad-looking blue whale fidgets in his seat, trying not only to stay awake but also find enough energy to reply to this question he seems to have no real interest in actually answering.

"Um… It means you and only you can save us sad-looking blue whales," the sad-looking blue whale says after adjusting himself. "Or should I say your heart. Only your heart can save us. Because, ya know… of how extremely sad-looking it is."

Daniel pauses contemplatively.

"But you can't see it."

"Sometimes I can. Just by looking into your eyes. They get a certain black glaze in them every once and a while. It's a lot like looking through a dark but recently Windex'ed window with night-vision goggles."

Self-conscious, Daniel glances away, his averted eyes suddenly looking damper than summer camp armpits.

"That's it," the sad-looking blue whale says almost jovially, or as jovially as a sad-looking blue whale who looks like he just finished watching *Titanic* can sound. Either way it seems to wake him up a little. "That's the look in your eyes right there. The one that lets me see how sad-looking your heart is."

"That look…" Daniel's brain says, but not in its own voice. It's another voice. One doing a spot-on impression of a person Daniel has spent a lot of energy trying not to think about over the past few years.

With that person now spotlighted front and center on the warped, uneven stage of his mind, forcing his mood to droop and sag even further than a bra-less pair of eighty-year-old breasts, Daniel slumps back into his seat. Feeling maudlin and introspective (or perhaps just self-destructive), Daniel, with a slouched and reckless despondency, recalls his mother, and somewhere, most likely on some dusty mantel in London, Daniel can feel Freud's ashes proudly swirling in their urn.

"That look…" his mom's voice repeats as Daniel's mind begins wandering.

"That goddamn look…"

Daniel was eleven or so. School was almost out and he was eagerly awaiting a phone call from his best friend, Stephen. Stephen and Daniel had met in pre-school and, despite having been in different schools ever since then, had managed to remain best friends. Stephen's family was rich. His grandfather owned a high-end sporting goods store in the center of Darien, Connecticut where Stephen's dad worked, and every summer, for the past four years, Stephen invited Daniel to go with him and his mom and his dad to Ocean City, New Jersey for a week.

Daniel loved going on vacation with the Zangrillos. Considering his own family never really had the money to go anywhere, Ocean City was always the highlight of Daniel's year. The Zangrillos rented a beach house close to the water and during the day they'd all schlep to the beach for lounging, boogie boarding and games. Then, at night, all four of them would go out to dinner and usually spend the remainder of the evening on the boardwalk. Every moment was dedicated to relaxing and having fun, and Stephen's mom and dad, knowing Stephen and Daniel had reached an age of maturity where they could take care of themselves—at least for a couple of hours without getting into trouble or being abducted, as well as probably wanting some time alone themselves—often let Stephen and Daniel venture out on their own, which was Daniel's first real taste of independence. He and Stephen would go mini-golfing, or to the movies, or sometimes, at the suggestion of Daniel's raging hormones, they'd wear sunglasses and go for walks up and down the shore while checking out women from behind the protection of their shades. Women that neither of them ever would've had the balls to talk to.

Daniel waited patiently that summer but the call from Stephen never came. Daniel was upset and disappointed but not angry. The Zangrillos had already done so much for him. They already spent so much money on him throughout the course of his friendship with their son, and Daniel just figured, for whatever reason, the Zangrillos couldn't afford to go to Ocean City that year. A few months later, when Daniel was at ends with his mother, although when wasn't he at ends with his mother, Daniel's mom snapped at him in a way she never had before, suddenly becoming vindictive and mean.

"You and that *look!*" she yelled at Daniel. "I'm so sick of seeing that *look* on your face every day. Your father and I do everything we can for you. We try to give you everything we never had and yet you still always look so goddamn miserable. It's so gloomy to be around. And you know what? You know why the Zangrillos didn't ask you to Ocean City last year? Mrs. Zangrillo called me and, on the verge of tears, she explained that they all love you so much but no matter what you guys did, no matter how much fun they tried to have, that you always just looked so goddamn miserable. And she said they were sorry, but that her and Mr. Z only have one vacation a year and they didn't want to spend it worrying if you were having a good time or not. That *look*, Daniel! You've gotta do something about that goddamn *look*..."

As his mom continued on, hundreds of thoughts tried to Three Stooges their way through the tiny, compact door into Daniel's mind. He didn't understand. He always had so much fun in Ocean City. He always felt so happy there. It just didn't make sense, so Daniel's first instinct was to believe his mom was lying. But although Daniel and his mom never got along, he knew she wasn't a liar. She was telling the truth. Still, Daniel couldn't process it, and so he walked away from his mom while she was still talking to him and went upstairs to his bedroom.

When Daniel opened the door to his room, he found a sad-looking blue whale as tall as his dad sitting on his bed. The sad-looking blue whale had its fins folded casually over its lap and stared at Daniel almost as if it'd been waiting for him. Even though Daniel had never seen a sad-looking blue whale close up before, he didn't feel scared. He didn't feel surprised or confused. He just stared back at the sad-looking blue whale, waiting for it to do something.

"Oooh, ooh, ooooh!" the sad-looking blue whale eventually cried.

And then, somewhere deep in his gut, Daniel felt the presence of a small, gift-wrapped blue box he'd never noticed before.

"Oooh, oooooooh!" the sad-looking blue whale cried, and then Daniel felt the ribbon untie itself and the top lift off the box.

"Ooooooooooooh!" the sad-looking blue whale cried again, and a warm, salty mist shot out of the box, alighting all over Daniel's insides. And just like that Daniel knew that he was different. For the first time ever, he knew there was something wrong with him ("That *look*, Daniel! That goddamn *look!*"). He wasn't sure what was wrong exactly, but he still felt the severity of it. He knew, whatever it was (*This wrongness*... his brain momentarily called it as it reached for a name), that it was heavy, and what was worse, that it would linger. That it would be with him for the rest of his life. That it was just as permanent as the color of his eyes and the shape of his slightly disproportioned head.

The sad-looking blue whale stood up from Daniel's bed, leaving a big, wet ass-print on the comforter.

"Oooooh, ooh, ooooh!" it cried, and left.

Daniel walked over to his mirror and he saw it. The look his mom was talking about. The look that prevented him from going on vacation with the Zangrillos. The look that would someday prevent women from ever coming up and talking to him. The look that, years and years later, one of his co-workers would describe as, "...just like Jack Nicholson from *The Shining*."

It was sad and miserable.

It was hopeless and defeated.

It was like looking into a collapsed mineshaft.

And Daniel hated it.

He tried smiling as he looked at himself in the mirror, but even after his best efforts, his face still looked despondently the same.

Daniel walked over to his bed and lay down. He stared up at the popcorn ceiling. A ceiling he would stare up at a thousand more times, feeling just as lost, cheated and helpless.

"That look..." Daniel hears his mom say, echoing all the way from his scarring past and into the present where he's lost at sea with the sad-looking blue whale.

"That goddamn look..."

Daniel rubs his face with his hands as if trying to thoroughly massage "that look" clean off it. Once he's done, he leans over the side of the boat and rinses his hands in the ocean, making sure there's no trace of "that look" left even on his fingers.

The water, sparkling like highly intoxicated aqua diamonds, sparkling like Laura's eyes, is cool and refreshing (*Also like Laura's eyes...*). Daniel impulsively splashes his face and sits up, letting the water run down his face and drip onto his beard and clothes. Momentarily relaxed and refreshed, he tilts his head back, closes his eyes and allows the sun to sadistically grin at him like the sick, flaming bastard it is.

"My mom saw sad-looking blue whales too," Daniel suddenly finds himself saying, hearing this sentence, this admission, not as if he just said it himself but more as some sort of spectator, as if he momentarily left his body and began floating above the bright-orange boat just in time to hear that other version of himself, that empty shell version of himself, even emptier than the empty Big Mac container, speak. And just as quickly as the delirious out of body experience happens, it ends and Daniel is slingshotted back into his body. When he opens his eyes, he finds the sad-looking blue whale staring at him now wide awake and looking even moderately interested in what he has to say.

"I think she saw even more of you guys than I do," Daniel continues. "You think she would've handled the situation a little bit better. Or I dunno... More delicately."

"What situation?"

"Or I guess now it makes more sense to me than ever why she talked to me the way she did," Daniel thinks out loud, accidentally tuning out the sad-looking blue whale—a rare feat for him and normally something he couldn't do if he tried. "Because you guys were probably there. Staring at her. Maybe even crying around her. And she knew that was going to happen to me, or that it was already beginning. And that it was her fault. That she passed that poisonous part of herself on to me."

Fagged and fatigued, like a war-torn flag from the losing side so filled with holes and tears that it barely manages to blow in the wind anymore, Daniel hangs his head and interlaces his fingers behind his neck.

"Why do you guys do it?" he asks.

Despite the question being somewhat vague and out of shallow left field, Daniel doesn't have to elaborate. The sad-looking blue whale knows exactly what he's asking.

"Honestly?" the sad-looking blue whale says.

Daniel gives a skeptical nod without lifting his head, unable to make eye contact with the sad-looking blue whale, as if he can tolerate hearing the answer but not seeing it in the sad-looking blue whale's eyes.

"I don't know why," the sad-looking blue whale says.

There's a brief silence between them, musty and stale, like the fart of an ashamed attic beginning to grow mold.

"Honestly?" Daniel says, now looking out over the watery morgue of the ocean that, at this hopelessly stranded point, will most likely house his waterlogged and bloated remains for all eternity. "Your answer kind of makes me want to punch you in the face."

"I know," the sad-looking blue whale says. And then, after another brief silence—pungent, but not as malodorous—and as if trying to somehow redeem not only himself but all sad-looking blue whales everywhere, the sad-looking blue whale delicately adds, "We don't follow everyone around, though. Just some people."

Daniel looks at the sad-looking blue whale with eyes even calmer than the ocean waves melodically rocking the bright-orange boat. Then his gaze falls onto the empty Big Mac container still giving him the silent treatment.

"Honestly?" Daniel repeats. "That kind of makes me want to punch you in the face even more."

"I know," the sad-looking blue whale says, and then anxiously straightens his fanny pack even though it's already perfectly centered around his waist.

"Your fanny pack makes you look like a tourist," Daniel muses.

The sad-looking blue whale glances down at his fanny pack and gives an unconcerned shrug.

"We're all tourists here," he waxes philosophically and gazes out over the ocean as if indicating the incredible vastness of the world that he and everyone else fleetingly inhabits.

Daniel, unable to help it, although not trying too hard to suppress it either, feels himself roll his eyes so hard he's surprised they don't come shooting out the sides of his head and skip across the ocean like disapproving, optical stones.

"What's in there anyway?" he asks.

The sad-looking blue whale stares down at the fabric pouch strapped around his waist like some big, hollowed-out slug made of synthetic blue fabric.

"Nothing important, really. This and that. Odds and ends. It's functional, sure, but it's also kind of a fashion piece," the sad-looking blue whale says.

"A fashion piece?"

"Yeah. I like to try and remain *en vogue.*"

A laugh almost explodes out of Daniel's mouth until he realizes the sad-looking blue whale isn't joking, that he's, in fact, dead serious about his fashion forward stomach attire, this startling realization clipping just the right wire to the amused contraction rising out of Daniel's diaphragm and, therefore, safely disarming it.

En vogue… says Daniel's brain.

90's R&B/pop vocal group, En Vogue…

"Free your minddddddd and the rest will follow…"

"Lock your heart in an empty Big Mac container, bury it beneath the ocean floor and the rest of the world will thank you…"

Those aren't the lyrics…

They should be the lyrics…

Bury your heart in an empty Big Mac container beneath the ocean floor… his brain says impatiently.

I'm trying…

Try harder…

Melting into the moment, easing as best he can into the taunting, endless minutes, Daniel leans so far back that he folds over the side of the boat like a human pancake, almost reaching the extremely flexible point where the top of his buzzed head touches the water.

Lying there like that, uncomfortably, but with the world turned upside down and suddenly seeming more friendly and less likely to hurt him than usual in its current alternative state, Daniel, despite enjoying the beautifully inverted vista, which his brain keeps describing to him as "topsy turvy," feels boneless and embarrassed. Embarrassed to be so wildly incompetent and incapable as an adult that he can't even kill himself the way he wants to, that instead of burying his heart in an empty Big Mac container beneath the ocean floor he's going to die of thirst while sitting across from one of the saddest-looking sad-looking blue whales he's ever seen.

Daniel lets out a long, upside-down sigh, and unable to take the pain in his back any longer, as well as the pressure building in his head, he unfolds himself and sits up. The blood quickly rushes back into his head, forcing black spots to swarm his eyes like blotchy moths drawn to the dark, flickering flames of self-hatred sulking in his skull.

After the spots fade, Daniel sees the sky is back where it's supposed to be, sitting tyrannically on top of the ocean with its big, fat yet horizontally lean ass, and after realizing he's returned to the same unfriendly world he's always been in, the very one he's trying to escape from, Daniel can't help but feel deflated and squandered.

Zip, zoop, zip, zoop…

Daniel heaves his gaze at the sad-looking blue whale unzipping his fanny pack and then quickly zipping it back up, over and over again, mindlessly, like a bored child with nothing else to do and no other way to occupy themselves.

Zip, zoop, zip, zoop, zip, zoop, zip, zoop…

"Dude…" Daniel says, aggravated.

The sad-looking blue whale cowers a little and stops.

"Sorry," he says.

They sit in silence.

Despite it sounding like something a college professor might say—one who's trying too hard to come off as profound in front of the curious, young minds they're responsible for molding—Daniel can't help but think about what the sad-looking blue whale said not long ago, the sage-like fact about everyone here being tourists, and the hint of truth to it that Daniel doesn't want to admit is there.

Zip, zoop, zip, zoop, zip, zoop…

Daniel looks back at the sad-looking blue whale who's resumed absentmindedly unzipping then zipping his fanny pack.

He stifles a scream.

If I am a tourist here, I sure as shit have seen enough… his brain says.

IT'S A HORRIBLE LIFE

THUD!

Daniel jumped in his booth and looked out the window. The sad-looking blue whale from the back door now had its head and fins pressed against the glass and was staring at Daniel with eyes like miniature manhole covers after a rainstorm.

"Oooh, ooh, ooooooh!"

The sad-looking blue whale's breath had fogged the glass so heavily that a circle of hazy pixelation censored its face, almost as if it were a criminal on a reality cop show. Taking this accidental vanishing act as a cue to move on, and simply refusing to let the sad-looking blue whale bring him down as he silently worshiped from behind the booth-shaped altar of his almighty junk food cathedral, Daniel pulled the mental shades down on the sad-looking blue whale and focused on his notebook. A thought was burgeoning in his head, ambiguously new and bubbling, like a bright-orange liquid over a Bunsen burner on the cheap movie set-laboratory of a mad scientist.

Daniel put his pen to the paper.

"My heart..." Daniel's hand wrote but then quickly stopped as he felt a small hamster bite of embarrassment sink its gnarly, yellow teeth into his confidence.

He was only two words in and the thought was already coming out cliched and banal. Instead of crossing out the words, Daniel put down his pen and sat back in his booth. He took a sip of his iced coffee to soothe the moaning disappointment in his head and glanced around the dining room at the morning's customers.

It was still mainly regulars at such an early hour, including a large group of elderly patrons scattered across three tables, a balding man who, when he wasn't reading one of about five newspapers, would occasionally ramble on about Vietnam or modern day conspiracy theories to anyone willing (or sometimes unwilling) to listen, and a homeless couple that lived out of their car in the Town Fair Tire parking lot across the street, a fact Daniel had learned from overhearing many of their loud and confrontational conversations with each other over the years.

These people, Daniel knew, as he stared at them with what his brain called "a dumb affection," these people were like him. None of them had escaped the daily grind of living. None of them came from money nor would they ever have substantial sums of it. None of them were bosses, executives or CEOs, but, instead, had spent the majority of their lifetimes taking a staggering amount of soul-berating orders. They had worked very hard for very little and, consequently, Daniel knew, with himself included in the group, none of them would die comfortably, or easily. Their deaths would mirror their sad, haggard lives. And this place, this McDonald's—where for hours you could sit comfortably as well as undisturbed as long as you bought something —was all most of them had left. Although it wasn't much, this refuge, this safe haven from the sad-looking blue whales quietly infesting their ramshackle, haunted-house lives like dismal, deep sea ghosts, this place was theirs, sticky floors, smelly bathrooms, dirty tabletops and all. And as much as Daniel came for the cheap, tasty and greasy food, he knew the reason he kept coming back was because he was silently accepted here, because he and the other regulars all shared the same communal hurt. They were all forced to live without ever feeling alive, and it made them feel slightly alive again—as well as slightly human—to see others like themselves braving out into the day for some peace of mind, small talk and cheap coffee with people who had lost in life like they had.

Daniel came here because he belonged here.

Belong… Daniel's brain quietly blurted out.

With a mild spark of excitement, Daniel sat up and grabbed his pen. After the words "My heart…" he jotted down the word "belongs." Then stopped.

This slowly-forming sentence, this whatever it was, Daniel didn't feel like he was writing it. More like he was decoding it from somewhere, like it was being sent to him from some faraway place and being picked up by his own internal antennae. It was exciting, but as much as Daniel wanted to know what this was exactly, as much as he wanted more of it to be revealed, Daniel knew he couldn't rush it. He knew, for once in his life, he had to be calm, patient, that if he kept doing exactly what he was doing right now—sitting in McDonald's, relaxing, taking it easy—the rest, eventually, would find him.

All he had to do was not scare it away.

Daniel sat back in his booth and, trying to be as quiet as possible, began biting his nails. He wondered where this was going, where his heart belonged. The Christian rock still playing over the speakers kept not-so-subtly telling him over and over that his heart belonged with Christ, but Daniel, despite being more lost and alone than he'd ever been in his entire life, still wasn't weak and lame enough to fall for that preachy load of bullshit.

He waited.

BAYYYBEE!!!

"OH MY GOD," Laura said. "I never showed you my boat."

Daniel and Laura were sitting on Laura's couch. It was around their fourth or fifth date and so far all of their dates had consisted of Daniel going to Laura's house, drinking wine and having sex which, as a hetero male, Daniel was more than okay with, but, admittedly, he was also beginning to feel guilty about. Daniel liked Laura. He wanted to take her out on a real date. A nice, romantic dinner with wine, which, Daniel hoped, would also end with sex.

"You have a boat?" Daniel said.

"Yeah, wanna see it?"

"Of course."

Laura grabbed Daniel's hand and led him outside through the back porch. They stood on the cement steps overlooking her back yard. *A wasteland*... Daniel's brain called it, filled with dead grass and littered with garbage. In the back corner, next to the remains of a tall wooden fence that was slouched over and ready to collapse, sat Laura's boat—small, metallic and, surprisingly, bright-orange.

"That's it," Laura said even though she didn't have to clarify. "I really need to be more careful with it. It's all the way over there because sometimes when it rains really bad the tide sweeps over from The Long Island Sound and floods my street, including my backyard."

"Shit..." Daniel said, because "shit" felt like the right thing to say.

"Yeah. Then after the water recedes I always find crap in my yard, hence all the litter. Last time it happened I woke up to find my garbage can totally gone but with someone else's in my yard."

"Please tell me you just kept it."

"Haha, yep," Laura said. And then, "Sorry. One sec. All this garbage is driving me crazy."

Laura walked down the steps and, barefoot, began picking up pieces of garbage in her yard. Daniel, finding her sudden impulse to pick up garbage cute and admirable, went back inside, put his shoes on, then walked out and helped her.

"That's a pretty intense color," Daniel said, referring to her bright-orange boat.

Laura laughed.

"I have this orange styrofoam shark on my key chain the same color."

"Oh yeah," Daniel said, recalling said styrofoam shark on her key chain.

"I saw that one day and was like, 'I'm gonna paint my boat that color.' Then I did."

"It looks like the color of Cheez-Its."

"Oh my god. I love Cheez-Its," Laura said, her arms filled with so much garbage she couldn't hold anymore. "Babe, there's a dollar store that's, like, a five-minute walk from here. Wanna go there and buy snacks and stuff?"

Something inside Daniel jumped. It was the first time Laura had called him "babe," he realized, which he liked, and which also made him realize that these dates of theirs were turning into something serious, that, no matter what, Laura would be a memorable part of his life, someone he would either be with for a long time or someone he'd never be able to forget about, for better or for worse.

"Yeah," Daniel said. "Let's go."

"I'm buying Cheez-Its," Laura said excitedly, and dumped all of the trash she'd gathered into her neighbor's garbage can that she now used as her own.

On their way to the dollar store, Daniel and Laura held hands. It was winter and Daniel felt cold but happy. Daniel wore sweat pants and his leather jacket. Laura wore a jean jacket, jeans and a hat that made Daniel think of a frumpy, denim lamp shade.

"I look like such a tool," Laura said, examining her own choice of wardrobe.

Daniel laughed. He was surprised but amused to hear Laura call herself a tool.

"Seriously, I'm wearing a Canadian tuxedo," she said with a huge smile crawling across her face (*A little girl's smile…* Daniel thought). "Why didn't you say anything?"

"Shut up, tool," Daniel said.

"Haha, I am a tool," Laura said. "A huge fucking tool. Thanks, baby."

"Baby," Daniel repeated.

"Bayyybee!" Laura fake-screamed in a weird, Southern-sounding accent.

Daniel and Laura walked into the dollar store, although, in all actuality, it was really more of a cheap-ass supermarket. The guy behind the counter had the physique of a flabby cinder block and greeted Laura and Daniel as soon as they entered. Laura greeted him back and Daniel smiled. He followed Laura down an aisle in the middle of the store. From the confident stride in her step, he could tell she shopped here often.

"I do a pathetic amount of my shopping here," Laura said, as if reading Daniel's mind. "But look, babe. You can't beat these prices."

Laura picked up two boxes of Velveeta mac and cheese and held them up for Daniel to see, her eyebrows raising up and down as if saying, "For dinner tonight?"

"Yeah, sure," Daniel said. "I can't even remember the last time I had mac and cheese."

Laura made a *Pffft!* sound with her mouth.

"I feel like I have this all the time," she said, smiling.

Suddenly feeling insanely happy for no real reason, which, consequently, only increased the insanity of this sudden happiness, Daniel pressed himself into Laura. Grabbing her ass with both hands, he playfully dry humped her leg while making grunt sounds. Laura laughed. She hit Daniel on his shoulder with one of the boxes of macaroni and cheese and tried to wrestle herself free from his grasp. In order to keep Laura from getting away, Daniel threw his arms around her and hugged her. Laura hugged Daniel back. They stood there in the aisle like that, naturally swaying back and forth to the rhythm of the generic love ballad playing from the speakers in the ceiling.

Pressed into Laura, dancing with her, Daniel felt himself breathing, or, rather, the ease of his breathing, finally feeling unlabored and natural, as if taken off some life support he never even knew he was on until this moment. Daniel kissed Laura—one, soft simple kiss on the lips, then they looked at each other.

"We need anything else?" Laura asked.

"I dunno. I'm trying to decide if I should get soda or not."

"Come on," Laura said.

She cradled both boxes of macaroni and cheese in one arm, then took Daniel's hand and walked him to the soda aisle.

"What kinda soda do you like"? Daniel asked.

"Whatever you like," Laura said.

Daniel grabbed a two-liter bottle of Coke.

"This okay?"

"Perfect", she said.

Daniel grabbed Laura's ass with his free hand and squeezed it again.

"Perfect," he said.

———

After dinner, cuddled up on the couch, Laura confided in Daniel for the first time. She told him about a manic episode she had a few years back. When she tried putting on all of the clothes in her closet and took off down the street she used to live on, running as fast as she could (which proved to be difficult considering the amount of clothes she was wearing), not knowing where she was going but still running, huffing and puffing and unable to stop, the mental image, as if it weren't humorous enough, making Daniel think of Forrest Gump.

"It's okay," Laura said, smiling herself as she noticed Daniel politely trying to hold back laughter.

"Then what happened?" he asked.

"My boyfriend at the time chased after me and tackled me to the ground and brought me home, literally kicking and screaming. But it wasn't easy for him because every time he got a hold on me, I'd slip out of that layer of clothing and take off again."

Daniel couldn't help it. He laughed out loud. He felt relieved when Laura did, too.

"Too bad the ending isn't so funny… One of my boyfriend's friends called the cops because he was worried about me. They thought I was going to hurt myself. Or maybe someone else. So the cops showed up as my boyfriend was bringing me home and by that time I was really losing my shit and screaming like crazy. Long story short, I was taken away and committed."

Having had no idea Laura had ever been committed, Daniel got really silent, respectfully silent, as if acknowledging the severity of what had happened. Then he put his hand on her knee, trying to show a physical display of love and support.

"Do you think you would've?" Daniel asked after they sat in silence for a bit.

"Would've what?"

"Hurt someone."

Laura got quiet. Her lips pursed together. Her eyebrows made this movement like they were trying to imitate the serious, contemplative scrunching of her lips.

"I don't know," she said. "Maybe. I was completely out of control. It was really scary."

They sat in silence. Laura's stomach, filled with both macaroni and cheese and Cheez-Its, gurgled. Weak rain pummeled the aluminum siding of her house as if trying to sound tougher than the drizzle it actually was.

"Moral of the story?" Laura said eventually, and seriously, in the tone of voice that made Daniel think of a seasoned shrink. "Don't take yourself off your medication."

"Why'd you stop taking your meds?"

Laura shrugged in a manner like she knew the answer but didn't really want to get into it, though she did anyway.

"Because I didn't like how I felt on it. And it gave me really bad acne. Like, *really* bad acne. So bad I was embarrassed to leave the house. But now I have this skincare routine I do every night that helps, so..."

"Are you still on meds?"

Laura nodded.

"Good," Daniel said. And then, trying to come off as deadpan, "I'm not a very fast runner."

Laura smiled. Daniel felt relieved, her smile prompting him to continue on with further humor to lighten the situation.

"I'd have to just let you go, ya know? Hope for the best."

Laura's smile widened and she punched Daniel in the arm.

"Isn't that what you're supposed to do?" Daniel asked. "If you love someone let them go, and if they come back they're yours forever?"

"Oh, so you love me now, huh?"

Daniel's intestines nervously twisted and tangled together like some kind of gross pretzel. He and Laura hadn't exchanged "I love yous" yet, although in that moment he realized he did love her. But the unexpected confrontation of his feelings for Laura, plus the added nervousness of how she might react if he told her he loved her only after a month or so together, made Daniel, instead, hold his hand up with his pointer finger and thumb closely together, physically indicating "a little bit."

"Well, I hate you," Laura said in a tone of voice that didn't sound like she hated him at all.

"Maybe I'll put a tracking device on you, though. Just to make sure."

Laura leaned in and bit Daniel's arm. Daniel screamed even though it didn't hurt. He leaned over and fell on top of Laura, pressing all of his weight into her so she couldn't move. Then he felt her arms wrap around his back, accepting him on top of her, enjoying the heavy closeness.

"That doesn't scare you?" he heard her ask after a minute. "The episode I had?"

Daniel paused even though he didn't need to, even though he already knew his answer. He shook his head.

"No," he added verbally, just in case Laura couldn't feel his head shake. "That doesn't scare me at all."

Laura began to cry.

Daniel stuffed his arms beneath her, between her back and the couch cushion, and kissed the side of her head. Her oily, unwashed hair left streaks on his glasses but Daniel didn't care or bother to wipe them off.

He wanted everything Laura had to offer.

The good, the bad, the ugly.

Even the greasy.

GREASY, CARDBOARD HEART-COFFIN

HOURS PASS in the ocean as painfully as beach ball-sized kidney stones. High above, the sun continues relentlessly catcalling Daniel with its macho heat, basting him with a bravado so bright and over the top that Daniel, much like an attractive woman walking by a line of ungentlemanly construction workers, begins feeling so uncomfortable in his skin that he wants to rip himself right out of it.

The sad-looking blue whale, however, despite sweating profusely, barely even seems to notice the burning machismo oozing from the sun. He sits in place stoically, like an enormous whoopie cushion with a small but damning hole poked in it somewhere, knowing it will never "whoopie" again but also having accepted this fate years ago, now so used to its state of flatulent impotence it can barely believe things ever used to be any other way.

Daniel, subtlety assessing the sad-looking blue whale as he looks out over the horizon, examining all sad-looking six feet of him, wonders how he does it, how he, or any other sad-looking blue whale for that matter, can exist in a such a state, like they're always being pistol whipped by gloom. A state that they not only never snap out of but seem content in, or even, maybe, enjoy.

The sad-looking blue whale pries his attention off the horizon and catches Daniel in the middle of his studious assessment. Daniel, playing the fool, the part he was born to play, looks away as if he hadn't just been gawking at the sad-looking blue whale.

"Hey…" the sad-looking blue whale says in the tone of a question.

"Mm?" Daniel replies coolly, pretending to wipe sweat off his brow even though he's not sure if there's any there or not.

"What made you write a novel about farts?" the sad-looking blue whale asks.

Daniel runs his hand through the slightly-tangled crop of bristly hairs that he calls his beard and mulls over the sad-looking blue whale's question.

"I dunno… I was a kid. Kids like farts," Daniel labors out of himself.

"But…" the sad-looking blue whale begins before trailing off.

"But what?"

"Nothing. I guess I was just wondering who'd want to read a novel about farts."

"*A* fart," Daniel says, and, suddenly annoyed, stops running his hand through his beard.

The sad-looking blue whale narrows his eyes, confused.

"But a fart can't read."

"No, you keep saying farts. But my book isn't about farts. It's about *a* fart. One, singular, lone fart contemplating its brief mortality."

"Oh…" the sad-looking blue whale says. And then, after a moment of furrowed contemplation, "Wow… 800 pages on one fart."

"500 pages," Daniel corrects him. "300 out of the 800 were just illustrations of the fart."

"How do you draw a fart?"

"Like this," Daniel says, and, suddenly feeling energized, makes quick and excited squiggles in the air with his pointer finger, which he then punctuates with a forceful forward stabbing motion.

The sad-looking blue whale's eyes narrow, either contemplatively or judgmentally, Daniel isn't sure.

"What?" Daniel asks, his energy suddenly drained by the sudden feelings of self-consciousness now consuming him.

"Nothing," the sad-looking blue whale says. "I'm sure it looks much more like a fart on paper."

"Oh…"

"It's just hard to picture. Ya know, when you draw it in the air."

And just like that Daniel feels his insanely sensitive ego shatter. Then the small janitor inside of him sweeping up the pieces with a push broom just as the janitor's had to do so many times throughout the course of Daniel's life, leaving Daniel to eventually rebuild his ego, to glue it back together incorrectly as he's always done, amorphous but still somehow missing pieces, losing pieces every time it happens, his poor sensitive shrunken ego not even half the size it used to be.

"I know it was a dumb idea," Daniel says in regards to his childhood novel.

"I wouldn't call it dumb. Maybe just..." The sad-looking blue whale pauses, looking for the right words. *"Avant-garde."*

Daniel makes a short, little, offended laugh.

"What?" the sad-looking blue whale asks.

"Isn't Avant-garde just French for 'dumb as shit?'"

"I didn't mean it like that—"

"Maybe we just don't talk about it anymore," Daniel interrupts.

"Yeah... Sure," the sad-looking blue whale says.

They sit in silence for a moment. And then, "Is it because talking about it reminds you that, despite your best efforts, your fart novel was the only thing in life you ever finished but that it was still really bad, and knowing that makes you feel like an enormous failure?"

Daniel stares at the sad-looking blue whale, right into his black beady eyes that make Daniel think of two small cities undergoing a power outage.

"Yeah..." Daniel says, stoically. "That about sums it up."

"Oh..." the sad-looking blue whale says. "Okay."

"And it's called *Passing Gas.* You keep calling it a 'fart novel,' which makes it sound sophomoric and crude, but in all actuality, it's really quite layered and sophisticated for—"

"I thought we weren't talking about it anymore," the sad-looking blue whale interrupts, then fixes his attention back out over the ocean, his muddled mind already moving on to other things, most likely involving *Titanic,* Daniel guesses, the thought of which prompting him to ask the sad-looking blue whale a question himself.

"Why *Titanic*?" he says in an incredulous and almost insulting tone of voice, like only idiots and prepubescent girls back in 1997 enjoy the film.

"Why *Titanic*?" the sad-looking blue whale echoes.

"Yeah. I don't get your obsession over it."

"Because," the sad-looking blue whale says matter of factly. "We're sad-looking blue whales, and *Titanic* is the saddest movie of all time."

Daniel makes a bland, disapproving gesture with his head and shoulders like, *"Yeah. Okay. Sure. Whatever."*

"What, you don't like *Titanic*?" the sad-looking blue whale asks.

Daniel thinks back to when his dad took him to see *Titanic* in theaters when he was in seventh grade. Right after the ship hit the iceberg, the screen went black. A few minutes later, the lights turned on and a manager walked in and announced they were having technical difficulties and that, hopefully, the picture would be back up and running shorty, and, if they liked, they could all go and get refills of popcorn and soda on the house, to which Daniel's dad muttered, "Jesus Christ. Just when we were getting to the good part." Daniel took their huge popcorn tub that was about three-fourths emptied and went and got a free refill. Fifteen minutes later, the movie picked back up where it left off and Daniel's dad got what he wanted and both he and his son watched the ship sink. It was really the first sad and dramatic movie Daniel had ever seen in theaters, or anywhere for that matter, and he remembers certain parts of it being hard for him to watch. It was difficult for Daniel to know this was true, that this had happened to real people, to real men and women and even children. It scared Daniel in a way to know that, yes, something like this, a tragedy of this scale, could somehow happen to him, that he wasn't exempt from disaster or death at a young age, and at least twice that Daniel remembers, he had to look away from the screen, hiding his face from his father, to let out a few unsolicited tears.

Yes, Daniel liked *Titanic*.

Even back in seventh grade when the movie was considered "gay" or a "chick flick" by the rest of the boys his age, Daniel knew it was a solid film. It was the first film to make him cry. Yes, it was a very sad movie indeed. Daniel, however, would just never let the sad-looking blue whale know any of this.

"It was fine, I guess," Daniel says, passive-aggressively seeking revenge on the sad-looking blue whale for making him feel foolish about his fart novel.

"Fine, I guess?" the sad-looking blue whale says disbelievingly.

"Yeah, I don't know. Just not my thing," Daniel says, then adheres his vision onto the horizon, abruptly ending this topic of conversation and giving the sad-looking blue whale a taste of his own sad-looking medicine.

And then, from out of nowhere, or maybe not nowhere, but from somewhere specific—some spiteful, vengeful place—the sad-looking blue whale says two words, verbally pulling the pin from a grenade stuffed with sensitive memories that shouldn't be trudged up: "Who's Laura?"

Daniel turns his head and wrangles the sad-looking blue whale with his pupils.

"How do you know about Laura?" he asks.

"You mentioned her before."

"I did?"

"Yeah. Briefly. You said her name."

"Oh…" Daniel says, then goes quiet.

"She's your ex?" the sad-looking blue whale pries, but casually, like a crowbar dressed in faded jeans and a graphic t-shirt bought at Target.

Daniel nods.

"Why'd she leave you?"

"What makes you think she left me? How do you know I didn't leave her?"

The sad-looking blue whale gently nudges the empty Big Mac container with his bottom fin.

"I don't think you'd be burying your heart in a Big Mac container beneath the ocean floor if you were the one who left her," the sad-looking blue whale reasons out loud. "He may be giving you the silent treatment, but he still says a lot just by sitting there in front of you. So? Why'd she leave?"

Dozens of small reasons immediately bum-rush Daniel, an overwhelming amount all flying around in his head like bats lit on fire, making it impossible for Daniel to focus on one long enough to give the sad-looking blue whale an answer. And it's only when Daniel looks up and his eyes meet the sad-looking blue whale's—dull, overcast and miserable—does he have an answer as to why Laura left him. The main answer stares right back at him, and in a way, as gut wrenching as the answer is, it's a relief. It makes this journey Daniel's on seem warranted, like this is definitely the right thing to be doing, like this is the only thing left for him to be doing.

"I made her sad," Daniel answers simply, and just like that all of the flaming thoughts in his head extinguish themselves and fall like charred bat-bacon rain onto the landscape of his mind.

The sad-looking blue whale nods as if this is an acceptable answer.

"Did she love you?" he asks.

"Jesus… Do you just sit around all day thinking of soul-crushing questions to ask people?"

"No," the sad-looking blue whale answers, not picking up on the sarcastic scorn in Daniel's voice. "Why?"

Daniel lets out a sigh so long winded it could extinguish all the candles on a ninety-nine-year-old's birthday cake.

"For a little while," he answers. "She loved me for as long as she could, I guess."

Daniel closes his eyes. He feels all of the reasons as to why Laura left him burnt to a crisp but still alive, still twitching.

"For whatever it's worth, I'm sorry she left you," the sad-looking blue whale says.

"Thanks," Daniel replies, too scared to tell the sad-looking blue whale that, at the risk of choking up, it actually means a lot to him.

"What about you?" Daniel asks, trying to change the subject in order to keep from possibly weeping.

"What about me?" the sad-looking blue whale says.

"You and your kind. Do you fall in love?"

"No. We have no need for it. We do however schedule meetings with members of the opposite sex and copulate quite often."

"Sounds romantic," Daniel says, deadpan.

"It is. We light a seaweed-scented candle, lie on a cold bathroom floor and cry *'Oooh, oooooh!'* over and over as we touch genitals."

Daniel unwillingly conjures this image in his head but then tries to banish it from his mind even faster than he accidentally let it slip in there.

"There's usually a copy of *Titanic* on VHS playing in the next room with the volume on full blast. Always VHS though. Never DVD or BluRay," the sad-looking blue whale says. "Not sad-looking enough."

"But you're not watching it," Daniel reasons.

A stupefied look washes over the sad-looking blue whale's face, like neither he nor any other sad-looking blue whale ever thought of this oversight before, and staring at the sad-looking blue whale currently immobilized in a sudden state of dumb shock, Daniel can't believe that this creature and his kind, all seemingly just as illogical and dense, are what rule his life.

"But surely the sound quality isn't as good on VHS," the sad-looking blue whale reasons back.

Daniel shrugs. Really, he could care less.

"It's been great, though," the sad-looking whale says. "Ever since the turn of the century we've been copulating and reproducing like crazy."

"Wow…" Daniel says, cracking a shit eating grin he can't hold in. "You guys sure you aren't *sperm whales?*"

"Yeah, positive," the sad-looking blue whale says matter of factly. "We're blue whales."

The shit-eating grin on Daniel's face bends almost gymnastically into a shit-eating frown, and the huge amount of disappointment he feels over his joke not landing almost makes Daniel begin to explain it to the sad-looking blue whale before deciding against such a pointless course of action.

"Anyway," the sad-looking blue whale says. "I guess I should be thanking you."

This confuses Daniel.

"Why?"

"Well, not just you. All humans, really. We sad-looking blue whales are thriving and it's all thanks to you and your kind evolving."

"I don't get it," Daniel says.

"We schedule the meetings to copulate and reproduce, but how much we actually copulate and reproduce depends on the quota we need to fill, on how many of your kind needs us. And for whatever reason, the more you and your kind evolve the more me and my kind need to copulate and reproduce. Which is great, because I love copulating. Especially the way I unexplainably burst into tears afterwards. That's always the female's favorite part, too…"

As the sad looking blue whale rambles on, Daniel mentally drifts off. He thinks back to numerous times when he'd be sitting in front of his computer in his parents' basement, drunk on wine and covered in cat hair while philosophically surfing the internet, deep in thought over what the internet actually was. And what was the internet actually? The internet was the entire history of mankind. It was everything mankind had ever learned all right there within his reach. Daniel could use the internet to answer almost any question he had. He could use it to pay bills. He could use it to buy Richard Brautigan books that had long since gone out of print. He could use it to buy food and then have the food delivered to his house. He could use it to watch TV and movies. He could use it to watch porn. He could use it to listen to music. He could use it to stay in touch with people he hadn't seen in years. He could use it to talk to strangers who seemed just as sad and lonely as him. He could even potentially work from home on it. The internet was something so great and powerful that a person would never have to leave the comfort of their home again if they didn't want to. But often, scrolling through social media sites and reading posts or status updates, or messaging back and forth with strangers online, Daniel would find that the vast majority of people out there felt scared and hopeless and alone just like him. People, most people, including Daniel, led coddled easy lives. They lived in warm houses with indoor plumbing and went to grocery stores filled with food they didn't have to harvest or kill. If they got sick, modern medicine was usually able to cure it, and if not, at the very least put up a fight. And yet, somehow, everyone was still unhappy or stressed or, most of the time, both. Twenty-one centuries of technological evolution and things had become so much easier yet no one was any happier. But the expectancy to be happy had become greater, and when people couldn't live up to it, when they couldn't be as happy as the world and its technology demanded them to, it was damn near fucking lethal. It was no wonder sad-looking blue whales ran the world, although now it made more sense than ever to Daniel why they did.

"...You okay?" the sad-looking blue whale asks Daniel.

"Yeah," Daniel says, not feeling okay at all. "I was just thinking."

The two sit in their familiar, oceanic silence. And then, a long while after, "Ohhhhhhhh... *Sperm* whale. I get it," the sad-looking blue whale says.

But doesn't laugh.

Or chuckle.

Or even crack so much as a sad-looking grin.

IT'S A HORRIBLE LIFE

DANIEL FELT time trickling through a constipated hour glass. Staring mindlessly at the swill of his melted iced coffee, which now looked more like the urine sample of a raging alcoholic, he yawned. A minute later, he yawned again. Not out of boredom, although he was beginning to feel himself becoming restless and impatient as he looked down at the sentence in his notebook, wondering where his heart belonged. Daniel yawned out of physical exhaustion.

Daniel hadn't slept well last night, or the night before. In fact, he seldom slept well ever. The sad-looking blue whales were always keeping him up throughout the night, kicking him in their sleep as they cuddled up close, or sometimes snoring so obnoxiously loud that Daniel could hear them even after he'd grabbed a pillow and blanket and moved to another room.

Daniel looked out his window to see the sad-looking blue whale was no longer there, fogging up the glass and staring at him. He didn't know where it had ninja-vanished to, nor did he care, and he didn't bother looking around for it either. Instead, he contemplated going home and trying to take a nap, but some nagging, forbidding part of him wouldn't allow it.

My heart belongs…

Daniel had to wait, had to find out where his heart belonged. And as he waited patiently, or as patiently as someone as impatient as Daniel could wait, a middle-aged McDonald's employee wheeled a middle-aged-looking mop and bucket into the dining area.

Daniel watched as the employee began mopping the floor meticulously, thoroughly, as if the floor were the surface of some abandoned laminate planet that she alone was responsible for cleaning even though no one populated it except her. She started at the far end of the dining area, then mopped her way closer and closer until, eventually, she was right beside Daniel.

"Excuse' me," she said in a thick yet charming Spanish accent while making a friendly, little head motion toward the floor underneath Daniel's table.

"Oh, sorry," Daniel said and lifted his feet.

The woman gave a few quick swipes underneath Daniel's table, even though she hadn't cleaned underneath any of the other tables, then said "Gracias" to Daniel. With her work now done, she walked over to the custodial closet in-between the two bathrooms. She put her mop and wheely bucket away and took out a wet floor sign that she placed down before hobbling, almost ogre-like, back up front.

Daniel stared at the wet floor sign. The cautionary cartoon man who was supposed to look like he was slipping looked more like he was break dancing. Daniel imagined a customer walking by the caution sign on the way to the bathroom when a break dancer suddenly comes from out of nowhere and sends the customer flying into the air, accidentally sweeping the customer's legs out from underneath them with their break dancing.

Daniel's brain registered this mental image as humorous and, correspondingly, felt some old, rusty machinery inside of him trying to get itself started, trying to rev itself up so it could produce a laugh, a chuckle, a chortle, an anything. But instead, the machinery began to cough and wheeze, like an old cartoon car struggling to make its way up a hill before giving up and dying, making Daniel inwardly frown, making him hate himself yet again, making him feel like nothing more than some pale, chubby graveyard full of smile miscarriages.

So many smiles… Daniel's brain mourned.

Dead before they even had a chance…

A girl with a tray of food walked into the dining area and sat down three booths away from Daniel. She was very pretty and looked like the type of girl who followed Carrie Underwood on Instagram, like the type of girl who always had a very well stocked refrigerator as well as very well stocked cabinets, like the type of girl who kept a list on her fridge of the things she was running low on, like the type of girl who had really neat and bubbly handwriting and only used pens that had purple or pink ink, like the type of girl who enjoyed baking so much that anytime she went to a party or holiday gathering she always brought some kind of homemade baked good.

Daniel liked her, or, rather, this fictionalized version of her his brain had created. He tried to look at her without looking like he was looking at her as she removed the clear lid off her breakfast container and began cutting her food into small, neat, manageable pieces. A few seconds later, however, a boy holding a tray of food walked over to the pretty girl's table and sat down across from her, blocking Daniel's view.

The boyfriend… his brain said bitterly.

There's always a fucking boyfriend…

Daniel scooted over into the corner of his booth to try and see if he could look around the boyfriend's head and still get a glimpse of the pretty girl.

He was able to. At least a little.

Daniel held his phone up in front of him so it kind of looked like he was staring at that and not the pretty girl. He watched her as inconspicuously as he could. He liked the way her jaw moved when she chewed, like every bite was really chewy, or really peanut buttery and sticky even though she was just eating pancakes. An observation, Daniel thought, that was really cute, like if he told it to her in a certain tone of voice, and with a certain impish look on his face, that it'd make the girl smile bashfully with a mouthful of food, that even though the observation made her feel just a little self-conscious she'd still find it sweet because she could tell Daniel found this trait about her endearing.

"I don't really like their pancakes," Daniel heard the boyfriend say after they'd been eating in silence for a few minutes.

"No?" the pretty girl said.

"No."

"Why'd you get them?"

"I dunno. I wanted pancakes."

"They call them hot cakes here," the pretty girl pointed out, and took a small, mouse-like sip of her coffee. *A nibble of coffee…* Daniel's brain called it.

"Hot cakes? Really?"

"That's what it said on the menu."

"Hm…"

"Are hot cakes any different than pancakes?" she asked.

"No, I don't think so."

"Did you want butter for them?"

"No, I'm alright."

"What about grape jelly? You ever try grape jelly on your pancakes?"

"No," he said, and stuffed a large forkful of pancakes/hot cakes into his mouth. "Is it good?"

"Yeah, I used to do it a lot when I was little."

"Why'd you stop?"

"I'm not sure," she said. "Good question."

The boyfriend swallowed his large mouthful, then grabbed his coffee cup.

"Do you want a refill?" he asked his girlfriend.

"You finished yours already?"

"Yeah."

"That was fast."

The boyfriend shrugged as he stood up.

"The refills are free," he said. "You want one?"

The pretty girl stared down at the lid of her coffee cup as if looking through it and measuring the coffee left inside with x-ray vision.

"No, thanks," she said. "I don't think I drank enough to warrant a refill."

"But they're free," he said incredulously.

"On the way out," she answered.

The boyfriend nodded and walked to the front to get his free refill. Daniel hoped he would never come back, that the pretty girl would get tired of waiting for him and eventually offer Daniel her missing boyfriend's hotcakes.

"I'd never leave you alone in McDonald's," Daniel would then say to the pretty girl after he sat down. "And to correctly answer your question, a hot cake is usually smaller and thicker than a pancake. And pancakes are usually thinner so they can be rolled or folded easier and be filled with sweet or savory fillings."

The girl would reach across the table and, smiling even more sweetly than the maple syrup on her now ex-boyfriend's hot cakes, she'd take Daniel's hand in hers.

"You're so smart," she'd say. "Take me home and have your way with me."

"After our hot cakes, baby," Daniel would reply. "After our hot cakes."

Then Daniel would smile and eat the hot cakes her ex-boyfriend had left behind. He and the girl would become boyfriend and girlfriend and he would never miss Laura again. He would never even think of Laura again. He wouldn't have to. He had *her* now. This new girl. This prettier pancake girl who he'd occasionally and playfully call "Hot Cakes." But as Daniel began imagining their life together (two daughters, three cats, an apartment in Manhattan, and every year on their anniversary Daniel made her hot cakes which he served to her in bed), the girl's boyfriend returned with his refill of coffee.

Daniel felt his heart deflate like a farting balloon. Not knowing what else to do, he just stared at the boyfriend, burning a hole into the back of his head, when it hit him like a wet wad of toilet paper being thrown into a brick wall—the past few minutes he spent daydreaming about the pretty girl were, essentially, how he spent the majority his life. Sad-looking day after sad-looking day, Daniel never had actual conversations with people. He only had imagined conversations with most people, especially strangers. Conversations Daniel could control, conversations where he was always funny and charming and, therefore, well received, much unlike most real conversations he had. And Daniel, smart enough to know better but too weak to ever enforce any kind of change, understood this was no way to spend a life while also simultaneously understanding how difficult it was for him to talk and connect with people when there were always sad-looking blue whales crying in-between every other sentence he tried to speak.

The sad-looking blue whales made it nearly impossible for Daniel to have any real conversations, so, instead, he settled for imaginary ones. It wasn't much, but it was the only way Daniel knew how to "connect" with people, it was the only way he knew how to feel connected to his humanity, which even the most reclusive of recluses, like Daniel, needed—to feel human, even if he had to fake it and lie to himself about it.

"What's with this music?" Daniel heard the boyfriend ask the pretty girl in regards to the Christian rock.

Daniel glanced up just in time to see the girlfriend shrug her shoulders.

"I don't know. I was wondering the same thing."

"It's kind of driving me crazy."

"Want to take the rest of our food and go? I'm kind of full anyway, I think."

"Yeah," the boyfriend said. "Let's go."

"Okay," the pretty girl said with a grin, as if she found her boyfriend's inability to tolerate Christian rock just as cute and endearing as Daniel did with the way she chewed.

The pretty girl and her boyfriend put the clear plastic lids back on their breakfasts and stood up.

"Be sure to get a free refill," the boyfriend said, holding up his coffee for the pretty girl to see.

"Okay," the pretty girl said, sounding like she didn't want a free refill at all, like she was going to get one just to appease her boyfriend.

The two of them walked away. Daniel, still feeling hurt, bitter and disappointed, wished he had packets of grape jelly to angrily hurl at them as they left. Then a rattling sound came from the back door.

Daniel turned and saw a sad-looking blue whale pulling on it, trying to let itself inside. Unsuccessful, the sad-looking blue whale momentarily gave up. It stood back, put its fins on his hips and stared at the door like a dad staring at the engine of the family car, unsure of how to fix it but still with a grave look of resolve in his eyes, like come hell or high water he was going to figure it out.

Something about the look in the sad-looking blue whale's eyes made Daniel uneasy. He was used to seeing them look sad, of course, but never so determined.

The sad-looking blue whale began pulling on the push door again, shaking it back and forth.

Daniel opened his notebook.

My heart belongs... his notebook still said, but then went nowhere fast, mindlessly trailing off like a dementia patient in the middle of a sentence.

As the sad-looking blue whale shook the back door, Daniel wondered what to do with himself.

He felt like he was always wondering what to do with himself.

BAYYYBEE!!!

IT WAS THE WEEKEND. Daniel and Laura were lounging around in sweatpants, trying to watch something on Netflix but failing because the show kept freezing.

"God dammit," Laura said eventually and got up off the couch to try and fix the internet on her computer.

After a few minutes, Laura gave up and shrugged. Daniel kind of shrugged back at her and tilted his head to the side a little as if saying, "Hey, what are you going to do? Right?"

"I'm sorry," Laura said, apologizing on behalf of the internet.

"It's okay."

"Still, it's annoying. I guess that's what you get though for being cheap and mooching off your neighbor's Wi-Fi."

Laura stood there at the foot of the couch for a minute with her hands on her hips, thinking.

"Want to take a bath?" she asked.

Daniel pictured Laura naked and wet. He smiled and nodded. Laura walked into her kitchen and began taking large pots out of her cupboards. Daniel walked over with a perplexed look on his face and left it there hanging on his face like a crooked picture until Laura saw it.

"Oh..." Laura said, grinning. "I can never get the bathroom water as hot as I want it when I take a bath, so I get water from the kitchen and fill the tub with it."

"Ah..." Daniel said.

"Like, the water in the bathroom is warm enough to shower with but the kitchen water is scorching for some reason, and I like the water so fucking hot it feels like it's going to melt my skin off."

Laura filled a pot and handed it Daniel.

"Go pour this in the tub and I'll fill another. Then you can come back and take the full pot and I'll take the empty pot and fill that."

"Assembly line," Daniel said, smiling.

"Assembly line," Laura repeated, smiling. "Two-person assembly line."

Daniel walked into the downstairs bathroom with the pot of hot water. He flipped a small steel lever thingy in the shower, presumably closing the shower drain, then poured the water into the tub. The lever he flipped didn't work though, and the water began funneling down the drain.

"Laura?" Daniel called from the bathroom.

"Yeah?" Laura called back from the kitchen.

"How do you close the drain?"

"You just flip the lever-thingy."

Daniel flipped the lever-thingy again, thinking maybe the drain was already closed when he entered and he'd accidentally opened it, but even after flipping it again the water continued draining.

Daniel walked into the kitchen and Laura held out the full pot for him to take.

"I can't get it to work," Daniel said.

"Can't get what to work?"

"The drain."

Laura just kind of stared at him for a second. And then, "How can you fuck this up? It's easy. Watch."

Laura walked into the bathroom and flipped the same switch Daniel had flipped but nothing happened. The water kept draining. She flipped it two more times. Nothing.

"What the fuck?" she said.

"'How can you fuck this up?'" Daniel sarcastically mimicked.

"What the fucking fuck?" Laura said. And then, "Hold on. I have an idea."

Laura went to the kitchen and came back with Saran Wrap.

"Huh? Huhhh?" she said, smiling, raising her eyebrows up and down.

"That's not gonna work."

"Yes, it will. Watch."

Laura ripped off two pieces of Saran Wrap and covered the drain with it as best she could. Then she poured the new pot of hot water in the tub.

"See?" Laura said, proudly.

"See what? It's still draining."

"No, it's not."

"Yes, it is. You can even kind of hear it."

Laura leaned her ear toward the shower.

"Maybe a little," she said.

"I think it, like, partially works."

"Well, we better hurry then."

"Timed bath," Daniel said.

"Timed bath," Laura repeated with a smile.

Daniel and Laura filled the tub with water. Laura grabbed a bottle of cheap champagne they bought the night before and a semi-large bar of dark chocolate she'd stolen from work. Then they took off their clothes. Laura dipped her foot into the tub, winced and quickly pulled it out.

"Shit," she said. "Okay. Maybe it's too hot."

"Ya think? It's steaming."

"We'll just wait a minute."

"Or forty," Daniel said.

Laura made a little laugh and took a swig from the champagne bottle. Then she looked down at Daniel's limp, dangling cock.

"Mmm..." she said and bit her bottom lip.

Laura began pulling on Daniel's dick. Not sensually. More so just tugging on it, stretching it, kind of like how Daniel used to as a little kid, randomly and mindlessly tugging on his penis, just kind of playing with it because it was there.

"Want a sip?" Laura asked, holding up the champagne.

Daniel took a big swig and gave her the bottle back.

"One sec," he said.

Daniel went to the kitchen and filled and poured a few pots of really cold water into the tub. Then he went to Laura's fridge, grabbed a single ice cube and dropped it into the tub just for comedic effect. Laura laughed and dipped her foot in again.

"That actually helped," she said. "It's cooler."

"I think it was the ice cube that did it."

"Definitely the ice cube," Laura agreed.

"It would've been even funnier if I came back with the rapper Ice Cube and just dropped him in the tub."

Laura laughed loudly. Then, very slowly, she lowered her naked body into one end of the tub. Daniel was next. He stepped in and began lowering himself into the water but stopped, hesitating before submerging his crotch.

"Oh my god. Just do it," Laura said.

"Fuck you. You don't have these."

"Pussy," she said.

"I'm gonna kick you in the pussy."

"Do it, bayybeee!" Laura playfully screamed.

"It's gonna be like boiling a hot dog…"

"Ew…"

Daniel fully submerged himself into the water. It was still really hot and he had to resist from standing back up, but after half a minute or so his body adjusted to the temperature. He and Laura sat there in opposite ends of the tub, facing each other, their legs woven into each other's.

"I think my fat ass is helping to plug the drain," Laura said.

Daniel smiled and drank some champagne.

"Like it's definitely helping hold the Saran Wrap down," she added.

Laura ate some dark chocolate. Then Daniel handed her the champagne and she took a modest swig.

"Damn, babe. These go so good together. Here. Eat a piece and then take a sip."

She handed Daniel some chocolate and then the champagne bottle. He ate the piece and drank some champagne.

"Shit…" he said.

"Right?"

"Definitely. Hand me another piece."

Laura did. Daniel ate the piece and took another sip. Then he handed the bottle back to Laura. As she drank, he looked at her pussy underwater and got turned on. Daniel maneuvered his foot toward her crotch and begin running his big toe up and down the front of her pussy. Laura stared at him, her eyes like smirking tsunamis.

Daniel slid his big toe into her pussy. Laura made a small sound and kind of began grinding her hips around. Daniel managed to work another toe inside her. Laura closed her eyes and grabbed and squeezed her left tit with her free hand that wasn't holding the champagne bottle. Daniel made a repeated thrusting motion with his foot, fucking Laura with his toes. Eventually, Laura came on them. She shuddered and the water around her rippled sensually.

"Fuck..." Laura said, blinking repeatedly, like she had something stuck in both of her eyes.

Daniel pulled his toes out of her. Laura put the champagne bottle down outside the tub and leaned forward. She cupped Daniel's balls with one hand and used the other to jerk him off underwater. Biting her bottom lip and making sexy little moans and grunt sounds, she watched what she was doing the entire time. Already insanely turned on, Daniel came fast.

"Baby..." Laura said as she watched his semen float to the surface.

"My semen looks like a drowning ghost," Daniel said.

"Haha, it does."

Daniel paused.

"I'm not sure if I just came up with that or if I've heard it somewhere."

"Where the hell would you have heard that from?" Laura asked as she sat back, relaxed, and grabbed the champagne.

"I dunno. A poem or something. Like, from a modern-day writer."

"When are you going to let me read your books?" Laura asked.

Daniel hesitated. He had two books of poetry published by an indie press but he was always hesitant to let those who were close to him read them.

"Sooner or later," he said.

"Oh my god. You're so fucking stupid."

"The fucking stupidest," Daniel agreed.

"I mean, you told me about them. So on some level that must mean you want me to read them."

Daniel didn't answer, and the two of them just sat there in the tub for a while, occasionally eating dark chocolate and swigging champagne as the water level slowly, but noticeably, lowered

"I'm thinking about maybe buying this house when my lease is up," Laura said after a while.

"Yeah?"

"Yeah. I have the option."

"Do it," Daniel said.

"Would you move in with me?"

Daniel was surprised by this question, although not scared by it. They'd only been dating a few months but, at the same time, it didn't feel like they were moving too fast.

"Yeah," Daniel answered casually, as if instead of Laura asking him to move in with her, she'd asked him if he wanted Italian for dinner.

"I mean, my lease is up in six months but you could move in before that if you want."

"What about my cats?"

"They can come, too."

Daniel smiled, nodded. Laura shivered. The water was halfway drained and not nearly as warm as it was before. Daniel was getting a little cold, too, but he didn't want to get out yet. He wasn't ready for their bath to be over. The dark chocolate was gone and there was only bubbly swill left at the bottom of the champagne bottle.

"Hold on," Laura said.

Laura got up out of the tub. Without toweling off, she ran out of the bathroom, dripping water everywhere. She came back a minute later with a digital camera. She made a face at Daniel that said, "Can I?" Daniel nodded and, suddenly feeling a little self-conscious even though he didn't mind having his picture taken, covered his cock with his hand.

"Ah, ah, ah..." Laura said in a very disciplinary tone of voice. "Move your hand. You're covering the best part."

Daniel removed his hand and held the champagne bottle to his mouth, taking a huge, long sip, finishing off what was left, posing for Laura. Laura took a few pictures of Daniel naked, draining the champagne, the dark chocolate wrapper on the lip of the tub, then looked at the pictures on her digital camera, smiling as she did so.

"Damn, babe," she said, sounding turned on. "I want to post these on the internet. But, like, privately. So no one can see them."

"Or I dunno," she added a second later. "Maybe I do want people to see them. Would you mind?"

Daniel shook his head. He was feeling drunk and spacey.

Feeling drunk and Kevin Spacey... his intoxicated brain said, making himself inwardly laugh.

"Well, maybe later we'll post some. We'll see. You getting out?" Laura asked.

"I think I'm gonna lie here until the water's completely drained. I really want to see this thing through."

Laura smiled.

"Okay, well I'm cold. So I'm gonna go get dressed."

"Okay."

"Baybeee," Laura said.

"Baybeeeee!" Daniel drunkenly screamed.

Laura wrapped a towel around her naked body and left, tracking more water everywhere.

Daniel closed his eyes and just lay there, somehow completely oblivious to the fact that he hadn't seen a sad-looking blue whale in weeks.

GREASY, CARDBOARD HEART-COFFIN

DESPITE REMAINING STAGNANT, sitting there with the posture of some dark monument commemorating not just the sad-looking blue whale sitting across from him but all sad-looking blue whales everywhere, Daniel, with absolutely nothing else to do, mentally and restlessly paces back and forth across the small, bright orange boat, being very careful on every pass to step over the empty Big Mac container lying in the middle of the boat's floor.

On one side of the boat, as far as Daniel's sun-drained, squinting mind can see, water.

Water, water, water…

Sad-looking blue skies…

Daniel's mind turns, pivots, and after taking a large and slightly cartoonish, burglar-like step over the empty Big Mac container, paces the short distance to the other side of the bright orange boat.

More water…

More sad-looking blue skies…

Daniel's mind, disappointed but not surprised, turns and heads back. It continues on like this, going back and forth, back and forth, until the sad-looking blue whale accidentally snaps Daniel out of his restless daze.

"Do you know you have a gap forming in-between your two front teeth?"

Daniel feels his slightly agape mouth quickly snap shut.

"Jesus…" Daniel says, not knowing what else to say.

"What?"

"I dunno. It's just… you can't do that," he finally gets out of him.

"Can't do what?"

"*That.* What you just did. Spit out every thought that comes into your head."

"Why not?" the sad-looking blue whale asks.

"Because it hurts people's feelings," Daniel answers, then inconspicuously runs his tongue in-between the gap in his teeth, trying to feel if it's expanded since the last time he explored the vast dental crevice however long ago.

"Hmm…" the sad-looking blue whale says.

"What?" Daniel asks, annoyed.

"Nothing, really. It's just that even though I follow you humans around all the time, sometimes I forget how sensitive you are."

"We're not sensitive," Daniel snaps. "It's just, how would you like it if I blurted out every thought I had about you? Like how gross and slimy and ugly you look. And how you smell like wet, salty garbage that just shat itself. That wouldn't make you feel very fucking good, would it?"

The sad-looking blue whale pauses, thinks. And then, matter of factly, he answers, "I know all that, though."

Daniel narrows his eyes as they wrestle with the gaze of the sad-looking blue whale's.

"You know all what?"

"That. What you said. I know all that. I know what I'm like and what I'm not like. And I accept what I am and what I'm not. But humans? Humans don't. Humans seem to think they're special for some reason. And when you accidentally remind humans they're not special, or perfect, their feelings get hurt. But sad-looking blue whales? We know we're not special or perfect. We know how gross, slimy and ugly-looking we are. We know that we smell like…" The sad-looking blue whale pauses, thinks. "What did you say we smelled like?"

Daniel forces himself to choke down the mild embarrassment stuck in his throat and answers, "Wet, salty garbage that just shat itself."

"Yeah. Wet, salty garbage that just shat itself," the sad-looking blue whale says with a shrug. "Who cares?"

Daniel studies the sad-looking blue whale who, to his surveying eyes, probing as far into their darkness as they can, looks sincerely unaffected by Daniel's harsh words.

"It really doesn't bother you," Daniel concedes.

"Why should it? Everyone is gross, disgusting garbage that shat itself. A lot of humans just don't know they are. And then there are people—people like you—who know it and feel it too much. Like on a subliminal, nagging level."

"A subliminal, nagging level telling me I'm garbage?"

"Yeah. But at the same time, you're still human. You're still stuck in a world filled with people who act like what they're doing is so important and so special and so unique, and whether you know it or not, that rubs off on you. That makes you want to be special and unique. That makes you want to be like them. And so you're stuck between knowing you're garbage deep down and wanting to be more than garbage high above. And I know it might not seem it, but you're better off for it."

"For what? Knowing I'm garbage? How is anyone better off like that?"

"Because, only once you realize what absolute garbage you are can you realize that you're no better than anyone else, and they're no better than you, and only when you realize how equal you all are can you be a real person, and only after you're a real person can you realize that you're not actually garbage at all, that you're important, that you matter, that you can make a difference, and if you can make a difference that means you can even change the world, and anyone who can change the world for the better can't be garbage. Even though, deep down, they still are garbage. We all are."

Daniel's head spins like a warped Beach Boys record (*Pet Sounds*) being scratched by a junkie's needle.

"That makes no sense," he says. "You're contradicting yourself all over the place."

The sad-looking blue whale shrugs again.

"Life contradicts itself," he says. "It's filled with paradoxes. The only constant is change. If something scares you then you should probably be doing it. The more you learn the more you realize how little you actually know. The only certainty is that nothing is ever certain. The more you fail the more likely you are to succeed. And the way we're all garbage but yet we're also still so beautiful."

"Beautiful garbage..." the sad-looking blue whale says to himself, as if coining the phrase right there and then.

The sad-looking blue whale pauses, letting this idea echo inside his head as he further mulls it over. "See? There's another contradiction."

The sad-looking blue whale unzips his fanny pack and takes out a blue pen and notepad. He jots something down—most likely his new revelation, Daniel guesses—then flips the notepad shut and puts it and the pen back in his fanny pack. After he zips it closed, the sad-looking blue whale patrols the horizon with his eyes, as if now suddenly expecting something of significance to appear after this realization, like the Titanic rising from its watery grave to come and rescue them.

Daniel, no longer waiting on anything or anyone to save him and the sad-looking blue whale, landslides into a moody, contemplative silence.

Beautiful garbage… his brain echoes.

"Hey…" the sad-looking blue whale says inquiringly, his eyes still focused dreamily on the horizon, waiting on The Unsinkable Ship he's watched sink on VHS, probably, thousands and thousands of times.

Even though the sad-looking blue whale won't look at him, Daniel can tell he has something on his mind, ever so precariously balanced there, like the sad-looking blue whale's not sure if he should say it or ask it, whatever it is, before it falls off and shatters.

"What?" Daniel says.

The sad-looking blue whale doesn't say anything.

"Just say it," Daniel says. "What?"

The sad-looking blue whale turns and mushes his eyes into Daniel's.

"Why are you doing this?" he asks.

Daniel averts his eyes and his shoulders slump. When he eventually looks back at the sad-looking blue whale, inconspicuously and out of his periphery, the sad-looking blue whale wears an expression of regret that doesn't quite fit the features of his face, almost like if he could take back asking Daniel that question, he would.

"Forget it," the sad-looking blue whale says. "I'm sorry. It's none of my business."

"Because I'm garbage," Daniel answers sharply, so sharply he's surprised his tongue didn't slice open the inside of his mouth.

Daniel's gaze falls upon the empty Big Mac container, upon his greasy cardboard heart-coffin, upon this stoic piece of, what most people would consider, garbage.

"I'm garbage," Daniel repeats. "And not beautiful garbage. Just regular garbage. Gross garbage. Lethal garbage. There's this poison in me and it affects everyone I come in contact with. It seeps out of me—specifically, out of my heart—and goes into anyone who's nearby. Maybe not right away, but eventually… Eventually, it always happens."

"That look, Daniel… That goddamn look…"

"And I can't do that anymore. I can't poison one more person just to watch them inevitably leave me because they can't handle everything wrong with me. Whatever's in me needs to die with me. I need to get my heart as far away from people as I possibly can and then put it in something where it'll feel safe and secure and happy just to make sure it never wants to leave. And then I need to bury it just in case it ever gets any ideas of trying to escape. It's the only thing left to do. After thirty-one years of nothing but selfishness, it's the thoughtful and kind thing to do. It's the humane thing to do. The *only* thing left to do. Enough is enough. I can't make one more person sad. I mean, can you imagine making everyone so sad that no one wants to be around you? Do you have any idea what that's—"

Daniel bites his tongue, pauses, and after his soliloquy of self-loathing he sees that the sad-looking blue whale appears extra sad-looking, like he just finished watching *Titanic* for the first time ever and is going to bawl at any second.

Aware of this, and perhaps even self-conscious over it, the sad-looking blue whale gazes back out over the horizon. Except now his eyes no longer patrol the waters as if expecting to see the Titanic. They're very cognizant and accepting of the fact that the ship is sunken and never coming back. Especially not to save him and Daniel.

Holy shit… Daniel's brain says in disbelief, stunned at the potency of the poison inside him, knowing it was strong but never knowing it was *this* strong.

I can't believe it…

I can't believe I *just bummed out a sad-looking blue whale…*

IT'S A HORRIBLE LIFE

EVEN THOUGH IT was summer outside, the sky, rather than staying its stereotypical and seasonal—albeit crowd-pleasing—shade of bright blue, had turned the shade of murky dishwater in some diner kitchen during the early bird rush, and the sun, submerged beneath the sky's nasty gray soup of disgruntled soap and leftovers, looked like a large, forsaken dinner plate desperate to come up for fresh air.

For someone looking to be inspired, the sky left Daniel sorely wanting. The afternoon was encroaching and he was beginning to feel hopeless. He couldn't think straight anymore (or even crooked or askew), and sitting there in his booth, becoming more and more frustrated with himself, Daniel felt like his mind, not always constantly creative but still seldom this dull and vacuous, had been replaced by something else. Something bland and cheap and unimaginative, like wind chimes made of empty beer cans and that his thoughts were just the sullen, aluminum clinks produced by whatever lame breeze that decided to casually blow by.

My heart belongs…

The unfinished thought on the mostly blank page looked like a long and unusual name spelled out in a field of fresh snow when Daniel's mind suddenly ran out of urine. And Daniel wanted to rehydrate and replenish his mind, to chug mental liquids chock full of cerebral electrolytes so he could finally finish this "name," this new identity, this answer to his problems, but he couldn't concentrate. The persistent sad-looking blue whale was still at the back door of McDonald's, pulling it, shaking it, rattling it, trying anything and everything to let itself inside.

Except, of course, just pushing the damn thing.

And as if that wasn't distracting enough, hot, musical loaves of Christ kept coming fresh out of the speakers hidden in the ceiling, one after the other after the other, steaming with evangelism so pathetically trite, cliched and over the top that Daniel felt like he was beginning to lose it a little bit.

Daniel gathered his things, walked to the other end of the dining room and sat in a booth as far away from the back door as possible. He put his headphones in again, played "Life in Vain" by Daniel Johnston and put it on loop. Even though the song managed to tune everything out, Daniel still felt a little "off," like things around him were changing, or, more specifically, like the McDonald's dining area was changing, gradually transforming from some safe haven to the waiting room of a doctor's office. One with a broken clock on the wall that had a missing minute hand and nothing but outdated magazines about trucks and fishing to read—literature, yes, but literature not even close to interesting enough to distract from whatever looming test results the patient was waiting to receive.

A long-time sufferer of sad-looking blue whales, this sensation was nothing new to Daniel. Countless times throughout his life he had experienced this locational metamorphosis before (although never in McDonald's—any place other than McDonald's, really), which always resulted in his mind venting to itself, or confiding in itself, softly, secretly, like someone lost and all alone in an enormous, underground cave whispering to themselves, *Holy shit. I'm just so sad and scared right now...* A confession that always existentially deflated Daniel to the point where he felt the need to reach out and tell someone, anyone, how he was feeling or else possibly risk going mad from having to keep the weight of this heavy and hushed sadness inside him.

Feeling this way now, this overwhelmed, like he was beyond lost and doomed, Daniel picked up his phone, ready to text either of his best friends, Dave or Greg—or possibly both—when his phone began vibrating in his hand.

It was Laura.

Daniel tensed up. Nausea brewed unlawfully in his gut like gastric moonshine. He hadn't heard from Laura since she called and told him she was moving to Miami, briefly, and then to Sweden, permanently, for a new job. Daniel ignored the call and let it go to voicemail.

Good... his brain said.

Don't be pathetic…

Pretend you're busy…

Pretend you have a life…

Pretend you just didn't skip work today…

After the call ended, his phone buzzed. Laura had left him a voicemail.

"Hey, Daniel. It's me. Call me as soon as you get this. We need to talk about something."

Her voice sounded strained and serious. Daniel walked outside, sat down on the sidewalk by some balding bush and called Laura. She picked up after the second ring.

"Screening my calls?"

"What's wrong?" Daniel asked.

Laura sighed into the phone. "I had this yeast infection, or so I thought. Anyway, I went to the doctor to get it checked out and, long story short, I have chlamydia."

Daniel felt even more nauseous. His heart was racing. He was glad he was sitting down.

Chlamydia? What's chlamydia exactly? Am I going to die?

"Over the last year I've only been with you and that other guy I was with two months before we started dating that I told you about."

"Did you guys use a condom?" Daniel asked.

"Did you and I use a condom on our first date?" she said.

Daniel skeeved. He wanted to vomit into the balding bush. He had chlamydia and was going to die from it.

"I need you to go and get checked out because I need to know whether or not I need to contact that kid and tell him he gave me chlamydia."

"How do you know you didn't have it before him? Were you tested?"

"Yes, Daniel," Laura said, sounding aggravated. "And apparently you don't just get it from having sex either. You can get it from just touching your partner's genitals and it can also lie dormant without symptoms for a while, so you can have it and not even know you have it."

"Okay…" Daniel said.

"Okay? All you have to say is 'okay?'"

"Jesus, Laura. What do you want me to say?"

"I don't know. How about, 'Sorry I gave you chlamydia.'"

"We don't know I'm the one who gave it to you. And I'm pretty sure I didn't," Daniel said, mentally flipping through the pages of his romantic past. The girls he usually slept with were girlfriends. He'd only had two one-night stands in his entire life. Laura, on the other hand, after Daniel asked her how many partners she'd had, just shrugged and replied, "I dunno… I've lost count at this point."

"Well, all I know is that I didn't have chlamydia before and now I do, and I've only been with you and that other kid after I last got checked, so someone gave it to me."

"Alright. Relax. I'll go get checked."

They mangled some type of goodbyes and Daniel hung up.

A sad-looking blue whale sat down on the sidewalk beside Daniel and put its fin around his shoulder. This was not the call Daniel had expected to get from Laura. When he saw her name on his phone his heart, although he didn't admit it at the time, did this little leap thing, like when a dancer in a musical jumped and gaily clicked their heels together, thinking maybe she was calling to say that she missed him or that she was thinking about him or perhaps even that she even wanted to get back together. But Laura didn't want to get back together with Daniel. Laura had chlamydia and was moving to Miami briefly and then Sweden permanently. Daniel was going nowhere. Daniel was going back inside McDonald's. The same McDonald's Daniel had pointed out to Laura when they were driving by it together for the first time and said, "See that? That's my McDonald's. That's where I do all my writing. I've probably spent at least a year of my life in there total. Probably more, actually." To which Laura replied with a scoff, "Wow… That's sad, babe. That's, like, really pathetic."

The sad-looking blue whale stood up and randomly walked off. Daniel got up, sulked back inside and sat down. He looked at the waterlogged receipt on the table that he was using as a coaster for what was left of his heavily perspiring iced coffee. At the bottom of the receipt was an offer. If you went online and did a survey you could win a McDonald's gift card. Daniel imagined Laura sitting there beside him and saying, "Oh my god, babe, we should do this," then stuffing the receipt inside her big yellow purse already stuffed with other receipts and coupons she'd saved promising her discounts or buy one get one frees.

Daniel crumpled the receipt for his iced coffee. He allowed himself to admit that he missed Laura, that he didn't want her plane to crash into the Atlantic as he had previously fantasized about on numerous past occasions. Daniel hoped Laura would be happy in Sweden with her new job and, eventually, her new boyfriend. He hoped her new boyfriend would be a happy person who made her smile a lot. Daniel wanted to call Laura under the pretense of asking her more questions about her STD, but really, he just wanted to hear her voice one last time. He wanted to say goodbye. He wanted to say sorry for making her so sad so often. He wanted to apologize for not knowing how to fight off the onslaught of sad-looking blue whales, for not being stronger somehow.

Poor Laura...

Poor all of the "Lauras" who had come before Laura... said Daniel's brain, which proceeded to then wonder how many girls he had unintentionally pushed away from him.

Instead of masochistically doing the math, Daniel kind of curled into the fetal position, or curled into the fetal position as much as he could while sitting in his booth, and just as he was about to Google "male chlamydia symptoms" on his phone…

THUD!

THUD!

Daniel jumped in his booth. His mind, startled, panicked and, therefore, insanely unreasonable, immediately pictured two condors flying into the window next to him, as if that was the most logical explanation given the unusually loud and booming nature of both sudden noises. But when Daniel looked outside, he saw a much more reasonable explanation—two sad-looking blue whales had their faces pressed up against the glass and were staring at him.

Daniel stared back and, while doing so, noticed something on the window.

No, not on the window…

In the window…

In front of their hideous, sad-looking faces fogging up the glass was a small hairline crack where one of the sad-looking blue whales had just slammed their heads.

Tiny and curved upwards, the crack looked like it was sadistically grinning at Daniel.

Oooh, ooooooh, oooooh… one of the sad-looking blue whales cried.

BAYYYBEE!!!

LAURA WAS A LANDSCAPE ARCHITECT. She knew a lot about different types of plants and trees. She also knew a lot about yoga and "natural" things and things that were "healthy," i.e. things Daniel knew absolutely nothing about. Daniel liked this about Laura, though. He liked that, as they grew closer, she wanted to share her knowledge of these things with him. He liked the way she lovingly tried to force vegetables on his mainly carnivorous appetite by sneaking spinach into her Sunday morning omelets or by putting some random green on his dinner plate even though he said he didn't want any.

Laura enjoyed cooking for Daniel, something she mentioned to him often. "Fattening up my man," she often called it, and even when she tried hiding vegetables in his food, Daniel enjoyed her desire to take care of him. To Daniel's surprise, Laura happily took on the part of the "well-behaved 1950's housewife" in the kitchen. The type of wife who wants to keep her man full and satisfied, leaving Daniel more than happy to play the part of the typical 1950's husband who let his wife do these things for him. It was insanely old fashioned, both of them knew, but they also both secretly got off on it for some reason that neither of them tried to understand. Almost like they didn't want to run the risk of spoiling it.

"Do you want the last burger?" Laura asked Daniel one night at dinner.

Laura's kitchen table was a black, metal, decoratively grated patio table. Daniel had dropped his fork and one of its points was stuck in its grating.

"No, thanks. That was very good, though," Daniel said while trying to liberate his fork. His plate was clean. Nothing but small streaks of ketchup and crumbs even though he didn't particularly enjoy Laura's burgers the few times she'd made them for him.

"Are you sure?" Laura asked. "I'm not hungry and I don't want any more." She grabbed his thigh and squeezed it. And then, very tight lipped and with her mouth clenched, "We need to fatten you up baby!"

"Bayyyyybeeee!" Daniel said.

"Bayyyyybeeeeee!" Laura screamed and then laughed, squeezing his thigh again, tighter than before.

"I'm good, thanks. I think I'm fat enough already," Daniel said.

Laura groaned.

"You're such a fucking woman."

Laura grabbed their plates and walked over to the sink.

"Come do the dishes. I'm gonna pack you this burger for lunch tomorrow. This way you don't have to spend money."

Daniel finally freed his fork from the hole in the table and got up and began doing the dishes. Laura packed him a lunch for the next day, then walked over to him and slapped his ass and squeezed it with both hands.

"This ass! This big fat fuckin *ASSSS!* Mmm! I love it. I want it bigger. I want it fatter, baybeee. Juicier! I want it to have celluloid and then I want you to sit on my face and suffocate me as a kind of foreplay."

Daniel smiled even though his hands were cold. The hot water had recently stopped working in Laura's kitchen sink so he had to clean the dishes with only cold water.

Laura slapped Daniel's ass and said, "Don't forget your burger for tomorrow. I put some spinach on it. Just eat it, please. Don't take it off."

"I won't," Daniel lied. He could already picture this spinach sprinkled on top of the garbage in the backroom where he worked.

"I'm gonna do this for you more often. You spend too much money on lunch from what you tell me. Money you don't even have," and then Laura laughed in a way that pinched Daniel's nerves, sending twinges of rippling aggravation throughout his body.

But Daniel mentally forged forward, trying to get over it, trying to get over himself and not let one small comment ruin their, otherwise, pleasant evening.

"Oh wait, I forgot. I got you something," Daniel said.

Daniel dried his hands on a wash cloth hanging on the stove's handle, ran over to his messenger bag and pulled out a gift wrapped present.

"Ooooh," Laura said as Daniel handed it to her.

"Don't let the wrapping paper fool you. It's not a real present or anything. I'm poor after all, remember?"

Daniel resumed doing the dishes. Laura curled up on the couch with her present and her glass of white wine leftover from dinner.

"It looks like a boy wrapped this," Laura said, smiling, as she rotated the present with her hand, critiquing the wrapping job.

"Haha. Fuck off," Daniel said.

"I think I know what this is…"

As Laura unwrapped her present, Daniel watched over his shoulder.

"I knew it," Laura said as she ripped the last of the wrapping paper off Daniel's two books of poetry. "Thank you, baby. I'm so excited to read these."

Laura began flipping through the pages.

"Just a reminder… One of the books is nothing but love poems and there's kind of some graphic stuff in there about me and past girlfriends. So you don't have to read that one if you don't want to."

"Damn," Laura said. "Your books are kind of long."

Daniel felt that same twinge he fended off just seconds ago. He could barely feel his hands. The sink water was fucking freezing.

"You don't have to read them if you don't want to. You just asked when you could read them so I gave you a copy of each."

"No. I want to read them," Laura said. "Thank you, baby."

"Bayybeee!" Daniel half-screamed.

"Bayyyyybeee!" Laura screamed.

She put down the books, walked over to the sink and gave Daniel a kiss on the cheek.

"Don't be mad…" Laura said out of nowhere. "Okay?"

"Okay," Daniel said, already feeling himself becoming upset over whatever she was about to tell him.

"I kind of want a cigarette right now," Laura admitted

"Sure. Go ahead. Smoke. If you want me to punch you in the tit."

"Babe…" Laura whined.

"It was your idea for me to help you quit."

"Oh, come on. Just one?"

"Read the contract," Daniel said, and with his hands busy washing dishes, he motioned his head to their smoking contract still taped to the front door.

Laura groaned. She picked up one of Daniel's books, wandered over to the couch, flopped down and began skimming the pages.

"It's not like that really matters anymore. I had one at work today."

When Daniel looked over his shoulder at Laura, she had this big, evil, satisfied grin on her face.

"I had a stressful day, so at lunch I went outside and had a cigarette."

"Laura…"

"What? Are you going to punch me in the tit?" she said in a confrontational, almost-challenging tone of voice that only made Daniel even more frustrated, like not only was she not taking her quitting smoking seriously but that she wasn't taking him seriously either. Daniel shook his head, feeling frustrated, powerless.

"You signed a contract," he said.

"Oh my god. It's one cigarette. Get over it," Laura said. "It's not a big deal."

"It is and it isn't."

"Babe, seriously. Stop being such a pussy."

Daniel gulped down his rage just like he had with the vegetables he'd eaten for dinner, the vegetables Laura had forced him to eat, and focused on washing the dishes. Laura got up, grabbed Daniel's other book of poetry and sat down on the couch with it.

"Which one has graphic stuff about you and other girlfriends in it?"

"Duhhhhhhhh, the one labeled love poems, smart guy."

"Hurrr hurrr," Laura said in a blatant, over the top "idiot voice."

"How graphic are we talking?" she asked.

"Graphic," Daniel replied. He was down to washing the last fork. Thank god.

"I feel like you wouldn't have given me this book of love poems unless you wanted me to read about you fucking other girls. I feel like you're trying to make me jealous."

"You asked for the books and so I gave them to you," Daniel said, then grabbed the hand towel hanging off the stove door again and dried his cold, aching hands.

"It won't work, though."

"What won't?"

"You trying to make me jealous by making me read about you and other girls. I'll probably get off on it actually."

Daniel didn't know how to react to this. His mind furrowed its untrimmed unibrow as he went over to the fridge and grabbed a beer.

"It's okay. Even if you are trying to make me jealous, I'll get you back when I write my memoirs," Laura said.

Feeling like he was being egged on, like Laura was trying to antagonize him, Daniel sat down at the kitchen table across the room from Laura and took a sip of his beer instead of inquiring about her memoirs like she wanted him to. When Daniel didn't press further with any follow up question, Laura continued on anyway.

"I'm going to write them someday. I've seen so much and I've been so many places I'd be crazy not to. It's going to include my relationships, too. I've had a lot of weird relationships and a lot of weird one-night stands. And you're going to have to read about them since I have to read about yours."

Daniel took another sip of beer and stared down at the kitchen table, pretending to pay only a vague amount of attention to Laura even though he was anxiously cliffhanging onto her every word.

"Like the guy I fucked before you and I started dating. I swear to god, babe, his dick had two pee holes. It was crazy. I'd never seen anything like it before."

Daniel looked at Laura's bed in the middle of the room and imagined her sucking off some strange guy in it, some guy who had two pee holes in his dick. His stomach contorted with jealousy.

"He kept telling me it was normal, that tons of guys had two pee holes, and I was like no way. I told him I'd seen a lot of cocks in my time and that I'd never seen one with two pee holes. Granted, one hole was smaller than the other, but still, it was there, without a doubt—a second small hole on the head of his cock. And when we finished fucking he even pulled out his phone and Googled his—" She paused briefly. "I dunno… I guess you'd call it a condition? Anyway, he pulled up stuff on it. It did have a name, but it wasn't nearly as common as he made it seem. Weirdest fucking pillow talk ever, though. That's for sure."

Another sip of beer, much larger than the last. Daniel looked through the window even though it was dark outside and he couldn't see anything.

"He couldn't cum," Laura said after a few seconds. She was holding Daniel's collection of love poems upside down in her hands and her eyes were far away, back in time, thinking of this guy with two pee holes. "He kept getting mad at himself and eventually he just gave up. I wonder if it's because he has two pee holes. Like if that makes it harder for him to cum for some reason. But why would it, I guess? There are more holes for the semen to come out of."

Daniel finished his beer. He got up, walked to the fridge and grabbed another.

"Whoa, easy," Laura said as Daniel cracked open his second beer in under three minutes.

"Hey," he said with a smug smile. "I'll curb my drinking when you curb your smoking."

"I had *one* fucking cigarette," Laura said.

"And I had *one* fucking beer."

Daniel sat back down at the kitchen table. He took his phone out of his pocket and checked his email just to have something to do rather than loiter in this new mounting tension between him and Laura.

"Thanks again for these," he heard Laura say, sounding more aggravated than grateful.

Laura dropped the books on the coffee table and got up and walked to her purse. After rummaging around, she pulled out her cigarettes and a lighter. Without saying a word, she walked out the front door. Daniel put his phone and beer down on the table and looked at their signed contract taped above its doorknob.

The door swung back open.

Daniel expected Laura—he thought it would be her returning to apologize—but instead, a sad-looking blue whale peeked its head inside. It ripped their contract off the door, crumpled it into a ball and threw it on the floor. Then the sad-looking blue whale left.

Daniel stood in place for a moment. He was caught off guard. He hadn't really seen, or thought about, sad-looking blue whales as of late. Daniel walked over to Laura's desk and grabbed the Scotch tape. He walked over to their signed contract, picked it up, uncrumpled it, and taped it back onto the door. As Daniel returned the tape to Laura's desk, he noticed her jacket hanging off the back of the chair. The very same jacket she wore to work every day. Daniel leaned in and sniffed. The jacket smelled like much more than one cigarette. In fact, it reeked off smoke.

"Ooh, ooooh, oooooooh!" Daniel heard the sad-looking blue whale cry from outside.

GREASY, CARDBOARD HEART-COFFIN

WITH HIS BURNT skin beginning to harden like leftover pizza crust, Daniel, more desperately than a Saturday morning cartoon character opening an umbrella over its head to fend off a plummeting grand piano, visors the sun with his hand as he looks up at the sky.

Despite being extremely bright and friendly in its overt blueness, like it would tousle his hair and call him "Sport" if it were able, Daniel finds something about the mild blue yonder endlessly yawning above them to be cheap, plain and inexpressive. Even the clouds seem lethargic to him, like amorphous, plump tricks too passively strung out on their own altitude to be shoved along by the overly demanding, and often cruel, pimp-wind.

"The clouds aren't moving..." Daniel says in a tone of voice that seems to limbo underneath the ambiguous pole of either a statement or a question.

The sad-looking blue whale squints his eyes at the clouds, almost straining them to the wrinkled, geriatric point where they're just about entirely closed.

"Hold on..." the sad-looking blue whale says.

The sad-looking blue whale unzips his fanny pack and takes out a pair of bi-focals. He puts them on and looks back up at the clouds.

"Hmm..." the sad-looking blue whale says during his now more focused examination.

"What? They're not moving, right? Like, I'm not crazy."

"Well, they're definitely not moving," the sad-looking blue whale says.

The sad-looking blue whale takes off his bi-focals and, contemplatively, bites down on the left end piece.

"What?" Daniel says. "Do you think it means anything?"

The sad-looking blue whale gives an unconcerned shrug and, as if having nothing more to say on the unusual and unmoving manner of the clouds, puts his bi-focals back in his fanny pack.

"We're never going to make it," Daniel says. "We're never going to make it to the bottom of the ocean. The sad-looking blue whales are never going to find us. I'm never going to bury my heart beneath the ocean floor. We're going to die out here like this."

Daniel waits for the sad-looking blue whale to speak up and console him, to disagree and assure him that everything is going to be okay, but watching the sad-looking blue whale obliviously rummage around inside his fanny pack, Daniel almost laughs out loud at himself, at his absurd and delirious expectation for this sad-looking blue whale to ever be anything more than just that—a sad-looking blue whale.

Seeking solace elsewhere, Daniel looks down at the empty Big Mac container only to find that, along with not speaking to him, now it won't even make eye contact with Daniel anymore, like it's turning a cold, cardboarded shoulder in his direction. The only consolation from all of this is the occasional breeze that, when it does decide to blow by, possesses a feminine kindness to it, taking pity on poor Daniel with its refreshingly cool and plump lips of gaseous mercy, momentarily making him forget about the railroad spikes of light constantly driving themselves into his already reddened temples.

"I feel like I'm losing it. I feel the sun is turning my skin into a straitjacket," Daniel says, and as if to prove to himself that his arms are still free and unbound, he begins mindlessly and therapeutically stroking his beard.

Daniel looks at the sad-looking blue whale to see the sad-looking blue whale already gawking at him.

"What?" Daniel asks.

"Your beard," the sad-looking blue whale says.

"What about it?" Daniel says and, self-consciously, stops running his hand through his caveman-like collection of crusty facial hair.

"Nothing, really. It just makes us look like we've been lost at sea for decades," the sad-looking blue whale says.

Daniel leans overboard and stares at his reflection in the water. His tangled crop of long and bristly ginger-brown hair is so comically large and novelty-sized his beard almost looks fake on him.

"I look like Tom Hanks in *Cast Away*," Daniel says. "I *feel* like Tom Hanks in *Cast Away*. Only more insane."

"Tom who?" the sad-looking blue whale asks.

"Hanks? …Tom Hanks?"

"Was he in *Titanic*?"

"No…"

"Oh," the sad-looking blue whale says, sounding disappointed. And then, almost inaudibly, as if he has no idea he's speaking out loud, "He should've been in *Titanic*."

Daniel imagines Tom Hanks in *Titanic*, cast as the wooden paneling that Kate Winslet floats on at the end.

Titanic... *Starring Leonardo DiCaprio, Kate Winslet and Tom Hanks as "The Wooden Paneling…"*

Tom Hanks in a door-shaped costume with Kate Winslet floating on top of him…

"Are you crying? Are you crying?! There's no crying! There's no crying in base-balllll!" Tom Hanks yells at Kate Winslet as she floats on top of him in his door-shaped costume…

"Cut!!!" James Cameron screams from behind the camera and, frustrated, begins massaging his temples…

"Wrong movie," Kate Winslet whispers to Tom Hanks in her sexy English accent…

"Oh…" Tom Hanks says, feeling embarrassed for ruining the take, but still somehow manages to win a Golden Globe (Best Supporting Actor) for his stunningly stoic portrayal of "The Wooden Paneling" anyway…

"Will there be any kind of award?" Daniel asks. "Or, I dunno… trophy?"

"For what?"

"You know…" Daniel begins, then stops to adjust himself, sitting up as straight and regally as possible while his sweat-soaked t-shirt clings to him tighter than all of his lifelong insecurities. Trying not to come off with a snooty air of importance, but somehow failing, at least a little, Daniel says, "For being The Chosen One."

"Oh… I dunno. Probably. If you want, I guess," the sad-looking blue whale says and, suddenly seeming uncomfortable, averts his eyes.

"I definitely wouldn't mind. I've never won an award or anything before."

"I won an award once," the sad-looking blue whale says. "For a short story I wrote."

"A *Titanic* fan fiction short story," the sad-looking blue whale elaborates after Daniel just sits there in a cold, uninterested silence.

"Where Jack and Rose both freeze to death in the water at the end," the sad-looking blue whale elaborates even further after Daniel's cold silence seems to mirror the freezing water that turned Jack into a teen heart-throbbing, human Popsicle.

Daniel lets out a small sun drunken laugh as he wraps his arms around himself and begins rocking back and forth.

"What?" the sad-looking blue whale asks.

"Nothing. I was just thinking I'd rather never read again than only be able to read *Titanic* fan fiction."

"It's all we're allowed to read, though," the sad-looking blue whale says. "Or write for that matter. The sad-looking elder blue whales back home are really strict about that sort of thing. Speaking of which, maybe don't bring up the fact that I'm working on a novel that isn't *Titanic* fan fiction. Ya know… if we don't die out here."

Daniel sighs. Still rocking back and forth, only faster now, and a little more psychotically, he says, "We didn't think this out very well, did we?"

"I definitely don't think it would've hurt to at least bring a book of crossword puzzles or something," the sad-looking blue whale replies.

"I was thinking more along the lines of food and water."

"Oh…" the sad-looking blue whale says. "Yeah. That too… But hey, if you're bored, and I know it's no crossword puzzle, I can read you my children's novel to pass the time. I have a copy in my fanny pack."

Confusion contorts the features all over Daniel's face.

"Your novel is a children's novel?"

"Well, one is. I have two separate books. The novel I'm working on now and the children's fiction novel I wrote a few years ago. Speaking of which, again, if we don't die out here and make it to the ocean floor, maybe don't bring up the fact that I wrote a children's novel either."

"Does everyone die at the end of that too?"

The sad-looking blue whale, dense in the vulgar vernacular of sarcasm, hesitates.

"Well, I don't want to spoil the ending, but… Ya know what? I'll just read it to you—"

THUMP!

Daniel gently lurches forward in his seat as the bright-orange boat comes to a sudden stop.

“Ow!” the sad-looking blue whale says as he grabs the back of his head with his fin.

Daniel blinks once.

He blinks twice.

He slowly stands up.

With his palm open and fingers spread, he reaches out and places a hand on the horizon.

“What the hell?” Daniel says as he tilts his head back, looking straight up.

“What?” the dazed sad-looking blue whale asks. “What was that?”

“The horizon…” Daniel says. “It’s fake.”

IT'S A HORRIBLE LIFE

IT'D BEEN AROUND fifteen minutes and the two sad-looking blue whales looming outside—the very same ones who'd slammed their heads against the window so forcefully that the sullen yet blunt impact left behind a small grinning crack in the glass—still hadn't so much as budged or blinked.

Daniel wanted to look away from this downcast tableau of the world's most blatant peeping toms, but there was something new in the sad-looking blue whales' eyes he was trying to comprehend. Something alarming, something lustful. Their eyes seemed to be bulging with a glistening dark hunger, an insatiability, like their eyes would be licking their lips if they had any and that Daniel was the meal they were currently salivating over.

One of the sad-looking blue whales put its fins flat up against the glass, leaning on the window with further desperation. The other sad-looking blue whale did the same. Under the weight of the additional sad-looking blue pressure, Daniel heard a small *tink* sound, like a teacup passing gas, and could've sworn he noticed the crack in the window microscopically grow.

Nervous, Daniel grabbed his things and moved across the dining room to a table against a wall with no windows. A few seats away, an elderly female patron sat alone, holding her cup of coffee as if it was a small, cardboard urn. Her table was covered in a bunch of newspapers and coupons she had cut out of them.

"Looks like rain," the old lady said, unprovoked.

Still busy settling down, Daniel couldn't tell if the lady was talking to him or to herself.

"Excuse me?" he said even though he'd heard her clearly, and in the split second that passed since wondering if she was speaking to him or not, Daniel realized that she was, in fact, talking to him, and any doubt as to whether she initially was or not just stemmed from the anti-social hope that a stranger wasn't about to try and strike up a conversation with him.

"Looks like rain," the elderly patron repeated. "I didn't think it was supposed to today. The weather station said it'd be sunny."

She raised the small cardboard urn to her lips and took a small, respectful sip. Daniel was untangling his headphones, desperate not to sink any further into the black tar pit of this elderly woman's oncoming small talk.

"I hope it doesn't rain," she said. "I walked here. If I had known it was going to rain, I would've drove."

Daniel glanced outside. The already dark sky was becoming even darker and the wind was rocking the street lights back and forth. It looked like rain alright, and noticing this, and being ever aware of his increasingly dreadful mood, Daniel began feeling anxious. He felt himself beginning to relive an old childhood fear he never fully grew out of. That he, Daniel, glum and hapless, was somehow altering the weather with his own shitty emotions, that the dark sky was simply just a reflection of what he was feeling on the inside.

"My children don't want me driving," the old lady said. "Can you imagine that? Your own children telling *you* you're not allowed to drive. I've been driving for over fifty years."

As hard as he tried, Daniel couldn't unknot his headphones. If anything, it seemed he was just tangling them worse.

"I didn't even bring an umbrella," she added. "And it takes me a while to walk places. I'm not as young as I used to be, ya know?"

Daniel looked at the old lady and smiled. Not out of politeness. Because he just successfully unknotted his headphones and was going to be free from this uncomfortable line of communication he'd unwillingly gotten himself into.

Daniel put his headphones in. He played the song "Story of an Artist" by Daniel Johnston and put it on loop, leaving the old lady alone with the Christian rock. Prompted by a morbid curiosity, Daniel looked back at his window to see the two sad-looking blue whales still standing outside, staring at him across the dining room. Daniel quickly averted his eyes to the table's surface covered in sugar. Staring at the leftover sugar, imagining himself cutting it into lines and snorting it, Daniel heard a muffled, prune-like voice rise up over the volume of his music. He took off his headphones and saw the old lady already looking back at him and pointing to the sugar on his table.

"I said, 'people need to learn to clean up after themselves.'"

"Oh. Yeah," Daniel agreed.

"I know the gentleman who left the mess. He does it all the time. And I tell him, too. I tell him every day to stop leaving a mess because then one of the nice Spanish ladies has to come and clean up after him. I tell him just because it's their job to clean up the dining room that doesn't mean we have to make it harder on them, but..."

The old lady threw her hands up in the air as if saying, "What are you going to do?" She grabbed her scissors and began cutting more coupons out of the newspapers. Watching her arthritic hands snip away at a coupon for orange juice, a sudden twinge of fear raked at the back of Daniel's head. He wondered if, at some point in her life, this old lady was ever like him, if she ever used to be introverted and quiet and tried to avoid conversation at all costs, but now, after years of neglect, after her husband had died and her kids had moved away and her grandchildren had gone off to college, loneliness had finally burrowed its way inside her. Under no circumstances could Daniel ever imagine himself starting a conversation with a complete stranger, but his life, now more so than ever, seemed to be on a similar trajectory with the old lady's. It was easy, almost too easy, for Daniel to picture himself as an old man, sitting in the back of McDonald's and sipping coffee. He had no wife, no children, no real friends to speak of, and so this was it, this would be the full extent of his future socialization, waiting for someone, for anyone, really, young or old, to walk by so he could verbally reach out with an offhanded comment about the weather, stopping the person dead in their tracks and forcing them to interact with him just so Daniel could feel the most minuscule of connections with another human being, just so he could be sure he still actually existed.

Suddenly feeling like a kindred spirit with the old lady, Daniel's anxiety transformed into sympathy, and instead of putting his headphones on and drowning her out again, Daniel surprised himself when he actually began talking to her.

"My girlfriend used to do that," he said, looking at the old lady's collection of coupons.

"Couponing?" she asked.

"Yeah. She lived for deals."

"Well, she sounds like a smart girl to me."

"Yeah. She definitely was."

"You keep referring to her in the past tense. Did it not work out between you two?"

Daniel hogtied the truth, put duct tape over its mouth and threw it in the trunk of his mind.

"She passed away," he couldn't believe he found himself saying.

The old lady tilted her head sympathetically and wrinkled her already-wrinkled brow the same way everyone does when they hear such news.

"I'm so sorry. That's just awful."

"Thank you," Daniel said while wondering what specific layer of hell he'd be burning in after he died.

"Was it sudden?"

Daniel nodded. "Car crash."

"Oh how horrible."

"Yeah... She was a great girl."

"I'm sure she was. It doesn't seem quite fair, does it? That some people lose their lives so tragically young and then there are old windbags like me that seem to be going on forever and ever. She's still with you though, ya know?"

"I know," Daniel said, even though if his fictional dead girlfriend were real he wouldn't believe that at all.

"She's with God now," the old lady added

Daniel forced out a sacrilegious, fake smile.

"I love this music," the old lady said, looking up toward the ceiling where the speakers playing Christian rock were located. "It's so much better than that awful modern stuff they used to play. Although, you're young. You probably love that sort of thing!"

The old lady laughed at herself and Daniel's fake smile turned into a work of non-fiction.

"Nah, not really," he said.

"Good. Good for you."

The old lady checked her wrist watch.

"Alright. It looks like it's time for me to be going." She began gathering her coupons and sliding them into a Ziploc bag. "It still looks like rain and I didn't bring an umbrella with me. It takes me a while to walk places these days. I'm not as young as I used to be, ya know?"

"Do you need a ride?"

"Oh no. That's very sweet of you, but I'll manage. I live close by. Thank you, though."

"Sure."

"Here..." the old lady said, looking through the tops of her bifocals at a coupon she was holding. "Maybe you can use this."

The old lady put a coupon down on Daniel's table. A coupon for a half-priced Big Mac.

"Oh cool. Definitely. Thanks so much. Have a great day."

The old lady draped her purse over her shoulder and pointed a finger at Daniel.

"I'm going to pray for your girlfriend. She's with God now. So don't you worry about her."

"I won't," Daniel said, inwardly cringing. "Thank you."

"Have a good day, dear. And be safe out there. It really looks like rain."

"Thanks. You too."

The old lady traipsed away. Daniel sighed to himself and wiped the sugar off his table. He wondered if he had chlamydia. He closed his eyes tight, sat very still and tried to see if he could somehow feel the STD coursing through his body, but all he could feel was this groping longing for Laura, for something familiar and comfortable to momentarily combat the low hanging, fog-like emptiness in the pit of his stomach.

Daniel picked up his coupon and stared at it like a long-lost puzzle piece, the one missing right in the center of the puzzle, but then, when you go to put the piece in, it doesn't fit, and only after looking at the piece more closely do you realize it doesn't belong to this puzzle. It belongs to another puzzle with a single piece missing, and instead of finding that puzzle and putting the piece back in its box, you bend it, you tear at its edges until it fits, until you're able to cram it inside the unwanting foreign puzzle that it doesn't actually belong to.

Daniel checked his phone. It was forty-five minutes or so until eleven-thirty when they started serving lunch, which, thanks to the old lady's generosity, he could now afford. Daniel decided that, even though he wasn't hungry yet, he would get in line at eleven twenty-nine and buy himself a Big Mac, filling the emptiness inside him any way he could.

Anything just to get from one moment to the next.

BAYYYBEE!!!

LAURA HAD eyes like small evangelical hemorrhoid pillows dipped in blue honey.

Daniel loved Laura's eyes and the way he felt like someone was holding a knife to his throat whenever they stared at him. It was scary looking back into those eyes, but also exciting, like anything—good or bad, great or worse—could happen. Laura's eyes, or, mainly, the unpredictability practically vibrating inside of them, was really the first thing that attracted Daniel to her. It was even one of the first things he loved about her, but now, months into their relationship, at that comfy, sweatpants-point where a relationship's two occupants really begin easing into the snug banality of each another, Daniel hadn't seen, or felt, that enthralling optical thrill of hers in a while.

It was early one Friday night. Daniel and Laura were lying on the couch— Daniel, sitting up, and Laura with her head resting on his lap —as they watched a DVD they'd already seen three or four times.

"Don't fall asleep," Daniel blurted out at random. As of late, Laura had been passing out around eight or nine o'clock, leaving Daniel, ever the night owl, wide awake, bored and restless in a house where there wasn't much else for him to do but read.

"I'm sleepy," Laura murmured.

"Well wake up," Daniel said. "Drink some coffee or something. It's Friday night for shits sake."

"I think DVDs put me to sleep."

"Then let's do something."

Suddenly, Laura's torso seemed to levitate upward from its horizontal position, like a vampire doing a single ab crunch in its coffin, and when her eyes mingled with Daniel's, they were flickering with wily, blue fire.

"I know what we can do," she said.

Laura got up and half-ran into the kitchen. Daniel followed. Laura opened a drawer and pulled out a Ziploc baggie that had a small amount of white powder inside it.

"Do you want to?" she asked, holding the baggie up for Daniel to see.

Daniel had never done cocaine before. In fact, all drugs had never really appealed to him in general so there was a lot he hadn't done—or had the will to do—but standing there with those magnificent eyes chiseling into his like ravenous, blue jackhammers, Daniel let a grin slip out the corner of his mouth.

"Sure," he said.

"Have you done it before?"

Daniel shook his head.

"Oh… Well, you don't have to do it if you don't want to."

"Let's do it," Daniel said.

"Yeah?"

"Yeah."

"Because, really… You don't have to if you're nervous—"

"Oh my god, let's do the fucking cocaine already."

Suddenly excited, and very much awake, Laura rushed over to her purse where she reached inside and pulled out a credit card and a dollar bill.

"Grab one of your poetry books."

Daniel grinned. He snagged one of his books of poetry off the coffee table and he and Laura sat down at the kitchen table. Daniel put his book down and Laura poured the cocaine onto its front cover.

"Whatever you do, don't sneeze," she said with a big smile.

Laura chopped the cocaine into three lines with her credit card even though there was only the two of them. Then she began rolling up the dollar bill, although now, up close, Daniel could see the dollar bill was actually a one-hundred-dollar bill.

"Ooooh. Fancy-ass rich bitch," Daniel said.

"Stop. Do *not* make me laugh."

Laura held the rolled up hundred-dollar bill to her nose. She leaned in and, in one very quick fluent motion, snorted the first line of cocaine. Then she sat back almost as quickly as she leaned in and her face scrunched up, making Daniel laugh.

"Whooooooo!" Laura said, trying to stretch her facial features back into their normal positions. She handed Daniel the rolled up hundred-dollar bill. "Just make sure not to accidentally exhale."

Daniel nervously made the mental note, then leaned in and snorted the second line of cocaine the same way he'd seen Laura do it. He jerked back up and winced, also the same way Laura had. He didn't know what he was expecting cocaine to feel like, but this wasn't it.

"It feels like a car just back fired in my throat."

Laura laughed and wiped her nose.

"Seriously. It tastes like gasoline or something," Daniel added.

"Yeah, sometimes people lace it with shit."

Daniel felt his heart begin to race but he wasn't sure if it was because of the cocaine or what Laura had just said.

"Lace it with shit? Where'd you get this from?"

"My brother got me some for my birthday earlier this year. This is all that's left. I've used it a few times before and I've been fine."

Daniel nodded and began to calm down.

"You've got some on your nose," Laura said.

Laura leaned in toward Daniel and wiped some cocaine off the tip of his nose. It felt like love as he watched her lick the bit of cocaine off the tip of her finger.

"You just ate my boogers," Daniel said.

"Ew, no I didn't."

"My girlfriend's a gross fucking booger eater."

"Your baybeee's a fucking booger eater."

"Bayyybeee!" Daniel fake screamed.

"Bayyyyy-beeeee!" Laura fake screamed, and then she and Daniel began laughing.

"I feel good," Laura added.

"Me too," Daniel agreed. "But I'm not sure if it's the cocaine or the excitement of doing cocaine."

"I think maybe it's both," Laura said, fidgeting in her chair.

"You're squirmy," Daniel pointed out.

"Squirmy wormy. I have all this energy all of a sudden."

"You were just about to fall asleep five minutes ago."

"I know, right?"

"Let's dance," Daniel said out of nowhere, surprising himself. "I want to dance."

Daniel stood up from his chair, as if punctuating his will to suddenly want to dance.

"You want to dance?"

"Yeah. Do you want to split the other line first?"

"Sure," Laura said, looking down at the line of coke. "Why did I cut it into three lines and not four?"

"Obviously because you're stupid."

"Really stupid," she said with a smile.

"At least you have pretty eyes. And pretty big tits."

Daniel began playfully batting at Laura's tits like he was a cat and her tits were big, fat, engorged mice.

"Ow, stop," she said, laughing, trying to swat away his hands.

Daniel stopped and, in a redneck accent, said, "Fine. Then split that there last line, woman!"

Laura grabbed her credit card and split the line in half. She gave Daniel the rolled up hundred-dollar bill. Daniel snorted his half, then Laura snorted hers and she and Daniel began uncontrollably smiling.

"You really want to dance?" Laura asked.

"Yeah. Why?"

Laura shrugged and smiled.

"I'm surprised. Not all guys like dancing."

"I do."

"Okay. Good. I like dancing, too."

Laura walked over to her computer and opened up YouTube. Knowing Daniel had an affinity for Katy Perry, she played her song "Teenage Dream." Laura turned around and stared at Daniel expectantly, those blue eyes of hers challenging him, saying, "Let's see what you've got."

Daniel held out his hand. Laura walked over to him and accepted it. Daniel pulled her in close and began moving around her to the rhythm of the music. Laura's eyes widened, seeming surprised but pleased over his somewhat competent ability to move fluently. She began a slow, gentle grind against Daniel's thigh, following his lead. Her mouth was opened slightly and her lips looked plump, wet and hungry. Laura closed her eyes and slowly ran her fingers through her hair as she began swaying her ass back and forth. There was sex beginning to move between them, hot, heavy and leaking pre-cum. Daniel reached behind Laura and placed his hand just above her ass. He pulled her in closer, and Laura, as if saying yes to this, began grinding on him even more forcefully. Daniel slid his hand onto her ass, grabbing a handful. A little moan slipped out of Laura's mouth and they both inaudibly laughed. Finding her too cute and irresistible, Daniel went in for a kiss but Laura pulled away. She waved her pointer finger at him playfully, as if instructing him "No. Not yet." Laura turned around and backed her ass into Daniel's crotch. She raised her hands into the air like a showgirl and slowly slithered up and down the front of his body. Daniel let her move all over him. He felt hot and flushed, like he couldn't hold in everything he was holding in any longer. Daniel reached around Laura and cupped her breasts, stopping Laura in motion. Feeling the need to taste her, Daniel leaned in and began kissing her neck as their hips remained in sync with each other. Laura put her hands over Daniel's hands still groping her breasts.

"The neighbors can see us," Daniel could barely hear Laura say over the music.

As if this was a dare on her part, Daniel slithered his hands down Laura's front. Soon, one of his hands was inside her panties. Daniel playfully twirled her pubic hair for a moment before running his finger up and down her cunt. Laura tilted her head back, resting it on Daniel's shoulder. She thrust her pussy into the pressure of his fingers but only for a moment before completely pulling herself free from Daniel.

"I want to wear a dress," Laura said firmly. "I want to look pretty right now."

The song ended. Daniel smiled and, trying not pant like the disgusting, out of shape man-ogre he was, he said, "Then go put on a dress."

"Yeah? You want me to dress up for you?"

Daniel nodded.

"I know just what I'm going to wear," Laura said and ran upstairs.

Daniel went over to the refrigerator and grabbed a cold beer. He held it on his flushed forehead for a second, trying to cool off, before cracking it open and taking a large swig. Then he went over to Laura's computer and made a playlist for them to dance to.

Not long after Daniel had compiled a short playlist, Daniel heard Laura's heavy footsteps booming across the upstairs hallway. He grabbed his phone, ran to the bottom of the stairs and began taking a video. Seconds later, Laura bounded down the steps wearing a green, low-cut, floral print dress. She stopped on the bottom stair when she noticed Daniel filming her. Her entire demeanor changed, shifting wildly and drastically from excited little girl playing dress up to bombshell vixen. Playing to the camera, Laura arched her heel and raised herself up onto one foot. Then she dropped one shoulder, closed her eyes and turned her head away, striking a pose. She pouted her lips and tousled her hair, making it messy, making it sexy, making it sexily messy, before turning and staring into the camera and, therefore, staring into Daniel.

As Daniel watched this through his iPhone, as he processed these different but equally enchanting levels of his girlfriend, his aching heart—gratefully aching for her and the fire-breathing magic she effortlessly exhaled—his aching heart prompted his mind to begin concocting a far-fetched story. It was years in the future and Laura had passed away giving birth to their daughter. Their daughter was a little girl now, and whenever she missed her mother, whenever she longed for this woman she never met, Daniel and his daughter would sit on the couch together and watch this video that Daniel was currently shooting. After one or two plays, his daughter would grab the phone from his hands and play it herself, watching intently, seeing the same things in Laura that Daniel did—the sweet playfulness juxtaposed alongside the sultry side his daughter yet couldn't fully understand. And so his daughter would study this woman that looked so much like her, trying to learn anything from her she could considering she'd never be there to teach her in person. "You remind me so much of her," Daniel would always mention to his daughter, feeling a catch in his throat, his heart broken but also so full of love he thought it was going to burst.

"What's wrong?"

Laura's voice catapulted Daniel back into reality. He stopped recording and saw Laura looking at him with concerned eyes.

"Nothing," he answered. "Absolutely nothing's wrong."

A little before midnight, Laura decided she wanted to go to the beach a block from her house. She and Daniel grabbed a couple beers and, still riding high on cocaine, they walked the short distance. They forgot to bring a blanket so they sat on the sand, very close, side by side, each borrowing the other's warmth.

"It's so cold," Laura said.

"Yeah, and this cold beer isn't going to help."

"I know, but I'm really craving beer."

"Me too," Daniel said as he cracked open a bottle and handed it to Laura.

"Don't litter the bottle cap."

"I'm not," Daniel said as he slid the bottle cap in his pocket.

Daniel opened himself a beer. He and Laura cheers'ed their bottles and began drinking. The waves were really loud, as was the wind. Daniel normally felt good when he was with Laura, but now he felt even better than he normally did. It was a dumb, simple happiness, although still powerful and potent, like he was finally exuding a severe and grinning positivity into the world around him, something he normally never did because he normally never felt this content with himself and this life he was thrust into.

"I think I love cocaine," Daniel said.

"Yeah. It's pretty great."

"I wish we had more."

"Me too, but it's probably best we don't. It's easy to lose control with it. At least for me."

"I can understand why."

"One time when I was in Amsterdam and high on cocaine, me and my girlfriends were at this strip cub and I entered and danced in an amateur strip contest."

"Oh," Daniel said, not sure how to feel about this newly shared information, even though he knew deep down that it wasn't a big deal and that he was stupid for not knowing how to feel about it.

"We did cocaine off your books," Laura said, smiling. "That's pretty bad ass."

"Haha, yeah," Daniel said, feeling better now that his precious ego had been stroked a little.

"You think anyone else has ever done cocaine off your books?"

"This one kid sent me a picture of him using one of my books to put weed on as he rolled a joint."

"Now *that* makes you a professional writer. When someone uses your book to help them do drugs. That means you made it."

"Haha. Yeah. I guess so."

"I liked them. Your poems, I mean. I read one of your books."

"Oh. Thanks," Daniel said softly, feeling embarrassed even though he knew this moment was going to come eventually.

"You don't have to thank me. I was happy to do it. You're talented."

Daniel took a modest sip of beer.

"It's always nervous dating an artist. I mean, knowing the person before knowing their art. Like one time when I dated this guitarist in a band and it turned out his band sucked, so of course I had to pretend I liked them. Which was tough because I was dating this person who had a dream I didn't really believe in."

"Are you pretending with me?"

"No. I really like what you do. It's different than most poetry I've read, but I enjoy it. Even though your poems are long. Like really, *really* long. You probably could've gotten some good use out of an editor."

"I did have an editor," Daniel replied dryly.

"Oh…" Laura said. "Well, what do I know anyway? I do read a lot, though. Man, I wish I had a cigarette."

Daniel stared bitterly at the waves. He took another sip of beer, much bigger than the last, and shivered.

"Oh come on," Laura said.

"Come on what?"

"You. You're being cold and distant all of a sudden because I offered you some advice. What? Did I damage your fragile, little male ego?"

A lot of the time when Daniel got mad, or offended, he shut down, or, more precisely, his mind shut down. Normally somewhat eloquent, his mind often drew blanks whenever he found it buzzing and vibrating with anger. So, being incapable of expressing how he feels, and also feeling stupid for shooting mental blanks, Daniel's mind, knowing time is of the essence when one is being confronted, usually just lashed back at whatever, he felt, had lashed out at him first.

In the moonlight, Laura's eyes—eyes that normally looked like small evangelical hemorrhoid pillows dipped in blue honey—now just looked dark and cold, like little wads of fish guts.

"Your face is breaking out," Daniel said, then hurled his gaze back out over the waves, punctuating his sentence with another sip of beer.

Laura punched Daniel in the arm as hard as she could, making beer dribble down his mouth.

"Fucking asshole! How about I just stop taking my meds then," Laura spat at him. "Ya know, if they make me too ugly for you to look at?"

Laura jumped up and left. Daniel sat there in the sand and finished his beer. Once he was done, he took the bottlecap out of his pocket and dropped it in the sand, an immature and unheard "Fuck you" to Laura.

In no rush to go back to the house and have to deal with the interminable silence, or, worse, a possible fight, Daniel wrapped his arms around his ankles and watched the lethargic waves. After less than a minute, he noticed something slowly rising out of the water, like a stealthy, Rambo'esque action hero about to unleash a world of pain on him.

Except it was no action hero. The figure rising out of the water was much more dangerous than a scorned action hero out to seek vengeance. It was a sad-looking blue whale, and it stared Daniel down, shooting machine gun-like sadness into his chest with the unlimited ammo of its dark, beady eyes.

"Ooh, ooh, ooh, ooooh!" it cried.

Daniel sighed. He picked up the bottle cap he purposefully dropped in the sand and made the short walk back to Laura's house, scared of what he'd be confronted with when he returned.

PART 2

"WHAT THE FUCK, *Daniel? Why haven't you called me back? Can't you hear it? Can't you hear it in my voice? This is serious, and I really need to talk to you right now. Please. Just call me, alright? I'll be by my phone…"*

GREASY, CARDBOARD HEART-COFFIN

"GEEZ..." the sad-looking blue whale says, still massaging the back of his head. "The horizon hurts."

Despite his craned neck beginning to ache, Daniel is still too stunned to relax his current giraffe-like posture as he stares up at the fake horizon.

"It's just a wall painted blue. Look. Even the clouds are painted on."

Careful not to capsize the boat, the sad-looking blue whale stands up and looks up at the towering length of the horizon. Seeing no immediate harmful repercussions happening to Daniel for touching the horizon, he works up the courage and places his fin on the wall, feeling it for himself.

"Hmm…" the sad-looking blue whale says.

Defeated, Daniel flops back into his seat, shaking the bright-orange boat. Almost losing his balance, the sad-looking blue whale makes a weird little yelp, wobbles, and places both fins on the horizon to keep from falling overboard.

"This isn't good," Daniel says, focusing all his attention on the empty Big Mac container.

"We've definitely drifted pretty far from the rendezvous point," the sad-looking blue whale admits as he sits back down.

"What are we going to do?"

"I dunno… I guess at this point I should probably call them, huh?"

"Who?"

"The sad-looking blue whales coming to get us."

"You mean, like, a call of the wild or something?"

"No. I mean like a phone call."

The sad-looking blue whale unzips his fanny pack, and as if reaching into some sort of zippered time machine instead, he pulls out an ugly, beige rotary phone. Daniel's eyes bulge like brown mushroom clouds. The sad-looking blue whale holds up the limp end of the phone cable, then looks at the plug, disappointed.

"Oh. Wait… You wouldn't happen to have a place to plug this in, would you?"

Daniel gawks at the plug. Then over his shoulder at the tauntingly vast ocean behind him. Then back at the sad-looking blue whale. He shakes his head.

"Yeah… I didn't think so," the sad-looking blue whale says. "Never mind."

The sad-looking blue whale coils the cable around the rotary phone and stuffs the phone back in his fanny pack. Daniel can't help but stare at the sad-looking blue whale in shock over his magician-like ability to pull a rotary phone out of such a compact pouch.

"What?" the sad-looking blue whale says when he notices Daniel staring at him.

"What else do you have in there?"

"Not much really. Or I guess I should say nothing helpful. Just a lot of junk. Trinkets. Odds and ends. Ya know, stuff like that. I enjoy collecting things. Some sad-looking blue whales say I have a problem. You know that TV show *Hoarders*? Well, look. I have the complete first season on DVD," the sad-looking blue whale says as he pulls the first season of *Hoarders* out of his fanny pack. "I've never watched it or anything—ya know, not sad-looking enough, *and* I prefer VHS's—but still, I like having it for some reason."

The sad-looking blue whale hands the DVDs to Daniel. Daniel examines the first season of *Hoarders* in his hands, rotating it, turning it over, as if making sure it's real and not some weird, slightly obsolete mirage of entertainment he's holding.

"Are you sure?" Daniel asks.

"Sure about what?"

"That there's nothing in your fanny pack that can help us?"

The sad-looking blue whale begins rummaging around inside his fanny pack again.

"Uhhhh… I have some Fruit Stripe chewing gum," he says and pulls out the red, yellow and green striped package of gum as if the dial on his time machine fanny pack is now set to the 1990's.

"How the hell is Fruit Stripe gum going to help us?" Daniel asks.

The sad-looking blue whale shrugs, and just as he's about to put the gum away, Daniel adds, quickly, "Well I never said I didn't want a piece..."

The sad-looking blue whale takes out the last two pieces of gum and hands one to Daniel. Daniel puts *Hoarders* down next to the empty Big Mac container and quickly unwraps his stick.

Gross... his disappointed brain says.

Lemon...

"What flavor did you get?" Daniel asks the sad-looking blue whale as he unwraps his own piece of Fruit Stripe Gum.

"Cherry," the sad-looking blue whale answers

"Do you maybe want to trade—?"

The sad-looking blue whale, knowing exactly where Daniel is going with this, and wanting nothing to do with it, crams the gum into his mouth and begins voraciously chewing.

Daniel grimaces and pops his piece in his mouth. Despite it somehow tasting the way the sad-looking blue whale looks, and not realizing how ravenously hungry he was until he bit down on the gum, he doesn't spit it out. He crumples the wrapper into a tiny ball and throws it in the ocean. The sad-looking blue whale sees this and, judging Daniel with his eyes for littering, crumples up his own wrapper and puts it in his fanny pack.

Daniel looks back up at the fake horizon. He closes his hand into a fist and knocks on the great blue wall. The horizon makes a hollow, metallic echo, as if Daniel just gave a good rattle on the empty stomach of some enormous metallic beast.

"Doesn't sound like there's anything behind it," he says.

The sad-looking blue whale only responds by tilting his head straight back and slightly to the side, as if the horizon's wearing a skirt he's inconspicuously trying to look up.

"How is this possible?" Daniel mutters under his breath, even though he knows the answer to his own question. As much as he doesn't want to say it out loud, as if making the thought concrete and real and factual, Daniel understands this construct, this great and miserable yet vastly impressive wall, is his handiwork, that he built it himself, deceptive inch by deceptive inch, with his own self-imposed limitations and constant negative thinking. And then, when the wall was complete, his inabilities, his lack of talent, the crappy hand he was dealt in the rigged card game of life—they all painted it blue and Bob

Ross'ed a bunch of happy-looking clouds for additional detail and authenticity.

Only you… says Daniel's brain.

Only you could be stuck at some dead end in the middle of the ocean…

With his gum somehow already having lost all its flavor, making it taste even more how the sad-looking blue whale looks, Daniel takes the small, non-flavored wad out of his mouth and sticks it on the horizon.

Pressed up against the painted-on blue sky, the wad of gum looks like a sad, stale star, so deliriously juiceless and confused that it missed its nighttime exit cue.

The bright-orange boat gently knocks against the horizon wall like the headboard of a bed an elderly couple is having sex in. Soft, lethargic, pleasureless knocks, one after the other after the other, persistently plunk their way into Daniel's ears, as if the old married couple, even with their bad hips, arthritic knees and achy backs, are sure to be going at it all night long.

And even though the lackadaisical ruckus is, by all means, relatively quiet and subdued, Daniel can't stand it. Each soft thump, each lifeless clunk, is, contrarily, a booming reminder of the horizon's inauthenticity, that the great blue expanse is nothing more than a great blue impostor, which, consequently, forces Daniel to think back on the life he failed to live. The very same failed life that constructed this fraudulent monstrosity in the first place.

Ruminating on this, unable to escape it, a mosh pit of nausea suddenly opens up in Daniel's stomach, wave after wave slam dancing in circles to the aggressive, ultra-violet music violently blasting non-stop from the sun.

Daniel leans over the side of the boat.

He vomits.

"Whoa!"

The sad-looking blue whale quickly leans forward to place his fin on Daniel's back but freezes when he's only an inch or so away, leaving his fin to awkwardly hover like a confused helicopter rather than touch down with the kind and supportive gesture as if suddenly thinking better of it, or perhaps, rather, just not feeling comfortable with the sentiment.

"You okay?" he asks.

When Daniel opens his eyes, he sees a large pinkish puddle that his brain describes as "flamingo chum" floating in the water. Feeling a little delirious, but also a little less queasy, he wipes a long string of saliva from his beard and allows his head to miserably hang over the side of the bright-orange boat. He listens to the boat knock against the horizon. The knocks sound like the old man giving it to his old lady is wearing nothing but black socks.

"Oh my god…" Daniel says as he closes his eyes and pictures the "horizon" towering up behind them.

"What?" the sad-looking blue whale asks. His fin still hasn't moved. It still has no idea what to do.

"I'm *Passing Gas*," Daniel says.

"Huh?" the sad-looking blue whale says, now looking just as confused as his fin.

"My novel? *Passing Gas*? I'm like the fart from it. I *am* the fart from it."

As if he had the right idea when he froze his fin in the first place, the sad-looking blue whale now fully withdraws his appendage from the vicinity of Daniel's back and sits up in his seat.

"I just hurtled through life with no idea what I was doing," Daniel says. "And, I mean, I guess everyone does that to some extent. But still. I never adjusted to the speed. Not even a little. I never stopped panicking and mindlessly grasping at whatever convenient but reckless thing that would only make me momentarily feel better. I never took the time to think about what I was actually doing. I never took time to plan ahead, to think about a future."

Daniel spits the taste of vomit from his mouth. The flamingo chum makes exotic, stripper-like gyrations that would almost be alluring if it weren't being performed by bile.

"Jesus…" Daniel says under his foul-smelling breath. "How can something as slow and painful as a life go by so fast?"

As if uncertain whether he has any more liquid volume to add to the ocean, Daniel slowly sits back up. He tries to move as little as possible but his attempt seems futile as the waves continue having their gentle way with the bright-orange boat.

"Do you know what I mean?" Daniel asks the sad-looking blue whale, holding onto both sides of the boat as if trying to keep it from rocking back and forth. "Does that make sense at all?"

"I don't know," the sad-looking blue whale says after a moment's hesitation, then sticks the tip of his fin in the water and mindlessly swirls it around, partially cooling himself off. He quickly retracts his fin, however, when he sees Daniel's vomit eerily floating towards him like jellyfish nightmares. "We sad-looking blue whales don't really pay attention to time," he adds. "We just kind of watch *Titanic*. And you know the saying—time flies when you're watching *Titanic*."

Silence. Nothing but the waves whispering among themselves and the bright-orange boat banging against the wall. At this point, the elderly man sounds like he's never going to come, and his old lady—that poor woman—she just lies there, patiently taking his brittle thrusting as her mind wanders hobo-like to other places more indicative of her age—bingo, sewing, trying to remember her mother's recipe for beef stroganoff, and so on and so forth.

Daniel begins feeling nauseous again. He tries focusing on a fixed point—his wad of gum stuck to the horizon—to make himself feel better.

A million real gray skies are better than one fake, bright blue sky... his brain utters hopelessly.

IT'S A HORRIBLE LIFE

AT ELEVEN TWENTY-EIGHT, Daniel got up from his booth and got in line. There were already five people waiting and Daniel hated them all equally, although, he knew, irrationally, for postponing his mouth-watering rendezvous with a now inevitable Big Mac.

Daniel felt energized as he waited in line, though, renewed even. Having something small to look forward to, something he knew he was guaranteed to enjoy, even if just for two minutes, or, who was he kidding, less than a minute considering Daniel ate like the Tasmanian devil with a tapeworm, made him feel okay in a simple and carefree floating kind of way, like he wasn't standing in line but, rather, levitating six inches off the ground, weightless and unburdened.

One by one, the people in front of him, all haggardly attired in sweatpants or leggings, or jeans that looked like they had been worn while working construction, ordered their food. Then, finally, it was Daniel's turn.

Daniel put the coupon down on the counter with an accidental yet authentically excited flare and asked, "Can I use this, please?"

The cashier, an unenthused and slightly lazy-eyed teenager who looked like he listened to Nu-Metal, grabbed the coupon and held it up toward the light, examining it like a bank teller trying to determine if the hundred-dollar bill they were just handed was counterfeit or not.

"Sure," he said tonelessly, as if his examination was all for show, as if he could've cared less whether the coupon was real or something Daniel had deftly drawn up himself to get a cheaper burger.

The wait was surprisingly short, and after Daniel was handed his small brown paper bag with the Big Mac safely nestled inside, he half-walked, half-ran back to his table, purposefully keeping his head down to make sure he didn't accidentally make eye contact with any of the sad-looking blue whales waiting for him outside.

The first bite was orgasmically hot and juicy. Grease leaked out one corner of his mouth and shredded lettuce and secret sauce fell and dripped from the burger's sides, landing on the strategically placed empty Big Mac container on the table to make sure nothing would go to waste. Daniel picked up some pieces of lettuce and shoved them in his mouth while he was still chewing. He knew how disgusting he must've looked, but although slightly ashamed over it, he didn't care. This was it, his moment of peace, his point of mouthwatering contentment. Let the onlookers stare, aghast at his slovenly public display of self-indulgence. It only lasted so long, and Daniel wanted to enjoy every second, and every bite, to its fullest.

As soon as the last mouthful cannonballed into his gullet, *it* happened, the same thing Daniel knew would happen, the same thing he had experienced a thousand times before—the post-McDonald's depression began settling in.

The Big Mac was gone, devoured with a regimented haphazardness, therefore, indignantly stranding Daniel at a point in time where he was the furthest possible distance from enjoying two more 100% beef patties slathered with secret sauce and sandwiched between a sesame seed bun, topped off with pickles, crisp lettuce, finely chopped onions and American cheese. Now, Daniel had nothing to look forward to, and as soon as he had digested his Big Mac, he would be empty again. Not wholly empty, but still, more than empty enough to notice that throbbing, pulsating and all-too-human void inside of him.

Daniel sat back in his seat, feeling both physically and emotionally disgusting. He looked at himself in his phone's camera and noticed that he had secret sauce in his beard. Daniel contemplated never wiping it away, leaving it there forever and completely owning it, as if showing off to the world and advertising what a disgustingly inept garbage-person he was, all the while pretending to be proud of it so it wouldn't hurt so much when others were naturally repulsed by him. But the fantasy of doing so was just like every single other one of Daniel's fantasies, short-lived and never acted on. Daniel grabbed a napkin and wiped the secret sauce from his beard.

The dining room was just about empty—most of the elderly

patrons tended to straggle on home around this time of day—and this was how Daniel liked it.

If life is a Big Mac, then isolation is the secret sauce bringing it all together... his brain waxed poetically, or food-drunkenly, then proceeded in wondering if what it had just said made any sense at all.

Daniel was constantly torn about being out in public. It made him feel less alone to be reminded he wasn't the only person on the planet, which was how he often felt while tucked away in his father's basement, but he also resented the presence of people whenever he went out. Or perhaps not their presence so much, but rather that no one seemed to acknowledge or recognize his own presence. Even though Daniel didn't want to talk to anyone, he still wanted them to acknowledge him, to find him handsome, to like and comment on the new band t-shirt he was wearing, or ask him about one of his tattoos. Daniel knew how absurd and contradictory this was, that it made absolutely no sense for a person to want to be left alone while also simultaneously wanting to be fawned over, leaving him utterly frustrated with the complicated mess of a human being he had somehow become.

Daniel hated being this way, so intensely anti-social while also yearning for affection, but at the same time, he felt there wasn't much he could do about it. A large part of why he avoided talking with others so often, he'd realized years ago, was because he was constantly having to rebuild his personality in order to communicate effectively, or pleasantly, with people. The sad-looking blue whales were constantly stripping Daniel of everything good-natured, positive and charming about himself. Not that there was a lot to begin with, but there was at least something there of substance. And whenever another person approached him—a relative, a friend, a stranger, a coworker, or even a McDonald's regular—Daniel always had to scramble to rebuild those enjoyable parts of himself that were taken away due to his daily interactions with the sad-looking blue whales. It felt like his personality was a castle made out of Legos the sad-looking blue whales kept repeatedly kicking over as soon as Daniel rebuilt it. And most of the time, unfortunately, Daniel didn't have the energy to search through the toppled remains of his personality. It was exhausting, not to mention he was sick and tired of doing so. (After all, how many times can a person rebuild the same fucking castle before they just stop?) So Daniel would be lazy. He wouldn't smile at or greet that coworker, or he'd sit at the occasional lunch with his friend, Dave, and let him do all the talking, or he'd stare at his phone, pretending to be busy, instead of conversing with that cute girl sitting next to him on the train.

"Oooh, ooooooh, ooh!"

Daniel craned his head in the direction of the booth he'd been sitting in earlier. The two sad-looking blue whales were still pressed up against the glass, crying, but there was another behind them now, on its tippy fins, trying to peer inside. And as if that wasn't bad enough, the same confused sad-looking blue whale remained at the back door, trying to figure out what it was doing wrong, why it couldn't get the door to open.

Trying, but failing, to think of a time when the sad-looking blue whales had ever been this fervid to get inside his McDonald's, Daniel ate the few remaining pieces of shredded lettuce that had fallen into the empty Big Mac container, then closed it shut. He held the container in his hand, feeling the lightness of it, feeling the overall emptiness of it.

"Oooh, ooh, ooooh, oooooh!" a sad-looking blue whale cried outside.

Daniel's eyes widened. The remainder of the thought arrived gently but heavily, like a morbidly obese bird alighting on a telephone wire in Daniel's mind. The telephone wire—stretching underneath the bird's immense weight, taut and ready to snap at any second.

Daniel scrambled for his notebook and pen. He opened up to the page where he last left off.

"My heart belongs…"

Daniel quickly put the pen down to paper.

"…in an empty Big Mac container buried beneath the ocean floor," his pen completed.

Daniel sat back in his booth and placed his pen on the table like he'd never have to pick it, or any other pen, up ever again.

Even though he'd only written the sentence once, something about its thirteen words seemed to fill his notebook entirely.

BAYYYBEE!!!

"WOW... LOOK AT THAT YACHT."

Daniel and Laura were sitting on the beach, holding hands. Daniel looked up from tracing the word "BAYYBEEE" in the sand and saw the yacht anchored off in the distance. The yacht was enormous, pristinely white, and made Daniel think of a large and elegant floating seashell.

"I wanna blow you on a yacht like that," Laura said. "While you're drinking champagne. And then, as I'm blowing you, you pour champagne down my ass crack."

"Mmm…" Laura said. "Fuck, babe. Do you want to have sex when we get back? It's been a couple of days, huh?"

Six and a half days… Daniel's brain calculated with painfully fast speed and accuracy. But then, rather than bringing up the exact number by saying it out loud and possibly angering Laura and jeopardizing finally having sex, Daniel, not wanting to seem to over-eager, just half-smiled and nodded.

"Good," Laura said. "Maybe I'll even let you come on my face."

Laura happily squeezed Daniel's hand. As she looked back at the yacht, a sad-looking blue whale who had come out of nowhere, as they were known to do, sat down in the sand next to Daniel. The sad-looking blue whale grabbed Daniel's free hand with its fin and squeezed it in the exact same manner Laura just had, although producing the exact opposite effect.

Daniel tried his best to ignore the sad-looking blue whale, but when he stared out at the yacht, an unavoidable sadness and defeat fell over him. He knew he would never drink champagne on a yacht like that where he would pour champagne down Laura's ass crack as she blew him. Daniel was just a stock boy. *A stock* man... his brain corrected him. But stock boy or man, it didn't matter. It didn't change the fact that Daniel was poor and couldn't give Laura the things he wanted to. They would never live a rich, extravagant life together. Despite Laura's decent paycheck, they would slum it for the most part because of Daniel's dead, financial weight, spending their free time between the dollar store, Ikea, and the occasional bar and/or dinner trip. And Daniel, used to slumming it, and because he had no ambition to chase money like the rest of the world, was okay with the inexpensive life laid out ahead of them like some cheap, sticky highway made of fly paper, or at least okay with it as he could be. The problem was, Daniel knew, that Laura was not okay with it. Laura wanted trips all over the world. She wanted excitement, adventure. She wanted cocks in her mouth and champagne poured down her ass and private yachts. And Daniel, as much as he would've liked these things too—minus the cocks in his mouth—and while acknowledging he didn't have the machinery inside to force himself through the sludge of a forty-plus hour work week which would be the only way he, an unskilled and slightly uneducated person, could finance such things, Daniel felt like he was letting Laura down, which, considering how much he loved Laura—and he did, he really did love her, backhanded compliments, frequent arguments and all—the knowledge that he was letting her down, and most likely always would be, became a mass-email open invitation to all of the sad-looking blue whales of the world.

"Ooh, ooh, ooh!" the sad-looking blue whale cried.

"What, babe?" Laura asked.

"Hmm?"

"Did you just say something?"

Daniel felt the sad-looking blue whale squeeze his hand again.

"No," Daniel said.

"What's wrong?" Laura asked.

"Nothing. Why?"

"You just sound sad is all. And you look sad too. Like really, really sad."

"Sorry. I was just thinking."

"Well stop. Stop thinking."

"Okay..."

"I'm bored," Laura said out of nowhere.

"You're bored? We've only been here five minutes."

"I know."

"And you were the one who wanted to come."

"I know, I know. Jesus… What? I can't change my mind?"

"No, you can. I'm just saying is all. Change your mind all you want. I don't give a shit."

"I hate you."

"I hate you more."

"Well I fucking loathe you."

"Oh my god. I am so going to cum on your face later."

"No, you're not," Laura scoffed.

"Yes, I am. It's not even going to be after sex. It's going to be out of nowhere, like when you're sitting on your computer at work and playing Minesweeper."

"Hahahaha, playing Minesweeper."

"And it's gonna be all the way from across the room too. Off the wall. Off the Ficus. Off the monitor. Nothing but your face."

"Haha. Your semen bounces like Flubber?"

"Yep. So you better watch the fuck out."

"Haha. 'Playing Minesweeper…'" Laura repeated. "No one plays Minesweeper anymore."

Laura squeezed Daniel's hand again, and as she did so, he could've sworn he felt the sad-looking blue whale's grip loosen.

"I love being so close to the beach," Laura said.

"Yeah. It's crazy how close by you are."

"I think I'm going to buy the house," she said after a moment of silence.

"Your house?"

"No. The house next door to me. Yes, *my* house."

"Oh… It's just you didn't seem so sure before."

"That's because my mom and dad are in Delaware. My brother's in Colorado and I have no real family or friends close by. Well, there is my cousin. He's not too, too far, but that's a whole other story… So before, all I had keeping me here was my job, really."

"And now?"

"And now I have you, idiot."

"Oh…" Daniel said with a dumb smile. "Yeah. You do have me."

"And I don't think it'd be that much more expensive than renting it. At least according to what the realtor said. Especially if you helped out."

"Yeah. I could give whatever I'm capable of giving."

"I don't know... It's just something I've been thinking of a lot lately."

"Well, I support whatever you want to do."

"I feel stupid," Laura said, kind of rocking back and forth, but whether because she was cold or restless or both, Daniel wasn't sure. "I feel stupid for bringing it up."

"Don't. I'm glad you did."

Daniel squeezed Laura's hand, and as he did so, he, without a doubt this time around, felt the sad-looking blue whale's grip loosen on his other hand. Laura, however, just stared off at the yacht.

"I wonder how much one of those costs," she said.

I would have to stock a trillion shelves to ever be able to afford something like that... Daniel's brain said about the yacht.

Ten trillion... his brain corrected itself, somehow suddenly good at math.

The sad-looking blue whale's fin clamped down on Daniel's hand with the grip a concerned mother has on her child's hand to prevent them from bolting away as they crossed the street, a very busy never-ending street where you never got to the other side and just always remained in the process of crossing. A process you'd been going through for so long you couldn't even remember why you began crossing the street to begin with, or what the other side would be like if you ever got there.

Daniel's focus shifted from the yacht to the horizon behind it. Suddenly, for whatever reason, it looked like cheap movie scenery rather than the actual horizon he knew, deep down, it was.

"Do you ever feel like the horizon's just a wall?" Daniel asked.

"What do you mean?" she said.

"Like in *The Truman Show.* Did you ever see that movie?"

"Yeah. Of course I have."

"You know when the horizon just turned out to be fake? To give off the illusion of there being something more out there?"

"It's not just a wall, though," Laura said matter of factly, then kind of laughed. "I know, babe. I've been all over the world. You just say that because you've never been anywhere."

"I know it's not a wall. I'm just saying sometimes it *feels* like a wall, like there's nothing more than this."

"That's because you feel trapped here in Connecticut because you don't have the money to move or travel even though you want to do both. And because you think so negatively, like it's impossible for you to do those things. And it's not. You just need to get a new job. You just need to get your shit together. That's all."

"The horizon's a wall if you want it to be a wall," she added. "It's as simple as that."

Laura had no idea what she was talking about, and she never would as far as Daniel was concerned. She had money and, as far as he knew, she'd had it her whole life. Maybe not excess amounts, but still more than enough to comfortably live off of without any major, pressing concerns. Daniel let go of Laura's hand under the pretense of having to scratch his nose, feeling mad and not wanting to hold it any longer. After a couple seconds, and after Daniel had scratched his nose and dropped his hand down by his side, Laura's hand found Daniel's again and held it against its will.

"Babe, what's wrong?" Laura asked, sounding frustrated.

"Nothing."

"You're doing it again."

"I'm doing what again?"

"Well, nothing really. It's just how you look. You look sad again. Like really, really, *really* sad."

"I'm fine," Daniel said after a moment of hesitation, trying to sink the yacht with his eyes, knowing deep down he wasn't fine and that, most likely, he never would be.

Laura shook her head.

"I tell him we're going to have sex and he's still miserable," she muttered to herself.

Before Daniel could verbally retaliate, he felt the sad-looking blue whale's grip squeeze down on his hand like it was trying to quash his bones into a fine powder. The pressure was so intense, so fracturing, he had to keep from screaming.

"Minesweeper," Daniel said after taking a couple deep breaths, trying to make Laura laugh again, but whether she ignored him or just didn't hear him, Laura let go of Daniel's hand and took her phone out of her pocket. She turned on the reverse camera and examined her reflection.

"Ugh…" she said, noticing fresh blemishes on her skin. "Sorry, but you're definitely not cumming on my face later. I don't want to risk breaking out more than I already am."

But Daniel knew, and he would've bet his life on the fact, that he and Laura weren't having sex later. The mood had been murdered, at least for her, and it would be another night of Daniel masturbating in the bathroom after Laura had fallen asleep early.

Laura humphed and put her phone away. She wrapped her arms around herself and rocked back and forth.

"I'm bored," she said.

Daniel stared down at the word "BAYYBEEE" he'd written in the sand. Using his newly free hand, the same hand that Laura just seemed so intent on holding only seconds ago but now seemed vaguely repulsed by, he crossed the word out.

"Oooooh, oooooh!" the sad-looking blue whale cried.

Daniel tried sinking the yacht one more time with his eyes, but, of course, failed.

"Let's just go home," Laura said.

"Okay," Daniel agreed after, what felt like, a long silence.

GREASY, CARDBOARD HEART-COFFIN

"HOLY SHIT..."

Daniel points past the sad-looking blue whale. Following the guidance of Daniel's finger, the sad-looking blue whale looks over his shoulder. Camouflaged into the horizon, painted over in blue and white, is a flight of stairs in the not too far off distance that ascends like a heavenly accordion up to a lone, gray door.

Daniel pushes away from the horizon with his foot and, leaning over the bow of the bright-orange boat, begins doggie paddling towards the staircase like it could disappear any second. The sad-looking blue whale just sits there, too sad-looking to help even though Daniel could by all means use some. Overly excited and eager, he paddles thoughtlessly and without precision, his complete lack of rhythm veering the boat this way and that, steering it straight one second and then right back into the horizon wall or out toward the ocean the next.

Eventually, however, after a superfluous amount of fevered paddling, Daniel manages to navigate the bright-orange boat over to the bright-blue staircase. He jumps to his feet and rushes onto the bottom stair but stops before going any further. Running on relief and excitement just seconds ago, Daniel stands there, panting. His eyes bulge with nervous apprehension.

"Well?" the sad-looking blue whale says from the bright-orange boat.

"Well, what?"

"What are you waiting for?"

"I dunno... It's just— I don't know what's in there," Daniel says, staring up at the door, which suddenly seems far away even though it's no more than one flight.

Daniel expectantly looks back at the sad-looking blue whale not budging from his seat.

"Aren't you coming?"

"Someone should stay here and watch the boat. Ya know, to make sure it doesn't float away," the sad-looking blue whale says, coming up with an excuse on the spot, albeit a valid one. He places both fins down on the bottom step, docking the boat in place.

Daniel turns back around, facing the stairs. Knowing anything has to be better than roasting in the sun one minute longer, he takes a deep breath and marches up the staircase.

When Daniel presses his ear close to the door in the horizon wall, he can hear a fast and fevered clicking sound coming from behind it.

"Hello?" Daniel says.

No answer.

Daniel gathers his courage and knocks on the door which, to his surprise, creaks open. The clicking stops. Then the brief sound of footsteps scurrying away.

Daniel takes a step back and looks at the sad-looking blue whale in the bright-orange boat. The sad-looking blue whale, now with only one fin lazily placed on the bottom step holding the boat in place, shrugs in response. Daniel leans closer to the door and peeks inside.

"Hello?" he repeats after his eyesight fails to penetrate the dense blackness, and when there's no answer, again, Daniel puts his hand on the doorknob and lets himself in.

Even with the sliver of sunlight leaking in through the open door, the room remains dark. So dark, Daniel can't see two inches in front of himself. Slowly staggering forward, dragging his feet across the floor that feels and smells like a large gym mat made of uncooked grade-F meat, Daniel sticks his hands out in front of him. He sweeps them back and forth and up and down, but after only a few steps, he still manages to bump his knee into something, bringing him to a stop. Daniel crouches forward and gropes the mystery object he just walked into.

A wooden chair... his hands inform his brain.

Daniel carefully reaches past the chair and comes across a small table. And on top of the table, some kind of dense plastic box with, what feels like, a keyboard.

A typewriter…

And to the right of the typewriter, Daniel's hands gropingly fumble across a large, Infinite Jest-sized stack of papers. Then he reaches above his head, finding what he was hoping for all along—a string dangling from the ceiling.

Daniel gives the string a tug and a lonely, lynched-looking light bulb turns on, bench pressing away as much darkness as it can. Enough, at least, for Daniel's eyes to be able to read the top page of the stack of papers. Enough light for him to see the exact same sentence typed over and over, psychotically filling the page from top to bottom.

"My heart belongs in an empty Big Mac container buried beneath the ocean floor… My heart belongs in an empty Big Mac container buried beneath the ocean floor… My heart belongs in an empty Big Mac container buried beneath the ocean floor…"

Stunned and unnerved, although definitely much more unnerved than stunned, Daniel lifts the top page to look at the one underneath it only to discover that it too is completely filled with his motto, his mantra, *"My heart belongs in an empty Big Mac container buried beneath the ocean floor…"*

Daniel flips through the large stack of papers. Page after page is all the same, *"My heart belongs in an empty Big Mac container buried beneath the ocean floor…"* typed over and over.

"Can you not touch those?"

The voice, like a disgruntled clap of thunder inside a brown paper McDonald's bag, stabs out of the shadows. Daniel retracts his hand and takes a nervous step back towards the door, ready to run, but also, for some reason, not wanting to.

"Sorry," Daniel says. "I knocked, but no one—"

"Daniel?"

Before Daniel can even begin to formulate a response, an old man—gaunt, wrinkled, bearded and pale, and clad in nothing but aged tighty whities—steps out from the shadows. His eyes are opened wider than a thirteenth story window that a suicide is about to leap out of, eyes that stare unmistakably at Daniel, oozing with recognition and disbelief, like his old eyes must be failing him, like this person in front of him, Daniel, can't surely be real. And although this old man seems to recognize Daniel, Daniel doesn't recognize him in return. But at the same time, he's not scared of the old man either. Nor does he feel uncomfortable around him even though he's wearing nothing but tighty whities that are no longer tight or white. His underwear, aged just as horribly as their owner, are the color of nicotine-stained dentures and their waistband is frayed and clinging onto his wrinkled hips not because they want to but, simply, because it's their job, because it's all they've ever known.

"Daniel…" the old man repeats, but this time not as a question. He says the name like it's a fact. "It's you. It really is you. I'm sorry. I didn't recognize you at first. The lighting…" he says and makes a gesture with his hand toward the dangling light bulb. A gesture he really doesn't follow through with, leaving his gesture and, therefore, his explanation for not initially seeing Daniel to die somewhere in the stale-beer air. Then the old man looks around the room, embarrassed.

"Messy… This place is so messy," he comes out with, as if he never noticed until now. "Here. Let me clean up. Sit."

The old man begins hobbling around the room, moving in and out of the shadows like a rheumatic crab as he snatches things up off the floor—a book, a record, another pair of ancient underwear.

"Go ahead, sit," the old man urges when he notices Daniel hasn't taken a seat yet.

Keeping an eye on the old man, although not out of suspicion or distrust, just more so out of curiosity, Daniel sits down in the chair he bumped into moments ago.

"It probably shows, but I'm not used to having company," the old man says as he picks yet another pair of yellowed tighty whities up off the floor. Then he pauses contemplatively. "In fact, I don't think I've ever had company."

The old man dumps the contents of his arms onto a spot on the floor that's out of the way and covers the small pile with a blanket that looks more like a prehistoric welcome mat, like the first welcome mat there ever was. Then he turns around and, standing akimbo, smiles at Daniel, making him uncomfortable. Daniel feels like the old man is waiting for him to say something but he has no idea what. All he has are questions. Dozens of questions he's too overwhelmed to ask. Questions he's not even sure if he should ask.

"Sorry again for kind of snapping at you before," the old man says, seemingly, just to fill the silence. "Ya know, about the papers."

The old man vaguely motions to the stack of papers on the desk with his head, giving them a little nod and, this time, completely following through with the gesture, as small as it is, successfully directing Daniel's attention to the intended target.

"You can touch 'em if you want," he says and makes a weird, hiccupy laugh. "I mean, they are yours after all."

"Oh," Daniel says, because his mouth and brain can't collaboratively figure out what else to say.

The old man's face changes. His eyes squint and all of the wrinkles on his face seem to squint along with them.

"You don't know where you are, do you?" the old man says.

Daniel hesitates, then shakes his head. The old man tries not to look hurt but Daniel can tell he is from the way his hands drop off his sides and the way his posture simultaneously slumps.

"It's just because it's so dark," Daniel says, lying, but also not lying at the same time in an attempt to hopefully not offend the old man any further.

The old man heaves his gaze up at the light bulb fighting off the oppressive onslaught of darkness.

"Yeah, it is pretty dark in here," he agrees. "Guess I'm just used to it by now."

"You don't have another light you could turn on or something?"

The old man makes a quarreled face, as if Daniel just gave him an enormous chore to do.

"One sec," the old man says, and hobbles off into the shadows.

From what little Daniel can see, the old man reaches up toward the wall and grabs a dark, pole-like abstraction that he pulls down on like a lever. Rusty, clanking, hollow-pipe sounds rattle above. Then, after a breathless moment, a small dot of light appears. Then another. Then two more simultaneously.

The dots float around the ceiling like luminous specks of lost dust. They look like they don't know what's going on. They just kind of float in place, looking half in control of their motions, half piss-drunk. But as they gradually drift a little bit lower, the luminous dots each seem to become more confident in themselves and their anarchistic-snowflake motions. They appear to be gaining their bearings, and, consequently, the more authoritatively they move, the more light they begin giving off. The light they exude isn't bright enough to completely illuminate the room but, still, it's bright enough for Daniel to accurately see and take in his surroundings.

The room, if that's what Daniel could even call it, is circular and arches upwards into the shape of a dome where the luminous dots first appeared. The walls are made entirely of dirt and hundreds of neatly-coiled cables and wires run up and down their length, going in and out of various fuse boxes labeled "HIGH VOLTAGE." There's barely any furniture aside from the desk and the chair Daniel's sitting in. Just two shelves. A large one the height of two stacked refrigerators, holding nothing but academic-looking leatherbound books, and another, much smaller, holding a collection of records, most likely, belonging to the victrola on the ground beside it. And most unusually, taped to a small portion of the dirt wall without any coils or cables covering it, is a picture of Laura. But not just any picture of Laura. A naked picture of Laura. Daniel's favorite naked picture of Laura. The one where she's standing sans panties in front of a mirror, holding her phone with her right hand and lifting her green and white striped shirt with her left hand, revealing her XXL water balloon-like breasts. It's the very same picture Daniel still masturbates to even though he and Laura have been broken up and even though she's moving to Miami and then to Sweden, where she'll eventually meet some tall, handsome, blonde Swedish guy who will date her and satisfy her not only sexually but emotionally as well, whereas Daniel would still be masturbating to this very same picture months from now if he weren't in this miserably long and drawn out process of trying to bury his heart in a Big Mac container beneath the ocean floor.

Without even realizing he's doing it, Daniel stands up and wanders over to the picture. Without asking for permission, he takes it off the wall. He holds it in his hands and stares at it longingly, admiring Laura as if she were dead. Although, in a way, she is. Just not to the entire world. Only to Daniel, considering he would never see her again.

"You did good, Daniel," the old man says, breathing his warm, mossy breath on the back of Daniel's neck.

Lost in Laura's blue-eyed reverie, Daniel hadn't even noticed the old man stalk up right behind him. He feels uncomfortable, like not only is the old man trespassing on the front lawn of this intimate moment but he's trampling the flowers as well.

Daniel tries putting Laura's picture back up on the wall but the tape doesn't stick and the photo falls and floats dead moth-like onto the floor, landing next to a box of tissues and hand lotion Daniel hadn't initially noticed, making him, somehow, and rightfully so, even more uncomfortable than he just was.

Instead of grabbing the picture and trying again, Daniel leaves it behind on the floor and walks back over to the chair and sits down. The old man picks up Laura's picture and carefully, precisely, tapes it back onto the dirt wall. Then he stands back, puts his hands on his hips again and admires the photo.

"Yeah... You did good alright," the old man repeats to himself.

With his head hung and, therefore, his eyes already aiming downward, Daniel notices, for the first time, the floor's dirty ham-hue and large amount of wrinkles. He presses the tip of his sneaker into the floor and rotates it like he's putting out an imaginary cigarette. The floor is rubber-like in nature, and has some give to it.

When Daniel looks back up, he sees the old man already looking at him. Always one to avoid eye contact, especially with strangers, Daniel reflexively stares at the luminous dots lingering around the ceiling just in time to see one go out, making the room dim considerably. Daniel keeps his eyes transfixed above, waiting for the dot to turn itself back on.

"What are those?" Daniel asks after the luminous dot doesn't return. "They remind me of lightning bugs."

"Want to listen to a record?" the old man asks in a tone very indicative of someone trying to change the subject.

Even though he doesn't want to, Daniel shrugs in a way that manages to say, "Sure. I guess."

The old man forces a smile onto his face—one that looks like it's been handcuffed to a radiator for thirty-one years—and walks over to his record collection. As if his choice was already made as soon as he asked the question, he grabs a record without hesitation, pulls it out of its sleeve and puts it on the victrola. The old man puts the needle down. The record hisses briefly and what Daniel immediately recognizes as "Devil Town" by Daniel Johnston begins playing.

The old man slowly, carefully and creakingly sits down cross-legged on the floor next to the victrola, then pats the empty spot on the floor beside him. Daniel hesitates then joins him. The two of them sit there with both of their heads leaned to the left, similarly leaned to the left, like they're doing impressions of each other without realizing it, and listen to the record.

Then, out of the corner of his eyes, Daniel notices the old man strain his neck and look up at the luminous dots.

"Enjoy the light while you can," he says. "Pretty soon it's going to be dark in here again."

The darkness filling the room is not the plushy, down comforter kind that anyone could ever comfortably count sheep in while waiting for sweet unconsciousness to wash over them like a warm syrupy wave of half-NyQuil, half-heated milk. It's a hopeless, bottom-of-the-well kind of darkness, elongated in the face and taunting. A maddening darkness arduously rung out of a dragon-sized raven that won't stop saying, "Nevermore... Nevermore..."

Daniel hasn't been under the darkness's tyrannical hospitality long at all and he can already feel himself starting to lose it, leaving him to wonder how someone like the old man could actually live under the oppression of its cold iron fist 24/7.

"How do you do it?" Daniel thinks aloud.

"Do what?"

"Live like this. In this darkness."

The old man pauses, thinks, and, accompanied along with a shrug, answers, "Same way you do, I guess."

Again, Daniel doesn't know what to say, so he opts for the virtue of silence.

"You can get used to anything really. It used to be brighter in here, though," the old man adds after Daniel doesn't respond. "Much, much brighter."

Daniel, as inconspicuously as possible—although he doesn't understand the reasoning for the stealthy pivoting of his neck—glances back up at the lightning bugs.

"Things weren't so bad back then to be honest," the old man continues. "Ya know, when things actually worked around here. When there was more light. Hell, it was even kind of nice. A little cramped, sure. But still, it was cozy. I had everything I needed, really."

"I'm sorry," Daniel finds himself saying even though he's not sure why. Something about apologizing just feels right. Polite even. Appropriate.

"Don't be. I get it, ya know? I understand what you're doing. And why you're doing it. Once you lose hope…" the old man says before trailing off.

Although Daniel never really thought about it before, he knows the old man is right. He can even pinpoint the exact moment he lost hope, and not just some hope but all hope, every last remaining shred, the grease-coated, savory memory of which prompting Daniel to stand up, walk over to the old man's desk and grab the top page from the stack of papers.

"My heart belongs in an empty Big Mac container buried beneath the ocean floor…"

"There's no coming back from that," the old man says, staring at the record player the same way a person who's deep in thought stares trance-like into a roaring fire. "Losing hope, I mean. Truly losing it. I guess that's what I was trying to say. And then, after you do lose hope, it's just a matter of how gracefully you let go of what little is left."

Only half paying attention to the old man, Daniel quietly thumbs through the stack of black and white self-published hopelessness, double-checking that each page is, in fact, filled with the same sentence. And then, just as he silently confirms to himself that every page very well seems to be, the old man's voice taps him on the shoulder.

"I'm sorry," he says.

Daniel places the page he holds back on top of the stack.

"You're sorry?"

The old man nods.

"Why?"

The old man hesitates, thinks. The victrola-fireplace is really hissing and crackling now as the old man gazes into it without blinking.

"I dunno," the old man says. "Something about apologizing just feels right. Polite, even. Appropriate"

Feeling a sudden and surprising closeness to the old man, Daniel contemplates rejoining him on the floor in front of the victrola before remembering the sad-looking blue whale outside in the bright-orange boat, waiting there with the dead boombox and empty Big Mac container Daniel still has to somehow bury his heart in beneath the ocean floor.

"Do you have any batteries lying around by any chance?" Daniel asks.

"No," the old man answers, sounding hypnotized, and as if on cue, another lightning bug goes out.

The two remaining lightning bugs float around the ceiling like a sparkling, dandruff ballet. They shine like they're trying their best, like they're trying to compensate not just for the loss of the two lightning bugs that went out before them but all lightning bugs that have come and gone before them. They float like a lonely, dimming tribute, like an in-memoriam montage slowly fading to black. And as Daniel basks in their meek yet comforting glow, a certain levity seems to wash over his current situation, or, more accurately, his predicament, like even though Daniel is lost in the ocean and sunburned and starving and thirsty and failing to bury his heart in a Big Mac container beneath the ocean floor, everything is still, somehow, okay.

But even if the lightning bugs are telling Daniel that he is, on some philosophical level, fine, their luminous whisper of reassurance does little to quell the hunger pains boiling like a tramp's boot in the impoverished cauldron of his stomach.

"What about something to eat or drink?" Daniel asks the old man. His mouth feels drier than a desert with a yeast infection.

"I don't eat," the old man says.

"You don't eat."

"Or drink."

"Or drink…" Daniel repeats. "How do you survive then?"

The old man, with his eyes still honed onto the victrola-fireplace, points his prune-like finger toward the ceiling.

"Light," he says in a distant, one thousand-year-old Cro-Magnon voice.

Daniel glances at the lightning bugs, then back at the cadaverous old man, and, suddenly, his decrepit, time ravaged, pale appearance begins to make sense.

"Why don't you just make more?" Daniel asks.

"Make more?"

"Yeah. Lightning bugs. Can't you just pull on that lever again?"

"I told you—things don't work that well in here anymore. It's finicky. I have to be careful."

Daniel turns his attention to the slice of light letting itself in through the open door like the annoying, scene stealing-next door neighbor in every sitcom ever but minus the applause.

"What about outside?" Daniel asks.

"What about outside?" the old man says.

"Why don't you just step outside for a sec?"

"I can't."

"You can't?"

"I can't…" the old man repeats.

Having had enough with the repetitious conversation, and seeing it's going nowhere fast, Daniel decides to drop it. Not knowing what else to do, but wanting something to do to fill the silence that's suddenly so tense it's just about screaming for a deep tissue massage, Daniel wanders over to the large bookshelf, grabs the first book he sees and opens to a random page.

Akin to those pages of a high school text book that had, unfortunately for itself, fallen into the bored, restless and unruly hands of a

D+ student slipping through the cracks of the system, the random pages Daniel opens to have been vandalized, scratched out with black pen to the point where all of the text is completely illegible.

Curious, but more so just mildly perplexed, Daniel turns the page.

On the top of the next page is the date "July 25th, 1995," and then, beneath that, in the exact same font and text size as the stack of type-written papers on the old man's desk, is a journal-like entry, which, unlike the pages before, is only sporadically crossed out instead of entirely, making the fevered, scribble marks somehow seem more thoughtful, more editorial.

Squinting his eyes in the dim, floundering light, Daniel begins reading the uncensored part of the entry.

"...If sticky had a smell, it would be this recycling center.

I don't like coming here. Everyone here, including Mom, especially *Mom, always looks so angry, so upset.*

There always comes a point when she yells at one of the machines too.

Either because a machine doesn't work or because it stops working or because it fills up before she's done using it.

Then Mom yells at the machine like it's not her fault it's full, as if the hundred or so empty bottles she deposited had nothing to do with it becoming full, like the machine itself is specifically out to get her and keep her waiting.

And an employee is never around to help, so she has to call for one.

The employee never arrives quickly either, which only makes her angrier with each passing second.

And if I ask her, 'Can't we just leave? Haven't we done enough?' she snaps at me.

She says, 'Do you want to eat tonight? Because, if so, stop your whining. This is the only way we can afford groceries right now.'

Then she says something about how lucky we are that Uncle Bobby leaves us all of his Beck's empties to begin with, that I should be thankful instead of complaining.

But I don't feel thankful.

This fat, old lady wearing a big, baggy Olympics t-shirt keeps staring at me and it's making me uncomfortable.

I hate this place and I know Mom hates it too.

And whenever we stand there, waiting for an employee to come and unload whatever machine is full, I can feel the recycling center hating us back.

'Wipe that goddamn look off your face,' Mom will usually say to me at some point when I'm bored and tired of waiting.

'That look, Daniel. I've told you about that goddamn look...'"

Daniel stops reading.

He remembers moments like these—too plentiful to count—so clearly, he feels like he just actually relived one. Not wanting to feel any worse than he already does, Daniel grabs another book off the shelf and leafs through the pages—the text still scratched out here and there, usually in groups of three or four paragraphs—looking for something lighter and happier to read and reminisce over. But as Daniel searches through the book, he begins to notice a disconcerting trend. That every entry he's able to read, every memory that's left behind for him to relive, is, in one way or another, a bad one, a sad one, a frustrating one, a scarring one. Daniel almost getting evicted from his first apartment because he failed to pay the rent on time three months in a row because he couldn't handle his dead-end job at Michael's Arts & Crafts and kept calling in sick, almost to the point where he got fired. Daniel having his first anxiety attack in a subway car on his way to see a punk show in Brooklyn where his friend, Greg, was waiting for him. Daniel's mom committing herself to a psych ward because she confided in Daniel's dad one morning that she wanted "to go to sleep and never wake up." Daniel's mom slowly, and painfully—so, so painfully—dying of pancreatic cancer.

Flipping through censored page after censored page, Daniel comes across nothing even remotely happy. Nothing hopeful or lighthearted. Just more of the same heartbreak, anxiety, shame, dread and self-hate. Daniel's heart begins racing. He can feel it panicking as a wave of heat that begins in his head quickly sweeps throughout the entirety of his body, a sensation that instantly forces him to begin sweating, and all of a sudden, it's like Daniel's right back outside underneath the blistering sun.

Even though he knows what he's going to find, even though he knows these discoveries are only going to crank up the heat wave of anxiety currently flushing through his body, Daniel pulls another book from the shelf. He flips through to find more text scratched out all throughout.

Daniel drops the book and grabs another. He flips through its pages. More vandalized memories. Only bad ones remaining. Daniel grabs book after book. He goes through them looking for just one that is left unmaimed. But book after book is vandalized. Book after book is scratched out, edited, censored. Nothing but bad memories, sad memories, shit memories, unwanted memories.

The old man ignores Daniel, remaining motionless with his knees tucked up into his chest as the victrola sputters music to him, exuding the warmth of melody. And after almost two whole shelves of books have been noisily flipped through and then tossed aside, Daniel, panting, blurts out a very fair and logical question.

"Why?"

Daniel watches the old man's shoulders rise and fall like two bony civilizations.

"Why'd you do this?" Daniel repeats, now holding open the most current book he's ripped from the shelf for the old man to see.

The old man finally pries his eyes off the victrola and looks over his shoulder at Daniel. As soon as his eyes lock onto the vandalized leatherbound book, they become heavy and sad.

"I didn't do it," the old man says.

"What do you mean you didn't do it?" Daniel says, recognizing the sudden authoritative and parental tone to his voice, like he's two seconds away from grounding the old man if he doesn't give him the answer he wants. "If you didn't do it then who did?"

"It wasn't just me," the old man answers after hesitating. "*We* did it…"

Daniel's eyebrows raise and his back straightens. The old man's words—soft, short and delicate yet sharp, like marshmallow thumbtacks—almost completely take all the air out of Daniel's lungs, and the book falls from his hand.

Daniel stands there, focused on the pale back of the old man, and for the first time he notices his ass crack peeking above the frayed-horizon waistband of his underpants.

Another lightning bug goes out.

Daniel hasn't moved. He can't move. He just stands in place, squinting through the flexing darkness at the old man whom he can barely even see anymore as the last remaining lightning bug illuminates the room like a chipped tooth sprinkled with fairy dust.

Feeling tired and weak, or even more tired and weak than he was already feeling thanks to the physical and emotional strain of this unsuccessful journey so far, Daniel sits down on the floor right in the middle of the mess of books. It's all gradually making sense to him. Why, as he grew older, he was never able to exude any vitality into the world. Why he could never seem to be anything more than some burned out movie projector with a short black and white film continuously flapping at the end of its reel.

Daniel feels cheated, and without even reading any of the books he threw on the floor, he can relive an entire lifetime of never sending anything positive or joyful back into society even though there was always a large part of him that wanted to. He just never understood why he was incapable of doing just that. But now it makes sense. His struggle to emanate that inner humanly light that others have. That light that brought humans closer, together. That light that made them want to stay. Daniel doesn't have that. Or he no longer has that. He has something else (*"That look, Daniel… That goddamn look."*), although, Daniel knows, there was a time when he once had that light. Years and years ago, as a child, before the sad-looking blue whales laid their grubby eyes on him. He could see that light shining out of his young self whenever his mom would occasionally bring out the family photo albums.

It killed Daniel to see himself like that as his mom flipped through page after page, smiling proudly and telling Daniel how cute he used to be. It was torturous to see himself filled with that divine light of simply being, of living unencumbered and free, and as much as that light diminishes for everyone as they grow older, most didn't completely lose it, or allow themselves to lose it (Had he *allowed* himself to lose it?), leaving Daniel to wonder about everything he's missed out on because of losing that bright, shining part of himself.

The record stops, the needle clicks and Daniel Johnston's voice seems to vanish all too poetically into the sour, brooding shadows. The hypnotic aura of the victrola-fireplace extinguishes itself and the room becomes filled with a hard to swallow silence.

Daniel hones in on the naked picture of Laura on the wall, at her eyes, at her smug, sexy, fishhook grin, at her breasts, at her exotic and untamed Brillo pad bush, and something inside of him snaps. He stands up, walks over to the shadow-covered area of where he saw the old man flip the lever and begins groping the dirt wall.

"What are you doing?" the old man asks with neurotically concerned eyes.

Daniel ignores the old man as his hands come across a baseball bat-sized lever running parallel with the dirt wall. Without thinking twice, Daniel yanks down on it. Sparks shoot out of the ceiling and, two molasses-seconds later, a lightning bug appears. But the collective, feeble light that it and the other lightning bug give off isn't bright enough, or sustaining enough, just as it hasn't been for the past fifteen years of Daniel's life.

"Daniel…" the old man says helplessly.

Daniel pulls down on the lever again. And again and again. More sparks shoot out of the ceiling but, unlike before, no lightning bugs appear.

"Daniel…" the old man says again, this time even more calm and tranquil, even more powerless.

But Daniel doesn't listen. He thrusts the lever downward as hard as he can, as if hoping the sheer force of his will alone will spawn more lightning bugs, dozens and dozens of them, then hundreds, all magnificently floating around, all emanating light.

Sparks explode from the ceiling and rain down onto the old man's desk. An ember lands on the stack of papers silently screaming, *"My heart belongs in an empty Big Mac container buried beneath the ocean floor…"* and the stack catches fire. But the old man doesn't notice, and neither does Daniel now repeatedly yanking on the lever, leaving no time in-between each desperate repetition to illuminate his dark self. Torrents of sparks fall like angry, burning rain, but still no lightning bugs are born from the short-circuiting madness.

The old man stands up. With his hands cupped over his mouth, he staggers backwards up against the wall and watches from the shadows, aghast. Daniel flips the lever so fast that he heaves with exhaustion. More sparks rain onto the old man's desk, one too many landing on the stack of papers, which officially ignites and goes up in flames.

Then the desk catches fire.

"Daniel!" the old man screams, and points at the fire usurping his work station.

Daniel stops when, from above, he hears a whoosh sound. He and the old man look up at the ceiling to see that it, too, has caught fire. With the proverbial floodgates now open, more embers fall from the ceiling. Some land on the numerous books scattered across the floor and, slowly, gradually, turn those into small but lethal-looking campfires. The entire room fills with fire, and smoke begins wafting down from the ceiling, the sheer heat making Daniel feel like his skin is melting off.

All of a sudden, Daniel feels a pair of hands grab his shirt. They drag him across the room and shove him out of the door. Daniel doesn't even realize the old man just saved his shell-shocked self until he stares back at him, standing hesitantly in the doorway, one hand behind his back and the other up over his head, blocking the sunlight that runs across him. Daniel finally snaps out of it. He runs a few steps down the staircase, expecting the old man to be right behind him but stops when he realizes he's not being followed. Daniel treks back up to the top step. The old man is still standing at the door frame, wincing, shielding himself from the sun. Daniel's not sure if his eyes are playing tricks on him or not, but the old man's skin seems to be boiling and bubbling in the natural light.

"Come on," Daniel says.

Smoke billows out of the door. Even though the room behind the old man is filled with flames, he refuses to budge.

"Come on," Daniel repeats and waves the old man outside. "What are you doing?"

Coughing, the old man extends a brittle hand out the door. In its grasp is Laura's picture. Daniel hesitates, then takes the photo, prompting the old man to force out that sad smile of his, the one that's been held hostage as if handcuffed to a radiator for the past thirty-one years.

"You really did do good with her, Daniel," the old man says.

Then the door slams shut. Above the roaring flames, Daniel hears a dead bolt click.

Smoke seeps through the cracks of the door. Then, seconds later, the muffled screams of the old man. As the ravenous flames dig into his wrinkled skin, eating him alive with their blue-tipped fangs, Daniel, moving with an eerie sedation, slides Laura's picture into his pants pocket and traipses down the staircase with the somberness of a tangled, lead slinky.

Daniel doesn't say a word or so much as make eye contact with the sad-looking blue whale after taking his seat in the bright-orange boat, even though the sad-looking blue whale is waiting on some kind of explanation as to what went on behind closed doors.

"What?" Daniel finally snaps when the sad-looking blue whale's eyes won't stop ripping into him.

"You— You have smoke coming out of your head," the sad-looking blue whale says.

Daniel leans over the side of the boat and looks at his reflection in the water. To his shock, he sees that the sad-looking blue whale is telling the truth. Smoke *is* coming out of his head, fervently puffing from each one of his ears like two Indians sexting each other via smoke signals.

IT'S A HORRIBLE LIFE

RELIEF BECAME THE SUPREME, reigning emotion crowning Daniel as he looked down at the sentence he'd just written, at his new motto, at his soon-to-be mantra, *My heart belongs in an empty Big Mac container buried beneath the ocean floor…*

It was a great idea, he thought, and a vaguely familiar one too, almost like he'd been trying to come up with it for years, like he'd been circling over it instead of coming in for a landing on its tarmac and, therefore, fully defining it and bringing it to life. But here it was out in the open, finally in front of him, staring at Daniel wide-eyed and smiling, as if saying, "Yes, we've found each other. At long last we're together."

My heart belongs in an empty Big Mac container buried beneath the ocean floor…

It represented the end of his life, an end Daniel knew was coming sooner rather than later, just never in what form. And that, Daniel realized, was where the relief he was feeling came in, in finally knowing how this fast-approaching end would present itself. Looking down at the sentence longingly, and placing his hand on it as if trying to feel the life of its pulse, Daniel knew things could be worse. That although maybe complicated and far-fetched, forcing him to exert a certain amount of effort he was normally against, burying his heart beneath the ocean floor would be much less painful than most other ways of exiting the planet, i.e. cancer, or being shot or stabbed. It'd also be a process he'd have control over, that he could take his time on or speed up according to however he was feeling. A process that seemed ceremonial as well, like a fitting farewell, as if somehow custom tailored for him by the years of built-up fast-food grease clogging his spiritual, and physical, arteries.

Relief... Daniel's brain said.

Relief that he'd, hopefully, never have to see or hear another sad-looking blue whale again. Relief that his grim lack of a future was now something he wouldn't have to try and navigate like the world's cruelest obstacle course. Because often, when Daniel did look ahead into his future, nervously and flinching, he didn't see much. Just more of the same sameness, tauntingly mundane and cruel, that he didn't know how to break free from. Everything seemed to be pointing in this direction, the direction of, *"My heart belongs in an empty Big Mac container buried beneath the ocean floor..."* which was a compass in and of itself, pointing him toward the ocean, directing him toward the end that he'd greet with wide open arms.

Daniel placed his arms on the table and buried his head in them. Despite being relieved, he still felt so weak, tired and unhappy that he couldn't bear the strain of seeing earthly things, alive or inanimate, around him any longer. Every moment was the equivalent of being in some pointless, exhausting battle where you had to continually keep your guard up in order to stay alive, and as he lay his head face down on the McDonald's table, much like a talkative child being told by a fed up teacher to put their head down on their desk and shut up, he could finally, after thirty-one years, feel his defenses completely drop and come crashing down as they hit the floor.

And then there was silence.

And then the sound of the back door opening.

The sad-looking blue whale at the rear door was now standing inside the McDonald's, staring back at the door with an expression of sedated shock on its face, either unable to believe it finally found a way to let itself in or that it'd been that easy this whole time.

Daniel sat there and watched the sad-looking blue whale. It hadn't seen him yet. It was still too busy taking in its new surroundings with a joyless and lost look on its face, almost like it had no idea what to do next, like it never planned this far ahead because it never thought it'd actually get this far ahead. Then the sad-looking blue whale finally noticed Daniel and their eyes firmly locked in some cold and unsettling visual handshake.

"Ooooh, oooh, oooooh!" it cried.

Daniel wasn't sure who was more stunned, him or the sad-looking blue whale. The last place on earth he was supposed to be safe from their kind had been compromised and it was only a matter of time before the sad-looking blue whale fully came to its senses—or what little senses it had—and joined Daniel, inviting itself over and sitting down in his booth like an old acquaintance it hadn't expected to bump into.

Everyone in the dining room had somehow dispersed without Daniel knowing, leaving just him, the sad-looking blue whale and the empty Big Mac container. Daniel looked down at the empty Big Mac container, almost pleadingly, as if seeking its help somehow, as if begging this inanimate box for advice on what to do next, and noticed an oblong grease stain on its lid that made him yearn for something undefined and distant, or maybe even non-existent. Daniel picked up the empty Big Mac container with both hands and, in a hum-drum deliriousness, made its lid flop up and down as if it were a puppet.

"'Greasy, cardboard, heart-container…'" Daniel made the empty Big Mac container say, feeling a sense of calm as well as another sensation he couldn't quite put his finger on. Daniel quieted himself. He focused, trying to determine what the feeling was precisely.

Appreciation? his brain ventured.

And the more Daniel tossed the idea around, it kind of fit. It kind of made sense. He appreciated the empty Big Mac container. And this was something, he realized seconds later, he had often felt with other inanimate objects. Not to mention with places as well, like late one night when Daniel was walking back to the subway station in Brooklyn after having seen this band, The Lillingtons, with his friend, Greg. Daniel was walking under a bridge that was keeping him safe from the rain he'd been trudging through for the past fifteen minutes. Daniel remembered stopping underneath. He remembered feeling calm and peaceful and safe as the city and rain echoed at him from outside. He remembered thinking, *I love this bridge…* Then the automatic realization that, yes, he truly did love the bridge. Because despite not being alive, the bridge had a presence. It even provided him with a type of company. And aside from maybe collapsing, the bridge couldn't hurt him either. Nor did it expect anything from him. The bridge was just there, and by simply existing and not hurting Daniel and, therefore, not adding more pain into his already pain-filled life, Daniel appreciated it. Old and rusty and wet, and shaped like the rib cage of some long-dead, enormous and mythological beast, he could look at it with love in his eyes. The same way he was now looking at the empty Big Mac container for similar reasons.

Interrupting his reverie, the first sad-looking blue whale to ever infiltrate a McDonald's took one step toward the wet floor sign and slipped and fell. Instead of getting up, however, it lay there on its back, staring up at the ceiling.

"You should help it up," a voice said after a moment.

Daniel looked over his shoulder but there was no one there. He looked around the dining room. Empty.

"In your hand," the voice instructed.

Daniel looked at his hand, or, more specifically, at the empty Big Mac container resting in his palm.

"Hi," the empty Big Mac container said, its lid opening and closing without any ventriloquist-assistance from Daniel whatsoever.

BAYYYBEE!!!

"HEY," Daniel said to Laura as he sat on her couch one Saturday morning. He was checking the balance of his bank account on his phone and hating himself and also low-key wanting to die in the depressing process of doing so.

"Mm?" Laura replied, as if barely listening.

Laura was unusually restless and sweeping the floor in nothing but bright orange yoga pants. It was unusually hot out and her small, adorable gut hung over the waistband of her pants and her large breasts drooped like the cheeks of an elderly basset hound as she was half bent over, running the Swiffer Wet Jet across the hardwood floors.

"Remember our first date when you asked me if I wanted to listen to some music?" Daniel asked.

"Kinda," Laura said, keeping her eyes focused on her cleaning.

"And then you brought your CD case over to me and told me to pick one?"

"Yeah."

"Do you remember what I chose?"

"Babe, are you asking me because you don't know or because you want to see if I remember?"

"The second one," Daniel said.

"Christ, you're such a woman."

Daniel picked up a chicken bone leftover on a plate from their dinner the night before and threw it on the floor.

"You missed a spot," Daniel said and pointed at the chicken bone.

"Babe..." Laura said, not even mildly amused, then quickly picked up the chicken bone and threw it away.

"Well?" Daniel said.

"Well what?"

"Do you remember what I picked?"

Laura shook her head.

"*In Utero*," Daniel said. "And then you put it on, but after, like, two and a half songs, you said you loved the album but that you weren't really feeling it. Like it wasn't good first date music or something."

"Well, I was right. It's definitely not."

"Were you scared that I was going to rape you if 'Rape Me' came on?"

Laura almost smiled without looking at Daniel. She was taking the dirty cloth off the Swiffer Wet Jet and replacing it with a new one.

"Actually, that would've been kind of hot," she said.

Daniel sat there on the couch, thinking.

"I agree, though," he said. "It's not first date music. You were right."

And then, not sure where he was going with any of this, Daniel mentally trailed off and stared down at the glass coffee table in front of him. The table was covered in empty wine bottles and empty glasses and dirty dishes from the night before. Laura had made chicken and Velveeta mac and cheese, and cheese was crusted onto the dishes. Daniel identified with the crusted cheese, like he was nothing more than a human version of said crusted cheese.

"Did you know Kurt Cobain originally wanted to name *In Utero* 'I Hate Myself and Want to Die,' but Krist Novoselic talked him out of it because he felt like it'd be irresponsible of them and he was worried that some of their fans might kill themselves if they named the album that?"

Daniel looked up from the crusted cheese. Somehow, without him noticing, Laura had taken off her yoga pants. She was now in nothing but light-blue striped panties that had a small bow near the waistband as she repeatedly ran the Swiffer Wet Jet over the same spot on the floor, trying to get rid of some defiant stain.

"Jesus. Why is it so fucking hot today?" she said.

"They still have a song called that, though," Daniel continued on, staring at the bow on Laura's panties. "It was supposed to be on *In Utero* but Kurt left it off because he felt like they already had too many 'noise songs' on the album. What did you put on after that?"

"Huh?" Laura replied, still having trouble battling the unruly mystery stain on the hardwood floor. "Ugh… It's like nothing wants to come up off the floor."

"What did you put on after Nirvana? Martin Sexton?"

"Babe," Laura said with a frustrated laugh. "How come when I take you out to dinner you just sit there all quiet and mute-like but now as I'm trying to clean you talk my fucking ear off?"

Daniel pictured him and Laura out at some restaurant. Laura sitting on one side of the booth and Daniel and a sad-looking blue whale sitting uncomfortably close on the other side.

"Sorry," Daniel said. And then, after a pause, "I talk to you, though."

"No. Not really."

"Remember when we went to Applebees and we played that trivia game on that touch screen by our table and we got the all-time high score? I talked a lot that night."

"Great, babe. Awesome. One time. *And* you were talking about the game."

Daniel sighed.

"Come watch TV with me," he said, feeling bored.

"I'm cleaning. If you want me to watch TV with you come help and make this go faster."

Daniel fell back into the couch and stared at the dirty dishes.

"Maybe I'll go to McDonald's and try to write," he said.

"Okay, but please do those dishes when you come back."

"I will," Daniel said and then just sat there on the couch.

"Are you going or not?" Laura asked after a few minutes.

"I guess not. I don't really feel like writing. In fact, I don't think I'm ever going to write again. I think I'm just gonna give up on poetry and become a door-to-door used condom salesman. Probably make more money that way too," Daniel joked.

"You have dreams. Not goals," Laura replied. "That's why you have no money. You need a career. Poets are great and all, but poetry is not a career."

"Unless you're really good at it," she added.

Daniel's eyebrows creased in confusion as he wondered if Laura had just insulted him or not. He put his phone down on the glass table next to a huge, flat piece of driftwood Laura had gathered on one of her walks on the beach and then brought home because she thought it looked nice. The piece of driftwood was covered in sea glass and sea shells Laura had also found on other walks. "Treasures," Laura called them.

Daniel knew Laura was right. Poetry was not a career. But Daniel knew a career wouldn't make him happy either. A career would just give him more money which would relieve a certain amount of stress from his life but that would also exhaust him and demand much more of his attention and, therefore, make him write less and allow him less time to do the things he loved and, therefore, greatly increase the plentiful visits of sad-looking blue whales.

"You need a new job," Laura said. "Your job now is not a real job."

Daniel nodded. His nod was his way of demonstrating he was listening to her even though he disagreed with her.

"I'm going to get a tattoo on my head that says, 'Born to take out garbage,'" Daniel joked, considering that taking out the garbage had always been one of his main duties with any job he'd ever worked.

Laura's bare foot stepped on something small, a pebble or something like that, Daniel guessed, and she swore out loud.

"Babe, you need to take your shoes off from now on when you come inside. This floor is disgusting. There's shit everywhere."

Daniel always took off his shoes. Laura was the one who never took off her shoes, but he decided against bringing this up. He didn't feel like fighting with Laura right now. He felt like he was always fighting with Laura. Even when they weren't fighting somehow.

A sad-looking blue whale wearing muddy boots on its bottom fins walked inside Laura's house, tracking mud all over. It sat down beside Daniel on the couch. Daniel tried his best to ignore the sad-looking blue whale by focusing on Laura instead. He looked at her gut and saggy tits. He looked at her nipples. They were large and puffy and wonderful and Daniel randomly imagined smoke coming out of them for some reason.

"I love you," Daniel said to Laura.

Laura didn't return the sentiment, but not because she didn't hear Daniel. It was just that sometimes Laura didn't say "I love you" back after Daniel had said it to her.

"I feel forced to say it. You shouldn't feel forced to say I love you," was how she defended herself whenever Daniel asked why she seldom said it back, which Daniel never understood. Why would saying I love you to someone you sincerely loved ever feel forced? Or like work?

All of sudden, Daniel realized the sad-looking blue whale was sitting on his lap.

"Ooh, oooh, ooh, oooooh!" the sad-looking blue whale cried.

"What, babe?" Laura asked without looking up from her cleaning.

"Nothing," Daniel said, already feeling his right leg begin to fall asleep underneath the sad-looking blue whale's massive, crippling weight.

"How'd this floor get so messy?" Laura asked. "Babe, send me your resume. I've reformatted and edited resumes for so many of my friends that I've become a pro at it."

The sad-looking blue whale shifted its weight on Daniel's lap, accidentally pinching Daniel's dick against his thigh.

"Ow," Daniel said.

"What?" Laura asked.

"I'll send it when I get back home tomorrow night," Daniel said.

"You're gonna forget. I'm just gonna text you and remind you. Remind me to text you and remind you."

"I would, but I'm probably gonna forget to remind you to text me and remind me to remind me to email you my resume," Daniel said, smiling like an asshole.

"You're such an idiot," Laura said, also smiling, but not quite like an asshole.

Laura caught her reflection in the window. Her smile immediately vanished and she groaned out loud.

"What the fuck? Why is this still happening to my face? Like, it shouldn't be happening."

Laura had been breaking out even more recently. Painful-looking, red blemishes all over her cheeks and forehead, like an unholy legion of fire-ants were trying to burrow out from underneath her flesh.

"Have you been doing your skincare routine?"

"Yes, I've been doing my skincare routine. You see me do it every night," she snapped back.

The sad-looking blue whale put its fin around Daniel's shoulder and Daniel inwardly cringed. He felt like a Santa Claus who had the biggest and saddest child ever on his lap, and all the child wanted for Christmas was for Daniel to be miserable *and* a new copy of *Titanic* on VHS, even though it got one just last year.

"Do the dishes," Laura suddenly commanded.

"I will," Daniel said, feeling especially pinned underneath the weight of the sad-looking blue whale all of a sudden.

"No. Do them now."

"Are you okay?" Daniel asked.

Laura laughed like an asshole.

"Yeah, I'm fine. I'm just tired of waiting for you to do the dishes."

"You let your own dishes sit for days," Daniel reasoned like an idiot.

"I make dinner and he doesn't do the dishes but somehow I'm the asshole," Laura said to herself. She was changing the cloth on the Swiffer Wet Jet again even though Daniel felt like she just did so.

"I never said you were an asshole. And if you have something to say to me, or about me, say it to me, and don't mutter it to yourself."

"Oh my god, I've already said it ten times. Do the fucking dishes! Please?"

Daniel wasn't sure what to do, or how to react to Laura's unusual, although frequently more common, mood. But rather than get into a fight, he decided to do the dishes. It took a few minutes for him to get up, for him to get the sad-looking blue whale off his lap, but after he had, he went right over to Laura's CD collection.

"I'm gonna put *In Utero* on if that's alright."

Laura stopped what she was doing. She was huffing and puffing a little and her face was flushed with sweaty redness.

"No," she said, firmly. "It's too depressing and loud."

Daniel just stood there holding the CD case, frozen like a little kid who had just been caught doing something wrong.

"And what's with you and all these depressing artists?" Laura asked.

"Oooooh, ooh, ooooooh!" the sad-looking blue whale cried.

Laura laughed to herself again. Or she laughed at Daniel, but in a "to herself" type of way.

"Seriously, though. Kurt Cobain. Ernest Hemingway. Sylvia Plath. Richard Brafftiagn..."

"Brautigan."

"*Brautigan*. Whatever."

"Don't forget Marilyn Monroe," Daniel said, annoyed and trying to sound as smarmy as possible.

"Oh my god, fuck that bimbo," Laura spat. "But really. Do you like anyone who hasn't killed themselves or is that your main criteria for art?"

"Did I do something?" was all Daniel could think of to say.

Laura put the Swiffer Wet Jet away in a closet. Then she grabbed her t-shirt off the back of the couch.

"Just put your music on," she said as she slid the shirt on over her head. "I'm gonna go upstairs and go through my closet like I've been meaning to."

"You just cleaned. It's the weekend. Relax a little and I'll do the dishes."

"Relax," she scoffed. "We adults have things we need to do, Daniel. Weekend or no weekend."

"Okay," Daniel said as Laura headed for the stairs. "I love you."

But Laura didn't return the words. She went to her purse, grabbed a pack of cigarettes, then bounded up the stairs, leaving Daniel and the sad-looking blue whale alone together.

She doesn't even try to hide it anymore... Daniel's brain said in regards to Laura's smoking.

Daniel put the CD case back down where he found it. He grabbed the dirty dishes on the coffee table, walked over to the sink and turned on the hot water. He let it run for a few seconds, then ran his hand through it. Except it wasn't hot. It wasn't even lukewarm. It was still just as cold, if not colder, than it had been the past few weeks. It was still just as cold, if not colder, than Laura. Just as cold, if not colder, than the sad-looking blue whale's eyes poking him from across the room like a thirty-foot-long frozen fish stick.

"Ooooooh, ooh, oooh!" the sad-looking blue whale cried, and kicked off its muddy boots across the room, splattering mud everywhere.

GREASY, CARDBOARD HEART-COFFIN

SMOKE STOPPED FUNNELING out of Daniel's ears like exhaust pipes with the trots right around the same time that smoke stopped seeping through the cracks of the lone gray horizon door. Even though the old man had stopped screaming some time ago, Daniel can still hear his helpless cries of agony echoing in his head. Daniel wonders if he'll ever be able to get these screams out of his head, which, even though it's now completely vacant of smoke, and who knows what else, throbs savagely.

Daniel can't remember the last time he had a headache this bad. Or if he ever has. He tries rubbing his temples but his amateurish attempt at a massage does little to alleviate any pain.

"Do you have any Advil?" Daniel asks the sad-looking blue whale.

The sad-looking blue whale glances at Daniel, almost flinchingly, then unzips his fanny pack.

"What happened in there?" the sad-looking blue whale asks as he begins rummaging around.

Daniel's been waiting for this question, not to mention contemplating how to answer it, ever since he sat back down in the bright-orange boat, but despite the internal debate, he's still not sure what to say. Solely because he's still not sure what actually happened. The whole thing, the entire bleak, two-watt experience that literally went up in flames, felt like some sort of fever dream, or like the trippy delusions of intense sunstroke, even though he knows it was neither.

So instead of answering the sad-looking blue whale, Daniel just rubs his head harder, as if trying to somehow knead the screams of the old man burning alive out of his head.

"Can you hurry?" Daniel asks, hoping that once his headache goes away the old man's screaming will vanish along with it.

"I'm trying," the sad-looking blue whale says. "There's just so much stuff in here."

Frustrated, and trying to clear some space in his fanny pack to ease and expedite the apparently arduous process of locating Advil inside the cheap and gaudy black hole strapped around his waist, the sad-looking blue whale begins pulling things out and setting them aside, one at a time, the most random assortment of crap imaginable —a left shoe with no laces, a cracked spyglass, a beer stein with no handle, a motor from a motorized tie rack, a scuffed hubcap, a motor'less motorized tie rack, a taxidermy beaver missing its two front teeth, a fishing pole with no fishing line, a blue kite with a hole in its middle, the door of a mini-fridge with a Mitt Romney campaign sticker on it, and, impressively, a Jean-Michel Basquiat painting that Daniel immediately recognizes as "Untitled (Skull), circa 1981."

Daniel gawks at the painting propped up in the corner of the bright-orange boat as the sad-looking blue whale continues foraging for Advil. He's seen it in pictures before dozens of times, but never up close and in person. Both painted and drawn in a monster mash of colors, the mangy skull makes Daniel think of a clown not wearing his makeup who took one too many pies to the face over the years. A clown who got laughed at, not with, one too many times. A clown finally at the end of the comically long handkerchief-rope he's been pulling out of his sleeve ever since he was born, and is now left with no other option except to seriously contemplate sucking on the cold, steel taste of a shotgun lollipop.

It looks familiar, the skull, and it's only when the throbbing and screaming in Daniel's head intensifies that he realizes who the skull reminds him of—the old man, burned alive, charred like a Fourth of July hamburger patty no one ever intended on eating.

"I'm not seeing Advil," the sad-looking blue whale says, peering into his fanny pack. "Sorry."

As if he didn't hear the sad-looking blue whale, or as if he'd completely forgotten about his need for headache relief altogether, Daniel, like a sunburnt Manchurian Candidate mesmerized by the old man's screaming, stands up, grabs the Basquiat painting and, using two hands, throws it as far as he can like it's a $110 million-dollar frisbee. The painting soars an impressively far distance, then skips across the water for a bit before coming to a rest on top of the sleepy waves.

When Daniel looks down at the sad-looking blue whale, the sad-looking blue whale is already staring up at him with eyes that seem to bulge the question, "What the hell?"

"Sorry…" Daniel mutters as he sits down, not sounding sorry at all. More so like he's apologizing in order to not look like any more of an asshole than he already does.

The sad-looking blue whale, seeming to accept his apology, or just feel entirely indifferent towards it, leans his head against the horizon wall and stares out at the painting slowly taking on water with a Titanic-like grace and dignity.

"It's okay," he says after a moment. "I never really liked it that much anyway."

"Not sad-looking enough," the sad-looking blue whale adds.

"Not sad-looking enough?" Daniel repeats, stunned that anyone could look at that painting and not consider the skull "sad-looking" or "tortured," especially considering how much the priceless work of art looks like it was painted by the old man's screams in Daniel's head.

"Well, I dunno. It's a little bit sad-looking, I guess. Just not nearly as sad-looking as all the rest of this stuff."

Daniel mentally processes all of the worthless crap surrounding them, noting that everything is either broken or scratched, or dirty or missing some key component. He wonders why the sad-looking blue whale bothers carrying around the additional weight of all this useless junk. Why he would make his life even more difficult and arduous and laborious than life already was to begin with.

"You never know when you're going to need it," the sad-looking blue whale comes out with, as if reading Daniel's mind.

"When the hell are you going to need a Romney emblazoned mini-fridge door?"

"When I come across a Republican who has a mini-fridge with a door missing," the sad-looking blue whale answers, simply.

Daniel laughs even though he's more annoyed than amused.

"What?" the sad-looking blue whale says, picking up on the hostility in Daniel's amusement.

"Nothing. It's nothing, really. I just think you're full of shit. That's all."

Daniel can feel himself smiling as he says this. A familiar smile. One he recognizes and knows all too well, confrontational and antagonistic in nature. A smile that's ready to pick a fight and then proceed to fight dirty, take cheap shots. Even eye gouge or throw a couple low blows if need be. Whatever hurts his victim the most.

"I'm full of shit," the sad-looking blue whale repeats, as if signaling Daniel to go on with his explanation as to why he, the sad-looking blue whale, has a blowhole positively brimming with metaphorical fecal matter, just knowing that Daniel is going to inform him as to why anyway.

"Yeah, you're full of shit," Daniel says. "All you ever do is go on about *Titanic*. About how sad it is. About how you and all the other whales worship it because of how sad it is. All of you sad-looking blue whales just wallowing in your sadness, or broadcasting about how sad it makes you as if you enjoy the sadness. But you don't. You don't like being sad-looking. You hate it. Deep down you want to be happy but the prospect of the unknown terrifies you because being sad-looking is all you've ever allowed yourself to be. And you, just like almost all humans, fear what's new and different and so you wade around in your misery because it's comfortable. Because it feels like home. But as homey as it can be, there's this subconscious part of you that knows better. That feels this hole inside of you begging to be full. This hole inside of you that *Titanic* alone can never fill. So you go around collecting all this crap. Holding onto it. Hoarding it. As if it's going to fill that hole somehow. But it doesn't. And so you just keep collecting more, trying to stuff more worthless crap into the hollowness inside of you, trying to secretly make yourself feel better."

Without missing a beat, the sad-looking blue whale grabs the empty Big Mac container and holds it up right in Daniel's face.

"Says the guy who goes to McDonald's almost six times a week."

Daniel's jaw drops without physically dropping. Angry and embarrassed, he snatches the empty Big Mac container from the sad-looking blue whale's fin and impulsively hurls it into the ocean.

As soon as the empty Big Mac container leaves his fingers, Daniel regrets what he's done. He doesn't watch it soar through the air but can still feel it gently plop on the water, and has to keep his entire body from anxiously convulsing in response.

The sad-looking blue whale stares at Daniel. Daniel stares back. His body is screaming at him to dive overboard and swim out after the empty Big Mac container, but he won't listen. He refuses because then the sad-looking blue whale would win whatever kind of fucked up game they're currently playing.

"Go ahead," the sad-looking blue whale says, but not in an "I dare you to" tone of voice. It's a sympathetic one, like he can see Daniel at war with himself.

Daniel almost says thank you, but before he knows it his body is crashing through the surface of the refreshingly cold water and he's swimming out toward the empty Big Mac container.

The sad-looking blue whale picks up the broken spy glass from his fanny pack, puts it up to his eye and watches Daniel swim toward the waterlogged container. The glass inside the eyepiece is cracked and there's a bunch of variations of Daniel swimming frantically.

All of them different, but, ultimately, all of them the same.

Holding the empty Big Mac container above water with one hand, trying to keep it dry, and using that same arm to tread the ocean waves like a vaudevillian cane with scoliosis, Daniel swims back over to the bright orange boat while towing the Basquiat painting behind him.

The first thing Daniel does as soon as he returns is hand the sad-looking blue whale the empty Big Mac container. Then the painting. The sad-looking blue whale receives both objects blandly, then extends Daniel a fin and hoists him aboard.

"Thanks…" Daniel says as he sits back down in his seat, still too embarrassed from his recent outbursts to make eye contact with the sad-looking blue whale.

The sad-looking blue whale ignores Daniel or just doesn't hear him. Either way, he stares with considerable focus at the retrieved work of art that seems to be holding up well after its salty little soirée in the ocean.

"I guess it is kind of sad-looking," the sad-looking blue whale admits after a moment of contemplation.

Daniel wrings out his t-shirt. He can't help but think of the old man as he stares at the skull painting, nor can he help the feelings of guilt that crawl around on all fours in the pit of his stomach, knowing that if it wasn't for him and his rashness, that if it wasn't for him and his desperate need for light, the old man would still be here, that he wouldn't have been burned alive—one of the most horrifically excruciating deaths Daniel's mind can think of. And it's this exact same type of guilt, Daniel knows, that convinced him to bury his heart in the empty Big Mac container beneath the ocean floor in the first place, the exact same kind of self-loathing shame he suffered through, and is still suffering through, after Laura left him.

Laura's picture… Daniel's brain suddenly remembers with a cerebral cringe.

Daniel reaches into his pants pocket and pulls out Laura's picture, or, rather, what's left of Laura's picture, which, unlike the painting, hasn't fared well from its dip in the ocean. Looking more waterlogged and prune-wrinkled than the crotch of a geriatric mermaid, Daniel allows himself to admit, albeit begrudgingly, that the picture, this last crumb of connection he has left to Laura aside from the boat he's floating in, is basically destroyed.

Daniel hangs his head and casually tosses the naked photo into the water where it floats on the ocean's surface like an erotic autumn leaf. Suddenly feeling crowded and claustrophobic, although not from all of the sad-looking blue whale's possessions surrounding him but rather by his own incompetence and natural ability to ruin everything —although still ready to blame it on, as well as calmly lash out at, the vast collection of inanimate objects in the boat because being angry at something or someone else has always been so much easier than being angry with himself—Daniel kicks some of the sad-looking blue whale's belongings away from him with his foot.

"Can't you put this crap away?"

With the enthusiasm of a child ordered to clean his room, the sad-looking blue whale slowly begins gathering his possessions. One by one, he puts his things back inside his fanny pack, clearing the bright-orange boat of everything except the Basquiat painting and the spyglass he keeps on his sad-looking lap.

But before zipping his fanny pack closed, the sad-looking blue whale glances overboard at the naked photo. He hesitates, and then quickly, without the brooding thirty-one-year-old man-boy sitting across from him noticing, the sad-looking blue whale plucks the ruined photo out of the water and slides it inside his fanny pack before zipping it closed.

IT'S A HORRIBLE LIFE

"YOU REALLY SHOULD HELP IT UP," the empty Big Mac container repeated.

At that jaw-dropping moment, the empty Big Mac container could've instructed Daniel to do anything—to stand up, drop his pants and give a little twirl—and he would've done it, thoughtlessly, robot-like and without hesitation.

Moving as if carried on the wind of the empty Big Mac container's voice, a voice that sounded like Buddha trying to pick lint out of his bellybutton but finding one of the noble truths inside instead, Daniel got up and walked over to the sad-looking blue whale who'd slipped and fallen onto the wet floor. He extended a hand out toward it. The sad-looking blue whale, looking unsure and skeptical, as if wondering if this five-digited olive branch reaching out was a trick or not, took Daniel's hand with its fin. Daniel hoisted the sad-looking blue whale up onto its bottom fins and the two of them stood there, bobbing up and down on the utter uneasiness of their current situation.

"There ya go," the empty Big Mac container said, and even though it didn't have a mouth, Daniel could tell it was smiling—a big cheesy grin.

Daniel walked back over to his booth and sat down with the rigidly nervous posture of a virgin crash test dummy.

"I'm sure he appreciated that," the empty Big Mac container said. "Daniel, right?"

"Yeah..."

"Nice to meet you, Daniel," it said, and then moved a little, as if trying to give a respectful bow.

"You too," Daniel managed to say. "Uh, do you have a name?"

"No," the empty Big Mac container said, simply.

Silence. Daniel hesitated. And then, "Did you want me to give you one, or…?"

The empty Big Mac container laughed to itself. Its laugh sounded like the doorbell to a house made of the space between stars.

"No, no. That's alright. I enjoy being nameless," it said.

"I've never felt the need to be defined, really," it added further.

"Yeah, okay. Sure…" Daniel replied.

The sad-looking blue whale, cautiously side-stepping the wet floor, finally made its first move and wandered into the center of the dining room, where it sat in its own booth not far away from Daniel.

"Ooooh, ooh, ooooh!" it cried.

"You don't like them much, do you?" the empty Big Mac container observed.

Daniel didn't even realize he was making a face, cringing, really, over the sad-looking blue whale's cry, until the empty Big Mac container had spoken up.

"Is it that obvious?"

"Just a little," the empty Big Mac container said, exuding another invisible grin.

There was something about the empty Big Mac container's unseeable smile, something infectious, something that made Daniel smile in return. Suddenly, he felt like this wasn't weird at all, like all objects were capable of talking and always had been, like if Daniel reached into the garbage and pulled out an empty fry container, he was certain it'd smile, greet him, and then ask how he'd been.

"Have you ever tried not viewing them as enemies?" the empty Big Mac container asked.

"Who? *Them?*" Daniel asked incredulously, and motioned his head toward the sad-looking blue whale sitting alone in its booth.

"Yeah," the empty Big Mac container said. "Them. The sad-looking blue whales."

Now it was Daniel's turn to laugh. "No… The thought never crossed my mind."

"That's okay." The empty Big Mac container's relaxed voice wore a necklace of prayer beads and open toed sandals, calmly illustrating that, although it disagreed with Daniel, it would drop the topic and leave it alone.

Light rain began spattering against the restaurant. The wind wailed and the bushes outside thwacked against the windows, swaying back and forth in such awkward, nonrhythmic motions that Daniel couldn't help but think of a drunken uncle dancing at a wedding.

"The sky looks like leaden cotton candy," Daniel thought out loud.

The empty Big Mac container seemed to shrug.

"It's not the end of the world," it replied.

"Then why does it always feel like it is?" Daniel asked.

Too busy taking in the grim scenery outside, Daniel didn't notice the empty Big Mac container sizing him up, as if visually downloading Daniel and learning everything there was to know about this bearded young man in a matter of seconds. Then it casually glanced at Daniel's opened notebook.

"What are you working on there?"

Daniel grabbed his notebook, slammed it shut and put it down beside him on his seat.

"Sorry," the empty Big Mac container said. "I didn't mean to pry."

"I'm sorry too. I just get weird about people reading my stuff. Or, ya know… things reading my stuff."

"It's personal. I get it."

Daniel couldn't be sure, but in that moment, he noticed the empty Big Mac container seemed to be radiating a warmth from inside itself, like it was this small and unusual campfire out in the middle of nowhere. Daniel felt drawn toward the empty Big Mac container. He wanted to warm his hands over it. He wanted to inch closer to its occult-like, comforting flames.

"What?" the empty Big Mac container asked.

"I don't know. I honestly don't know. Sorry… I didn't mean to stare."

"It's fine," the empty Big Mac container said, smiling, which, for an inanimate object, it seemed to be doing a lot.

"It's just that I—" Daniel paused, trying to nail down the specificity of what he was feeling inside. "I feel comfortable around you, I guess."

"Thank you. I feel comfortable around you too."

"Really?"

"Of course."

Daniel didn't know what to say.

"That shocks you?" the empty Big Mac container asked.

"Yeah. No one's ever said that to me before."

"That look, Daniel...

"That goddamn look..."

And all of sudden, Daniel felt—all too familiarly—that muddy, sloping descent inward. He was sinking back into the darkest, most claustrophobic parts of himself, gradually and in no real rush, like an elevator stopping at every floor of a two-hundred story tower of terror on its way down to the doom-ridden basement. The elevator music, however, was surprisingly upbeat and jazzy, pointedly contradicting the murder scene-ambiance and making the hopeless downward ride that much more of an unnervingly hostile mind-fuck.

"Are you okay?" the empty Big Mac container asked.

At first, Daniel wasn't sure if he should share what he actually wanted to share with the empty Big Mac container, so it came as a surprise when he felt himself reaching for his notebook.

Daniel laid his notebook out on the table next to the empty Big Mac container. He opened it to a very specific page, not out of guilt or fear, he realized, but actually wanting to be honest and open with the empty Big Mac container, especially considering the plans he had in store for it.

Daniel didn't say a word as he waited for the empty Big Mac container to read his fourteen-word swan song. He just bit his bottom lip, wanting to grab it and then stretch it up all the way over his head so he wouldn't have to look the empty Big Mac container in its non-existent eyes.

"Hmm..." he finally heard the empty Big Mac container say.

"I just wanted you to know," Daniel said.

"Thank you, Daniel. I appreciate that."

And just like that, Daniel's plans felt inherently wrong, like a crime against nature, even, like he was going to scalp a dove. Not that it was going to stop him. Daniel's mind was made up. He had to—and would—bury his heart in an empty Big Mac container beneath the ocean floor.

"Can I ask a very simple yet very complicated question?" the empty Big Mac container said.

Daniel nodded half-heartedly.

"Why?"

Daniel's eyes changed after the empty Big Mac container's question. They darkened, as if staring inward and seeing something they didn't like. Something dead and rotting. Something that had expired too soon. Something Daniel never figured out how to properly mourn because doing so was never a conceivable, realistic option, just more of a far-fetched "nice idea," like winning the lotto, or going to the gym regularly and getting into really good shape.

After a brief moment of indolent reflection, Daniel's eyes returned to their state of sullen normality. He shifted in his seat and shrugged off the question as if he didn't know the answer, even though, in all actuality, he did.

My heart belongs in an empty Big Mac container buried beneath the ocean floor…

Although it hadn't initially struck him as such, technically, Daniel supposed, the idea could be construed as suicide. Even though he wouldn't be the one burying his heart beneath the ocean floor (he'd be too dead to), and even though he wouldn't be the one removing his heart and putting it in the Big Mac container (not that he knew who would be doing so yet, but whatever—he could figure out the semantics soon enough), none of this would be done against his will.

It was suicide, yes, but it didn't feel like suicide. It felt like fate, and, more importantly, like it was the mature and responsible thing to do—to dispose of this heart of his properly, to get this poisonous, toxic lump of fatty tissue as far away as possible from everyone else on the planet. To bury it in the only thing strong enough to keep it locked up until both disintegrated—a greasy, cardboard heart-coffin where it would feel so safe, and so at home, that it would never even think of trying to escape like Daniel imagined it, somehow, might try to.

It was suicide, but it wasn't. Was it self-pitying? Yes. But it was also self*less*. Daniel didn't know what to do with his heart anymore, how to fix it, how to care for it, and he didn't have the energy or desire to try to do either, so the least he could do, he figured, was make sure it was never able to hurt anyone ever again.

THUD!

THUD!

Daniel's head jerked up. Looking across the dining room, he saw two more sad-looking blue whales, ones that had wandered from god only knows where, standing out in the rain with their faces and fins pressed up against the glass.

"Oooh, ooh, oooh, ooooooh!" the sad-looking blue whale that had infiltrated McDonald's cried upon noticing its baleen brethren peering into the dining room.

Thunder cracked like a battery-powered dominatrix whip. Rain battered the outside of the restaurant and, inside, the lights briefly flickered on and off. Feeling like it was getting colder, and considering he left his hoodie in his car, Daniel inconspicuously leaned in closer toward the empty Big Mac container, pilfering some of the warmth it miraculously exuded.

It felt like wearing a hoodie, only cozier.

BAYYYBEE!!!

DANIEL SAT at the kitchen table, drawing with a black Sharpie on a piece of cardboard as Laura sat next to him, feverishly cutting coupons out of the Sunday newspaper for when they'd go shopping together later in the day.

"You're such a ninety-year-old lady," Daniel said.

"Haha, fuck you."

"You cut coupons out of the paper and fall asleep at 8:30. I'm dating a senior citizen."

"Babe..."

"All this work just to save five cents on a can of tomato paste."

"I'm gonna save, like, ten dollars when I'm done with all this."

"Uh huh."

"Wow, see? One dollar off toothpaste. Oh my god, I'm so excited about this."

"For someone who makes a decent amount of money you sure are a cheap ass."

"Maybe you should be watching me and learning a thing or two considering you're constantly spending money you don't have."

"Hah. Got me there."

"Did you look for jobs today?"

"I looked yesterday."

"But did you look for them today?"

Daniel hesitated. "Uh, I looked for them yesterday."

"Jesus, Daniel. You're sitting there drawing when you could be looking for work. Why'd I re-do your entire resume if you're not even going to try and look for a new job?"

Daniel still had his job, albeit a shit one, and didn't want to look for another. He didn't want to jump through all the hoops and kiss all the required asses just to find another low-paying, but possibly less degrading, dead-end job, but he knew it was important to Laura that he do just that. And so Daniel, like any good boyfriend, or, perhaps, like any weak-minded and whipped boyfriend who wanted to have sex again, had caved. And who knew? Maybe Laura was right. Maybe he did need a new job. Maybe if he got a slightly better job he would finally be able to fully support and take care of himself.

Laura grabbed her work laptop and put it down on top of Daniel's drawing.

"You said you worked with kids for a little while in-between college semesters, so why not look for something like that?" she suggested.

"Okay," Daniel said, even though he really couldn't imagine himself doing that again, let alone getting hired without any kind of degree or certification.

Daniel flipped open the laptop. He absentmindedly perused for jobs online, not really looking, more so just giving off the illusion of looking. Laura snipped away with her pink scissors and then slid different coupons into different Ziploc bags.

She has a system… Daniel's brain marveled.

My girlfriend has a couponing system…

Good god…

"Your face seems to be clearing up," Daniel said to Laura as he sarcastically typed "ROCKET SCEINTIST" into the search bar of the job site he was currently on, accidentally misspelling "scientist" and inwardly laughing at himself in the process.

"Yeah, well, it'd better be clearing up," Laura said almost threateningly.

"What's that mean?"

"Nothing. It just means that it'd better be. I don't think you understand how bad it was."

"No, I guess not. Do you have any pictures?"

"On my phone, I think. My doctor asked me to take some. But there's no way in hell you're ever seeing them."

"Oh, come on."

"No, Daniel. In fact, I'm going to fucking delete them as soon as I'm done with this."

"What? Do you think if your face ever broke out like that again that I'd leave you or something?"

"I don't know. Maybe."

"I don't date you just for your pretty face."

"No. Just for my pussy and big tits."

"Yes, exactly. Just don't break out on your pussy or big tits and we'll never have a problem."

"You're not seeing the pictures," she said, unamused.

"Alright, fine. Whatever."

Daniel typed "BRAIN SURGEON" into the job site's search bar and clicked ENTER, finding a lot more results than he expected there to be in the Tri-state area.

Laura's phone vibrated. She glanced at it, opened it up, read her text, texted something in return, and put her phone down. Then she sat back in her chair and sighed.

"I'm bored," she said. "I think I'm gonna go smoke. You want to come outside with me?"

Laura had been smoking a lot recently. Almost feverishly. She went through about three packs a week, Daniel estimated, and he'd basically given up and resigned himself to the fact that Laura wasn't going to quit like she'd promised.

"I can't go outside with you. I have to sit here and look for a job even though I already have one."

"Your job is not a job, babe," Laura said with a scoff.

"I get up early, commute ninety minutes and do something I hate for people I hate. That's not a job?"

"You're a stock boy," she said as she grabbed her cigarettes. "Your job has 'boy' in the title. You need a new one."

"Are you ashamed of me or something?"

"You really want me to answer that?"

Before Daniel could even think of how to begin to answer her question, Laura pushed her chair back, got up and walked out through the back porch. As soon as she was gone, Daniel closed the laptop. He sat there for a moment, feeling like an overflowing septic tank of sad and shitty emotions, before picking up his black Sharpie, ready to spitefully continue work on his drawing. But before Daniel could put the marker to cardboard, he noticed Laura's phone left behind on the table.

Daniel glanced at the back porch, then quickly snatched up Laura's phone. He punched in her password (they knew each other's passwords considering they had "nothing to hide from each other," or so Laura had said) and went inside her photo album.

Daniel quickly scrolled through, seeing the occasional picture of he and Laura together, the occasional sex video that he and Laura had taken, the occasional screen shot of some shoes or dress that Laura wanted to buy. He scrolled carefully, not wanting to go too far past when they started dating at the risk of seeing only god knows what, and eventually found what he was looking for—photos of Laura's acne-covered face.

It was even worse than Daniel imagined. Laura's cheeks and forehead looked like they had been stung by a plague of wasps. She was all puffed out and red. There was pus. But Daniel didn't feel grossed out by it. He only felt empathy that this person he loved had to go through such an embarrassing, frustrating ordeal.

All of a sudden, Laura's phone buzzed in Daniel's hand and a message labeled only with a phone number simultaneously appeared at the top of the screen.

"Well I'm not going anywhere, so definitely keep in touch," the message read. "Hope to see you soon."

Before Daniel could even debate whether or not to go into Laura's messages, he found his thumb, moving with a mind of its own, press onto the message, which took him right into the conversation.

The conversation was short, but judging from its content, or the abrupt lack thereof, it looked like there had once been more to it.

"This guy doesn't sound like a real man and like he doesn't know how to treat a woman," the exchange began. "But you know I do. If you change your mind, let me know. Maybe we can get coffee sometime. I miss seeing you."

To which Laura replied, "Thanks, but even though I'm not sure what I want, I don't think coffee would be a good idea right now. I don't want to hurt him."

"Well I'm not going anywhere, so definitely keep in touch. Hope to see you soon."

Daniel heard the back porch door swing open. He quickly closed Laura's phone and put it back down on the table where she left it. But it wasn't Laura coming back in from smoking. It was a sad-looking blue whale.

The sad-looking blue whale sat down in Laura's chair. It picked up her phone and punched in her password. It opened up the conversation Daniel just read and held the phone in front of Daniel's face.

Daniel closed his eyes and turned his head as if he'd just been sucker punched. Although, in a way, he had been.

"Ooooh, oooooooooooooooooh!" the sad-looking blue whale cried, then put Laura's phone back down on one of the Ziploc bags filled with coupons.

Stunned, dazed, and not knowing what else to do, Daniel opened one of the Ziploc bags. He reached inside and took out a few coupons, stealing just enough so their absence wouldn't be noticed. He got up and went to the downstairs bathroom. Daniel dropped Laura's coupons in the toilet and flushed. As he stood there watching the water swirl, he felt the sad-looking blue whale's presence underneath the door frame.

"Leave me alone," Daniel said to the sad-looking blue whale.

"Um, okay… But are you alright? You're trembling."

Daniel turned to find Laura standing outside the bathroom, holding her lighter and pack of cigarettes.

"I thought you were smoking," he managed to say.

"My lighter died. What's wrong?" she asked.

You really are ashamed of me… Daniel's brain wanted him to say.

But instead of speaking up, Daniel just stared down into the toilet. A lone, straggling coupon for toothpaste was still floating in the bowl, staring up at him with its waterlogged savings.

"Nothing," Daniel said, and flushed the toilet again.

GREASY, CARDBOARD HEART-COFFIN

DANIEL'S not sure how much longer he can take it.

At this point in their journey—if one could even call getting lost at sea and eventually bumping into a fake horizon wall a journey—his head feels like a dilapidated building that the ghost of the old man is supernaturally squatting inside of, haunting him with his screams of agony. And sitting there across from the sad-looking blue whale—*still* sitting there across from the sad-looking blue whale, who's now busy occupying himself by looking through the broken spyglass out over the ocean—and inconspicuously staring at him and the gloom splattered all over his sad-looking face like dark, wet bird shit, Daniel, just like he's been unable to fathom so many times before, can't believe how much he's hurting right now, how much physical and emotional anguish he's in. Not even in the self-pitying "Why me?" kind of attitude he usually reflects upon these thoughts with. It's more of an awe this time around, a truly stunned disbelief that not only can one human being hurt this much but also—and more shockingly and appallingly—that a human being is *allowed* to hurt this much by whatever superior forces may or may not be out there, governing our small, silly and inconsequential lives from far beyond the stars.

It's fucked up... Daniel's brain keeps repeating to itself.

So incredibly fucked up that even if there were a billion words in the English language, Daniel would still never be able to come close to articulating the incredible vastness of the pain he's feeling. And at the same time, and which Daniel finds even more incredibly fucked up than all of that, is how just one word can sum up the way he's feeling, and the way he has been feeling, for so long now—shitty.

That's it. One small word encapsulating the pain of the last fifteen years of his life. It's reductive, sure, and yet somehow it isn't. Daniel feels, and has felt, shitty, and it's that annoyingly simple just as much as it's that annoyingly complex. Like life itself—one huge contradiction after the other until you eventually die from the mundane and maddening illogicality of it all.

Trying to stifle his pain even the slightest bit, Daniel has a stroke of genius, or perhaps, rather, a delayed fap of common sense. He grabs the Basquiat painting and holds it over his head like a neo-expressionist beach umbrella, creating a small yet still decadent area of much needed shade over his body.

Being so fried from the sun, Daniel immediately notices a difference, something almost like a Winterfresh coolness breathing over him. Daniel lets out a quivering sigh of relief, and with his own personal needs temporarily met, he directs his attention towards the empty Big Mac container.

After returning to the boat, Daniel was worried he had possibly ruined the empty Big Mac container by tossing it overboard—the last thing that could go wrong for him, really—but from what he can tell, the only part that got wet at all was its bottom, which seems to be already drying thanks to the sun toiling above them.

Daniel finds himself fighting off the urge to apologize to the empty Big Mac container. As much as he wants to, he feels overly self-conscious about talking to a once animate but now inanimate object in front of the sad-looking blue whale. And while stifling that apology as best he can, Daniel notices about a dozen or so more sprout up in its place and begin swirling around inside him. The urge to apologize to Laura. The urge to apologize to the novel he was working on but now, obviously, will never finish. The urge to apologize to his father who spent the majority of his adult life taking care of Daniel, who was, in fact, still taking care of Daniel as he and the sad-looking blue whale rowed off in Laura's bright-orange boat, only to have his son that he sacrificed his adult life for, ultimately, throw his own life away.

And as tired of life as Daniel is, and as much as he wants his own to end, it still seems like a waste for something that's so cherished by others—such as life—to be squandered. He wonders if things could've been different, if it ever could've been possible for him, at some point, to shake off the terrors of a meaningless life and an empty future that the sad-looking blue whales kept endlessly crooning about.

"I wish I tried harder," Daniel finds himself thinking out loud.

He squirms in his seat. Even though the painting isn't very heavy, and even though he hasn't been holding it up for very long, he can still feel his shoulders beginning to tire and ache.

"I wish I hadn't wallowed in the shadows of your crying for as long as I did. I wish instead of letting you and your crying run my life that I fought back a little more. I wish I had taken more small but productive steps forward rather than remaining paralyzed and immobile. I wish I had learned that just because you were crying all day one day didn't necessarily mean you would be crying the next.

"And I wish I had been kinder to myself, more compassionate. I wish I had understood how impossible it was to gracefully live alongside you guys and I wish that I could've forgiven myself for not always trying my best or being at my best. I wish I had seen then what I'm starting to see now—that maybe I had more control over you guys than I ever thought I did. That maybe I wasn't completely and entirely helpless.

"But as much as my fault as it was, or is," Daniel continues, "I still hate you so fucking much."

"All of you," he adds, like cherry laced with rat poison daintily being placed atop a sundae.

When Daniel looks up from the empty Big Mac container, he expects to see some form of hurt or regret or compassion crammed onto the sad-looking blue whale's face alongside the usual sad-lookingness, but the sad-looking blue whale isn't paying as much as a dollop of attention to Daniel. He's still busy looking out over the ocean through the cracked spyglass.

"Hey," Daniel says, aggravated.

"Hmm?"

The sad-looking blue whale lowers the spyglass but keeps his focus curiously directed out toward the ocean.

"Did you hear what I said?"

The sad-looking blue whale shakes his head, his eyes now even further away.

"Jesus," Daniel says. "What? What's out there?"

"I'm not sure. It looks like this really small light that keeps moving around," he says. "Here."

The sad-looking blue whale hands Daniel the cracked spyglass, then points at the real horizon. Daniel holds the spyglass up to his eye and tries his best to follow the vague guidance of the sad-looking blue whale's fin.

It takes a second, and it's hard to see as it competes with the overzealous sun still shining far too bright for Daniel's liking, but floating out over the water not too far away, shrinking and dimming as if floating further and further from the bright-orange boat clunking into the horizon wall, Daniel spots, what his charred mind immediately recognizes as, a lightning bug.

IT'S A HORRIBLE LIFE

IN THE HALF hour that passed, Daniel and the empty Big Mac container hadn't exchanged a single word, but despite the silence between these two strangers, which, normally, would've made Daniel feel awkward and tense, like whenever he had to share the elevator with a co-worker that he seldom spoke to, a harmonious, Zen garden-like atmosphere had fallen over the dining room. Even the storm outside seemed less ominous and threatening, less like the entire world was coming to an end. So much so that Daniel had almost entirely forgotten about the sad-looking blue whales staring at him through the McDonald's windows, not to mention the one who had let itself inside, invading his once impenetrable fast-food-fortress.

At first, Daniel thought that perhaps the sudden sanctitude had something to do with the Christian rock still issuing itself from the speakers, the berating relentlessness of it, one song after the other, like audible Communion wafers trying to save the souls of his sinful ear drums, ear drums that were used to much more aggressive songs of worship (complete with heathenistic swear words and all), but the longer he just sat there, the longer he let himself exist in this pious yet grease-scented divinity, the more he wanted to lean in closer to the empty Big Mac container.

Daniel's rational mind couldn't comprehend how, but the empty Big Mac container really did seem to be emanating a giddy warmth, almost making him feel like he was on drugs—LSD, he kept thinking, not that he'd ever done it before—or that carbon monoxide was accidentally leaking into the restaurant and poisoning him.

"You don't smell anything, do you?" Daniel asked, flaring out his nostrils.

"No," the empty Big Mac container replied. "Why?"

"Never mind. I don't know what I'm talking about."

"Ooooh, ooh, ooh, oooh!"

Daniel turned his head just in time to see the sad-looking blue whale get up from its seat, walk to the back door and prop it open. Rain and cold air gushed inside, snuffing some of the warmth wafting from the empty Big Mac container.

"Oh hell no."

Daniel stood up and stormed over to the back door. He undid the latch propping it open, closed the door and locked it. Then he walked back over to his booth and sat down. Perplexed, the sad-looking blue whale stared at the door. It grabbed the handle and pulled on it over and over. Then, when that didn't work, the sad-looking blue whale, exercising crude, neanderthal logic, repeatedly rammed its shoulder into the door, trying to bust it open.

"Dumb ass..." Daniel muttered in regards to the sad-looking blue whale.

"That's got to be exhausting," the empty Big Mac container said.

"What?"

"Disliking them so strongly."

"Disliking them? Try hating them," Daniel said.

The empty Big Mac container seemed to nod to itself thoughtfully.

"Well, in that case, that's got to be even more than exhausting," it finally came out with.

Daniel opened his mouth, fully intending to defend himself and argue with the empty Big Mac container over what it had said. But then, upon realizing soon after the empty Big Mac container was right, that it was, in fact, insanely exhausting to hate something so dispassionately and so consistently—not to mention when he already had so little energy to begin with—he shut his mouth and pursed his lips tight. Loathing the sad-looking blue whales came naturally to Daniel the same way breathing or walking did. It was something he had learned when he was young, something he had taught himself, and ever since then, there seemed to be no real reason for him to unlearn it. It felt justifiable to hate something that was bringing you nothing but constant pain and displeasure. Natural even, like no other person in their right mind would ever think otherwise.

"It's like you can't accept them," the empty Big Mac container insightfully stated after Daniel had gone silent. "Or you just refuse to. I'm not sure which."

"Why should I accept them? Would I just accept a brain tumor or something else bad for me?"

"Well, you wouldn't deny a brain tumor, I hope. You would have to accept it at some point. And then, after you did, you would try to do something about it. Just hating something, whether it be sad-looking blue whales or a tumor, gets you nowhere. It only makes you sicker. Things can only get better once you accept them."

"Oooh, ooh, ooh, ooooooh!" the sad-looking blue whale cried as it went back to pulling on the back door.

Very unsettlingly, the sad-looking blue whale's cry spread over Daniel like peanut butter, the chunky kind—the kind only sociopaths enjoy—and he shivered in his seat.

"The reason you hate them," the empty Big Mac container continued, "the reason you're angry with them, is because you're holding onto this idea of a life without them, a life that other people get to live but you don't. And by focusing on that perception of how your world should be but, ultimately, isn't—meaning, a world without sad-looking blue whales—you're denying how things truly are and creating a world of suffering for yourself in the process."

Staring down at the table, something inflated and warped began floating through Daniel's head, moving curiously of its own accord.

The truth... Daniel's brain said in regards to the mental U.F.O. circulating his skull's airspace.

Daniel shivered again and wrapped his arms around himself.

"It's freezing in here. How are you so warm?" he asked the empty Big Mac container.

The empty Big Mac container took a contemplative, sage-like pause. Not because it was drawing a blank, Daniel could tell, but rather as if to emphasize the importance of the answer it was about to give. Daniel's curiosity inched him closer to the empty Big Mac container's warmth.

"I pass a lot of gas," the empty Big Mac container finally answered.

Daniel sat bolt upright in his seat. His lip curled in disgust and his brow furrowed in confusion. This was not the answer he was expecting, and before he could think of how to reply to this startling, flatulent confession that sent him reeling, the empty Big Mac container's lid began flapping up and down and a surprisingly loud and booming guffaw let loose from in-between its animated, cardboard jowls.

"What?" Daniel asked. "What's so funny?"

"I'm just messing with you," the empty Big Mac container managed to get out mid-laugh.

"You're just messing with me?"

"Yeah. I haven't been passing gas. But man, you should've seen the look on your face."

Daniel couldn't help it and chuckled himself.

"I really thought I was warming myself on your farts for a second there."

For a moment, as the two of them laughed together like children, it all went away—the storm, the sad-looking blue whales, Daniel's plan to bury his heart beneath the ocean floor, the fifteen-plus years that had gotten him to that point. The rough edges of life had been sanded down, and Daniel could finally, albeit momentarily, hold onto what was his, and what had always been his, without hurting.

As their laughter winded down, the sound of the rain rapping against the windows returned, as did the Christian rock sermonizing from the speakers in the ceiling. But unlike before, none of it felt severe or threatening. Daniel slid back into his seat and relaxed himself. He felt tiny and imagined, like a thumbnail-sized Loch Ness Monster, this tiny hoax of existence, and accordingly, suddenly, everything felt ridiculous. Especially himself. Daniel felt the most ridiculous of all. He couldn't believe he had ever taken a single minute of this life so seriously, let alone the entire past fifteen years. Life, Daniel thought, was a board game, cheaply manufactured in China and missing pieces. The rules were unclear because they didn't matter, because the whole thing was rigged to begin with. It took no real skill to play, just patience. Patience and an epic sense of humor to laugh at the clawing futility of it all.

Daniel put his elbows on the table and leaned in toward the empty Big Mac container.

"But really, though…"

"How am I so warm?" the empty Big Mac container asked.

Daniel nodded.

"Because. I learned to love the emptiness inside me."

The answer burned like incense in Daniel's musty head. He didn't understand it, and he didn't try to. Instead, he let the answer waft around inside him, occasionally tangling and twisting with the maudlin saltiness of, *My heart belongs in an empty Big Mac container buried beneath the ocean floor…*

"You don't seem scared at all for someone about to spend eternity alone," Daniel said.

The empty Big Mac container shrugged. "Once you realize you have everything you need, and that you always have, not much scares or agitates you."

The incense funneling around in Daniel's head grew stronger, both in scent and boldness, wrapping itself around Daniel's escape plan, his mantra, *My heart belongs in an empty Big Mac container buried beneath the ocean floor…*, squeezing the life and color out of it with a primal anaconda-like pressure.

Daniel looked up at two of the sad-looking blue whales staring at him through the window. At some point, two more had wandered over and were standing behind them, also looking in.

"I really am sorry," Daniel said to the empty Big Mac container. "Ya know… about what I have to do."

"I know you are," it replied. "I know you are…"

BAYYYBEE!!!

DANIEL AND LAURA were walking down the beach.

"Look," Laura said.

Laura ran over to a gardener's glove that was half sticking out of the sand and picked it up.

"Oh my god, babe. This is a perfectly good gardening glove."

Daniel almost felt himself smile, finding it cute that Laura was so excited over, essentially, finding trash on the beach, but for the past week and a half or so, the corners of his mouth had been weighed down by the text Laura had sent to either her ex-boyfriend or her ex-hookup, which had said, "Thanks, but even though I'm not sure what I want, I don't think coffee would be a good idea right now. He's not a bad guy and I don't want to hurt him."

Daniel hadn't done anything since seeing the text he was never meant to see. He'd just been idling, as if stuck in highway traffic in a car filled with sad-looking blue whales, a car in which the AC didn't work while it was ninety degrees outside. A car with the windows all rolled down only to absorb the heat raging off the fourteen-wheeler stuck beside it. Daniel, sweating. The sad-looking blue whales, sweating. The salty mash-up of odors creating an olfactory Molotov cocktail of offensive perspiration that had exploded inside of, and was currently burning up, Daniel's nostrils.

The truth was Daniel didn't know what to do. The predicament had, of course, and all too predictably, herded hundreds of sad-looking blue whales into his life as of late, and their constant crying at all hours of the day had essentially numbed Daniel, leaving him to drift along like a littered candy bar wrapper in a stream, flowing over this rock, bouncing off that one, going over a small dip of a waterfall, but never reacting to any of it. He and Laura had even been speaking less and when they did speak it was only formalities ("What do you want to watch?" "What do you want to eat?"). Daniel was torn between fighting for this person who, seemingly, didn't want him and just flat out giving up. But thanks to the sad-looking blue whales, he was incapable of pulling the trigger on either.

"I've been wanting to garden again," Laura said as she inspected the glove for imperfections. "Ya know, when it gets nicer out."

"You're really gonna keep it?"

"Why not? We could still find the other one," Laura said as she slid the glove onto her left hand. "Look. It fits."

"Save yourself the trouble and just cut off your other hand now because we're not going to find the other one."

"Jesus. Why do you have to be so negative all the time? We could find it. Come on, let's look."

Laura held out her hand wearing the glove for Daniel to take.

"I'm not holding onto the hand that's wearing that gross-ass glove."

Laura rolled her eyes and held out her other hand. Daniel hesitated, then took it, and they continued walking. He wondered what the hell he was doing here, with Laura, and then *here* here, on this beach, on this planet that seemed consistently indifferent to him and his fledgling presence.

"Jesus," Laura said as they walked. "There's fucking garbage everywhere."

Earlier, toward the beginning of their walk, Daniel had noticed it too, the surplus of trash littering the shore and floating in the water. But now, he couldn't take his eyes off three sad-looking blue whales boogie boarding in the surf. Or, rather, trying to boogie board. The waves were far too small and weak to propel such large blobs of schmaltzy fat forward so they all just kind of floated there, waiting on a large wave that would never come as he and Laura were waiting on a left-handed glove that would also never come.

"I can't take this anymore," Laura said in regards to all of the trash. "Hold on."

Laura let go of Daniel's hand and began walking around, frantically picking up trash off the beach as if it were going to run away from her if she didn't get to it quickly enough. Daniel watched. Every time Laura bent over her ass crack popped up out of her sweat pants. But not sexily. He felt more like he was looking at some plumber's hairy ass crack, which, consequently, not to mention surprisingly, made him feel something he'd never felt before—a small revulsion toward his girlfriend.

Laura walked over to Daniel with her arms cradling a big pile of garbage.

"Here, could you hold this? I'm out of arms."

Laura dumped her load of garbage into Daniel's arms. Daniel felt angry. Angry at Laura for dumping damp, sandy trash into his arms without asking and mad at himself for mindlessly extending his arms out and taking it in the first place for whatever reason.

"I could see your ass crack," Daniel suddenly found himself saying in an accidental but clearly confrontational-sounding tone of voice.

"What?"

"Every time you bent over. I could see your ass crack."

"So?" Laura said.

Daniel didn't say anything. He knew he was being stupid. He didn't know why he said that. And as soon as he said it, he knew it was going to make Laura mad. Maybe not so much what he said, although what he said could possibly be perceived as insecure and controlling, like a boyfriend telling a scantily clad girlfriend to cover up, but more so it was the tone of voice he knew he'd said it in that was going to set Laura off.

"Oooooh, ooooh!" Daniel heard one of the sad-looking boogie boarding blue whales cry.

"What? You think I care if someone sees my ass? Because I don't. I don't give a flying fuck," Laura said, her calm tone of voice being contradicted by the blue flames shooting out of her eyes.

Laura grabbed her sweatpants and pulled them down around her ankles. Daniel's heart jumped—a small kickflip it didn't land. He glanced down at her untamed bush of black pubic hair as if confirming, yes, she really just pantsed herself in public.

"See? I don't care. And if this bothers you, you need to get the fuck over it."

Laura pulled her pants back up. Then, pissed off, she stormed away and resumed picking up more trash. Wondering if anyone just saw what happened, Daniel perused the beach but saw no one in sight, so he stood there holding her pile of garbage, which, normally, he would've tried to parlay into some kind of metaphor about his own life if he wasn't currently so upset and downtrodden.

Back in the water, the sad-looking boogie boarding blue whales were still there, although now there were a few more of them. Not really boogie boarding, though. Still just kind of lethargically floating. Staring at them, Daniel couldn't help but wonder what the fuck was wrong with him even though, for the most part, he already knew the answer. He also knew he should apologize to Laura, but instead, he kept telling himself it's okay, that he'd do it later when they got back to her house despite knowing the longer he waited to apologize, the more he put it off, the less likely he was to actually follow through with it. So rather than listen to his better judgment and apologize to Laura as soon as she walked back over to him with a new pile of garbage cradled in her arms, Daniel didn't say a word.

"There's a garbage can this way," Laura said and hurried off in the direction they'd originally been walking before she stopped to pick up trash.

Daniel followed a few feet behind. They walked for around five minutes before reaching the trash can. Laura dumped hers in first. Then Daniel dumped his. Without saying anything or checking in with Daniel, Laura began walking back towards her house. Breathing in the odor of the garbage, Daniel knew his time with Laura was running out. He could feel it, like there was some doomsday clock counting down inside of him that began ticking as soon as he first saw Laura at the front door of her house, barefoot, smiling and wearing her navy-blue sunflower dress, like it was destined to end poorly just like every other relationship he'd entered into.

Trudging down the beach with sand slowly filling his shoes, Daniel glanced ahead at Laura to see her ass crack out. He wondered if she did it on purpose, then randomly imagined himself living alone in some abandoned motel on the moon, roaming down the dark halls, sleeping in a different unmade bed every night, and felt a sense of relief thinking of the isolation, of the distance between himself and other humans and, therefore, the distance between him ever feeling disappointed in himself again because there just wasn't enough of him to ever fully satisfy his significant others.

"Holy shit," Daniel heard Laura say just before they were about to walk off the beach and turn back onto the street.

Laura began a slow jog towards an older man headed in their direction. Daniel saw a glove in the older man's hand. A gardening glove. The right to Laura's left.

"Does this belong to you?" the old man asked as Laura approached him, still wearing the other glove.

"No. I found this glove down on the shore and picked it up because I thought I might find the other."

"I did the same thing," the old man said with a smile.

"No way," Laura said, and laughed.

"Well, here you go," the old man said, and held the other glove out, offering it to Laura.

"Aw, are you sure?"

"Yeah, I'm sure. I already have another pair kind of like these. It just seemed like a good glove and I didn't want it to go to waste."

"Thank you."

Laura took the glove and put it on. Then she held up her gloved hands and rotated them around, back and forth, showcasing the gloves to herself and the old man.

"Ah, a perfect fit," he said.

"Where'd you find this one?" Laura asked.

"Oh, down the beach a ways," the old man said, looking over his shoulder in the direction he came from. "What about you?"

"Back that way."

"Quite the distance."

"Yeah, quite the distance," Laura said, sounding highly amused.

"I wonder if they missed each other," the old man joked.

"Haha, maybe. But not anymore thanks to us. Thank you again."

"My pleasure. You have a good evening."

"You too."

The old man nodded and smiled at Daniel as he walked by him, and Daniel, in return, politely nodded and smiled back. Laura was looking at her gloved hands in a happy, childlike disbelief and wonder. Then, as if remembering she wasn't alone, she locked eyes with Daniel and the wonder on her face disappeared.

"What?" she asked. "Why are you staring at me?"

Daniel hesitated, then, finally reaching a point where he was too overwhelmed by everything, including what he learned last week—i.e., Laura's uncertainty of their relationship—he worked up the courage to say, "I know you're embarrassed of me."

"I never said that. But speaking of which, are you embarrassed of *me*?" Laura asked, brilliantly turning the conversation around on him. "You complained about my ass being out, you complained about me picking up these gloves."

"You complain about me all the time."

"That's because you need fixing."

"I need fixing?" he said, taken aback.

"Yeah, Daniel. Newsflash, okay? You need fixing. And you're crazy if you think I'm going to waste my time with some boy who doesn't have his shit together. Time is running out for me if I ever want to have a family, and so if you want to be with me then you need to make some changes."

"And what about you?

"What about me?

"You don't think you need to make any changes?"

Laura laughed to herself.

"I make almost six figures and I'm about to buy a house. What changes do I need to make?"

And as if that was the end of the conversation, Laura turned and walked off, even though Daniel wasn't ready for the conservation to be over.

Antagonistically, he blurted out, "I saw your pictures."

Laura stopped dead in her tracks while Daniel's gaze firmly locked on the sad-looking boogie boarding blue whales.

"What pictures?"

"The ones you sent your doctor. You know, when your face broke out."

"I deleted those."

"Yeah, but I saw them before you deleted them."

"So you went into my phone without asking me?"

With Daniel's betrayed eyes burrowing into her, challenging her, Laura, who only one second ago seemed about ready to explode, now seemed concerned. She became quiet, timid, as if momentarily backing down and not wanting to find out what else Daniel may or may not have seen while going through her phone.

"I'm going back," she said finally. "Are you coming or are you just going to stand there?"

"I'm just going to stand here," he answered, looking back at the sad-looking boogie boarding blue whales who had an unusually enormous wave sneaking up behind them.

Laura rolled her eyes and walked off. The enormous wave scooped up the sad-looking boogie boarding blue whales and practically hurled them ashore where they crashed down, wiping out right in front of Daniel's sneakers. Standing there, just like he told Laura he would, he listened to the ticking of that goddamned doomsday clock counting down inside of him, wishing he was strong enough to do something, anything, to make things better between him and Laura before it was too late.

"Ooh, ooh, oooooooh!" one of the sad-looking boogie boarding blue whales cried.

And it took everything left inside of Daniel not to cry right back.

GREASY, CARDBOARD HEART-COFFIN

IT WAS the sad-looking blue whale's idea. A smart one, Daniel admitted to himself, although not so much in its originality but rather the speed in which the sad-looking blue whale came up with it.

As soon as Daniel saw the lightning bug, he knew they had to somehow follow it, and after vocalizing this thought, the sad-looking blue whale, without missing a sad-looking beat, took the Basquiat painting from Daniel and began ripping the canvas off its wooden frame.

Daniel sat back and watched. He didn't know what the sad-looking blue whale was up to, but this normally slow and lethargic creature was moving with such speed, confidence and assuredness that Daniel didn't bother to ask and, therefore, possibly risk slowing him down, whatever he was doing.

It was only after the sad-looking blue whale had broken off a large single piece of the canvas' wooden frame, as well as having torn two small slits in the painting itself—one all the way at the top, the other all the way at the bottom—that Daniel realized what the sad-looking blue whale was crafting.

"Hold this up," the sad-looking blue whale said, and handed Daniel the six-foot tall wooden beam that, just moments ago, had been physically supporting a once priceless work of art.

Daniel held the splintered beam vertically. Then awkwardly, carefully, the sad-looking blue whale rose onto its bottom fins and slid the Basquiat painting down over the makeshift mast, giving their bright-orange boat the sail it never knew it needed.

"Is that supposed to be a sail?" Daniel said, even though he already knew the sad-looking blue whale had constructed just that.

Rather than waste time by responding, the sad-looking blue whale sat down and pushed off the horizon wall with his bottom fins, propelling the bright-orange boat back out toward the ocean. Then he unzipped his fanny pack and rummaged around inside, eventually pulling out a cracked hubcap that he submerged and held underwater behind the boat.

"Do you really think this is going to—"

Before Daniel's doubtful lips could even utter the word "work," a merciful and voluptuously fat chested breeze blew past the bright-orange boat, puffing out its sail like the cheeks of Dizzy Gillespie taking a breathalyzer test.

The boat jolted forward. Daniel clung to the mast he was holding, trying to keep it perfectly upright, and the sad-looking blue whale, looking through broken spyglass and trailing the lightning bug, steered the boat by altering the direction and angle of the hubcap-rudder in the water.

And it was like that, miraculously MacGyver-like, that Daniel and the sad-looking blue whale began trailing the lightning bug back out into the ocean. And even as Daniel sits here now, clutching onto the mast for dear life as the sad-looking blue whale does all the hard work, he can't believe this is happening. He just stares back behind them at the fake horizon wall, watching it become more and more realistic-looking the further away the wind propels them, and yearns for a simpler, more pain free time in which he wasn't wise enough to know better.

Much to Daniel and the sad-looking blue whale's good fortune, the wind blows ravenously, like the ocean is an enormous bowl of scorching hot, Atlantic-flavored soup that has to be cooled off before it can be tasted.

Daniel, with the form and grip of a koala-naval officer, manages to keep the mast perfectly upright despite his tired and aching muscles, while the sad-looking blue whale, who still has the cracked spyglass affixed to his eye, trails the lightning bug, giving it chase, losing it every time its bright and bulbous ass dims, but somehow picking it back up whenever it flashes back on.

Daniel, admittedly, has no idea where the lightning bug is leading them, or if it's even leading them anywhere at all, but he keeps his concern to himself that the only reason they began chasing it in the first place was out of sheer desperation, because both he and the sad-looking blue whale silently projected a seagull-like instinct to not stray too far from land onto the lightning bug, like that, specifically, is where it's going to lead them.

All of a sudden, the sad-looking blue whale lowers the spyglass and pulls the hubcap-rudder out of the water.

"What?" Daniel asks. "What's wrong?"

"I lost it…" the sad-looking blue whale says.

As Daniel's spirits sag, so does the sail. The wind loses its appetite, or, perhaps, just begins craving something different, something heartier, altering its course and leaving Daniel and the sad-looking blue whale behind as it heads back east for some Chinese. The bright-orange boat coasts to a slow, choppy stop, and without the coolness of the wind, Daniel is thrust right back into the sun's smothering, carnal embrace.

"Who knows if it was actually leading us somewhere anyway," Daniel says after a solemn, bobbing moment, trying to make himself feel better in whatever way he can, even if it involves lying.

The sad-looking blue whale rotates his fin in circles, the one that had been holding the cracked spyglass up to his eye, trying to work out the soreness. He stares down at the boombox for a moment, then presses PLAY, hopelessly, desperately, only to get the same dead, robot-like click. The sad-looking blue whale hangs his head as a heavy, cinder block sadness Daniel's never seen on him before sags from the corners of his mouth.

"I watched a man die two nights ago," the sad-looking blue whale says.

Daniel immediately and uncomfortably escorts his eyes down toward the empty Big Mac container.

"A young man. He hanged himself right in front of me," the sad-looking blue whale continues. "Which I've seen before. But still… you just never get used to it. Or I dunno… at least *I* don't. Especially the silence afterwards. That's always the worst part. The way the quiet always seems to scream at you through a bull horn about what just happened. The fact that a human life was lost. And not even just lost. That it was taken of its own volition and that you're partially responsible.

"He was probably in his mid-twenties or so, with this medium-length, shaggy brown hair and a sallow face. It was around noon and

I'd just let myself into his bedroom as he was changing into this ceremonial, pristinely white Marine uniform. He stopped as soon as I entered, and with one leg in his pants, he turned and looked over his shoulder at me, at this sudden intruder, calmly but also stoically, like he'd been expecting me. Then he just finished getting dressed.

"I stood there by the door, knowing what was about to happen but wishing it weren't. Wishing, if this had to happen, that I had at least shown up ten minutes later after the deed had been done. This way, he wouldn't have stared me in the eye as he kicked the upright cinder block out from underneath his feet, keeping eye contact with me the whole time as he writhed and convulsed, as his face changed color, as spittle flew out of his mouth. And I couldn't look away from him. I had to look him in the eye as this was happening. Doing otherwise just would've felt cowardly, ya know? Like if my kind and I had pushed this young man to the point of no return then the least I could do was look him in the eye as he finished himself off. It only seemed fair, especially considering that, most likely, not much else in his life had been. I felt like I owed him that much.

"He did it in his closet. He hanged himself with this black leather belt, and only after his body had finally stopped moving, after it had reached "complete stillness"—that moment when the body looks frozen in the air—did I finally move. I never move around before that. Never… It just feels too disrespectful.

"So, I did what I always do next—I searched for a suicide letter. Most of the time, if I'm not there watching the victim write it and see where they place it afterward, the suicide letter is usually found in the same room as the body, left in an obvious place where anyone could stumble across it, sometimes formally folded and propped up against something, the writing neat and legible, the letter long and rambling but still eloquent and clearheaded, as if it wasn't a rushed decision the person had made but one they'd given a good amount of rational thought to. And other times the suicide letter is just a short sentence scribbled on the first piece of paper the person could find—a receipt, an envelope, a Post-it—and it's usually a little bitter, or angry, or self-loathing, or, a lot of the time, all three at once. But either way I could see this type of suicide letter the young man had written—or maybe suicide note would be more apt—I could see that this suicide note was written quickly, that his decision had been a snap one. And all I could think about was how if he'd just gone to bed and made it to the next morning then maybe he would've woken up and been glad he didn't go through with killing himself the night before, even if he still wasn't totally happy or enthused with the idea of being alive.

"His suicide note was on the nightstand by his bed. It was written on a piece of torn-in-half printer paper. In black pen. In typical male handwriting, small and scrunched up and rushed-looking, as if not caring about legibility at all.

"'Thanks for nothing.'

"That was all it said… 'Thanks for nothing…'

"After I read it, after I was physically able to let the letter leave my fins, which was hard for some reason—I didn't want to put it down—I put the letter back exactly where I found it and I stared at him hanging in the closet. I looked at this young man, or what was left of this young man, and in the process, I noticed something on his left leg. Or not really on his leg. It was in his pants. This covert yet snake-like bulge that ran almost halfway down his left leg. So I walked over to the bedroom door and I closed it and locked it. Then I went over to the young man and unzipped his pants.

"I haven't seen a lot of male human genitalia—I have no will or reason to—but it was, by far, the biggest I've ever seen. Freakishly big, so hunkering large that his underpants weren't strong enough to contain it and so it just kind of dangled out the left leg-hole like a girthy string of white sausages. And as I'm staring at it, as I'm looking at this monstrous penis of his, all I could think about was how some woman had once taken that inside her—some woman whom he most likely loved—and that no other woman would share that pleasure or intimacy with him ever again. And I dunno… I know this is probably sounding weird, or perverted, but it just seemed like a waste. And it made me wonder what else he had to offer. What else he was blessed with, or good at, that he essentially threw away.

"It was just…" the sad-looking blue whale pauses. "Sad…

"So sad that I put my fins up to my face and, for the first time in my life, I cried. I finally reached this point I'd felt coming for a long time. Or maybe not a point, but an end, like I couldn't do it anymore, like every time I saw a human kill themselves a piece of me died along with them. And after seeing so many take their own lives, there was just nothing left of me."

The sad-looking blue whale looks like he's somehow watching one-hundred different movie screens all playing *Titanic* at the same time. He looks like he's going to cry.

"Why are you telling me this?" Daniel asks. His tone is sympathetic and curious, and if he were to look over the side of the bright-orange boat at that big, glossy mirror of H2O called the ocean, he'd see that he appears to be on the verge of tears as well.

The sad-looking blue whale shrugs.

"I guess I just wanted someone to know that about me. Ya know… before I die out here."

Daniel kind of nods. With the wind now miles away, deliriously salivating over thoughts of impending Kung Pao chicken, he lets the very bottom of the mast slide into the side of the boat and leans the upper-half on his shoulder. He wants to do something to remedy their dire situation but doesn't know what to do. Most likely because there's nothing he can do.

Daniel looks out across the water. The ocean is suddenly as motionless as a dog with a treat balanced on its nose, leaving the bright-orange boat, like the floating, miniature milk bone perched atop the ocean's wet and patiently waiting snout that it is, unusually stagnant.

To Daniel, the end feels closer than the occasional fat man with bad breath and pit stains who'd fall asleep on him during his train ride to work, like this is the calm before some unforeseen storm, like any second now the ocean is going to snap its jowls and devour him and the sad-looking blue whale whole, finally finishing them off. But it's largely thanks in part to this sudden quiet and tranquility that's fallen over the ocean that allows Daniel to feel this new sensation inside of him, like a radioactive New Year's Eve ball dropping into the center of his chest, like there's this slowly-descending lump the size of a baby's skull moving its way through his torso, which, initially, Daniel self-diagnoses as pure, raging anxiety. But the more he focuses on it, the more he inwardly pokes and prods, it becomes clearer and clearer what the lump actually is—a compressed wad of giddiness and delirium, thoughtlessly mashed and rolled together like Play-Doh in the tiny, booger-coated hands of a toddler.

Daniel can't help it.

He begins laughing.

Daniel wraps his arms around his waist and keels over. Tears stream down his face. He laughs so hard it begins to hurt. The sad-looking blue whale who has, undoubtedly, never laughed in his entire life just stares at his companion, unsure of what to do.

"What? What's so funny?" the sad-looking blue whale finally asks.

"This," Daniel says in-between laughs, and makes a grand gesture with his hands toward the ocean surrounding them. "Look at this."

"Look at what?"

"*This.* Look at all this nothingness."

Daniel laughs harder. He hurls the sail overboard, which lands with a belly flopping splat on the water. He swipes the cracked spyglass from the sad-looking blue whale, stands up and, deliriously, sarcastically, looks at all the nothingness surrounding them.

"Look!" Daniel screams in-between laughs. "Look at the nothingness!"

The sad-looking blue whale pivots his head back and forth, taking in all the nothingness and trying to see what's so funny about it.

"I don't get it," he says.

"You don't have to get it. There's nothing *to* get. And there's nothing to get because there's absolutely nothing here. There never has been either. Just look! Nothing but nothingness! Nothing but emptiness as far as the eye can see!"

Still standing, Daniel goes into another small fit of laughter that makes the bright-orange boat teeter back and forth.

"I mean, you have to laugh at it. You just have to or else you'll go crazy. It's just so messed up how everyone expects to be happy and full. But they can't be. I can't, you can't. No one can. Unless you're an idiot. Unless all of this nothingness is somehow imperceptible to you.

"It's a joke," Daniel continues. "A sick fucking joke. There's nothing out there. Nothing in the entire world that will ever completely fill you or me or anyone else up. And I'm just understanding that. I'm just seeing that now."

He puts the cracked spyglass up to his eye.

"Look!" he screams again. "Nothingness! Nothing but—"

The radioactive New Year's Eve ball stops in the area just below Daniel's rib cage. He freezes. Out in the distance, amidst all the blatant nothingness, Daniel sees something.

"Holy shit…" Daniel mutters, his tone hard and flat, like a cement Pog stuck to the roof of his mouth.

"What?" the sad-looking blue whale says.

"Holy shit!"

Daniel drops the cracked spyglass onto the boat's floor. He gets down on his knees, leans over the side of the bright-orange boat and begins paddling with his hands.

"Come on!" Daniel screams at the sad-looking blue whale who's just sitting there, confused.

"What? What is it?" the sad-looking blue whale asks. "What'd you see?"

"A boat," Daniel says. "I saw a fucking boat!"

IT'S A HORRIBLE LIFE

AS THE STORM outside spastically carried on, time inside McDonald's became bold and daring. Feeling acrobatic, it balanced itself on its hands, both minute and hour, then scuttled around Daniel in overly excited—yet still languid and wobbly—counter-clockwise circles. The sensation made Daniel feel as if he was trapped inside some sort of large Jell-O mold. One that forbade both past and future from permeating its gelatinous walls, turning both perceptions of time into these dream-like things skulking around outside the Jell-O mold's perimeter. And even though Daniel wasn't sure what was going on exactly, he was okay with it. He was okay with everything, really. The Christian rock, the feral storm, the sad-looking blue whales—none of it bothered him. None of it hurt him. It was all just there (there in the same simple way Daniel was), entangled in this womb-like moment they so happened to be sharing together.

Daniel rolled his Simpsons pen up and down the opened page of his notebook, moving it back and forth over *My heart belongs in an empty Big Mac container buried beneath the ocean floor…* This was something he used to do as a little kid in school, he remembered, a joyous little act of rebellion against the mind-numbing, hum-drum prattling of his underpaid teachers who didn't want to be there any more than he did.

"You seem quite at peace all of a sudden," the empty Big Mac container observed.

Somehow, Daniel had almost forgotten about this fast-food container that had recently come to life. They hadn't spoken in a few minutes—or maybe it'd been hours, who knew—but however long, the silence didn't uncomfortably ride up into the ass crack of his consciousness like it normally did whenever he found himself in the presence of new acquaintances.

"Yeah. I guess I am kind of at peace," Daniel admitted.

"But not because you're going to kill yourself," the empty Big Mac clarified.

"No…" Daniel said, surprised.

The empty Big Mac container seemed to nod to itself knowingly.

"It's nice, isn't it?" the empty Big Mac container asked.

"What is?"

"Being here," it said after a moment of reflective silence. "Here, and nowhere else."

"Experiencing eternity," it added, its voice sounding seated in the lotus position.

Daniel donned his philosophical astronaut's helmet, untethered himself from the statement at hand and allowed his brain to space out, mulling it over.

Eternity… his brain echoed.

Before Daniel could agree with the empty Big Mac container that, yes, this was indeed quite nice, his pen slipped from his fingertips. It sped away from his notebook, rolled off the other side of the table, bounced off the seat and clattered onto the floor.

Daniel contorted his body and peeked below where the atmosphere was dungeon-like and otherworldly. His pen lay on the floor next to a ripped open sugar packet. Twisting and turning his already-inflexible body even further in order to retrieve his pen, Daniel's periphery caught sight of, what he initially perceived to be, a small, petrified orange bat hanging upside down from the table's underside. And as if going along with the uncomfortable curvature of his corkscrewed mid-section, as if following its warped lead, Daniel's heart wrenched itself in one-hundred different directions.

It wasn't just gum, Daniel realized, but a familiar piece of gum, hardened, just like its owner's affection toward Daniel inevitably had.

Daniel sat up, leaving his pen behind on the floor. His brain began playing a slideshow of Laura. Some of the slides were out of focus, and some were even upside down, but they were all unmistakably of her, and the longer this presentation of lost love went on, the more Daniel hurt, the more he winced every time his brain made a click noise and another memory was projected onto the old, tattered screen behind his eyes. And just like that, any remaining crumb of hope, any naive, lingering dust bunny of faith that he may ever see Laura again, was Hoovered right up out of his overloaded system.

She was gone. It was over. And Daniel was alone.

"Oooooh, ooooh, ooooh!" the sad-looking blue whale who had infiltrated McDonald's cried.

Outside, the electrified skyscape spewed sparks larger and more bulging than Zeus' varicose veins. Seconds later, the lights in McDonald's went dark, the Christian rock converted itself to a cult-like silence, and all that was left to be heard was the rain jackhammering itself against the roof and windows.

Thanks to the past that came flooding back into his head, time became top-heavy, lost its balance and toppled over. The Jell-O mold fortress caved in. Memories invaded and eternity was lost. And all that Daniel was left with was the rotisserie-style warmth of the empty Big Mac container trying to heat the entirety of the dining room.

"Where'd you go, Daniel?" the empty Big Mac container asked.

"I don't know what you mean," Daniel said, knowing full well what the empty Big Mac container meant.

"I know you still miss her," it said, its voice calmly wafting out from in-between its corrugated lips like burning sage. "And although it's okay to occasionally go back and visit the past, albeit briefly, it's never a good idea to bring the past back with you."

Daniel shifted in his seat and forced himself to sit up straight. He knew he should've been surprised that the empty Big Mac container seemed to be reading his mind but, for some reason, he wasn't.

"It just really hit me that she's gone," Daniel allowed himself to admit out loud. "I'm having trouble believing it."

The empty Big Mac container seemed to nod understandingly. "Our rational minds can never understand what happens to us, or why, but if we keep our hearts open, we can always find our own intuitive way."

Daniel rolled his eyes.

"You don't even have a heart," he said bitterly.

"True," the empty Big Mac container agreed, "but soon enough it looks like I'll be having yours."

Although the empty Big Mac container stated this mournfully, Daniel's ears, despite being Q-tipped clean earlier that morning, were now clogged with thickly-hardened layers of contempt, and the innocent statement spoken by the soon-to-be greasy, cardboard heart-coffin just ended up sticking a red-hot poker of rage into the small of Daniel's back.

"Oooh, ooooooooooh!" the sad-looking blue whale cried.

Just as Daniel's head swiveled in the sad-looking blue whale's direction, a fine mist geysered out of the blowhole on top of its head. Even though the droplets that parachuted downward were physically nowhere near Daniel, he still felt this abnormal sensation, like those tiny, liquid paratroopers—the thousands upon thousands of them, all glistening in the dimmed dining room as brightly as stale Milk Dud shavings—were, somehow, alighting all over his insides, coating the most private and vulnerable parts of his being in a warm, salty, and not to mention highly unwelcome, froth. It was invasive and unsettling, like the equivalent of some stranger's sour breath curdling on the back of his neck. Daniel couldn't stand it. So much so that he stood up and stomped over to the only sad-looking blue whale who had ever infiltrated his McDonald's.

"Get out," Daniel snapped, and pointed unmistakably at the back door.

Confused, the sad-looking blue whale looked up at Daniel. Then at the back door. Then at Daniel again.

"Out!" Daniel screamed.

He could feel himself beginning to lose his temper. His hand that wasn't pointed at the back door was knotted into a fist.

"I said, get out!" he repeated when the sad-looking blue whale hadn't so much as budged.

"Daniel..." the empty Big Mac container pleaded.

"No. They follow me everywhere—to work, to the bathroom, to the grocery store, to bars. And I'm sick of it. This, *this* is the only place I have left, and with what little time I have left, I'm going to enjoy it. I refuse to let them ruin this place for me the same way they've ruined everything else.

"Now I'm going to say it one more time," Daniel said, blitzing the sad-looking blue whale with his frenzied eyes. "Get... the fuck... OUT!"

With cinematic timing that perfectly harmonized with the booming severity in Daniel's voice, the sky made a tremendous noise, like a metallic football field being ripped in half, and light strobed through the darkened dining room as if from the flash bulb of some intergalactic paparazzi. But nevertheless, still dazed and confused, the sad-looking blue whale only blinked absently at Daniel, and those soft, delicate, ocular flaps of fatty tissue, or, more so, their inability to conceal the belligerent vacuousness secreting from behind them, sent fifteen years of pent-up frustration surging through Daniel's exhausted body. And just like that it all came out at once—through his open-palmed hands that shoved the sad-looking blue whale right out of its seat.

If the sad-looking blue whale appeared confused before, then now, propping itself up on the dirty, latte-colored floor tiles when, just seconds ago, it had been in its seat minding its own business, thinking of *Titanic*—the part where the musicians keep playing as the ship goes down—the sad-looking blue whale seemed totally perplexed. In even more shock was Daniel. Appalled at his trembling self and unsure of what to do next, he hung his head, walked back over to his booth and sat down.

Vaguely aiming his vision at a coffee ring on the table, Daniel couldn't coerce himself to look the empty Big Mac container in the eye. He felt too ashamed, too embarrassed. No one spoke. No one budged.

Eventually, Daniel heard the sad-looking blue whale pick itself up, then the sad shuffling of its bottom fins heading toward the back door.

"Oooh, oooh, ooooooooooooooooooooooooooooh!" it cried, and left.

Something about the sad-looking blue whale's last cry—the tone of it, viscous and ominous, like a death threat wheat-pasted onto someone's front door with semen—made Daniel's entire body nervously vibrate.

"Perhaps the question you need to be asking yourself—" the empty Big Mac container began.

"Don't," Daniel interrupted. "Just don't. Alright? I can't listen to your mystical bullshit one second longer."

"I'm sorry," the empty Big Mac container said after a brief moment of eloquent silence. "I didn't mean to upset you. I'll do whatever you need of me. Whatever makes all of this easier on you."

"Good. In that case do me a favor and keep your mouth shut. I just want fuckin' peace and quiet, alright? Is that so much to ask for before I kill myself? To suffer in peace?"

Daniel expected the empty Big Mac container to say something in return, but its lid remained closed. The warmth it exuded also died off, vanishing so suddenly it was like someone had flipped an invisible switch on it. Once talkative and insightful, the empty Big Mac container became just that—just another ordinary Big Mac container, one out of a million made from 100% recycled paper, including 40% post-consumer, or at least so it was written on its side.

Daniel felt a wrecking ball-sized lump of guilt crashing into the walls of his throat. A part of him wanted to apologize to the empty Big

Mac container, but now, considering the way it looked as if it were posing for some weird still life, the notion of doing so seemed completely absurd. Had the empty Big Mac container even talked to him in the first place, he wondered, or had his grief-stricken, frazzled mind just been playing tricks on him this whole time?

When Daniel finally looked up, he saw that, much to his delighted surprise, all of the sad-looking blue whales that had been outside—the very same ones who had been peeking in like Daniel was in some reverse aquarium—had wandered off. Now that he was thinking of it, he also hadn't seen another customer in, what he presumed to be, hours, nor had he seen an employee or heard the regular, chaotic, fast-food din coming from the cash registers, deep fryers and milkshake machines up front. The McDonald's had apparently turned into a ghost town, making Daniel, of course, its lone phantom resident.

It's everything we've ever dreamed of… Daniel's brain said.

And then, seconds later, *So why aren't we happy?*

Watching the rain streak down the windows like slug tears, Daniel became very aware that he was alive. He thought of all the things his body was doing just to currently keep him going—pumping blood, producing cells, sending nerve impulses, inhaling, exhaling—and how, soon, all of that would come to a stop. The drama of life would be over and he, and his body, would finally be at peace. The idea soothed him. The rain soothed him. The sky the color of the Unabomber's dirty socks soothed him.

Blindly, Daniel plucked the orange gum off the table's underside like a piece of dried up, low-hanging fruit and popped it in his mouth.

The hardened dollop of lost flavor crunched against his teeth like granola Trident.

Laura… Daniel's brain said, simply.

BAYYYBEE!!!

DANIEL LAY on Laura's couch. Laura was at the end by Daniel's feet, kneeling over the armrest and scrolling through Hulu on her computer set up on a nearby table.

"*Property Brothers*?" Laura asked.

"I think I want McDonald's," Daniel said, zoned out and looking at Laura's ass. She was wearing boys' basketball shorts, and her ass was aimed at him like some big, fat, sexy cannon.

"You always want McDonald's," Laura said without taking her eyes off her computer. "How are you not a million pounds by now?"

Daniel shrugged.

"So how about it? McDonald's? We're gonna go get McDonald's, right?"

"No, babe," Laura said, and even though he couldn't see her face, Daniel could tell she was smiling a little.

"Yes. I want McDonald's. I want a Big Mac."

"No, babe. You don't have the money," she said, although now in a tone of voice that made it clear she was no longer smiling.

"How about Taco Bell? I want Taco Bell. You wanna get Taco Bell?"

"No, Daniel. No fast-food. I'm gonna make us dinner in a bit. That's why we went grocery shopping before. Remember?"

"McDonald's," Daniel said. "Taco Bell."

"No, babe."

"Where are your keys? I'm gonna go get a Big Bell."

"A Big Bell?"

Daniel sat up and began running his hands over Laura's ass as if it were now a big, fat crystal ball made of ham.

"Yeah. A Big Bell—two soft tacos from Taco Bell placed inside a Big Mac. Like one soft taco placed on top of each hamburger patty. I'm gonna go get one and then come back here and tie you down to a chair and eat it right in your fucking face."

"Haha, you're such an asshole."

"But seriously, how good does that sound?"

"That sounds revolting."

"That doesn't sound revolting at all. But ya know what *is* revolting?"

Laura glanced over her shoulder and smiled at Daniel, asking him what.

"Your face!" Daniel said, smiling a huge shit-eating grin.

"Haha, asshole..." Laura said again and turned her attention back towards Hulu.

Daniel wrapped his arms around Laura's waist and fell backwards on the couch, dragging her along with him and making her fall back on top of him, like a botched German suplex. Daniel buried his face in Laura's neck and kissed her. Laura held onto his hands around her waist. Somewhere outside a dog was barking. Daniel felt happy and then felt even happier because he knew Laura was feeling happy too.

"You know I'm kidding, right?" Daniel said after a little while.

"About the *Big Bell*?" Laura said, saying the words "Big Bell" in a doofy-sounding voice.

"I mean about your face being revolting."

"I know, babe."

"Your face isn't revolting. It's beautiful. Like a still life of a Big Mac. Like an old Victorian portrait of a Big Mac."

"Haha. Like it's just a Big Mac on a stool and there's all this empty black space around it that would normally be taken up by a larger human model."

"Exactly. Yes. That's what you look like to me."

"Thank you, baby."

"Bayyyybeeee!" Daniel half-screamed.

"Baybeeeeee!" Laura half-screamed, then craned her neck, turning it as far as she could so she could kiss Daniel on his lips.

"You taste good," Daniel said. "You taste like you."

"You taste good too," Laura said. And then, after a few minutes of comfortable silence, "So... McDonald's or Taco Bell?"

"Yayyyy!" Daniel screamed, and over dramatically threw Laura off of him so he could find his sneakers.

Laura drove them to the McDonald's near Daniel's house, or "*his* McDonald's" as he often referred to it. Daniel ordered a large Big Mac extra value meal and Laura ordered a medium Quarter Pounder extra value meal. The dining room was empty except for an elderly lady sipping coffee and cutting coupons out of newspapers splayed across her table. When Daniel and Laura were both finished eating, Laura came and sat down next to Daniel on his side of the booth and held his hand and rested her head on his shoulder.

"We're *that* couple," she said. "We're a 'same side booth' couple."

"Haha, kind of. We didn't eat on the same side at least. We're just digesting on the same side. So it's not as bad."

"Yeah. I guess that's true."

"Look," Daniel said, and pointed at an elderly lady cutting out coupons. "That's going to be you someday."

"Haha, fuck you."

"Someday? What am I thinking? That already is you," Daniel corrected himself.

Laura laughed, then surprised herself when a burp squeaked out of her.

"Oooh! Shit... Excuse me," she said, covering her mouth with a fist.

"I've never wanted you more. You're so sexy when you're stuffed with McDonald's."

"Ugh... I don't feel sexy."

"Well you look it. You're glowing. You have a post-McDonald's glow."

"You sure it's not the ceiling lights glistening in the sweat I perspired while eating?"

"Hahaha, that's exactly what your glow is. Mmm... I love it."

"I sweat while eating fast-food. I hate myself," Laura said as she reached into her purse and pulled out a pack of gum.

"The Food Sweats would be a great name for that band we're never going to start," Daniel said.

"Haha, it would. But wait, don't we already have another band name? Remember? We came up with it while watching *Property Brothers*?"

"Oh. Open Floor Design Plan."

"Haha, yes. Open Floor Design Plan."

"*Muuuuusical guest,* Open Floor Design Plan!" Daniel said in the voice of former Saturday Night Live announcer, Don Pardo.

Laura laughed. She popped a piece of orange-flavored gum into her mouth, then adjusted her head, really nestling into Daniel's shoulder.

"I like you like this," Laura said.

"Like what?"

"Like this. I dunno… Happy, I guess. I feel like this is how you're supposed to be all the time. Or, ya know, most of the time."

"And I'm not like this most of the time?" Daniel said, even though he knew he wasn't.

"You just have this look about you sometimes," Laura said. "I don't know how to explain it. But I've said all this before."

"That look, Daniel…

"That goddamn look…"

Not sure what to say, Daniel squeezed Laura's hand and kissed her on the side of her head. Then he grabbed the empty Big Mac container. Using his hand, he made its lid flap up and down.

"*Muuuuusical guest,* The Food Sweats!" Daniel said, using the empty Big Mac container as a puppet.

"Haha. But I thought we were Open Floor Design Plan?"

"Yeah, but if we're The Food Sweats this guy can be our mascot," Daniel said in regards to the empty Big Mac container.

"True, true. The Food Sweats it is."

"That's right, woman. Listen to your man," Daniel made the empty Big Mac container say, flapping its lid up and down again.

Laura gasped, pretending to be offended, and lightly elbowed Daniel in his ribs.

"Ow! Shit… I didn't say it. He did."

All of a sudden, Laura got silent. She hung her head and began scraping away at the chipped nail polish on one of her fingernails.

"Are you sure you can handle me?" she asked point-blank.

Daniel watched as flakes of navy-blue nail polish fell onto her lap.

"Where'd that come from?"

Laura shrugged.

"I love these moments of ours. These nice moments, but the problem is they never seem to last. I don't know… Maybe I'm too much for you."

"You really think that?"

"I want to know what *you* think."

Daniel took a beat. Suddenly feeling foolish for holding the empty Big Mac container, he put it down on the table. He felt like clutter. Or, more specifically, like clutter in Laura's life, like he was this untidy lump of emotions that she'd never understand and, therefore, be able to properly deal with, leaving him to pile up in her mind only to create this inevitable mess that would drive her mad. He didn't feel like her boyfriend. He felt like a chore, like something to be dealt with, something that needed to be resolved.

"Yeah, of course I can handle you," he said. "Are you sure you can handle *me*?"

"I don't know," she answered. "I mean... yeah, I guess. If you go on medicine. I think you'd be a lot better on medicine."

Daniel solemnly nodded to himself. He knew he had to grow up, he knew he had to get better, but, at the same time, a part of him wondered if he'd ever be good enough for Laura or if she'd just always be picking at him, wanting him to change something new about himself every month. To Daniel, that seemed quite plausible, and the potentiality made him more nervous than he would've cared to admit.

"I think you'd be happier is what I meant to say," Laura added. "Not better. Ya know, if you were on something."

Unable to look Laura in the eye, Daniel allowed the empty Big Mac container to cradle his attention. It had a grease stain on its top that looked like the shape of some European country he couldn't think of.

"Ugh... This gum loses flavor so fast."

Laura took the piece of orange gum out of her mouth and stuck it underneath the table.

"Dude. Don't do that," Daniel insisted.

"Well, this is *your* McDonald's, right?"

"Yeah. So?"

"So now every time you sit here it'll be like I'm here with you."

Daniel felt himself smile. At that moment, he knew he'd do whatever it took to be with Laura. Whatever it took to make himself better, to make himself the man she needed, and, more importantly, the man he knew he needed to be. He kissed her on top of her head. He picked up the empty Big Mac container and held it up in front of her face.

"I love you," Daniel made the empty Big Mac container say.

Laura laughed.

"God, you're such a tool," she said instead of saying "I love you" back.

PART 3

"MY COUSIN'S DEAD, *alright? There! My cousin's fucking dead! He hung himself and I'm all alone and you're ignoring my calls like a selfish piece of shit! I don't know why I'm surprised, though. I must be an idiot. That's it… I must be a goddamn, fucking idiot for ever thinking you could be any sort of real man and put our differences aside and just be there for me right now. But no. So fuck you, Daniel. Alright? Fucking… fuck… you! I'm so glad I dumped your sorry ass!"*

GREASY, CARDBOARD HEART-COFFIN

THE SEA HAS WOKEN UP. It's yawning and stretching its legs. It's adjusting its balls. It's rubbing the sleep from its dehydrated eyes, all of this fresh new motion making it much more difficult for Daniel and the sad-looking blue whale to row the bright-orange boat.

Daniel stops paddling. His arms are tired. Unable to use his appendages as oars any longer, he surveys the yacht they've been creeping up on, which is now only one-hundred yards or so away.

The yacht looks like a large and elegant seashell crowd surfing atop a sea of pumping, blue fists. It's covered in sad-looking blue whales who are all dressed in colorful bathing suits and bikinis. Sad-looking blue whales who are drinking alcohol from large, expensive-looking bottles and dancing to party music.

"Hey!" Daniel screams.

Daniel stands up and waves his exhausted arms over his head, trying to get the attention of the sad-looking blue whales aboard the yacht.

"Hey! Over here! Help! Help!!!"

But the music only seems to blast louder. Daniel watches one male sad-looking blue whale do a body shot off of a female sad-looking blue whale. All of the sad-looking blue whales cheer. Another female sad-looking blue whale takes her bikini top off and swings it above her head like a fabric helicopter blade, prompting all of the sad-looking blue whales to cheer even louder.

"Fuck…" Daniel says, and drops his arms. "They can't hear me."

Daniel plops down into the bright-orange boat, wondering how the sad-looking blue whales can all be so sad-looking and blue but still look like they're having so much fun at the same time.

"Come on. Let's get closer…"

"I've been thinking about what you said," the sad-looking blue whale says.

Daniel gnaws on the insides of his cheeks, waiting for the sad-looking blue whale to go on.

"About the nothingness," the sad-looking blue whale continues. "About how there's nothing out there to fill up on."

Daniel makes a frustrated facial expression that seems to say, "Yeah? So? What's your point?"

"And you're right," the sad-looking blue whale continues. "There is nothing out there to fill up on."

"Yeah," Daniel replies. "I know."

"But I always thought you weren't supposed to try to fill up on things," the sad-looking blue whale indirectly argues. "I always thought you were just supposed to learn to live with it."

"Live with what?"

"Ya know… The emptiness. Because what could fill all of this up? Like, what could fill the staggering and unending emptiness of simply being alive?"

"Nothing," Daniel says after a second.

"Yeah," the sad-looking blue whale says. "Nothing."

"Yeah…" Daniel says, but still feels like he and the sad-looking blue whale are arguing somehow even though they seem to be agreeing.

"Are we agreeing or disagreeing?" the sad-looking blue whale asks.

"It doesn't matter," Daniel says, annoyed. "Let's just get closer before they sail off or something."

"Okay…"

Daniel and the sad-looking blue whale put their respective hands and fins in the water and continue paddling toward the yacht in silence.

Daniel and the sad-looking blue whale paddle up to a ladder hanging off the side of the yacht. The sad-looking blue whale grabs the bottom rung, docking the bright-orange boat in place.

"Okay," Daniel says. "I'll be back."

"Don't be long," the sad-looking blue whale says, sounding and looking like a skittish only child who's watched *Home Alone* one too many times.

"Okay," Daniel says.

"But still look for batteries for the boombox."

"Okay…"

"But don't forget about me either."

"I'm going," Daniel says, and begins ascending the ladder.

When Daniel climbs over the side of the boat and sets foot on deck, the sad-looking blue whales are too busy partying to notice him. They walk past him with drinks in their fins. They make out. They do more body shots off each other. They grind against each other on the dance floor to the loud, horrible, bass-thumping music.

Suddenly stuck in place, as if physically malfunctioning and therefore unable to make himself move, Daniel feels the fun the sad-looking blue whales are having. Or rather, he feels it going on around him, like their fun is doing cartwheels past his face, the gust of wind it kicks up blowing across his nose and eyes and beard. So close but, ultimately, eluding Daniel by centimeters and leaving him untouched by it, which, in this case—and just like the millions of other cases throughout the course of his life—might as well be miles.

But something about the fun the sad-looking blue whales are having looks off to Daniel. *Staged…* is how his brain describes it, as if the sad-looking blue whales are just going through the motions of drinking, dancing, partying and hooking up, like they don't really want to be doing this at all, like they'd much rather be sitting in sad-looking blue bean bag chairs and watching *Titanic* while snacking out of large cardboard tubs filled with buttered krill instead. And now, watching them even more intently, Daniel notices a superfluous lifelessness in their black eyes. He hears the silicone in their big breasted, but ultimately fake, laughter. But regardless of how staged their fun may seem, it makes Daniel think of everyone else in the world, of all the people continually going out and dancing in expensive and trendy clubs, of all the people going to rooftop parties with their friends and meeting new people and randomly hooking up in bathrooms and feeling exciting new things. The staged fun right there in front of his face makes Daniel think of all the people in the world filling up on life, and he wonders if maybe, just maybe, it is actually possible to combat the empty nothingness of life after all. Standing there, watching the sad-looking blue whales party, Daniel, again, finds himself wishing he'd tried a little harder, that he actually made attempts to reach out to the world and the people in it. And all of a sudden, Daniel feels like maybe it's not entirely the fault of whatever celestial being that programmed him, connecting all of the wrong wires inside of him, or just having left too many wires unconnected. It was his fault too. It took work to feel connected, to *be* connected. Work that Daniel never really put forward, that he let the sad-looking blue whales prevent him from attempting.

A sad-looking blue whale rushing to the dance floor accidentally bumps into Daniel, spilling beer from a red SOLO cup onto Daniel's arm and derailing him from his speeding train of thought.

"Shit..." Daniel says.

The music becomes louder. Unable to take feeling left out any longer, and finally feeling able to move again, Daniel walks towards the back of the yacht, stopping at the first door he comes across.

Daniel glances back toward the dance floor where the sad-looking blue whales are all partying. They're too busy having fun, or fake fun, to pay him any attention, so he turns the handle and lets himself inside.

Standing in a hallway pulled straight out of a five-star hotel, Daniel closes the door behind him. The hallway is long and lined with white carpet, and at the very end of the hall, past the numerous doors on both sides, stands a sad-looking blue whale in a black suit, holding a clipboard.

The sad-looking bouncer blue whale shoots a skewed look down the length of hall. Daniel inwardly panics, almost retreating back through the door he entered from, but then calms himself and begins walking down the hallway like he's supposed to be here.

"Hi," Daniel says as he stops in front of the sad-looking bouncer blue whale.

"Name?" the sad-looking bouncer blue whale says.

"Uh, Daniel..." Daniel says in a tone of voice like he's not sure what his name is.

The sad-looking bouncer blue whale lowers his dark black sunglasses and peruses the list on the clipboard.

"I'm not seeing your name here," he says after a second.

"Oh," Daniel says, trying to sound surprised. "That's weird. Hmm... Could you maybe check under 'The Chosen One?' Yeah, it might be under that."

"'The Chosen One?'" the sad-looking bouncer blue whale repeats.

"Yeah. Or, I dunno... Maybe just 'Chosen One.'"

The sad-looking bouncer blue whale gives his clipboard a slow but studious check.

"C-H-O…"

"Yeah, I know how to spell. I'm just still not seeing it on here. And it's a really short list."

Daniel glances past the sad-looking bouncer blue whale and sees a golden placard on the door beside him that reads "V.I.P." But the "I" is scratched out and has a "D" written in above it.

"Are they expecting you?" the sad-looking bouncer blue whale asks.

"Uh, yeah. They should be."

"Wait, a minute," the sad-looking bouncer blue whale says and lowers his sunglasses even further. "Open your eyes nice and wide for me. Try not to blink."

Daniel opens his eyes as wide as he can. The sad-looking bouncer blue whale pulls out a small flashlight, shines it in Daniel's eyes and leans in close, examining them.

"Wow. Yeah… Okay," the sad-looking bouncer blue whale says and clicks his flashlight off. "You're good to go."

The sad-looking bouncer blue whale unhooks a dingy-looking velvet rope from in front of the door.

"I'm good to go?"

"Yeah. You check out."

Daniel hesitates then, takes the two steps over to the door and puts his hand on the golden door knob.

"So, I'm going to go then…"

"Enjoy," the sad-looking bouncer blue whale says.

Daniel turns the handle, but instead of opening to a luxurious suite like he expected, the door opens to a pitch black, waterless water slide.

"Oh yeah… All V.D.P. riders must ride feet first," the sad-looking bouncer blue whale says. "You must lie on your back at all times. Do not sit up while riding the slide. Riders assume all risk of injury due to misuse of this slide or failure to follow these rules. Do you understand?"

"I think so."

Daniel sits down and stretches his legs into the slide. He feels right away that not only is there no water in the dark tunnel but that the bottom surface seems to be lined with sandpaper.

"Uhhh—"

"I'm really not supposed to keep this door open, sir. Are you going or not?"

Daniel hesitates a moment before nodding.

"Okay then. Enjoy."

Daniel pushes forward with his hands, trying to propel himself forward. Naturally, though, he stays in place on the rough, scratchy surface, curled up and with his head hung low.

"Sir?" the sad-looking bouncer blue whale says, growing impatient.

"Sorry," Daniel says and scooches forward on his ass.

Daniel hears the door slam shut behind him and finds himself submerged into a warm and abrasive darkness.

He sighs.

If I'd known that burying my heart in an empty Big Mac container beneath the ocean floor was going to be this miserable, I would've just hung myself… his brain says.

Daniel can't see where he's going.

For however long, he's been dragging his ass down this endlessly winding water slide (still sans water), navigating the darkness as best he can but still bumping his head on the ceiling whenever he rounds one of the slide's many twists and turns he can never see coming.

The palms of Daniel's hands are rubbed raw from the sandpaper coating the slide's bottom. He worries he's going to wear a hole through the seat of his pants any second now, if he hasn't already. And just as he contemplates quitting, just as he begins imagining the mechanics of, somehow, climbing back up to where he came from, fearing that this waterless water slide may never end, Daniel sees a glimmer of light coming from below, forcing him to trudge forward and endure the raspy burning of the sandpaper a little while longer.

Flushed, Daniel finally emerges from the waterless water slide. He's so relieved to be free from the oppressively scratchy darkness that it takes him a minute to notice the table only a few feet away. A table with the most surprising and unusual cast of maudlin characters seated around it, playing cards.

Richard Brautigan.

Sylvia Plath

Kurt Cobain.

And Ernest Hemingway.

These players, these legends, these men and women among men and women, all share the same aloofness of the sad-looking blue whales who were too busy partying to notice Daniel when he first stepped aboard. None of them sense his arrival, nor do they so much as take note to his sudden presence punctuating the room—a room like the back of a butcher's shop, where, in-between breaking bones and hosting high-stakes poker games, the greasy wheelings and dealings of the Italian mafia seedily transpire. However, off in the far corner, lounging ever so exotically on a velvet sofa, and donned in her iconic, light-ivory cocktail dress—the very same one that was blown above her waist from the raging hormones of a randy subway car rushing by below, just dying for a split-second glimpse of starlet camel toe—lies the ever vigilant and keen Marilyn Monroe.

Marilyn's dipping a potato chip into a glass of champagne but stops as soon as she sees Daniel. Her Technicolor eyes study him for a moment, almost like he's some human monologue she's trying to memorize. Then, with a shutter speed-bat of her lengthy lashes, Marilyn diverts her attention back to the action at hand. She fully submerges the chip into the champagne and pops it in her mouth.

"You in?"

Back at the card table, all of The Players are now staring at Daniel expectantly.

"Excuse me?" Daniel says.

"I said, are you in?" Richard asks in a voice that doesn't fit the man it's coming out of. His voice sounds like it should be coming out of a felt puppet on a children's morning TV show rather than a bespectacled, hippie'ish-looking older man. His voice should be teaching children their ABC's. Not inviting Daniel to play cards.

"Oh... No, thanks."

"Well don't just stand there. Take a load off, weary traveler," Richard says and pulls out the empty chair beside him.

Intimidated, Daniel hesitates, then wanders over and sits down.

"Richard," Richard Brautigan says and extends his hand, which Daniel shakes.

"I know," Daniel says, grinning. "Daniel."

"Daniel. Nice to meet you, Daniel. That maudlin, blue-eyed handsome devil to your left is Kurt. That brunette, psych ward-bombshell is Sylvia. And that's just Ernest."

"Knock knock," Ernest says to Daniel, smiling, suddenly vibrating in his seat with such excitement he looks like he might explode if Daniel doesn't answer the door. Kurt and Sylvia, however, groan and roll their eyes, their pupils moving in such accidental yet perfect unison that they look like synchronized swimmers diving into the backs of their heads.

"Uh, who's there?" Daniel asks.

"The old man."

"The old man, who?"

"*The Old Man and the Sea*!"

Ernest slaps his knee and laughs like a crazed prospector. Not wanting to seem rude, Daniel churns out a polite smile. To his side, Daniel hears Richard laugh. Not with Ernest. At him. Definitely at him.

"You sure you don't want in?" Richard asks Daniel as he grabs a new deck of cards out from underneath his hat.

"I'm good. Thanks."

Ernest sweeps all of the old cards off the table and Richard begins dealing, throwing card after card with only the vaguest hint of aim and precision and never coming close to forming something that resembles a pile in front of anyone. Not that the other players seem to mind. Kurt, Sylvia and Ernest grasp at whatever random cards come their way. Richard "deals" until he's all out. Then he grabs the leftover cards the rest of The Players haven't taken and organizes the absurd amount into a hand as best he can.

"What are we playing?" Kurt asks.

"Deuce to Infinity Unlimited Grab Bag No Backsies," Richard says.

"Didn't we play that yesterday?" Sylvia asks.

"Hey, Sylvia. Knock knock."

"No, that was Deuce to Infinity Seven Card Stud Grab Bag No Backsies."

"Sylvia. Knock knock?"

"Who goes first?" Kurt asks.

"I think it's my turn," Sylvia answers.

"Sylvia. Knock, *knock?*"

"New guy, could you get the door for me?" Sylvia says, aggravated and unable to concentrate as she studies her hand.

"Uh, who's there?" Daniel asks Ernest.

"A movable."

"A movable who?"

"*A Movable Feast*!"

Ernest cracks up again. Daniel forces another polite smile, which, this time, comes out a little crooked. Sylvia puts seven cards down on the table, three face up, four face down.

"My turn?" Ernest asks.

"If you can go two seconds without making a fuckin' knock knock joke, then yeah, it's your turn," she answers, reorganizing what's left of her cards.

Ernest licks the back of a queen of hearts and sticks the card to his cue ball forehead.

"Ahhhhhhh," Richard says, smiling. "Well played, sir."

Richard throws six cards on top of Sylvia's, then rips a seventh card in half and puts one half in his right pants pocket and the other in his left pants pocket.

"I'm out," Kurt says and drops all of his cards on the floor under the table.

Sylvia and Richard moan as Kurt lights a cigarette.

"He always folds," Richard explains to Daniel.

"Hey," Kurt says with the cigarette between his lips. "No one here gets to judge me for folding."

"Then he always says that," Richard explains further.

"Well, it's true. All of us folded in the ultimate sense," Kurt elaborates.

"At least I fuckin' folded with some sort of style," Sylvia chimes in. "I mean, I know most men are completely unoriginal to begin with, but I would've at least expected more out of you three."

"Sure, Betty Crocker. Like you were the first person to stick their head in the oven like some kind of sad, candle'less birthday cake."

"Even if I wasn't, the way I went out was a million times less trite than blowing your head off with a fuckin' shotgun."

"What about with a revolver?" Richard says, grinning like a sarcastic pot brownie.

"At least it's not as overtly macho as a fuckin' shotgun."

"Well, shit. My brains still flew out of my head like bats flying out of some haunted belfry, man."

"How about you?" Kurt asks Daniel.

"Me?"

"Yeah. How'd you do the deed?"

All the action stops. The room becomes very quiet and still as all eyes fall on Daniel.

"Oh... Uh..." Daniel gulps. Then the truth just kind of warbles out of his mouth like a one-handed drum roll. "I haven't yet... Done it, I mean."

The Players all continue staring at him, once curious but now confused.

"But I'm on my way to doing it," Daniel says. "I guess..."

There's a pause.

"Just please don't say you're going to do it with a fuckin' shotgun," Sylvia quips.

Everyone smiles, and any hints of possible judgment Daniel thought he may have seen in the eyes of The Players vanishes.

"No. I'm, uh… I'm burying my heart beneath the ocean the floor?" Daniel's voice unexpectedly trills up at the very end of the sentence, turning the already weird and unusual sentence into a now weird and unusual question he seems to be asking himself.

"You're burying your heart beneath the ocean floor?" Sylvia repeats.

Daniel nods.

"In a Big Mac container," he adds.

"What the hell's a Big Mac container?" she asks.

"McDonald's, man. Fast-food. Hamburgers. Over ninety-nine billion served," Richard explains.

"Greasy capitalism at its finest," Kurt adds. "Over ninety-nine billion arteries clogged. What a country!"

Sylvia kind of nods to herself, taking it in, processing it like a poetic computer.

"Original," she says to Daniel. "I'll give you that much."

"Yeah, man. Totally. Hey, did you hear that, Marilyn?" Richard says, looking over his shoulder. "This guy's burying his heart in a hamburger container beneath the ocean floor. Is that wild or what?"

In such prestigious company, Daniel had somehow forgotten about Marilyn. He looks at her splayed out on the couch, dramatically posed as if recovering from the vapors. Despite being addressed, she doesn't turn and look in their direction. Rather she stares off ahead, dreamily, as if gazing through some invisible window overlooking the Hollywood hills that only she can see.

"I heard, darling," Marilyn says, but unlike the others she doesn't sound amused or impressed.

Richard laughs to himself.

"She's always on her own planet, man," Richard says to Daniel. "Far, *far* out on her own planet."

"Sad-looking blue whales?" Sylvia asks Daniel as she throws two cards over her shoulder. "Hit me."

Richard pulls another new deck out from underneath his hat and deals Sylvia five more cards.

"Yeah," Daniel says, somehow only now just grasping the complete lack of logic and rules to the game they're playing.

"Too many sad-looking blue whales and not enough of anything else," Kurt says.

"You're not kidding. No matter what I did, no matter how many fuckin' poems I wrote, there was still always a little space left around me, just a little bit of emptiness."

"And then they just slide their way right inside it."

"No way to keep them out, man. No way, no how."

"Knock, knock?"

"I got to the point where I was so crowded by them I couldn't even feel the excitement of creating music anymore. Or even listening to it, ya know? It was just them piling into the nothingness. Filling it. The only things that were ever capable of filling it really."

"Knock knock?"

"I never wanted to write another word as long as I lived I got so tired of them. I just wanted to get the fuck away, man."

"Did it work?" Daniel asks.

"Did what work?" Kurt says.

"I dunno... Folding, I guess. Do you still see them?"

Kurt nods.

"But they keep their distance more than they used to. And they act different now, I'd say."

"Yeah. They're still sad-looking, but it's like they're trying to look happy-looking or something," Sylvia says.

"That's better than sad-looking all the time, right?" Daniel asks.

"It is and isn't. I don't know. It's hard to explain. It just kind of evens itself out into..." Kurt pauses, flipping through the pages of the one subject, college-ruled notebook of his mind, looking for just the right scribbled down word to use.

"Nothing?" Daniel says.

"Yeah... You don't feel happy looking at them. Or sad. You just feel nothing."

A bummed, jailhouse silence fills the room. Ernest tries to remedy the situation the only way he knows how.

"Hey, new guy. Knock knock?"

"Who's there?"

"For whom."

"For whom who?"

Ernest opens his mouth, but the punchline, obvious and lame, stays perched on the tip of his tongue.

"Never mind... I fold," he says, removing the card still stuck to his forehead and throwing it and the rest of his cards down.

"Yeah. I fold too," Richard says.

"I guess I win then," Sylvia says, not sounding glad or excited at all.

"I'm sorry," Daniel says, examining all their faces. "I didn't mean to bum everyone out."

"Nah, man. It's not your fault. This always happens."

Everyone sits in silence, until, to Daniel's surprise, a revolver comes tumbling out of the waterless water slide. And although the firearm's arrival surprises Daniel, it doesn't seem to shock anyone else. The Players, all four of them, stare at the revolver like it's a fully loaded newspaper delivered to their front doorstep. Ernest walks over to the gun, picks it up and wanders back over to his seat.

"Who wants to go first?" he asks, giving the gun's chamber a festive spin, like it's a roulette wheel on some morbid game show.

There's a tense silence. All eyes dart back and forth between each other, each person waiting for the other to speak up. Daniel doesn't know exactly what's going on although he still has a pretty good idea. Enough to the point where he almost can't breathe he's suddenly so nervous.

"I'll go first, man," Richard says and holds his hand out over the table.

Ernest places the revolver—a .44 Magnum, Daniel can see—in Richard's grasp. Then Richard takes off his hat and tips it toward Daniel.

"Daniel, my friend. *Watashi no yūjin.* It's been a real privilege, man. I'll see you on the flip side. I'll see all of you on the flip side." Richard laughs to himself a little. "Far out."

Richard puts the revolver in his mouth. Before Daniel can stop him, a loud, booming gunshot goes off, and Richard rag dolls out of his chair.

Silence.

"Hand me the gun?" Ernest eventually says.

The gun lies on the floor close to Daniel's feet, but in an almost catatonic-like state of shock, he can't move. Growing impatient, and seeing Daniel's too stunned to budge, Ernest gets up, grabs the gun and sits back down.

Staring at the gun in his hand, he says, "Don't worry, New Guy. He'll come back tomorrow. And so will I. We all will."

Ernest puts the revolver up to his temple.

"Knock, knock..." he says, and pulls the trigger.

Daniel's eyes are closed and his head's turned away as he listens to Ernest's body tumble out of his chair.

"It gets easier to watch, believe it or not," Daniel eventually hears Sylvia say over the slight ringing in his ears.

Daniel opens one eye, then the other. Kurt pulls out another cigarette and lights it so casually it's like the famous author who had sat next to him just didn't paint the walls with the very same legendary brains he once used to write remarkable prose.

"Wait a minute," Kurt says, and exhales a puff of smoke. "So you didn't fold yet?

Daniel hesitates, then shakes his head.

"Then how'd you get down here?"

Daniel shrugs.

"Maybe it's because I'm The Chosen One," he insecurely reasons.

Kurt grabs the gun off the ground and places it on the cards covering the center of the table. His somber, lost puppy dog-eyes pout in the gun's direction like the drastic key change that the gun is.

"Yeah... I used to believe I was The Chosen One too."

"Used to?" Sylvia says.

Kurt cracks a devilish grin. He delicately grips the revolver with his thumb and pointer finger and gives it a spin. The gun comes to a psychic stop pointing right back at him.

"I guess that's why I'm here now," Kurt says, staring into the barrel of the gun. "I guess that makes this here my kingdom. What a martyr! What a savior I am! Singing from the pit of my burning, nauseous stomach! Suffering to save the souls of millions! The Chosen One I am indeed!"

A delirious little laugh wriggles out of Kurt's mouth. He grabs the gun and holds it in the open palm of his hand.

"The Chosen One..." he says with scorn. "Cling to your pain too long and you become an erratic, moody baby. Cling to your pain too long and your pain becomes you. Or you become your pain. Doesn't matter either way, though."

Kurt's fingers tighten around the gun's handle.

"They're still listening to me, though? Right?"

Daniel gulps. Then, timidly, he answers, "Yeah... They're still listening to you."

Kurt nods to himself.

"Guess I'm just one of those narcissists who can only appreciate things when they're gone."

Kurt holds the gun up to his head.

"To The Chosen Ones," he says with a smile that glistens with flannel-tinged teenage angst. "What would the unchosen do without us?"

Kurt puts the gun in his mouth. Another thunderous crack ravages Daniel's ears, forcing him to jump in his seat even though he knew it was coming. Kurt tips over in his chair and the same unsettling silence moves right back in.

Sylvia sighs.

"We throw quite the party, don't we?" she says.

Daniel feels sick to his stomach as he watches Sylvia pick up the gun.

"It's no oven, but it has to do, I suppose," she says, looking at the gun in her hand. "Do you think it'll hurt?" she asks after a moment of silence.

Daniel doesn't know what to say. His mouth just kind of hangs open.

"Maybe for a split second," he finally gets out.

"No. I meant you. Burying your heart in a…" She pauses. "What are you burying your heart in again?"

"An empty Big Mac container."

"An empty Big Mac container…" Sylvia repeats softly. "I used to be obsessed with how I would first do it. I'd spend hours contemplating various methods—slitting my wrists with razors, shooting myself in the head, drowning, hanging—and then I'd wonder how much each method would hurt. I'd think about how long it would take. That was what always scared me—the pain beforehand. I knew the razors would take too long, and that a bullet to the brain was too cliche, and, worse yet, overtly masculine. Drowning just downright terrified me. Noose knots were too miserable to tie, and then you had to find a support structure strong enough to hold you. Jesus… Escaping those incurable sad-looking blue whales was such hard work.

"Even *this* feels like work to me," she continues, clutching the revolver. "The simple, split-second action of pulling the trigger back. That's how exhausted I still am from years and years of being hollowed out by their eyes. I couldn't stand those eyes. Eyes that felt like an owl's talons clenching my heart.

"Please don't tell anyone I used this," Sylvia kindly asks of Daniel, referring to the gun. "What would my feminist readers think?"

Daniel has no idea who he would tell, maybe aside from the sad-looking blue whale, but he nods regardless, confirming his promise.

"They're still reading me, aren't they?" she asks.

"Yeah. Of course they are."

Sylvia's mouth contorts into something that resembles a smile. She holds the gun up to her head. Daniel turns away and closes his eyes.

A split second after the gunshot goes off, Daniel's able to hear the faint, whisper-like splatter of Sylvia's brains re-decorating the wall.

"Come here, darling."

Daniel opens his eyes just in time to see Marilyn sit up on the couch and sleepily stretch her arms above her head. She delicately kicks off her heels and pats the empty seat beside her.

Daniel hesitates, then walks over and sits down next to Marilyn. Nervously, he glances at the floor, trying his best not to gawk at her feet that look like beautiful, five-headed, porcelain doves.

"I'm kind of glad they're gone for now if I'm being honest," Marilyn says. "I'm so tired of watching them play that silly game every day."

Daniel self-consciously nods to himself.

"Do you mind if I change into something more comfortable?" Marilyn asks.

Daniel shakes his head. Marilyn stands up and walks behind a changing screen, leaving her heels behind on the floor. Daniel watches her dress eventually drape over the side of the changing screen, a fabric whisper hinting that the starlet, the silver screen legend, the most beautiful woman to have ever existed, the sex symbol that millions upon millions of men have fantasized about—and still fantasize about to this day—is completely naked only a few feet away from him.

Not wanting to feel perverted, Daniel ogles his sneakers. He literally twiddles his thumbs, trying to not only distract himself but also appear innocent, as if he's not currently having certain thoughts raving in his head like a bachelor party.

"It's okay," a voice says a few seconds later, although not Marilyn's. The voice is softer and sounds much less sure of itself. "You can look now."

When Daniel looks up, he sees a little girl in a faded blue Sunday dress and knee-high socks. Except the elastic band of one of the knee-high socks is worn and has lost is tautness, leaving the sock to sadly droop around her ankle. Daniel recognizes the girl immediately. It's Marilyn, but it's not Marilyn.

It's Norma Jeane—Marilyn as a little girl.

Norma Jeane walks over to the couch and gets comfortable beside Daniel, her short legs dangling adorably off the side. She grabs the bag of potato chips and holds it upside down, making sure there aren't any left, and frowns when none come tumbling out.

"They always go so fast," she says. "I love potato chips. Don't you?"

"Yeah," Daniel says. "Sure."

Norma Jeane drops the empty bag on the floor and smooths out the skirt of her rumpled, ratty-looking dress.

"Yes. This is just so much more comfortable," she says about her new outfit. "Not nearly as elegant, but still… much more comfortable. I like being Her—and I won't lie, I like the attention she receives. Well, most of the time—but still, it can be tiresome to say the least. But She is who *they* want," Norma Jeane says, and makes a little head motion toward the table where The Players were seated. "I don't think they'd want to be hanging out with a little girl all day, so I give them what they want. You have to do that once you belong to the world, I'll have you know. 'Give the people what they want.' That's the famous saying, right? But actually doing so gets old much faster than most think."

Norma Jeane lies down on her side and rests her head on Daniel's leg.

"You don't mind, do you?" she asks.

"Uh, no. You can lay on me," Daniel says, trying not to sound anxious, trying not to sound like she's caught him off guard.

"Oh, well that's good. But I mean that I'm not Her right now. You don't mind that, do you?"

"No," Daniel says again. "You can be whoever you want to be."

"Thank you, darling. I appreciate that. I wish more people had said that to me. Say, is there any more champagne left?"

In the bottle on the floor by his feet, Daniel estimates at least two glasses-worth are left inside.

"There's a little."

"Could you pour me a glass, please? And pour yourself one too."

Daniel hesitates, and as if feeling his reluctance, Norma Jeane adds,

"You don't have to worry, darling. This is just an outfit I'm wearing. I'm not actually seven-years-old."

Daniel waits for Norma Jeane to lift her head off his lap to allow him to move, but when she doesn't, as if she's too comfortable to do so, Daniel just kind of leans to his side, trying to disrupt her as little as possible. Racking his body, he grabs the bottle of champagne and pours it into the two glasses on the nearby end table. Daniel takes one glass for himself and hands the other to Norma Jeane who still doesn't sit up.

"Thank you, darling. Cheers."

Norma Jeane raises her glass and Daniel clinks it with his. He takes a sip, but she only cradles hers.

"Were they talking about folding again?" Norma Jeane asks.

Daniel looks back over at the now empty table. The bodies of all The Players are gone and the walls are completely clean of their blood, not to mention the spattering of their brilliant brains.

"Yeah," he answers, surprised at himself for not being more nonplussed at the sudden disappearance of all things grim and gore.

"They always do," she says. "Every time they play they talk about it. I can't help it, so I space out, think about other things, which probably comes off as rude, although I don't mean to be. They're perfectly fine people, and I really don't mind them. I just wish they'd talk about something else for a change."

"They had so much," Daniel finds himself saying as he reflects upon the lonely table and blood-free walls. "All of them. I don't get it."

"Don't get what?"

"Why they folded. Why anyone who had so much would throw it all away like that."

Silence. Instead of answering, Norma Jeane carefully takes her first sip of champagne.

"You had everything," Daniel says softly.

Norma Jeane raises her champagne glass and rotates its stem back and forth between her fingers.

"I didn't have everything. People just thought I did. The truth is I spent my entire life trying to convince myself I was actually a person, which, believe me, is a very sad and lonely way to live. Imagine the entire world loving you but still being unable to love yourself. Imagine the emptiness. Imagine what it would feel like if the love of the entire world still wasn't enough to fill you. Imagine the isolation, darling."

"Is that why you did it?"

Daniel inwardly cringes, immediately regretting the invasive question and wishing he could take it back.

"If you even did do it on purpose," he says, recoiling. "I don't know. I wasn't there. I don't know what happened."

Norma Jeane sits up. She chugs her entire glass of champagne and wipes her mouth with her forearm, just like a little girl would. She slides off the couch and places the glass on the floor. Then she kicks off her shoes and steps her tiny feet into the heels Marilyn left behind. She wobbles a bit at first but sticks her arms out and regains her balance.

"The truth is, darling, that you'll never have everything, and that you'll never feel full, until you learn to love yourself. And I just couldn't figure out how to do that. At least not as an adult."

Norma Jeane stares down at her feet in the oversized heels, but sadly. Quite the opposite of a little girl standing in her mother's shoes. More as if she knows for certain that she's going to grow into them someday and she's currently mourning just that fact.

"That's why I think the answer lies in here," she says as she begins walking around the room in the heels, staggering every other step and keeping her arms outstretched, trying not to fall. "In this little girl I used to be. Or perhaps, rather, in the little girl I was supposed to be before I was forced to grow up so fast. I think that's why I like wearing this outfit so much. I think that's why it feels so comfortable even though I can't keep it on forever. Because being a young child is really the last time you feel comfortable in your own skin. You're just allowed to be whoever it is you are. You're allowed to *like* yourself, appreciate yourself. Well, if you're lucky. If you have good parents, I suppose. Either way, then you grow up and everything changes. Everything gets ruined because now you need to have a purpose, you need to have value. You need to be pretty or smart or strong. You need to constantly be producing and giving something to a ravenous, ungrateful world, and so it's no longer okay for you to just be a person like when you were younger. Back when you never really wanted much. But now? Now you have to be an asset. Now you have to contribute. And not just occasionally either. *Ohhhhhh* no." She giggles, almost deliriously. "You have to contribute all the time. Because if you don't? Boy, then are you in trouble. Then you're made to feel even worse about yourself than you already do. You're made to feel less than, like you're not good enough. And so of course all adults feel empty. Of course they feel the vast, unfillable nothingness. It's because they're not allowed to just 'be' anymore. They have to now *be* something else."

Norma Jeane trips over herself, yelps and topples onto the floor. Daniel jumps up to help her, to make sure she's okay, but stops as soon as he hears her laughing.

"Wow... Whoever invented these things sure was silly," she says, picking up the one high heel her foot fell out of and rotating it in her small hand as she examines it.

"I guess I'm still not sure if I did it or not. I guess I don't know if I —" She pauses. "Folded... The whole thing is just one big blur when I reflect back upon it, but it wouldn't surprise me if I did, and it wouldn't surprise me if I didn't either. It just happened because I was sad. Because I couldn't be me, because I didn't know *how* to be me, and because I didn't know at the time that was all I had to be—just me. Nothing but me. A person and nothing else. But now it's too late for that, I suppose."

Norma Jeane drops the heel onto the floor and stares at it.

"Boy... People sure do allow silly things to happen to them when they're sad. And *do* silly things to themselves when they're sad. Kind of like burying their heart in a hamburger container beneath the ocean floor."

Norma Jeane gives Daniel a wry, little smile. Daniel kind of smiles back, trying to look wry himself, trying to hide the sudden pang of not only sadness but guilt he feels sprout up inside him like knife-flowers.

Norma Jeane kicks Marilyn's other high heel off her foot. It flies across the room and accidentally hits Daniel in his shin.

"Oops!" Norma Jeane says. "Sorry."

"It's okay," Daniel says, smiling it off. His smile, although small and crooked, is real, he knows. It's genuine and proper. But as soon as he acknowledges this, the smile disappears, or, rather, it kills itself, Daniel ventures, especially considering the intentional and violent manner in which he feels it rip itself from his face.

Norma Jeane yawns.

"I think I'm getting sleepy," she says.

Norma Jeane stands up and wanders behind the changing screen. Daniel watches the white dress slide down behind it and looks away. Seconds later, he hears the bare footsteps of Marilyn approaching him.

"It's okay, darling. You can look."

And there she is again, the most beautiful woman that ever existed. She's not quite smiling, and she's not quite frowning either. Her facial expression is neutral, is that of nothingness.

A luminous nothingness… Daniel's brain says.

"I don't mean to be rude," Marilyn says, her voice sounding like a white-satin hammock swaying in-between two palm trees, "but I think it's time."

Daniel stands up.

"Time?"

Marilyn reaches behind one of the couch cushions and pulls out a pill bottle.

"Time," Marilyn repeats, holding up the pill bottle and giving it a little rattle.

Marilyn unscrews the cap and pours a large amount of pills out into her palm.

"I wish I could be her all the time, but I can't. I have to be *Her*, I think. Or perhaps just me. Or at least as much as this place will allow me to be me. I don't know… It's all rather confusing at this point, darling. Considering where I am and what I've done. Or, rather, what I might've done."

Marilyn pops the pills in her mouth and gulps them down without water, but still does so with the relative ease of someone who just downed them with a mouthful of water. Then she curls up on the couch. Using her hands as pillows, she closes her spotlight eyes. As soon as they're shut, Daniel swears that the room gets darker.

"For what it's worth, darling, I hope you don't do it," she says.

"Do what?" Daniel says, even though he knows exactly what she's talking about. He's just not ready for her to stop talking. He just wants to hear her voice a little longer. He loves her voice the way certain people love nature.

"You know, darling…" she says, drearily, fading fast.

Daniel wants to rush over to her and shake her. He wants to keep her from falling asleep, from folding, but he just stands there, feeling the gloppy mess of affection he has for her drip and ooze down into the pit of his stomach where it forms an unhappy puddle.

Shit… says Daniel's brain as he watches Marilyn's eyelashes flutter, suddenly remembering the point of coming aboard this yacht to begin with.

"Uh, Marilyn? I mean, Ms. Monroe?"

"Mm?" Her voice sounds a like lone bubble floating to the surface in a glass of flat champagne.

"Do you have batteries by any chance?"

"Behind the couch cushion…" she says before drifting off.

Daniel hesitates, then walks over to the couch. He reaches behind the cushion and fishes around until his hand comes across something long, slender and cool.

Daniel pulls out the mystery object.

It's a vibrator.

But not just any vibrator.

Marilyn Monroe's vibrator.

Daniel's anxiety skyrockets. Beginning to perspire, he fumbles around with the sleek, female orgasm donor, struggling to find out how to open it and access the batteries. Finally, Daniel realizes he needs to unscrew the vibrator into two separate pieces. Looking over his shoulder, Daniel bangs one half of the vibrator into his palm and a battery comes out. Then he does the same with the other half and another falls out. Daniel pockets the batteries and screws the vibrator back together. He carefully places it behind the couch cushion where he found it and makes his way back over to the waterless waterslide, already dreading the rough ascent.

Before he climbs inside, and before he can turn around to whisper goodbye, Daniel hears it—a harsh, grating, crunching, like the sound of a mother trash compactor regurgitating garbage into the eagerly awaiting, hungry mouths of her baby trash compactors.

The noise is coming from Marilyn, he realizes.

She's fast asleep.

And snoring like a son of a bitch.

———

Just like when he first stepped aboard the yacht, Daniel, now back on deck, remains more unseen and unnoticed than the credits dutifully rolling by at the end of a porno. The party's still raging on, and the sad-looking blue whales still almost seem to be having fun.

The batteries Daniel took from Marilyn's vibrator bulge visibly in his pants pocket, and even though they're not inside anything electronic, even though they're not being powered in any way, he swears he can feel them emanating a low yet steady hum, like they're alive, like they have tiny and acidic alkaline minds of their own.

That's the sound of freedom... Daniel's brain says.

The sound of relief...

The sound of the impending end...

"The end is nigh..." Daniel's brain says, even though his brain has

no real idea what "nigh" actually means because it's spent its entire existence only using contextual clues to understand its definition rather than just outright learning it.

Daniel closes his eyes and tilts his head back. He basks in the sun. Suddenly knowing he won't have to feel it for much longer, and that after that he'll never feel it again, the sun momentarily feels good on Daniel's burnt skin. He remembers it wasn't always this way, that the sun wasn't always this much of an abusive boyfriend to him, that, in fact, he'd spent many painless—and even enjoyable—hours underneath its glaring supervision. Standing there and feeling his rage towards the sun subside, Daniel almost even feels sentimental towards it. But sentimentality, Daniel knows, is just not wanting to fully let go of something, or to have already let go of something and to want, at least, a little piece of it back. And even after spending time with The Players, and even after spending time with Marilyn, Daniel still knows what he wants.

My heart belongs in an empty Big Mac container buried beneath the ocean floor…

Just as Daniel's about to make his way back to the ladder on the hull of the yacht where the sad-looking blue whale is, hopefully, still waiting, something drunkenly bobs past his face. Daniel almost swats at the floating speck until he sees it blink once, then twice.

The lightning bug…

The lightning bug floats past Daniel and alongside the cabin of the yacht until it arrives in front of another ladder, one that rises all the way up to the yacht's roof. The lightning bug flies in a little circle and then begins its ascent, floating past rung after rung and, eventually, disappearing up over the roof and out of sight.

Following the same impulse that got Daniel to where he's currently standing, the very same one that made him paddle after the lightning bug in the first place, when he believed, either out of desperation or instinct, that it somehow knew where it was going and, therefore, that it'd lead him and the sad-looking blue whale to some type of safety, or relief, Daniel glances over his shoulders, making sure no one is watching him. When he sees that, yes, that's still very much the case, he walks over to the ladder. Daniel puts his hands on the rungs and takes a deep breath, which feels rehearsed to him, like he's suddenly in a movie, and begins his ascent. It's a short climb, and as his buzzed and burned head rises over the yacht's roof like a cuckolded sun with a ball gag in its mouth, Daniel freezes in place.

A sad-looking blue whale in a tuxedo, with one fin on his waist and with the other holding onto a sweating bottle of champagne, has his eyes closed and his head leaned back as he's being fellated.

Daniel's eyes are immediately able to process and register the sad-looking blue whale, as well as the scandalous act he's caught him in the middle of receiving, but who, or perhaps what, that's currently performing the act on the sad-looking blue whale is an entirely different story.

Daniel can feel his eyes squinting and unsquinting, zooming in and zooming out like an 1980's home camcorder struggling to focus and, therefore, clearly register this abstractly familiar figure. It takes a few seconds before it happens, and the wavy figure that comes into muddled focus turns out to be Laura, but a distorted version of her, waterlogged, wrinkled and slightly bleached of color, just like, Daniel realizes, her naked picture he accidentally took into the ocean with him.

Laura's striped green t-shirt is pulled up above her deflated airbag breasts and her uncooked bacon arms are wrapped around the sad-looking blue whale, holding the area where his ass would be if he had one as her head mechanically moves back and forth, back and forth, slobbering over the sad-looking blue whale's cock, occasionally swerving and erotically pivoting while glistening drips of drool fall from her mouth.

With a mechanical stiffness, the sad-looking blue whale pours champagne onto Laura's back. A magical, endless, sparkling stream of it, as if coming from a never-ending, bottomless bottle, rushes down and funnels through her crooked ass crack. Just as Daniel is about to look away, just when he feels like he can't tolerate watching one second longer, the lightning bug, which he'd momentarily forgotten about, flutters from out of nowhere and, like an obtrusive younger sibling with no sense of boundaries or privacy, flies around in front of the sad-looking blue whale's face.

The sad-looking blue whale stops pouring champagne and swipes at the lightning bug disrupting his moment of slobbery euphoria. But even though the sad-looking blue whale becomes distracted, Laura never does. If anything, she speeds up, moving with such a smooth and unadulterated force that she looks like she's trying to suck the sad-looking blue whale's dick clean off his body.

Whether involuntarily or not, the lightning bug swishes underneath each one of the sad-looking blue whale's lumbering swings. As if receiving the disgruntled message loud and clear, it finally floats away out of harm's reach. But nonetheless, it floats towards Daniel, and before he can duck down and hide, the sad-looking blue whale, originally tracking the slow-blinking exodus of the lightning bug, locks eyes with Daniel. And everything goes to shit.

"Mother fucker!" the sad-looking blue whale screams.

Panic seizes Daniel and he freezes in place just as he did when he first stepped on deck. The sad-looking blue whale crouches down and gropes for his pants down around his fins. But he's not just fumbling for his pants terror-stricken Daniel soon realizes when the sad-looking blue whale grabs a revolver holstered to his belt. The sad-looking blue whale aims at Daniel. Without informing his brain they're going to do so, Daniel's hands instantly let go of the rungs. Daniel falls back off the ladder and crash lands on the deck. After composing himself, he looks up just in time to see the sad-looking blue whale's furious face peer over the roof. Daniel doesn't think twice. He stands up and hurls himself overboard. A gunshot goes off. The blaring house music stops. In a stunned and confused silence, the sad-looking blue whales stop partying and look around the yacht, wondering what the hell just happened.

A beat later, a confetti canon goes off.

The sad-looking blue whales all throw their fins into the air and cheer wildly. The horrible, bass-thumping dance music blasts back on and everyone continues dancing as if they'd never stopped.

Daniel's body submerges a good twenty feet or so after hitting the water's unfriendly surface. Instead of racing up for air, he starts swimming. He kicks his legs. He flails his arms, trying to make an unseen underwater getaway, or at least trying to get himself as far away from the yacht as quickly as possible.

With a sub-par lung capacity, Daniel doesn't make it far. He rises to the ocean's surface and takes a big gasp of air but never stops swimming.

Fuck it... Daniel's rattled and panting brain says.

The sad-looking blue whale can come to me...

Daniel swims and swims and only looks back when he's too exhausted to physically exert himself any further. Much to his relief, he sees the sad-looking blue whale already paddling the bright-orange boat after him.

Daniel can't make out much else on the yacht—he definitely doesn't see any sign of the sad-looking blue whale who wanted to shoot him—but, for the first time, he does notice the name of the yacht painted on its side in navy blue lettering.

A name he's not sure how he missed before.

The Limbo.

"Are you okay?" the sad-looking blue whale asks after hoisting Daniel back inside the bright-orange boat.

Daniel searches himself for a gunshot wound with his hands. He doesn't find any, nor does he feel pain anywhere. Regardless, a large part of him expects to be like, "I guess he missed me," and then, after speaking too soon, a steady, cartoonish stream of bright-red blood begins pouring out of him.

"What happened?" the sad-looking blue whale asks after Daniel fails to answer his first question.

The partying sad-looking blue whales pretending to look happy, the waterless water slide, The Players, Marilyn and Norma Jeane, wrinkled Laura sucking off a sad-looking blue whale while getting champagne poured down her warped ass crack—it all feels like too much to recount, it all feels too strenuous to retell, especially right after his brush with death. So, instead, Daniel reaches into his pants pocket, takes out the batteries and holds them up for the sad-looking blue whale to see.

"Let's just hope they still work," Daniel says.

The sad-looking blue whale takes the batteries and looks them over.

"They're drenched," he says.

Daniel shoots the sad-looking blue whale an angry, disgruntled look, one he receives loud and clear.

"Yeah… Let's just hope they still work," he repeats.

The sad-looking blue whale places the batteries in his lap and grabs the boombox. He removes the battery hatch and replaces the old batteries with the new ones, then places the boombox down in-between him and Daniel. Both of them hunch over it and look at each other.

"I'm scared," the sad-looking blue whale says.

"Oh fuck this," Daniel says.

Daniel's impatient hand jabs out toward the boombox and his pointer finger hits the PLAY button.

And it happens.

Again.

The same dead click.

All the air seems to leave Daniel's body. He collapses back into the boat, his arms draped over the sides. The sad-looking blue whale doesn't move, his hopeless eyes remaining anchored on the boombox.

"No…" Daniel says, firmly, after a long and utterly defeated silence.

"No, what?" the sad-looking blue whale asks.

"No," Daniel says again, this time even firmer than before. "Just no."

Daniel grabs the boombox. He takes the batteries out then puts them back in, pressing into them, making sure they're locked in place. Daniel snaps the hatch back on. He places the boombox back down and gives the sad-looking blue whale a "Here we go…" look before pressing the PLAY button.

At first, Daniel just hears a small little hiss. Then a sound like a hi-pitched, tree queef musically blowing through a crystallized spiderweb wafts out of the speakers, proceeded by a voice, like a wheel of Munster cheese slowly rolling across a Canadian landscape coated in their sappiest and sugariest maple syrup…

"Every night in my dreams,

I see you,

I feeeeeel you…"

Daniel knew this moment had to come if they ever wanted to summon the sad-looking blue whales from their underwater kingdom, but instead of the relief he thought he would feel when this moment happened, when he and the sad-looking blue whale finally got the boombox working, every organ, every fiber, every molecule of Daniel's being shudders. And trying to earmuff the auditory assault currently shanking his ear drums like they're no-good prison snitches, Daniel does all he can do—he covers his ears with his hands.

The sad-looking blue whale closes his eyes. Even though he's now sitting upright, he still manages to have the posture of melting candle wax.

"Turn it up," the sad-looking blue whale says.

Reluctantly, and fighting against every screaming instinct in his body, Daniel turns the volume up as high as it will go, then immediately recovers his ears.

"How long do you think it's going to take for them to find us?"
"Is it on repeat?" the sad-looking blue whale asks.
Daniel looks at the menu display on the boombox and nods.
"Good," the sad-looking blue whale says.
Then leans back in his seat.
And smiles.

IT'S A HORRIBLE LIFE

DANIEL DIDN'T KNOW what he was waiting for.

He knew what he had to do next, what he *wanted* to do next (*My heart belongs in an empty Big Mac container buried beneath the ocean floor...*) but, regardless, for some dull, edgeless and vague reason, he couldn't pry his ass out of the booth to actually follow through with it.

It was so quiet in McDonald's Daniel could've heard a French fry drop. The power was still out, leaving him to feel as if he was sitting in some sort of ultra-hip, contemporary cave, one complete with an open floor design plan and just the right amount of natural light that young, modern day, hipster cave dwellers would expect from such a home. Outside, the rain had tired itself out. Coming out of the gate too strong, too fast, it was catching its breath as it tiptoed across the roof and polka dotted the window panes with translucent measles. And hanging low to the ground like a vaporous and all-encompassing straight jacket, a fog swaddled the buildings and parking lots. It restrained the street lights and trees. Somehow, without Daniel hearing, it had dragged them off kicking and screaming, and now there was only silence—silence like a nightmare trying to patiently imagine itself into existence, silence like a mental illness insidiously passing itself onto future generations.

For Daniel, staring at the fog through the windows was like staring at the musty emptiness inside himself. He no longer felt human. He felt more like an outline of a human, like back when he was in kindergarten and, as an art project, Daniel's teacher had all of the students lie down on a large piece of paper which she then traced each student's outline onto, intending for the students to color in the outline with their underdeveloped self-images.

Not counting food, Daniel couldn't remember the last time he felt full, or even close to full, and on the rare occasions when he did add something positive and substantial into his system, all it took was one cry (*Ooooh, oooh, oooooh!*) to hollow him back out again. Emptiness seemed to be his natural state, he thought, although, really, it was more like a near-emptiness. Because no matter how bad things got, no matter how gutted Daniel became, there always seemed to be this mocking speck that lingered in the vast emptiness of his being, this .1% taking up space inside him, like a dead gnat in the back of a cement mixer truck, which, drastically contrasting the old adage, "Something is better than nothing," ended up making Daniel feel even worse off than if he were to be entirely empty. And while not only failing to provide enough spiritual nourishment, this lone, lingering kernel of positivity, rattling around inside him without ever moving as it quietly tried to pop and expand into something bigger and better—but failing, always failing—only forced Daniel to notice the emptiness that much more profoundly. It became a pinprick of a reminder that he was capable of total contentment, just as all humans were, but that, ultimately, he was nowhere near close to attaining it.

So Daniel did what he had been programmed to do since birth—he consumed. He funneled himself full of whatever he could get his hands on. The somewhat healthier options always succored him much longer than the metaphysical junk food he often shoveled into his ready and willing maw, but still, inevitably, healthy or not, his consumptions never failed to evaporate without a trace. But because this method kind of worked, because it faithfully unleashed a torrent of that classic feel-good hormone, dopamine, to his brain, and because it was easier and more convenient to stuff himself to the rafters with what he wanted rather than what he needed, Daniel, like billions of others, stuck to this lifestyle of voracious, non-stop gobbling. It was as if his soul was eternally high and there weren't enough 7/11's in the world to satisfy his epic, unending case of the munchies. A fate that left Daniel constantly longing for more. More of this, more of that. Anything at all to fill the empty slough of space in the bowels of his problematic gut.

Daniel coaxed his eyes toward the empty Big Mac container, trying to sneak a spy-like glance as it nestled on the table like the suspenseful ellipsis at the end of the sentence, *My heart belongs in an empty Big Mac container buried beneath the ocean floor...*

Daniel felt an apology clambering its way up his throat like a fat kid struggling to climb the rope in gym class. He wished he hadn't snapped at the empty Big Mac container. He needed someone, or, in this odd case, some*thing* to talk to. An anxious boiling was brooding beneath the surface of his skin, and the more he tried to calm it, the more he tried to simmer himself down, the more this restless seething reminded him that, despite his best efforts, despite years of striving for some sense of normalcy, despite all of the inner battles he had fought to be one of them—*them*, the ones who weren't silently under siege from the sad-looking blue whales—Daniel was reminded that he was different, that he was, essentially, a sad-looking blue whale in human drag. And it was this very same volcanic truth, he realized, the same one he had known about and tried to suppress his entire adult life, that was suddenly rising to the surface, ready to erupt.

Out of nowhere, the speakers in the ceiling crackled like a rat biting into an electric Rice Krispies treat. A few seconds later, an all too familiar frequency oozed downward, goopily stretching itself towards Daniel's ears like an audible string of salt water taffy tragically adorned with dozens upon dozens of the most mournful vowel in the English language.

"Ooooooooooooooooooooooooooooooooh!" the speaker cried.

Shock and dismay flogged Daniel in the back of his buzzed head, not only because he couldn't believe what he was hearing, but also because he couldn't believe how quickly he found himself suddenly yearning for the squeaky-clean chords of Christian rock. Daniel scrambled for his earphones, accidentally putting the left one in his right ear amidst his panic. Then, after correctly affixing both to their proper places, he scrolled through the iTunes library on his phone to Daniel Johnston and hit shuffle. But instead of lo-fi Beatles'esque melodies, instead of pre-school instrumentals that sounded like they needed a tetanus shot, dozens of microscopic O's wafted from the dime-sized speakers and forayed their way into Daniel's ears with the cavalier nonchalance of an army of smoke rings.

"Oooooooooooooooooo—"

Daniel ripped out his earphones and threw them across the table. At a loss, he put his hands on the side of his head. He had no idea what was going on, what the hell was happening to his McDonald's. As the ceiling speakers bellowed a cetacean sadness, the effervescent toiling beneath the freckled terrain of his desert-like skin only seemed to be getting angrier by the second. Meanwhile, the fog surrounding his once impenetrable fast-food fortress had grown tangibly thick and noxiously gray. Any lingering signs of civilization outside had been swallowed whole and Daniel had no idea if they would ever come back or if this—this claustrophobic cage of unwholesome murk—was his new permanent reality.

Daniel slid out of his booth and began pacing back and forth through the dining room. The thought of going outside and trying to find his car seemed unsafe, too risky. The fog, like the foul breath of a boneyard, was too unnatural. As long as Daniel was in McDonald's —*his* McDonald's—he would be okay. Even with the power out, even with all of the employees mysteriously gone, even with the dirge of crying whales crooning down from the ceiling, Daniel was safe here. Safer than anywhere else in the world, he figured, even more so than his own home.

Just as he began calming down, just as the boiling below his skin gave the vaguest hint of turning down the flames and beginning to simmer, Daniel noticed a shrouded figure in the fog, lurking toward the Golden Arches. Transfixed, and with his heart suddenly beating like a maraca in a paint shaker, he stopped pacing and stared through the window. The top-heavy mystery guest eerily lumbered forward, almost drunkenly, almost like its feet were tied together. Closer... closer... closer it inched, taking its time as it shuffled along with a zombie-like sense of urgency.

Daniel held his breath. His asshole nervously puckered. The figure was beginning to take shape, to reveal itself. Daniel squinted. The fog parted like elevator doors made of cranky smog and, all too predictably, out from the murkiness stepped a sad-looking blue whale.

But before Daniel could breathe a sigh of relief that something much more sinister hadn't emerged from the fog, he noticed a flat piece of, what appeared to be, cardboard strapped to the sad-looking blue whale's face. A mask, Daniel realized after squinting his already strained eyes even further, although, at this hazily obscured point, he still couldn't tell of what.

Daniel hurried over to the window and pressed his face up against the glass. With a closer look, and with the sad-looking blue whale still trudging forward, he could see it clearly now. The sad-looking blue whale was, in fact, wearing a mask, and it was of Daniel.

Daniel with that look on his face.

"That look, Daniel...

"That goddamn look..."

BAYYYBEE!!!

WHEN DANIEL LET himself inside Laura's apartment one night, she was curled up on the couch in sweatpants, crying.

"What's wrong?"

Daniel dropped his stuff and sat down next to Laura. He put an arm around her and she collapsed into him like an overwhelmed, blonde avalanche.

"Family stuff," she said.

"What kind of family stuff?"

"My cousin. He's been talking about killing himself again."

"Jesus," Daniel said, not knowing what else to say, and also completely unaware Laura's cousin had such tendencies.

"Yeah. And I'm the one he reaches out to when he's feeling like this."

"Does the rest of your family know?"

"Yeah. He's..." Laura hesitated. "Disturbed... He fought over in Afghanistan and when he came home he wasn't the same."

"And I assume he's tried getting help?"

"Yeah. He sees a shrink and goes to meetings and stuff. And he's on medication. But it's not enough. The guy has seen friends die right in front of him. He's shot people. How does anyone get over that?"

"I have no idea. I don't think I could."

Laura sniffled.

"Me neither."

"That's got to be stressful for you too, though. Being the one he turns to when he's unraveling like this."

"Yeah," Laura said, wiping more tears from her eyes.

"Does he talk to anyone else in the family?"

"Kind of. But not really. He really only opens up to me."

"Well, he's lucky to have you then. He's lucky you guys are so close."

Laura shrugged.

"We are, but we aren't, ya know?"

Daniel didn't, and he shook his head. Laura suddenly seemed nervous about what she was going to say next.

"He likes me," she finally said.

"Well, yeah. Of course he does."

"No... He *likes* me. Like, he has a small crush on me."

"Oh..."

"Don't go getting weird on me or start judging me!" Laura snapped.

"I'm not. I'm not doing anything. I'm just sitting here, listening."

"Okay," Laura said, wiping her Rankin & Bass red nose with a tissue. "Sorry."

"But even before the war," she continued, "he's always been a little off. He's not bad. He's just different. And I've always been nice to him because it seems like not too many people are, and so he likes me because of it."

"How do you know he *likes you* likes you?"

"Because he's told me. He's told me a few times. The whole family knows. It's this whole weird and awkward thing. He used to send me these flirtatious Facebook messages, but he doesn't anymore. Now he mainly just talks to me about his love life and stuff, about how much trouble he has getting a girlfriend."

"Because of his PTSD?"

"That definitely hasn't helped, but no, there are other things."

"Like what?"

Laura sat there, silent.

"It's okay. You don't have to tell me if you don't want to," Daniel said.

But Laura had this exhausted look on her face like she did want to tell him. She took a breath, stared at the floor and said, "He has a really big dick."

Even Daniel felt embarrassed now, not to mention jealous, although he tried his best not to let it show that he'd suddenly, although, more so immaturely, lost just a tad of sympathy for Laura's cousin and his enormous cock.

"So? Wouldn't that help him find a girl?"

"No. It's, like, really big, Daniel. Like freakishly big. Like big to the point where it just hurts the girl. Big to the point where he has trouble wearing certain pants. And I know so because I have old friends who have more than seen it, if you know what I mean. It's a real problem for him. It makes him self-conscious. It makes him hate himself more than he already does and so he just keeps to himself, which is a horrible idea because he's already insanely lonely and has no friends and he has all these fucking mental health problems and I don't know how to help him but I feel like I should be trying harder to help him because he doesn't live too far from me and it's all too much and work is crazy for me right now and my boss got mad at me today and yelled at me in front of everyone..."

Laura trailed off into a wailing wall of tears. Daniel cradled her, allowing her to burrow further into his chest, and ran his hand up and down her back.

"I know," he said softly. "I know. That's a lot."

Daniel gave Laura a kiss on top of her head and her greasy hair smudged his glasses as per usual. He thought about Laura's cousin and mentally tried to picture the insane amount of sad-looking blue whales currently infiltrating his life right now. He thought about how unfair the situation was to her cousin, how unfair life was in general, and how relentless life always seemed to be.

"I need more tissues," Daniel heard Laura say. "I've got snot all over my fucking face."

Daniel got up and handed Laura the box of tissues. Then he got her a glass of water for no reason other than it just felt like the right thing to do. Laura accepted the glass as if she'd asked for it and Daniel sat back down beside her and put his arm around her. Laura took a sip of water then blew her nose.

"Ugh... I'm disgusting," she said.

"No, you're not. You're rightfully upset. That's all a lot to handle."

Laura kind of nodded.

"I don't know what to do."

"I think you're doing all you can do."

"I guess."

"Just so long as he isn't making you uncomfortable anymore."

"No. Not really."

"You promise?"

Laura nodded again.

"I just don't want him to kill himself. It would destroy me."

Laura took another large gulp of water.

"Thank you," she said after swallowing it down, proceeding to add a sentiment that caught Daniel completely off guard. "You're a good man."

Daniel sat upright, pleasantly stunned.

"You really are. I appreciate you. It's nice having someone who loves me and will actually listen to me. I've never had that before. At least not like this."

"Of course," he said. "Anytime. I love you."

Laura got the same look on her face that she had on before, like she wanted to tell Daniel something but that she was nervous to.

"I stopped taking my medication," she finally came out with.

Daniel was taken aback.

"Why?" he asked. "Why would you do that?"

"Because I don't like how I feel on it. And because it was making me break out and look ugly again."

"So you just quit cold turkey? Without letting your doctor know?"

She nodded.

"Jesus, Laura."

"Please don't scold me right now."

"I'm not. But that's not safe. You can't do that."

"I know. But I feel so subdued when I take it. I don't feel like me."

"Then you need to talk to your doctor and figure something else out."

Laura took another sip of water.

"I'm sorry," she said. "I know I've been a lot to deal with lately. I know I've been a little manic and bossy and restless and all over the place. It's like I see it happening, I see myself saying or doing certain things but I can't stop myself from doing them."

Daniel had noticed a drastic change in Laura from when they first started dating, but he never imagined this could be the reason why.

"Are you going to talk to your doctor soon?" Daniel asked.

"Yeah," she said.

"You promise?"

"I promise. I'll make an appointment tomorrow."

"Thank you."

Laura finished her glass of water.

"More?" Daniel asked.

"Yes, please."

Daniel took her glass, but before getting up, he leaned in and used his pointer finger to scoop a stray piece of booger off Laura's nose.

"Ew, stop. What are you doing?"

"You had a boog."

"Ew. Don't touch my boogers. You're gross," she said, smiling, like she loved the fact that Daniel just touched her boogers.

Daniel held up the booger on the tip of his finger.

"Go ahead. Blow on it. Make a wish."

"Haha, that's eyelashes you idiot."

"Ohhh, yeah. My mistake. How could I forget?"

Laura laughed. She seemed to be feeling better.

"I'm gonna go get you more water. You want anything else from the kitchen?"

"Fuck the water. Bring beer, please."

"That's my girl."

Daniel kissed Laura on her forehead and got up. As he was heading off into the kitchen, he heard her voice call out after him.

"I love you…"

Daniel stopped. He looked back at Laura and smiled.

"I love you too," he said, suddenly feeling better than he had in a long time.

GREASY, CARDBOARD HEART-COFFIN

IT SEEMS ironic to Daniel that a song titled "My Heart Will Go On" could make him wish that his heart would do the exact opposite. That it would, quite simply, stop beating. That his entire body would then proceed to follow his heart's lead and completely shut down so his ears wouldn't have to listen to one more menopausal note, so they wouldn't have to be subjected to one more drum fill that sounds like a three-pound vulva being dropped down a short flight of stairs, so his ears wouldn't have to hear this overly hormonal string-cheese section ever again.

"Do you think they'll be here soon?" Daniel asks, half-screaming so he can be heard over the intensity of the song's climactic, warbling, mating call-vocals.

"Hard to say," the sad-looking blue whale half-screams back at Daniel. "I'm not sure how far we've drifted from the rendezvous point."

"Maybe we turn it off for a little bit," Daniel suggests.

"Mm, I don't know… I think we should keep it on. Just to be sure."

"Well, can we at least turn it down a little?"

"Mm, I don't think so. We should probably keep it turned up all the way. Just to be sure."

Suddenly not sure what's worse, being cooked alive by the sun or listening to one more verse of "My Heart Will Go On," Daniel shoves his fingers deeper in his ears as the song fades to its miserable end and then immediately swells back up like a swollen ankle to its even more miserable beginning.

"It's just that I'm not sure how much longer I can take it," he says, and really meaning it too.

"Hold on," the sad-looking blue whale says, sounding frustrated, like he's had enough of Daniel interrupting his listening party.

The sad-looking blue whale unzips his fanny pack and fishes around inside. After a couple seconds, he pulls out a Discman and some black plushy headphones that he hands to Daniel.

"I'm not sure what CD's in there, but maybe you can use it to drown out Ms. Dion," the sad-looking blue whale says.

Daniel looks at the Discman and headphones in his hands. He freezes as he feels his brain slowly beginning to do the situational math.

If the sad-looking blue whale had a Discman this whole time, and if the sad-looking blue whale knew he had a Discman the whole time, and if the Discman actually works, which means it currently has functioning batteries inside it, then that means the sad-looking blue whale has had functioning batteries on him the whole time. Batteries, the one thing we've been in dire need of ever since we left, the one thing we needed to summon the sad-looking blue whales but didn't have…

Daniel puts the headphones on.

He presses PLAY on the Discman.

"My Heart Will Go On" by Celine Dion begins pumping out through the headphones as well.

Calmly, but quickly, Daniel hits the STOP button. He takes off the headphones and drops them and The Discman into the ocean as the sad-looking blue whale watches, confused.

Daniel presses the PLAY button on the boombox, pausing the song.

"What?" the sad-looking blue whale says.

The punch happens so fast, like lightning sharting its pants, that Daniel doesn't even realize what he's done until he feels the pain radiate through the bones of his fist, until he sees the sad-looking blue whale's head jerk back, making him lose his balance just long enough to lean too far over the side which he then topples over, his bottom fins kicking up to where his head was just moments ago, sending up a moderate-sized splash. Instinctively holding onto the sides of the bright-orange boat that's rising and falling from the swells of the sad-looking blue whale's sudden departure, Daniel leans forward, looking as far over the side of the boat as he can. Bubbles scurry to the surface, and then, seconds later, the sad-looking blue whale's head bursts above water. Gasping, he flails his fins in an attempt to stay afloat, but when that doesn't work, he panics. The sad-looking blue whale makes desperate lunges for the side of the boat but his hectic, unorganized movements only leave him stranded in the water.

They really don't know how to swim… says Daniel's brain.

They never learned…

"Too sad-looking to have ever learned…"

Still gasping and flailing, and with its tiny, panic-stricken eyes bulging out, the sad-looking blue whale keeps rising to the surface only to quickly sink right back beneath it. As Daniel watches the sad-looking blue whale struggle, he thinks about the batteries, about how the sad-looking blue whale made this entire journey so much more difficult than it had to be, which, consequently, parlays into Daniel thinking about all the other sad-looking blue whales who have come before, about how they always made everything else in his life so much more difficult than it had to be. He thinks about the numerous times he fantasized about killing one of them. A hammer-bludgeoning was usually Daniel's go-to fantasy. The sickening thuds, the act of physically beating them to death, like fatally tenderizing a really sad-looking hunk of rancid meat. Years of anger, frustration and resentment releasing itself through the blunt end of the hammer, occasionally switching it up and using the pointed end. But as often as Daniel thought about doing so, he never could follow through with it. Something about it felt wrong, like Daniel would be killing off a piece of himself in the process, and whether or not that was actually true Daniel never figured out, but that theory—the one that the sad-looking blue whales were part of him—combined with the fact that he was non-violent (minus, perhaps, the recent punch to the sad-looking blue whale's face) had always kept Daniel from fulfilling one of these revenge fantasies. And now here he is, watching a sad-looking blue whale die right in front of him. And the best thing, Daniel knows, is he doesn't have to get his hands dirtier than they already are. The hard part is over. All he has to do now is not act and he'll assist in finally killing off a sad-looking blue whale. And being stalked by sad-looking blue whales who were notorious for draining him of his energy and desire to move, Daniel is more than used to not acting, to sitting back and doing nothing.

And that's why Daniel feels stunned when he notices himself leaning forward.

And that's why he's even more stunned when he feels his forearm submerge itself into the cool ocean water and grasp around.

And that's why he's even more than stunned when he feels his hand interlock with the sad-looking blue whale's desperate fin, when he somehow hoists the six-foot-tall sad-looking blue whale out of the water with the sudden strength of a mother lifting a car off her toddler who's pinned underneath.

The sad-looking blue whale kind of half-flops, half-collapses into the middle of the boat. Daniel, as if he's done all he has to do, sits back in his seat like a massive, fatty lump of non-emotion and watches the sad-looking blue whale cough up water. Instead of making sure the sad-looking blue whale's okay, Daniel grabs the empty Big Mac container off the floor to keep it from accidentally getting crushed. Safely holding the empty Big Mac container with his left hand, Daniel looks at his right. His knuckles are already starting to swell from the punch he threw, so he sticks his hand into the ocean water, icing it off.

Daniel sighs.

He leans forward and presses the PLAY button on the boombox.

Celine Dion, still just as loud, belt'y and Canadian as ever, picks up right where she left off.

The ardor of the waves' constant belly dancing slows down considerably as the day nears its end, and the bright orange boat, greatly excited and seduced by the motion of the ocean throughout the course of the day, consequently calms down along with it like a strip club patron down to his last crumpled dollar bill.

Daniel can barely keep his eyes open. Although, initially, the Canadian crooning molesting his ear drums was driving him to a point of insanity, its inoffensive, warm milk-instrumentals now almost act as a lullaby. Daniel would love nothing more than to drift off, and just as he's about to do so, the song's volume lowers dramatically. Daniel opens his eyes and sees the sad-looking blue whale hunched over the boombox with the tip of his fin wrapped around the volume knob.

"Sorry," the sad-looking blue whale says. "I didn't mean to wake you. I, uh… I just wanted to say thanks. Ya know… for not letting me drown."

Daniel looks at the empty Big Mac container. Although he feels completely justified in his actions, he also feels a little bit of shame and guilt swirling around inside him, making it difficult to look the sad-looking blue whale in the eye.

"Although it was your punch that sent me sprawling overboard to begin with," the sad-looking blue whale adds bitterly.

Glancing down at the empty Big Mac container, and immediately feeling a familiar comfort as soon as he does so, Daniel says, "You should really learn how to swim."

The sad-looking blue whale falls silent for a second, reflecting on this suggestion. And then, along with a nod, he says, "Yeah... Probably."

Silence. Daniel and the sad-looking blue whale sit in the bright-orange boat like two strangers sitting at some weird, pointless bus stop in the middle of the ocean.

"Why didn't you tell me you had batteries?" Daniel finally asks.

The sad-looking blue whale shrugs.

"I didn't think of it. I have so much stuff in there it's hard to remember it all."

The sad-looking blue whale fixes his attention out over the ocean, as does Daniel. The bright blue monopoly in the sky is slowly crashing as its sole investor, the sun, sinks into the horizon, allowing its vacant realty to be overtaken by a decadent orgy of pussy pinks, autumn oranges and flamboyant lavenders that sensually grope at each other with their floating, cottony hands. And while voyeuristically peeping at this hot, cirrus-on-cirrus, slow-motion action going on above him, Daniel feels a calmness and a tranquility and every other synonym for "peacefulness" ever throw themselves into a blender in his brain and then hit the purée button. After it's "soup," the blender lifts itself and pours the smoothie over Daniel's brain, coating it, filling in all the cracks and crevices, and just like that, just as simply as that, Daniel feels happy. He feels grateful to be alive. He feels like the world is beautiful again, as if anything is possible. He feels like he could stand on the bright, glimmering highway the sun has painted across the surface of the ocean leading all the way up to the bright orange boat. He feels like he could wave goodbye to the sad-looking blue whale and, with no hard feelings, wander down its glittering pavement, letting it lead him someplace new and beautiful and kind.

"It's stunning," Daniel finds himself saying out loud.

The sad-looking blue whale rallies his downcast eyes toward the sunset. And then, after a small pause, "Meh..."

And just like that the orgy in the sky comes to an end, leaving everything to suddenly appear sperm-soaked and cold. The clouds all grow hard, unfriendly edges and their backs turn to each other as if the post-orgasmic remorse and embarrassment is settling in. And even though Daniel knows this is the exact same sunset he was looking at just seconds ago, he also knows it isn't. Because, now, he's seeing it through the sad-looking blue whale's eyes. Because that is what the sad-looking blue whales did best—force him to unwillingly see the world through their drenched and obstructed perspective.

Just when Daniel thinks he can't feel much worse, an all too familiar click hiccups out of the boombox. The music stops, Celine Dion's voice goes back to the hell from whence it came, and all to be heard are the waves gossiping amongst themselves.

"The batteries died," the sad-looking blue whale says, needlessly stating the obvious.

"Yeah…" is all Daniel can say.

"What'd you do with The Discman?" the sad-looking blue whale says in that tone of voice when someone asks a question they already know the answer to but still need to hear the answer spoken aloud to confirm and believe their own shit luck.

"I tossed it overboard," Daniel says, feeling like a shackled magician being lowered into a cold and impossible tank of water.

"Yeah…" the sad-looking blue whale says. "That's what I thought you did with it."

IT'S A HORRIBLE LIFE

IT WAS the same look that ruined his life—a projection of the slop-encrusted empty trough smack dab in the center of his soul no one could eat out of even if they wanted to. It repelled women, it kept friends from calling, it prevented co-workers from saying good morning, and now, that look, that goddamn look Daniel had been polluting his surroundings with for years, was turned back on him, flimsy and two-dimensional, yes, but still just as dejectedly potent as it'd ever been, if not more so.

Daniel couldn't look away. Considering it was all he could focus on, the mask seemed to float through the fog, headed straight for him like some sort of decapitated apparition. And just as Daniel came across a dollop of courage, just as he began formulating a plan to gather his shit and make a break for his car out the back door, another figure forced its way through the dramatic curtain of Jack the Ripper'esque fog haunting the McDonald's perimeter. Then another figure appeared. Both bulbous on top and narrow down below as they languidly waddled forward.

Daniel staggered away from the window. He had a strong hunch of what else was steadily approaching, so it didn't surprise him, it only appalled and alarmed him further, when two more sad-looking blue whales, each wearing a Daniel mask like the one before them, emerged from the fog.

The sight gut-punched the wind out of Daniel. Desperate, he turned to the empty Big Mac container for help, or, at the very least, for some kind of explanation as to what was going on. But either giving Daniel the silent treatment or, perhaps, just following the orders Daniel had originally given it, its Pac Man-shaped mandibles remained closed, and all Daniel could do was watch helplessly as the first sad-looking blue whale, like a horribly bruised hockey player slamming himself into the boards, splayed itself up against the window.

The sad-looking blue whale remained like that, frozen in place as if plastered to the glass by its own desperation to get inside. Its mask was firmly pressed into the pane and the eyes bored a hole into Daniel. Staring at himself in, what felt like, a sadistic funhouse mirror, Daniel couldn't move. Even though the pupils perforating him from the outside in weren't real, there was nothing fake about the sad and defeated hopelessness power drilling out of their faux yet potent pupils.

"That look, Daniel...

"That goddamn look..."

It was Daniel's first time seeing it the way everyone else always had—a helpless mirage of a human being looking back at him. And as if that wasn't bad enough, as if one look—*that look*—wasn't already too much to bear, just then the two other sad-looking blue whales wearing Daniel masks thwacked themselves up against the windows.

Either too dimwitted to understand the concept of glass, or just overly obsessed with getting inside, the sad-looking blue whales didn't allow something as annoyingly tangible as a transparent wall to deter their spirits. They forged ahead, bouncing off the windows and staggering back. Then, determined, they tried again, and again and again, their Daniel masks rebounding off the clear surface obstructing them each time but, nonetheless, never dissuading them and their bumbling Laurel and Hardy slapstick efforts.

The trembling under Daniel's skin intensified, and the bawling coming out of the ceiling speakers, playing like the soundtrack to some foreign film that was shot entirely underwater, got louder. Meanwhile, out in the fog, more shadowy apparitions appeared. Coming forward from every direction, dozens and dozens of sad-looking blue whales wearing Daniel masks swarmed the McDonald's. Unknowingly, Daniel had backed up against the far wall, distancing himself from the windows thronged by sad-looking blue whales. He didn't know what to do. The sad-looking blue whales wouldn't stop emerging from the womb-like grayness. Everywhere he looked he saw himself, but not just himself, the worst version of himself. He was forced to look into his own eyes, an entire brown plague of them, almond-shaped and inclement and buzzing with loss and regret.

Daniel couldn't handle it. He was shaking so badly he couldn't feel his body anymore. Weak and noodle-legged, his back slowly slid down the wall until he found himself seated on the floor. From this lower vantage point, Daniel could barely see the fog outside any longer. His view was obstructed by the hundreds of masks pressed up against the glass, all trying to squeeze past each other, all trying to get inside somehow, the commotion of which making the masks appear to bob up and down, creating the illusion of waves, as if Daniel was lost and floating in an unruly ocean of his own inherited sorrow.

Staving off seasickness on dry land, Daniel couldn't have been more relieved when, for no apparent reason, the choppiness of the peering masks quelled into a pond-like serenity. The sad-looking blue whales' heads turned and stared in the same direction, at a singular sad-looking blue whale transfixed by something—a smudge, a stain, a who knows what—on the window pane in front of it.

The crying coming out of the speakers stopped and everything became quiet and still. Confused as to what was going on, Daniel found the strength to pick himself up off the floor. He was too far away to tell what had caught the attention of the singular sad-looking blue whale, but after noticing the window's location, how it was right beside the booth Daniel had first seated himself in upon entering the dining room earlier this morning, a sense of doom prominently announced itself, dainty yet foreboding, brittle yet penetrating. Daniel's mind was jolted back in time to only a few hours ago, when he was seated in his booth with the two sad-looking blue whales glaring at him from outside. He recalls their blunt-instrument heads slamming into the window (***THUD! THUD!***), and then, even more alarmingly, the thin, horizontal crack left behind in the glass, slightly curved upwards on both ends like a sinister smile of things yet to come.

The pensive sad-looking blue whale lifted its Daniel mask, granting itself a clearer view of the smug hairline fracture its sad-looking brethren had left behind earlier in the day. Then, with the speed of a coked-out hammer, it slammed its head into the glass.

THUD!

Daniel jumped. He tried to speak out, to scream "No, stop!" but his voice was gone. All he could do was watch as the sad-looking blue whale did it again.

THUD!

And again and again.

THUD!

THUD!

Daniel turned his attention to the other sad-looking blue whales, all studiously still, all watching this violent action with curious awe. Then, among the pod, Daniel noticed one sad-looking blue whale suddenly parallel its face to window before it. It reared back its Daniel-covered head and banged it into the glass.

THUD!

The sad-looking blue whale briefly hesitated, most likely stupefied by the unexpected pain, but then thrust its head forward into the exact same spot. More sad-looking blue whales turned to watch. Even though they were all masked by that look, that goddamn look, Daniel could still see the sad-looking gears turning in their heads, unoiled and clunking but still moving nonetheless. Low-wattage light bulbs appeared over their heads only to explode into pieces a split-second later. Inspired, another sad-looking blue whale slammed its glistening blue dome of misery into the window before it. Then another a few feet away followed suit, doing the same. Sharing a mob mentality, all hell officially broke loose and every single sad-looking blue whale capable of wreaking havoc on the windows did just that—they bashed their heads into the glass, and the ones that couldn't, the ones stuck in the second, third, fourth and fifth rows of this sad-looking heavy metal concert, tried bum rushing the transparent barricades, ready to storm the metaphorical stage as they cried out into a fog that was now so dense it gave off the appearance of night.

"Oooooh, oooooh!"

"Ooooh, ooh, ooooooh!"

"Ooh, oooooooooh, ooooooh!"

"Ooooooooooooooooooooooooooh!"

Cracks began appearing everywhere in the windows, then rapidly growing and elongating like spindly erections. There was no stopping this now, Daniel knew. Things had spiraled too far out of control and showed no signs of slowing down, which, consequently, reminded Daniel of how he arrived here, how his life had completely gotten away from him, unpredictably sidewinding away over the years like a snake. Although, Daniel knew, there was still one very last thing he could control—how he expired.

My heart belongs in an empty Big Mac container buried beneath the ocean floor…

As the windows continued losing the war waged upon them by

the sad-looking blue whales, and as more rifts appeared in the glass than there were worried thoughts in Daniel's head, Daniel grabbed the empty Big Mac container and his notebook off the table. Just as he closed his eyes and tucked his head into his shoulder, as if feeling it coming, a window shattered. Glass cascaded down like crystalized rainfall, sprawling across the table, booth and floor, and coming up just short of Daniel's sneakers.

Pressing his back up against the far wall, Daniel stared at the decimated window in horror. Sad-looking blue whales were already spilling inside, and as they tried to untangle themselves from the bloated, knotted mess of each other, another window lost its strength and collapsed, making the sound of pearly white baby teeth clattering across the dining room.

No longer muffled by glass barriers, *Oooohs* freely rang out into the dining room, allowing grief-drenched decibels to heckle Daniel's ear drums. More ransacked windows shattered and fell. Toiling with their cumbersome bodies and ungainly fins, highly unsuited for such physical activity on dry land, the sad-looking blue whales struggled climbing inside. More so than anything else, they ended up being shoved forward by the impatient masses behind them and then squeezed out like big, fat globs of maritime toothpaste. The sad-looking blue whales rolled off the tabletops and plopped onto the floor, or on top of each other. Mounds formed. Some were already starting to drag themselves out of such heaps. Others, the more helpless ones pinned below, only cried and wailed as further sad-looking blue whales piled on top. In almost no time, however, despite all the confusion, despite all the flotsam and jetsam flopping around and trying to sort itself out, sad-looking blue whales began slowly rising to their bottom fins. Once upright, they gained their bearings and straightened their crooked Daniel masks that had, somehow, remained strapped to their faces. Then they turned and unmistakably stared that look at Daniel.

Face to face with himself, or, rather, himselves, Daniel's delayed instinct was to run, but not only were sad-looking blue whales now flanking him from the front of the restaurant, wafting into the dining room like a gaggle of swollen lymph nodes, like a barrage of outdated heat-seeking missiles, but back outside they had swarmed the rear exit as well. Daniel was stuck, and the sad-looking blue whales were catatonically closing in on him, ambling in his direction with outstretched fins.

But through the unending din of *Oooooh* that made Daniel's entire body writhe worse than a burn victim's, Daniel's brain delivered him a reminder, one whispered softly but profoundly, the shrewdness and quiet confidence of which making it audible and helping it rise above the rest of the noise.

My heart belongs in an empty Big Mac container buried beneath the ocean floor…

Assuredly, Daniel tucked the empty Big Mac container underneath his bearded chin and flipped through his notebook. He found where he'd jotted down his escape plan—a.k.a., his only current purpose for still living, a.k.a., the last thing on earth he had left to do—and tore the page out in one clean motion. Daniel discarded his notebook onto the floor, then held the proclamation out in front of him.

"Back! Back!"

Daniel swung the page back and forth like a torch. To his surprise, the sad-looking blue whales stopped dead in their tracks, shielding their Daniel-faces with their fins. Daniel kept swinging. Always keeping the page extended at an arm's length, he shuffled along the wall, trying to clear a path toward the back door. The sad-looking blue whales carefully resumed their advancement, inching after Daniel while still keeping a safe distance so as not to be burned by the one thing giving his maimed life a sense of purpose. Daniel took his time. Step by step, he worked his way toward the rear exit, the horde of sad-looking blue whales maintaining their sluggish pursuit, rearing back every time Daniel whooshed the page past their faces.

When he finally reached the back door, Daniel slammed the page face up against the glass, forcing the sad-looking blue whales outside to recoil. Daniel kicked open the door. He saw a gap in the startled pod of sad-looking blue whales reeling backwards and made a break for it, taking off and burrowing through while wildly helicoptering the page above his head.

Daniel ran through the heavily fogged parking lot in the direction he presumed his car to be. He literally bumped into its trunk, more relieved than he ever thought he'd be to see the damaged bumper still barely hanging on from an accident years ago.

As soon as he got inside, the fog magically lifted. Daniel threw the empty Big Mac container onto the passenger seat, stuck the keys into the ignition and slammed the clutch into reverse. He hit the gas and the car gunned backwards, feeling and hearing a few thumps as the car screeched to a stop. One unfortunate sad-looking blue whale in particular careened into the air, cartwheeled miraculously across the roof and then plopped down on the front windshield. The mangled sad-looking blue whale slowly lifted its miserable head. Its mask was still on and Daniel's own miserable eyes stared back at him.

"Oooooooooooooh!" the mangled sad-looking blue whale cried. And then—*pop!*—one of the mask strings snapped and Daniel's face slipped off to the side.

Daniel furrowed his brow. His switched gears into drive and slammed his foot on the gas, sending the sad-looking blue whale flying off the front hood as Daniel peeled out of the parking lot. He heard a tumbling behind him, the sad-looking blue whale's ragged body coming to a rolling stop, but he didn't look back. It would've hurt too much to see his McDonald's in the rearview mirror growing smaller, shrinking, and even more excruciatingly, becoming no longer his.

BAYYYBEE!!!

THE STORM ARRIVED like Mother Nature's SWAT team. The sky turned the color of poisoned seals, and the battering-ram rain pounded relentlessly against Laura's roof.

"Wow, babe. My street's already beginning to flood."

Laura was looking out the window and watching the storm. Daniel got up from his seat on the sofa and joined her. Water from The Long Island Sound had risen over the beach and was now cascading down from the top of Laura's street. The tires from both of their cars were already halfway underwater and Daniel could barely see traces of lawn, concrete or pavement left anywhere.

"Holy shit," Daniel said.

"See? I told you my street floods when there's a storm."

"I never said I didn't believe you, asshole."

Daniel leaned in and playfully bit Laura on the neck.

"Ow! Shit… Stop. I want to watch this."

"I hope my engine doesn't get flooded."

"It'll be fine. My car's always fine when this happens."

"Yeah, but your car's a Jeep, and so it's higher off the ground than mine."

"Haha. Oh, yeah," Laura said.

"Guess we're not going anywhere anytime soon."

"Definitely not. This sucks. I'm starving too, and we have nothing to eat really."

"Hey, want to order a pizza?" Daniel joked.

Laura laughed.

"The pizza delivery guy pulls up to my door in a tugboat or something," she said.

"And he only gets a tip if he's dressed like The Gordon's Fisherman."

"God, that would be such a dick thing to do."

"I didn't bring any clean clothes with me. Or comfy clothes," Daniel said, looking down at his jeans.

"That wouldn't be a problem if you would just move in here with me."

"But you never asked me to move in with you."

"What are you talking about? Yes, I did."

"No, you didn't. You've only brought it up hypothetically, like if you buy the house then maybe I move in here."

"You don't have to wait until then if you don't want to. This way the next time this happens you're not stuck in jeans."

Daniel quickly lowered his eyes so Laura couldn't see the sad hesitation bobbing up and down inside them.

"What?" she asked, sounding offended. "You don't want to live with me?"

"No, it's not that. I'm just surprised you seem to want to live with me."

"That's stupid. Where would you get a stupid idea like that?"

"Because I read your text message."

Daniel couldn't believe he said it out loud. He hadn't planned to. It just jailbroke right out of him.

"What text message?" Laura asked.

Daniel had the text message memorized. It'd been easy considering the text had been haunting him for weeks.

"'Thanks, but even though I'm not sure what I want, I don't think coffee would be a good idea right now. I don't want to hurt him.'"

"You were going through my messages?" Laura said.

"He texted you when I was looking at your acne pictures."

"And you clicked on it?"

"It was an accident."

"Oh yeah. I'm sure it was."

"Can we talk about the real problem here?"

"The real problem?"

"Yeah. That you're talking to other guys behind my back?"

"Oh my god. I'm not talking to other guys. *He* texted *me*. And I told him no, so I really don't see why you're complaining."

"Because you said you weren't sure if you wanted to be with me.

Do you have any idea how that feels? Especially when I'm in this relationship 110%?"

"Oh stop being so dramatic."

"And you stop belittling everything I say in order to evade the issue at hand. If the tables were turned here, you'd be just as hurt."

"No, Daniel. I wouldn't. Because I'm stronger and not co-dependent like you."

"Laura..."

"Daniel..." Laura mimicked in his pleading and exhausted tone of voice, pissing Daniel off, making him want to grab a coaster from off the coffee table and throw it at her, the coaster sticking into her forehead and her blue eyes widening in shock as a stream of blood trickles down her forehead and onto the tip of her nose where it drips, drips, drips off. "And by the way, you're not in this 110%. Most of the time you're so distant and far gone it's like I'm alone anyhow. Plus, you're broke, you have bad credit and you're a stock boy. You work a job that high schoolers and old retired people work. So, yes, I'm sorry but I have some doubts."

"But I'm looking for work."

"I know—"

"I'm doing what you've asked of me. And I can't help it if I get sad sometimes."

"But, once again, you do nothing about it. You just flounder in your misery and expect it to get better."

Daniel felt like his head was stuck in a quid of chewing tobacco, like he was being gummed to death. He couldn't think straight and felt exhausted. All he did know was that he wanted to leave. He could feel his body's anticipation to turn around and begin gathering his things but stopped when his brain reminded him that the storm had turned the entire neighborhood into a large dunk tank.

"You want to leave," Laura said. "I can see it. You talk about being here 110% but you want to run away when things get tough."

"But things are tough all the time."

Laura surprised Daniel when she had nothing to say to this, or, at least, nothing new left to say. And all of a sudden, she looked exhausted too.

Laura walked over to the window, lifted the blinds and peered outside.

"I didn't tie my boat up," she said to herself.

Daniel sat on the couch and put his head in his hands.

Fuck your boat... his brain managed to say, and then panicked, unsure as to whether it said that to itself or accidentally said it out loud. Daniel knew he was in the clear when Laura didn't verbally lash out at him. She just continued gazing out the window as if more concerned about her bright-orange boat than her darkly-bruised relationship.

How can you love someone so much but, essentially, just feel like enemies with them all the time? his brain wondered.

A sad-looking blue whale entered through the front door wearing goggles, arm floaties and an inner tube.

"Ooh, ooooooh, ooh!" it cried, as if needlessly announcing itself.

Daniel watched water drip off the sad-looking blue whale, feeling like the wet mess it was leaving all over the floor. Desperately, Daniel glanced up, hoping to see an enormous paper towel coming to wipe him out of existence, but, instead, all he saw was a long crack in Laura's beige-painted ceiling. He'd never noticed it before, but something about the fissure momentarily made him feel less lonely, less ill-fated, like maybe, just maybe, if he was patient enough, and if he traced his eyes along its jagged path for just long enough, that the anemic stripe in the ceiling would, eventually, split open, allowing some hidden truth to come tumbling out and land right in Daniel's lap. And then, and only then, could Daniel finally be at peace. Then, and only then, could he tolerate another minute inside this god forsaken flesh cage that was his human body.

"I started looking for a new job," Laura said. Her arms were folded, accidentally pushing up her already prominent breasts, and she was staring at the floor.

"Okay," Daniel said. "Good."

"But not around here," she admitted.

Silence. Daniel felt waylaid, like he'd just been hit in the gut by someone swinging a sack of doorknobs.

"So you're leaving?"

"I don't know. If I get something good, I guess. I can't stand my job anymore, and there's not much around here for what I want to do. At least not in the pay range I'm used to. And besides, everything in these parts is so expensive anyway."

"Wait. Why would you ask me to move in with you when you're planning on leaving?"

"I'm not planning on leaving, really."

"It sure as shit sounds it."

"Well in that case, you come with me. Would you do that? Would you come with me?"

The words that left Daniel's mouth, the words that were blabbered out by his soft, flabby heart instead of his brain, came out so fast he didn't even really have to time to reflect on the question Laura had asked.

"Of course I would," he answered.

Laura kind of nodded, looking as if she was about to cry.

"You're sure you'd want me to, though?" Daniel asked.

"I just asked, didn't I?"

"Even though you have all these doubts?"

Laura hesitated, then sat down next to Daniel. Her arms were still pushing up her chest like a freckled push-up bra and Daniel couldn't help but stare as Laura squirmed in place, trying to get settled.

"I just get nervous sometimes, and then I panic," she said once she was cozy, once her ass had found the groove in the plushness of the sofa it'd been looking for. "I know it's not fair, but I don't know… I just do it."

Amidst the turbulent silence that followed, Laura noticed a Cheez-It stuck in-between the couch cushions. She grabbed it, ogled it for a moment, then popped the Cheez-It in her mouth. But before she could so much as bite down on it, Laura grimaced, leaned forward and spit out the Cheez-It into the palm of her hand.

"Did you just try to eat an old Cheez-It you found in the couch?" Daniel asked.

"I'm hungry," Laura reasoned, "and I thought it was from when I was eating them earlier."

"But it wasn't, was it?"

"This one's, like, at least a few days old," she said, grinning with her eyes as if laughing at herself.

Looking into those grinning eyes of hers, Daniel felt like he would never break up with Laura. No matter how bad or miserable or combative things became between the two of them, he would always let her talk down to him and try to change him for the rest of his life. He was in too deep, his love for her too strong, and even though she doubted him, or, rather, his ability to be a "man," Daniel knew, despite not having the strength to leave, that he had the strength to brave her confrontational love for him and, also, love her back selflessly, flaws and all, and then maybe, one day, she'd finally see that his undying love, loyalty and support was what made him, Daniel, her boyfriend, a real man, and not necessarily whatever else she envisioned the characteristics of said real man to be.

Laura dropped the moist Cheez-It onto the coffee table. Daniel began laughing and, suppressing laughter herself, Laura leaned her head on his shoulder as the storm outside continued to wail as if trying to break into the house.

"I'll stop talking to him," Laura said after a little bit.

Daniel didn't have to ask who she was talking about.

"Thank you," was all he said.

"And I'm sorry I didn't tell you that I began looking for a new job. It's just that I saw you looking and I thought, 'Maybe I should look too. Maybe I can do better for myself too.'"

"And I'm sorry if I didn't seem more supportive about it. It just kind of felt like you were leaving me behind when you told me."

"I know, but I'm not. I do really want you to come with me. Okay?"

Daniel nodded and kissed Laura on top of the head.

"It'll be nice," she said. "Ya know, to get out of here. To go someplace new and different."

Daniel glanced at the sad-looking blue whale who had managed to find him despite the flood. It stood by the door, struggling to take off its arm floaties. Daniel imagined himself and Laura moving somewhere far away and the sad-looking blue whales never being able to find him ever again. It was a nice idea, but like most nice ideas, it didn't last long. No matter where he moved, Daniel knew the sad-looking blue whales would find him. It might not be right away, but, eventually, they'd track him down.

They always did.

It was what they were born to do.

"Baybee!" Laura fake-screamed.

"Bayyyybeeee!" Daniel fake-screamed back.

"Bayybeeee, baybeeeee!"

"Bayyyybeee, bayyybeeeeeeeeeee!"

Laura began laughing. Daniel smiled.

"Did you want to tell me something?"

"Haha, oh yeah. The storm is over. I want to go out on my boat."

"Now?"

"Yes. Right now. I miss the water. I miss being out on it."

"Okay."

"Really?"

"Yeah. Let's go."

Laura hugged Daniel and ran upstairs. Her footsteps sounded tantrummy even though they weren't. Daniel followed after her. Laura opened her second story bedroom window to reveal her bright-orange boat floating right outside it.

"The storm flooded the entire world. Everyone's dead except you and me," she said to Daniel.

"Cool," Daniel said.

Laura climbed out the window and into the boat. Daniel followed her.

"Look. Everything's gone," she said.

All to be seen were the tops of numerous houses peeking above an endless expanse of lethargic water. Poking up here, protruding there, the rooftops looked like pointy, angled tombstones in a large, navy-blue cemetery.

"Shit," Daniel said. "The world is just a giant puddle now. You think my McDonald's is okay by any chance?"

Laura smiled, as if finding Daniel's childish hope endearing. She shook her head.

"Sorry, baybee," she said.

"Bayyybeee!"

"Bayyyyybbeeeeee!"

Laura began rowing the boat. She wore a green tank top and her pale arms looked unusually toned and stronger than usual. As she rowed, Daniel could see the burgeoning of black hair underneath her armpits. He felt drawn to it, this sandpapery pit stubble of hers, like he wanted to brush his face against it in the manner of a cat showing affection.

"It's so peaceful, though," Laura said after she had maneuvered the bright-orange boat past the cemetery of rooftops.

"Yeah, and all it took was for the entire world to drown."

Laura shrugged her shoulders without ruining the fluent momentum of her rowing.

"I'm okay with it."

"Yeah, me too. I feel like I should be more freaked out or worried or something."

"Haha, me too."

"Where are we going, by the way?" Daniel asked.

"I don't know. Why? Do we have to be going somewhere?"

"No. I guess not," Daniel answered.

"Besides, there's nowhere left to go."

Laura threw the oars overboard. Daniel's ears enjoyed the thwack *sound they made as they bitch-slapped against the water.*

"My arms are tired. Use the engine," Laura said.

Daniel turned around and revved the engine, the very same engine that wasn't there just seconds ago. The boat jolted forward, the sudden jerking motion reminding Daniel of how people jump during the cheap scares of a horror movie, and then took off. Laura's hair blew back into his face and tickled his nose, making Daniel feel like he was going to sneeze.

"Sorry," Laura said, proceeding to wrangle in her hair with a sexy cowgirl prowess and then tie it in a ponytail.

"I like your hair up," Daniel said.

"Yeah?"

"Yeah. You have nice bone structure."

"I wanna bone your structure."

"Haha, nice."

Daniel and Laura smiled and hi-fived.

"We don't hi-five nearly enough," Laura observed audibly. "We should hi-five more."

"I'll hi-five you if you take your shirt off."

"Okay," Laura agreed.

Laura slid her green tank top off over her head in one fluent motion and threw it overboard.

"I didn't expect you to throw your shirt overboard," Daniel said, staring at Laura's breasts that were gleefully jiggling as the bright-orange boat cruised across this newly formed water world.

"You're such a boy," Laura said in regards to Daniel's almond brown eyes groping her chest.

"Normally when you say that, you say it like it's a bad thing, but right then you said it like it was a good thing."

"You being a boy?"

Daniel nodded. Laura stared at him, thinking, or, perhaps, plotting something.

"What?" Daniel asked.

"Remember when we did coke off your books?"

"Yeah."

"Remember when I went upstairs and put on a dress?"

"Uh huh."

"Well, I want to do that again. I want to look pretty," she said. "I want to feel *pretty."*

"Okay," Daniel said.

He and Laura hi-fived. Laura stood up and went behind a changing screen propped up in the back of her tiny, bright-orange boat. Daniel watched as her shorts were draped over its side. Then her panties. Her period panties, Daniel noticed—the skin-toned granny panties that looked like they had a raspberry jam stain on the crotch.

A moment later, Laura appeared back from behind the changing screen. She wore a navy-blue dress covered in sunflowers and her blonde hair was even blonder and tied up in pigtails. It was Laura, yes, but a different version of Laura—four-feet tall and with two of her front teeth missing.

Laura as a little girl.

Laura sat back down across from Daniel.

"There. I feel pretty now," she said. "And much more comfortable."

"You look adorable," Daniel said.

"Thank you, bayyybe."

"Bayyybeee!"

"Look. Look how far out we are. I told you the horizon wasn't fake," Laura said, looking at the horizon.

Daniel looked at the horizon along with Laura. The clouds roamed by like a magnificent herd of marshmallow animals with no particular place to go.

"We must be pretty far out. I haven't seen any house tops in a while," Daniel said.

"We're probably out in the ocean by now. Cut the engine."

Daniel turned the engine off and the boat came to a puttering stop. Laura wrinkled her nose, closed her eyes and tilted her head back, soaking in the sun. Her greasy hair glistened like it was spun in a Rumpelstiltskin sweatshop.

"I missed this," she said.

"It is really nice out here. Plus, it will be hard for any sad-looking blue whales to find me. They can't swim, ya know."

Laura began picking at a small scab on her knee.

"How come you never talk about them?" she asked.

Daniel kind of shrugged.

"They're not much fun to talk about."

"Yeah, but you've never talked to me about them, like, at all."

"Sometimes you're not an easy person to talk to," Daniel surprised himself by saying out loud. Perhaps because of the very unthreatening costume Laura was suddenly adorned in. Regardless, Laura seemed to wilt in front of him.

"I wish I knew you when you were little," she came out with.

"Me too. We would've been best friends."

"Aren't we best friends now?"

"Yeah. I'm just saying, I guess. Plus, it would've been nice to know you before I met them. I wish you could've seen me like that. Ya know, the way I used to be."

Laura examined her dress and straightened it with her hands.

"I get it. I think I understand why you cling onto all of that stuff. Espe-

cially now," Laura said and playfully flapped the skirt of her dress a little, indicating her current elementary state.

"All of what stuff?"

"I dunno. Your innocence, I guess."

"Oh..."

"I'm sorry they took it away from you when you were so young. Ya know, for whatever it's worth."

"Thanks."

"But maybe that's why you cling onto it? Maybe that's why you're having trouble maturing and becoming a real adult? Because you feel robbed."

Daniel didn't know what to say. He didn't want to say anything. He just wanted to color on the floor of his childhood bedroom. He wanted to draw on those pieces of cardboard that his dad would bring home from the library where he worked. Large, TV tray-sized pieces of cardboard. Daniel loved those. He missed decorating them, covering each and every piece with cartoons and little stories and video game cheat codes. He missed the way he kept them in the small narrow space behind the TV cabinet and how he'd pull one out and put his food on it whenever he wanted to sit on the floor in front of the TV and eat dinner. And then, after they'd gotten too old and flimsy, Daniel would throw them out and ask his dad for some more cardboard from work. "I'll see what I can find," his dad would always say, and then, in two to three days, there he was, coming home through the front door with a fresh stack of cardboard pieces tucked under his arm.

Daniel looked up and saw Laura drawing, what appeared to be, a large snake on a piece of cardboard suddenly splayed across her lap.

"Cool snake," Daniel commented, craning his head in order to try and see her drawing right side up.

"It's not a snake."

Laura kept drawing. She was so focused she was biting her bottom lip. Daniel hoped that if he and Laura ever had a little girl that their little girl would do that when she colored, too, just like her mom.

"Then what is it?" Daniel asked.

"It's my cousin's cock," Laura answered flatly.

Daniel's eyes widened. There was something very jarring and disconcerting about hearing a little girl say the word "cock," costume or no costume.

"Really, though. This is how big it is," Laura said. "This is, like, to scale."

Laura stopped coloring and stared down at her drawing sadly.

"He's not going to make it," she said. "The sad-looking blue whales—they're going to get him."

"You don't know that. Maybe they won't," Daniel lied.

Laura frowned and threw the cardboard and crayon overboard.

"No one ever has a chance. We all lose that something special we used to have. That scintilla of youth. That luminous emptiness that gets bludgeoned out of us. You're not the only one, Daniel."

Laura stood up.

"I'm going to change. You can't stay like this too long. You can only visit occasionally. Or else you turn into you."

"Into me?"

"Well, not you specifically. But like you, I guess I should say. An adult-child."

Daniel internally winced as Laura got up and went behind the changing screen. She returned seconds later, her enormous breasts hanging off of her chest like pineapple-sized Christmas ornaments, as if making her transformation back from little girl to woman 110% clear, and sat down across from Daniel.

"I stopped taking my medicine again recently," she admitted.

"I know," Daniel said after a pause.

"How do you know?"

Daniel shrugged.

"I can just tell."

Laura hesitated, and then, nervously, she asked, "Do you really think we're good for each other?"

High above, thunder clapped and lightning struck like a gloomy overture. Daniel and Laura both tilted their heads back and stared up at the unfriendly sky.

"I don't care if we're good for each other or not," Daniel said. "I love you."

GREASY, CARDBOARD HEART-COFFIN

AS IF GOING through some elegant form of puberty, the night sky is pockmarked all across its crude oil-face with shimmering acne. The moon, levitating regally as if ruler of all these celestial whiteheads bulging big and bright, shines with a beautiful but slick and greasy glow, so throbbingly full of itself it looks ready to pop at the hands of its own vanity any second now.

Staring up at the moon, Daniel's thoughts drift, carefully, gropingly, to Laura, to how he and she used to walk down the beach by her house at night, holding hands and looking at the stars.

Daniel reflects back on how clear and numerous the stars always were those nights, and how, despite his best mental efforts, he could only vaguely remember the last time he had seen stars so plentiful and bright prior to those walks with Laura. It was some snippet of memory from back when he was a kid, a flash of him lying on wet grass somewhere and staring up at the sky. A time, he would've guessed, a few years before he began living under the saturated stare of the sad-looking blue whales.

The stars were extraordinarily beautiful at that moment, Daniel remembers. Even as a child he thought so, although not with the one-dimensional appreciation of beauty most young children have. His appreciation then, in that specific moment, in that snippet of prepubescent time, was more mature. Yes, he appreciated the pretty way they shone and sparkled ("Ooooh! Ahhhhh!"), but the most beautiful thing about the stars to Daniel was how many there were, and how far away they were. The way their magnificent number and scale made

Daniel realize how small his childish world was, the way the stars made him feel so small and insignificant. And many years later, admiring those same stars with Laura, and admiring those same stars here and now while sitting across from that tyrannical eyesore of blue gloom, the sad-looking blue whale, Daniel again feels small and insignificant. But it's a welcomed feeling. One he's more than okay with because, Daniel realizes (or has he always realized it and only now is he giving it proper thought and consideration after hearing something the sad-looking blue whale said earlier on in the day), that only when you feel small and insignificant can you ever feel the true size of the universe, only then can you feel how big and enormous it is, and only after acknowledging its massively impressive scale can you feel special and lucky enough to be a part of something so vast and incredible. And then, feeling that inclusion, feeling that gracious awe and wonder of being a part of something so big, can you truly feel alive, can you learn to live with the vast nothingness, or the never-ending emptiness of simply existing.

"I wish I had been braver," Daniel finds himself saying. "Or I dunno… Stronger."

"Or maybe both," he adds.

"What do you mean?" the sad-looking blue whale asks.

Daniel pauses, collecting his thoughts and arranging them as carefully as a young boy arranges small, plastic green army men, prepping for a battle where, imaginary or not, the stakes still feel high, like life or death.

"There's this part of me that wishes I had just kept it all to myself," Daniel finally says. "Like every creative thing I've ever done. I wish I hoarded it all away instead of sharing it with people. Because after I did, it always became something else. Like I was seeking their approval. Like I always began making something for myself, and always for different reasons—because I was bored, because I was inspired, because I couldn't stand reality any longer, because there was something inside of me I just needed to get out or work through, because there was nothing else to do—but then, after I was finished, I would always find ways to share whatever I'd done. These personal ideas of mine, I'd want people to like them even though I'd tell myself it didn't matter if they did like them or not. But deep down, it always did matter. I let it matter because I didn't know how else to reach out or connect with people. I didn't know how to feel included in the world. So that was my way—sharing those things I'd created. But most of the time they were never well received, or acknowledged, and because I didn't know how to do otherwise, I let everyone's disapproval spoil my feelings towards all those things I'd made. I felt like when they rejected my creativity they were rejecting me and my attempts to reach out and connect with the world and feel human. Art always starts off as this self-serving purpose but then, as soon as you share it, it transforms. It becomes a cry for attention. Or some weird kind of attempt at an emotional connection you don't know how to make any other way. And I hate myself for doing it. For corrupting so many beautiful and private thoughts because of this loneliness-induced, lifelong brain fart that kept me from remembering that the reward was in doing it and not if, or how much, people liked it. I wish I had been more secure in myself to hoard it all away. And who knows? Maybe all those unspoiled poems, short stories, unfinished novels and drawings would've been enough to keep me company and keep me feeling full and then I wouldn't have spent my entire life feeling so goddamn lonely and rejected and left out. Maybe that would've been enough when nothing else ever was. Maybe then I would've seen that I still belonged here."

He pauses. And then, "I think the more you try to fit in the further you just drift away from yourself and your humanity."

Daniel sighs. Without even moving, and despite the sudden nighttime coolness, he feels the days' worth of sunburn on his forehead and neck and all over the rest of his body. He feels the dryness in his throat. He's thirsty. So goddamn thirsty. Surrounded by millions of tons of water and unable to drink a drop of it.

Daniel leans forward and presses the play button on the boombox only for it to make the same, dull, lifeless click.

"What are we going to do now?" he asks.

At a loss, the sad-looking blue whale shrugs. Daniel can't help it. Suddenly, surprisingly, he feels sorry for the sad-looking blue whale. Guilty even, because, in a way, he knows he did this to the sad-looking blue whale, that it's somewhat his fault for their current situation. And even though his hand still kind of hurts from punching the sad-looking blue whale in the face, even though he was that furious at him not long ago, Daniel can't stand seeing him so hopeless and deflated. Not to mention there's just something about being so close to the end of his life, whether it be the sad-looking blue whales finding him and burying his heart, or whether it be the two of them remaining undiscovered and dying of thirst, that makes Daniel want to be at peace with what little time he has left, even if that means being kind and considerate to a sad-looking blue whale.

"What about your novel?" Daniel says.

"My novel?"

"Yeah. The children's fiction novel you told me about."

"What about it?" he asks.

Daniel pauses, wishing the sad-looking blue whale would've taken the hint and began telling it instead of forcing Daniel to actually make the request out loud, a small feat he finds difficult to do despite wanting to make amends.

"Read it to me," Daniel musters out.

The sad-looking blue whale's eyes light up as much as a pair of black eyes underneath a night sky can light up.

"Really?"

"Sure. You said you had a copy, right?"

"Yeah. Okay. One sec..."

The sad-looking blue whale unzips his fanny pack, and after the typical amount of rummaging around inside, he pulls out the manuscript, as well as a lighter, which he flips on and uses to illuminate the first page.

"It's called *The Happy-Looking Blue Whale,*" the sad-looking blue whale says.

Once there was a boy.

A very sad-looking boy who had a hole in his chest where his heart should've been. And the boy looked very sad-looking not just some of the time but all of the time because he didn't know how to fix the hole in his chest where his heart should've been. And not only did the sad-looking boy not know how to fix the hole in his chest where his heart should've been, but his mom didn't know how to fix it either. Or his dad. Or his brother or sister. Or his doctors. Or his pet dog, Sniffles. Or his pet cat, Mittens. Or even his pet goldfish, Goldy, who, for a goldfish, seemed to possess a far superior intellect than most regular goldfish and would follow the sad-looking boy's finger whenever he traced it up and down the glass of Goldy's fishbowl. But not even having such a smart and special goldfish was enough to fix the hole in his chest. And so, too sad-looking to do much else, the sad-looking boy spent the majority of his time standing on the shore of his family's beach house, alone, staring out over the dreary ocean and the broken-looking sky until one day when a happy-looking blue whale walked out of the water and approached him.

"Hi," the happy-looking blue whale said to the sad-looking boy.

"Hi," the sad-looking boy said to the happy-looking blue whale.

"You have a hole in your chest where your heart should be," the happy-looking blue whale said.

"I know," the sad-looking boy replied.

"Does it hurt?"

"Not in the way you'd expect it to," the sad-looking boy said. And then, after diverting his attention to the sky above, "The sky, does it look broken to you? Or I don't know... Fake?"

"No," the happy-looking blue whale said. "It looks very real. Not to mention bright and blue and happy, and kind of like it's singing!"

"Oh..." the sad-looking boy said.

"The hole in your chest," the happy-looking blue whale said. "Why don't you fix it?"

"I don't know how," the sad-looking boy replied with a shrug.

"Oh..." the happy-looking blue whale said.

"Maybe you could help me?" the sad-looking boy asked.

The happy-looking blue whale smiled and, looking extra happy, he said, "I can try. I do know a lot of great and powerful sea creatures. Here. Hop on."

The happy-looking blue whale crouched down and the sad-looking boy climbed onto his back.

"Here, take this and put it over your nose and mouth so you can breathe underwater," the happy-looking blue whale said and handed the sad-looking boy a magical sea shell.

The sad-looking boy placed the magical seashell over his nose and mouth and the happy-looking blue whale walked into the water with the sad-looking boy clinging tightly to his back.

The happy-looking blue whale swam to an underwater shark kingdom. Inside the castle, the sad-looking boy and the happy-looking blue whale were brought to The Shark King who was seated on top of an enormous pile of gold coins he was in the middle of counting.

"10,001, 10,002, 10,003..." The Shark King was saying to himself.

"Excuse us, your majesty," the happy-looking blue whale said.

"What? Oh yes, hello. What do you want?" The Shark King said without looking up at his visitors.

"We were wondering if you could help us,"

"...10,002? ...10,005? Um... Uh... Oh, darn it! You made me lose count!"

"I'm sorry, your majesty," the happy-looking blue whale said.

The Shark King glanced at the sad-looking boy and began counting his gold coins again.

"You do know you have a hole in your chest, don't you, young human? 1... 2... 3..."

"I know, your majesty."

"Actually, we were wondering if that's something you could help us with. Considering you're such a wealthy king, maybe there's a way you could help him fill the hole in his chest?"

"7... 8... Fill the hole? Well of course I could fill the hole in his chest. Look at all of this" he said and motioned down to the enormous pile of gold coins he sat on. "Gold coins, money, wealth, there's nothing they can't fix! Here..."

The Shark King swam down to the sad-looking boy and handed him a large finful of gold coins. The sad-looking boy put the gold coins in the hole in his chest where his heart should've been but the gold coins spilled out. He tried again and again, but no matter what, the gold coins kept falling out of the hole in his chest where his heart should've been.

"It's hopeless," The Shark King said. "If gold coins won't fill the hole in your chest where your heart should be then nothing ever will!"

Then he swam back up to the top of his enormous pile of gold coins and resumed counting.

The happy-looking blue whale, not looking as happy as before, consolingly put his fin on the sad-looking boy's shoulder.

"Come on," he said. And the sad-looking boy climbed onto the happy-looking blue whale's back and he swam off.

Next, the happy-looking blue whale swam the sad-looking boy to the mermaid kingdom.

"Excuse me, your highness," the happy-looking blue whale said to The Mermaid Queen.

The Mermaid Queen was sitting on her throne and looking into a very elegant hand mirror as she applied bright red lipstick. At the sound of the happy-looking blue whale's voice, she glanced away from her mirror, but only for a split second to see who had spoken to her, and then immediately looked back at her reflection.

"Oh, I didn't even see you there," The Mermaid Queen said. "Were you waiting long?"

"No, not at all."

"Then what is it? What do you want?" she asked, still carefully applying lip stick even as she spoke.

"Well, I'm sorry to bother you, but considering you're such a great and beautiful queen, I was wondering if it wouldn't be too much trouble for you to help my friend here," the happy-looking blue whale said.

"What friend?" The Mermaid Queen asked and then moved on to applying eyeliner

"My friend right here, of course."

The happy-looking blue whale nudged the sad-looking boy and the sad-looking boy gave a sad-looking, little wave to The Mermaid Queen.

"Where? I still can't see him," she said without looking away from her mirror.

"Your highness, I think perhaps maybe you need to look away from your mirror in order to see him," the happy-looking blue whale said.

"Well that certainly isn't going to happen again," she replied. "So, get on with it already. What is it? What does he want?"

"Well, you see, your highness, my friend has a hole in his chest where his heart should be, and we were hoping you knew how to fix it somehow."

"Of course I know how to fix it. Don't be silly. Here, use these," she said and, without looking away from her mirror, The Mermaid Queen threw lipstick and eyeliner and eye shadow and foundation (all waterproof of course) down to the happy-looking blue whale. "Apply those to his face, AND to the hole in his chest, and he will be beautiful and he will never feel empty or sad again."

The happy-looking blue whale did the best he could and applied the makeup to the sad-looking boy's face, as well as the hole in his chest where his heart should've been.

"Well?" the happy-looking blue whale asked after he was done.

The sad-looking boy, made-up and glamorous and ready for his close up, only looked at the happy-looking blue whale and gave a little, defeated shrug.

"Nothing…" he said. "I feel the same."

The happy-looking blue whale frowned a little.

"If being beautiful doesn't fix the hole in your chest where your heart should be then nothing will," The Mermaid Queen said, who was now brushing her hair as she gazed into her mirror.

"Thank you for your time, your highness," the happy-looking blue whale who was suddenly looking not-so-happy said, and then the sad-looking boy climbed onto his back and they were off.

"I'm beginning to feel hopelessly broken," the sad-looking boy said.

"Don't worry," the less than happy-looking blue whale said. "I know of one more place. I should've just taken you here to begin with. THIS king will know what to do."

The less than happy-looking blue whale swam the sad-looking boy to the kingdom he came from and lived in; the happy-looking whale kingdom.

The Happy-Looking Blue Whale King was much larger than The Shark King and The Mermaid Queen. He was at least the size of the Titanic, and, considering no throne on the planet would've been big enough for him, he just leisurely floated above his kingdom while shoveling finfuls of krill into his enormous and cavernous mouth.

"Your majesty," the less than happy-looking blue whale greeted his king.

"Hello, my subject," The Happy-Looking Blue Whale King said as he chomped up and down on a disgusting mouthful of krill. "How can I help you?"

"It's my friend. He has a hole in his chest where his heart should be and we were wondering, considering you are such a large and powerful leader, if you could fix it somehow?"

"I am quite large and powerful, aren't I?" The Happy-Looking Blue Whale King said proudly.

The less than happy-looking blue whale gave the sad-looking boy a little nudge.

"Oh... Uh, yes you are, your majesty," the sad-looking boy said.

"I got that way by eating krill all day long," The Happy-Looking Blue Whale King said.

"Now let me see... Let me see..." he continued, examining the sad-looking boy. "Is that it right there? That tiny hole in your chest? Is that all you need fixed?"

"Yes, your majesty," the sad-looking boy said.

The Happy-Looking Blue Whale King gave a great, big laugh. Krill fell out of his mouth and rained down onto the less than happy-looking blue whale and the sad-looking boy.

"My dear boy, I can fix that easily!"

"Really?" the sad-looking boy said excitedly.

"Of course," The Happy-Looking Blue Whale King said. "Easiest thing in the world. Take a finful of krill and shovel it into the hole in your chest where your heart should be."

The sad-looking boy's spirits sagged. He didn't think krill was going to work but he gave it a try and followed The Happy-Looking Blue Whale King's instructions anyway. Just as he feared though, the krill simply spilled out of the hole in his chest.

"No, not like that!" The Happy-Looking Blue Whale King screamed. "More! Morrrrrre!!! You need to keep doing it! Shovel more and more in! And never stop," he said and shoveled an enormous finful of krill into his own mouth, showing the sad-looking boy how to do it.

"See?" he said as more krill fell from his mouth. "Like that!"

The sad-looking boy tried over and over, cramming krill into the hole in his chest where his heart should've been as fast as he could, but it never stayed, and when it did, it was only momentarily, and he never truly felt full either, or like the hole had been fixed.

"Hmm..." The Happy-Looking Blue Whale King said when he noticed the sad-looking boy having trouble. "More and more krill usually works for me."

The sad-looking boy put his face into his hands and began crying.

"Come on..." the now completely sad-looking blue whale said. "Let me take you home."

The sad-looking blue whale swam the sad-looking boy back to the beach. After arriving, they sat in the sand together side by side. The sad-looking blue whale expected the sad-looking boy to burst into tears again, but he didn't.

"I guess nothing will ever fill the hole in my chest where my heart should be," the sad-looking boy said.

"I'm sorry I couldn't help you," the sad-looking blue whale replied, sounding genuinely heart broken.

The sad-looking boy looked up at the sky. He stared at it and stared at it until, eventually, unlike earlier in the day, it didn't seem to look broken, or fake.

It almost looked blue.

It almost even looked happy.

The sad-looking blue whale put his fin around the sad-looking boy's shoulders and they sat together in silence, watching the waves go in and out, in and out, in and out.

Somewhere, off in the distance, a lonely seagull made a lonely sound.

"That's it?" Daniel asks.

The lighter goes out and the sad-looking blue whale crams it and the manuscript back inside his fanny pack.

"That's really how it ends?" Daniel presses on.

"Why?" the sad-looking blue whale asks. "Is it bad?"

"It's not bad... It's just..." And then Daniel trails off.

"What?" the sad-looking blue whale demands.

"The ending. You just might want to think about changing the ending. That's all."

"Why?"

"Because," Daniel says, getting upset, either at the sad-looking blue whale for peppering him with incessant one-word questions or at himself for ever thinking that a story written by a sad-looking blue whale could've ever been anything other than 110% "sad-looking."

"It's sad," Daniel continues. "It's so goddamn sad. It's *too* goddamn sad."

The sad-looking blue whale makes a face. Not mad, or confused. More so contemplative, like he's trying to understand where Daniel's coming from.

"How?" the sad-looking blue whale asks.

"How?" Daniel says, incredulous. "Because this little boy is left with a hole in his chest that nothing can ever fill. How is that not sad? How is that not the saddest fucking thing ever?"

The sad-looking blue whale pauses, contemplates, and then answers, "Because. He learns a lesson that most human adults never do. A lesson most human adults don't ever seem to be aware of. It's like what we were talking about before. What could ever fill the staggering, unending emptiness of simply being alive?"

"Nothing," Daniel answers, simply, quickly.

"Yeah," the sad-looking blue whale says. "And that's what the boy learns. There's not enough of anything that will ever fill any of us. He's beginning to realize you don't try to fill the emptiness. That, instead, you live with it. Or not even with it. In it. You learn to live in the emptiness."

Daniel scoffs.

"That's the dumbest thing I've ever heard. How could anyone ever be happy like that?"

"Because. Emptiness isn't a bad thing. Emptiness is the just space that takes over once you stop trying to distract yourself. Once you stop eating krill, or watching *Titanic*, or doing whatever else, emptiness is what moves in right after.

"Emptiness *is*," the sad-looking blue whale adds.

"Is what?" Daniel asks, thinking the sad-looking blue whale just hasn't finished his thought.

"No. Like, it *is*. Emptiness, I mean. Emptiness is the natural state of existence, the natural state of being.

"Emptiness *IS*," the sad-looking blue whale emphasizes like a blue-in-the-face Maharishi.

Despite making no effort to, Daniel can't wrap his head around what the sad-looking blue whale is sermonizing. There's also the large stubborn part of him that doesn't want to understand and, therefore, possibly risk agreeing with a sad-looking blue whale (whose kind are his natural born enemies and so what could he ever learn from them anyway?). And so, after the long day he's had—the longest of his life—Daniel mentally storms out in the middle of the conversation.

And that's when he hears it. The worst, most damning sound imaginable.

Thunder.

Daniel and the sad-looking blue whale look up at the sky. Just as Daniel hopes that the worst won't happen, that the thunder is further away than it sounds, a torrential downpour begins cascading onto his face. The fast, pummeling drops are cool and refreshing, but as Daniel looks down at the floor of the boat, as he watches the rain water pool around his sneakers, he also quickly realizes this rain is lethal.

"You don't happen to have a lifeboat in that fanny pack of yours, do you?" Daniel screams over the sound of the rain.

The sad-looking blue whale shakes his head.

"But I might have something else…" he answers.

The wooden paneling is large and intricately carved, like whatever it used to be a part of was, most likely, very elegant. Daniel lies on it belly down. The sad-looking blue whale floats in the water beside it, clinging to its side, keeping himself afloat.

Daniel watched in awe when the sad-looking blue whale took the door-sized piece of wooden paneling out of his fanny pack. The way he hoisted it above his head with surprising, brute-like strength, and then tossed it overboard. Because Daniel knew how to swim, the sad-looking blue whale instructed him to go first. Daniel grabbed the empty Big Mac container, abandoned ship and swam the short distance to the wooden paneling that he carefully slithered onto.

The sad-looking blue whale hopped out next. Daniel extended his arm and grabbed the sad-looking blue whale's fin to keep him from sinking under, but when he tried to hoist the sad-looking blue whale onto the paneling alongside him, the large wooden piece began tilting back and submerging. The sad-looking blue whale rolled off seconds before the paneling capsized and held onto its side where he floats now, watching the bright-orange boat that's so flooded with rain water it's barely even visible anymore.

Daniel can't believe how fast the bright-orange boat filled up. He watches it sink with mixed emotions. The bright-orange boat was Laura's. She was going to take him out on it when summer arrived. And even while he's stranded out here in the ocean, caught in a downpour, helplessly floating on some ornate hunk of wood, something about losing the bright-orange boat still manages to hurt despite

Daniel having more serious matters to worry about. It pains him to watch his last connection to Laura slowly sink out of sight. It makes their break up feel final, even though it has been for months now.

The rain is so heavy, Daniel doesn't even see the exact moment when the overtly orange dinghy that brought them this far into the ocean completely, and unceremoniously, submerges out of sight.

"It's really over now," Daniel finds himself saying out loud, staring at the spot in the ocean where Laura's bright-orange boat was floating just seconds ago.

The sad-looking blue whale reaches underwater with one fin, and a second later, his fanny pack flops onto the wooden paneling. Daniel tucks the empty Big Mac container underneath his chin and holds onto the sad-looking blue whale as he begins rummaging around inside his fanny pack. Eventually, he takes out a picture—Laura's picture. The one Daniel accidentally waterlogged and then discarded in the ocean. The sad-looking blue whale holds it out for Daniel to take. Daniel stares at Laura's bleached, wrinkled face. Somehow, she still looks beautiful.

"Thank you," Daniel says to the sad-looking blue whale, touched.

He takes the picture and gives it a pained and longing look before sliding it in his pants pocket. Then he shimmies to the side of the wooden paneling, making room, and holds out his hand.

"Come on."

The sad-looking blue whale shakes his head.

"Too much weight," he explains.

"What else do you have in there?" Daniel asks and motions with his head to the sad-looking blue whale's fanny pack lying on the wooden paneling like a pregnant puddle.

"That I could float on? Nothing I know of."

"Well… then we'll take turns."

The sad-looking blue whale shakes his head again.

"Why not?"

The sad-looking blue whale hesitates.

"You're not The Chosen One," he says.

"What?"

"You're not The Chosen One," he says a little louder. "There is no Chosen One. I made it all up."

Daniel's eyes flatline as they stare at the sad-looking blue whale. He's too stunned to say anything, too confused to comment.

"You were doubting yourself earlier. You weren't sure if you wanted to go through with this or not. And I'm sorry, but I couldn't risk you changing your mind. I'm in trouble. I'm in a *lot* of trouble. It's the elders back home. They were going to send other sad-looking blue whales to come and arrest me. They were going to imprison me because I couldn't do it anymore, because I couldn't tolerate the idea of making just one more person so sad. And then I met you. And you were already so sad. You were already willing to give it all up anyway, so I took advantage of that. I hoped if I could bring you home myself and present you and your sad-looking heart as a sacrifice that the elders would forgive me. Or at least go easier on me."

"There's no Chosen One…" Daniel mutters.

"No," the sad-looking blue whale says.

"So what am I?"

The sad-looking blue whale either shrugs or shivers, Daniel isn't sure.

"Why do you have to be anything other than just what you are?" the sad-looking blue whale answers.

Some part of Daniel's brain knows this is a valid question but he's too drenched, exhausted and devastated to give it any real thought.

"But I see you guys all the time," he comes out with. "All the time, every day."

Very flatly, the sad-looking blue whale replies, "Do you really think you're sadder than everyone else? Do you really think you suffer *more* than everyone else?"

In a defiant act even colder than the ocean itself, Daniel shoves the sad-looking blue whale's fanny pack into the water and shimmies back into the center of the wooden paneling, claiming his territory while also instructing the sad-looking blue whale that he's no longer welcome on it.

"I'm sorry," Daniel barely hears the sad-looking blue whale say through the assault rifle-rain.

Daniel rests his head on the wooden paneling with the empty Big Mac container only inches from his face. It's so drenched and rain-battered its lid looks like the roof of a ramshackle house that's about to cave in.

As Daniel closes his eyes, hoping that, somehow, he'll fall asleep, he can't help but wonder if he'll ever open them again or if these are his final moments on earth. And while these types of thoughts may be terrifying enough to keep most people on the planet up all night, Daniel finds them so soothing, so lush and comforting, he drifts right off to sleep.

It's still dark out when Daniel wakes up. The rain has calmed to a drizzle and the wind gently sashays around him. The wooden paneling is shaking, which Daniel first attributes to the mild ocean waves, but only after glancing at the sad-looking blue whale does Daniel understand the source of its vibrations.

The sad-looking blue whale has turned a new frostbitten shade of blue and is shivering in the water. To his own surprise, Daniel feels a panic rise up into his throat. He can't ignore the genuine concern he feels for the sad-looking blue whale, not to mention the corresponding guilt that tags along with it for letting him stay in the frigid ocean water this whole time.

"Hey…" Daniel says, shaking the sad-looking blue whale, trying to get his attention.

The sad-looking blue whale slowly swivels his head like a rusted weather vane, and when his eyes finally meet Daniel's, they look confused, like he has no idea who Daniel is.

"Come on," Daniel says. "We're trading spots."

Before Daniel can slither into the water, the sad-looking blue whale pries one of his fins off the wooden paneling and, with a surprising quickness, wraps it around Daniel's wrist. His fin is so cold Daniel almost yelps.

"You must do me this honor," the sad-looking blue whale says. "Promise me you will survive. That you will never give up. No matter what happens, no matter how hopeless, promise me now, and never let go of that promise."

Daniel feels his breath leave him. He can't believe his ears. He can't believe that a creature who's stolen so much life from him just spoke to him from his heart and told him to strive for that very same life, to fight for it, to not give up on it, as if life is, after all, something too precious to be squandered. To hear all of that at once is too much for Daniel, and a single tear streaks down his cheek.

"I promise—"

Daniel's voice gives out. It quivers and fades when a small, fluttering light catches his eye. The light disappears as soon as Daniel swerves his head in its direction, looking for it, but then reappears seconds later, closer than it was just seconds ago. The lightning bug flutters over to Daniel and alights on the hairy helipad of his forearm.

Daniel stares at it, this little winged light bulb, and then, correspondingly, feels an equally small light bulb go off in the dimmed cinema catacomb-archives of his mind.

"Wait… Were you just quoting *Titanic*?" Daniel asks.

Daniel turns and looks at the sad-looking blue whale. His eyes are open, but, essentially, they're closed. His grip on Daniel's wrist has loosened and the wooden paneling has stopped shaking. The sad-looking blue whale isn't there anymore. He's gone somewhere far away, walking up the Titanic grand staircase where Leonardo DiCaprio and Kate Winslet are both waiting for him, greeting him with casually outstretched hands and "We've been expecting you" smiles.

Daniel feels a weird numbness prickling the entirety of his body, a numbness, he knows, that has nothing to do with the drizzling rain or freezing cold, but rather the numbness of feeling too many things at once. The numbness of a complete emotional overload, his mind short circuiting and his body crashing all at once.

Daniel looks at the lightning bug blinking on his forearm in, what looks like, S.O.S. Morse code. Then he looks at the sad-looking blue whale's fin still clinging onto his wrist. Daniel extends his arm out over the water and gently shakes it. The sad-looking blue whale's fin slides off and his rigid, mannequin-body slowly sinks underwater and out of sight.

Daniel glances back at the lightning bug on his forearm. He raises his now free hand high above his head and brings it down on the lightning bug as hard as he can, stinging the hell out of his sunburned wrist but, at least momentarily, forcing himself to feel something again.

Daniel leaves his hand in place for a moment before lifting it. Through the rain and drizzle, he's just able to see a little black smudge on his palm, which he wipes off on the wooden paneling.

Daniel lays his head back down next to the empty Big Mac container and closes his eyes.

He goes right back to feeling absolutely nothing at all.

IT'S A HORRIBLE LIFE

DANIEL DIDN'T MAKE a conscious decision to drive to the beach by Laura's house. It was just where he ended up, the same way a blackout drunk arrives back home without any recollection as to how they got there until they look outside the next morning and see their car parked across the lawn. Daniel blinked and there he was, standing barefoot in a dune, his socks and sneakers off to the side and his hands holding onto the empty Big Mac container.

It was most likely some hushed, romantic reverie that had brought him back to these familiar sands, that or a desperate last hope to see Laura, to bump into her going for a walk on the beach just as they used to do together so often. But Laura was nowhere to be found. She was most likely at home only a few blocks away, Daniel figured, packing for her new life in Miami, and then Sweden.

The only sign of life anywhere to be seen was a sad-looking blue whale. The sad-looking blue whale wore a fanny pack and held a cinder block as it stood all alone on the shore, staring off into the horizon. The cinder block had a rope tied around it and the other end of the rope was dramatically tied around the sad-looking blue whale's bottom fins.

Daniel had seen thousands and thousands of sad-looking blue whales in his lifetime, but he'd never seen one so hopelessly lost to the point where it appeared more than ready to take its own life. Daniel never even knew that sad-looking blue whales were capable of taking such drastic measures against themselves, or that they'd possibly ever dream of doing so. He thought they reveled in that sadness, that sadness that made him want to turn and run in the opposite direction whenever one approached. But unlike all of the other sad-looking blue whales Daniel had ever met, something about this sad-looking blue whale in particular made it seem approachable.

Probably the cinder block… Daniel's brain reasoned.

Or the fanny pack…

But most likely the cinder block…

Daniel figured his brain was right. After all, he was holding onto his own metaphorical cinder block. It wasn't as big or as heavy as the sad-looking blue whale's, but it—the empty Big Mac container—still symbolized the same type of ending, an ending they both planned on taking control over instead of letting it take control of them.

So Daniel couldn't believe it, especially after the riot in McDonald's he just escaped from, when he found himself trudging through the sand toward the sad-looking blue whale, stopping just far enough away to not be creepy, but also just close enough to be social. Daniel had made up his mind. He was going to try something he had never tried before, something he had never even contemplated trying before.

Quite simply, for the first time in his life, Daniel was going to try talking to a sad-looking blue whale.

"Hey," Daniel said to the sad-looking blue whale in a tone of voice as if the sad-looking blue whale wasn't currently holding a cinder block tied to its fins.

The sad-looking blue whale turned its head slightly and mushed its eyes into Daniel's. Then it looked back out over the horizon.

"Hey," the sad-looking blue whale replied in a tone of voice that wasn't unfriendly but that was still very indicative of the cinder block tied to its fins.

Although it wasn't easy, Daniel suppressed his shock. He wholeheartedly didn't expect the sad-looking blue whale to talk back, and so the two of them just stood there in silence for a moment, listening to the water lap against the shore like the tongue of some tired, old dog slurping water out of its bowl.

"I'm going to do it," Daniel said after a little while.

Again, the sad-looking blue whale turned its head just enough to look at Daniel.

"Do what?" it asked.

Daniel held up the empty Big Mac container without taking his eyes off the water.

"Bury my heart in this empty Big Mac container beneath the ocean floor," he answered. "I don't know how yet, but I'm going to do it."

"Oh…" the sad-looking blue whale said. And then, in the quiet moment that ensued, it contemplated the tone of voice Daniel had just spoken in, realizing it wasn't sad or defeated like it'd expect someone to say that sentence in, but, rather, a tone of mild relief.

"I never knew you guys talked," Daniel admitted. "I just thought you all… ya know, cried."

Daniel shivered. Even though he'd stopped trembling since his escape from McDonald's, he couldn't shake this feeling of inescapable chilliness as of recent, as if he had cold mayonnaise chugging along through his veins.

"We speak when we're spoken to," the sad-looking blue whale said. And then, after an ashamed moment of silence, "Which isn't very often.

"Or ever, really," it further elaborated.

Daniel nodded to himself.

"Is that why you're going to do it?" he asked.

The sad-looking blue whale shifted uncomfortably, its strained fins trembling from the heaviness of the cinder block it was holding.

"Why don't you just put it down for a minute?" Daniel asked.

Again, the sad-looking blue whale gave him no answer.

"Unless you're scared that as soon as you put it down you won't be able to follow through with it anymore."

The sad-looking blue whale's continued silence was all the answer that Daniel needed. Unlike it, Daniel was ready. He knew he was. His mind was so erratic over thoughts of burying his heart in the empty Big Mac container beneath the ocean floor that he found himself having trouble being able to focus on anything else.

"You seem okay with it," the sad-looking blue whale said. "Resolved, even."

"Yeah. I guess I am," Daniel said, lightly tossing the empty Big Mac container back and forth between his hands.

The wind blew gently. A few seagulls flew past overhead. Standing there next to each other, Daniel and the sad-looking blue whale looked like a weird married couple.

Then Daniel's phone began vibrating.

He took it out of his back pocket to see Laura was calling. Daniel felt his heart twitch and held his breath. He looked over his shoulder to make sure she wasn't there on the beach, that she hadn't seen him somehow, but Laura was still nowhere in sight. Daniel let his phone ring. Eventually, it went to voicemail. He held the phone up to his ear and played the message.

"Daniel, it's me. Please call me back as soon as you get this, okay? It's an emergency and I really need to—"

Daniel hung up. He clutched his phone, then hurled it as far as he could into The Long Island Sound.

"My ex-girlfriend gave me Chlamydia," Daniel said to the sad-looking blue whale. "Well, most likely."

"Oh..." the sad-looking blue whale replied.

"It's too much," Daniel said, trance-like. "The emptiness, it's too goddamn much."

"So you're really going through with it?"

Daniel nodded.

"You're sure?"

Daniel nodded again.

The sad-looking blue whale became sad-lookingly pensive for a moment, almost at war with itself, as if wrestling over some slick and greasy thought that its mind couldn't get its fins on and pin down. Then, just like that, the sad-looking blue whale let go, both mentally and physically. The cinder block thudded into the sand and, suddenly, the sad-looking blue whale appeared at ease.

"I'll help you," it said to Daniel.

For the first time since they began talking, Daniel and the sad-looking blue whale looked each other in the eye.

"I know how to bury your heart in an empty Big Mac container beneath the ocean floor," it said.

Daniel hesitated. He wasn't used to a sad-looking blue whale being kind to him. It almost felt like a trap, but then again, he reasoned, what danger could this sad-looking blue whale put him in that was any more severe than the danger Daniel was already ready and willing to put himself in?

"Are you sure?" Daniel asked.

"Yeah. I'm sure," the sad-looking blue whale replied. "How about tomorrow morning?"

"Okay. Sure," Daniel agreed. "I know a boat we can borrow."

"Good," the sad-looking blue whale said, bending over and beginning to unknot the rope tied around its bottom fins. "I'll bring the Celine Dion."

"The Celine Dion? Why?"

The sad-looking blue whale kicked its bottom fins free from the rope. It stood up straight, looked Daniel dead in the eye, and as if the answer couldn't have been more obvious, it replied, "Because. It's the saddest-looking song there is."

BAYYYBEE!!!

DANIEL WOKE up from his Laura-infused dream with an enormous hard-on. He rolled onto his side and began kissing her neck. Laura moaned softly, sleepily, but responding positively.

Daniel forged on.

He ran his hands up and down her body. Laura was in nothing but panties and her skin was smooth and nice and warm from sleep. Daniel rolled himself on top of her. She welcomed him by spreading her legs and making room in-between her. They kissed and Daniel massaged her breasts with his hands.

"Wait, babe. Wait," Laura said. "I really have to pee first."

Daniel fell back onto his side of the bed. Laura sat up, looked at his erection and licked her lips.

"Mmm…"

Laura leaned in and kissed Daniel's cock once, twice, three times, and then deepthroated it, making herself gag in the process. When Laura removed her mouth from Daniel's cock, her lips were smiling and wet with sexy drool. Then she took Daniel's hand and put it on his cock and moved his hand up and down, prompting him to touch himself.

"Now hold that thought," Laura said in regards to Daniel's erection.

Laura rolled out of bed and ran to the bathroom. She left the door open and Daniel could hear her peeing—a hard, powerful stream, she really did have to go. Suddenly feeling even more turned on, he lay there in bed, naked, stroking himself to the sound of her pissing.

The toilet flushed and Laura walked back into the bedroom. Her panties were gone and Daniel took in her wilderness of pubic hair with great adoration. Instead of immediately climbing on top of him like Daniel thought she would, Laura walked over to her nightstand and checked her phone. Daniel felt a twinge of irritation peck at his nerves. He moved to her side of the bed and kissed Laura's leg but her focus remained on her phone. Daniel playfully reached for her phone with the intent to take it but Laura swatted his hand away.

"Oh my god, stop. You're so annoying. One second," she said.

Daniel rolled back onto his side of the bed. He grabbed the bed sheet, pulled it over him and turned onto his side, facing away from her. Seconds later, he felt Laura getting back into bed. She cuddled up next to him, spooned him and then reached around him and grabbed his cock. Then Daniel heard her make a pouty sound with her mouth.

"Aw. What happened, baybee?" Laura asked, stroking his dick, trying to make it hard again.

Daniel kind of shrugged, feeling mad and upset but also trying his best to suppress his temper so as to avoid another fight, and also unsure if what he was feeling was warranted or not.

Laura kissed Daniel's shoulder. She continued stroking him but he couldn't get hard in her hand. He didn't want to get hard in her hand. Laura sighed, let go of his cock and rolled onto her back.

"We need to feed you better, baby," she said, giving up. "Maybe if you ate healthier this wouldn't have happened. And then maybe if you felt better you wouldn't look so miserable all the time too."

Daniel didn't know what was happening, but he suddenly felt himself rolling out of bed. Feeling as if someone else were controlling him, he searched the bedroom for a t-shirt and shorts. He heard Laura talking to him but her voice was far away and distorted-sounding, like someone talking or screaming in a movie after an explosion.

Daniel dressed himself and floated downstairs. His body alighted in a chair at the kitchen table. He picked up a marker and continued working on his latest drawing he'd started a few nights ago. Sitting there in the early morning hours, doodling, Daniel felt as if he was wearing really big headphones that weren't playing music. Noise canceling headphones that mercifully muted the static-filled soundtrack of daily life. He felt removed from everything and everyone, and blissfully so, leaving this large and exhausted part of him that never wanted it to end, that never wanted to hear another human voice as long as he lived.

"HEY!"

Daniel's head snapped up to see Laura standing across the table from him. She had on a big, baggy t-shirt and her eyes were furious. He had no idea how long she'd been standing there or even how long it'd been since he'd left the bedroom.

"What the actual fuck? You're just gonna sit there and ignore me?"

"I didn't hear you," Daniel answered honestly.

"You didn't hear me?"

Daniel shook his head.

"Are you joking? I can't tell if you're fucking being a smart ass now or not."

"I wasn't joking."

Laura huffed and sat down in the chair across from him. Then she stood back up only to sit back down seconds later, as if she didn't know what to do with her angry body.

"Everyone warned me about this," Laura said softly, as if it were a thought she accidentally let slip out. But Daniel knew it wasn't an accident. She wanted Daniel to hear what she'd just said. She wanted him to feel the cards stacked against him so she could gain some kind of argumentative leverage for the fight they both knew was coming.

"I don't know what's happening," Daniel said. "One second we're about to have sex and the next you're insulting me and now we're fighting?"

"Insult you? When'd I insult you?"

"You said I was always so miserable-looking."

"Babe, that's not an insult. That's a *fact!* You always have this look on your face like someone died."

"That look, Daniel...

"That goddamn look..."

"It was the way you said it. With hate. And like you were sick and tired of it. And of me."

"I *am* sick and tired of it. It's draining, Daniel. And I have had enough of it. You need to go on medication."

"Speaking of medication, are you on yours?"

"Oh fuck you. We're not talking about me. We're talking about you."

"I know. We're always talking about me."

"Yeah, because you don't have your shit together and you need to if you want to be with me."

"I don't know what's happening," Daniel said, frazzled. "But it's like you're always on the attack. You're always criticizing me. It's exhausting, always feeling like you're being picked apart."

"That's what I do, babe. That's the way I am. I see problems and I fix them. I make them better."

"I'm a problem?"

"Oh my god, you're *so* sensitive. See? I can't say anything to you without offending you."

"You're always criticizing me. You do it all the time."

"Because there are things about you I need you to fix if you want to be with me."

"Like what?"

"Like finding a better job. Like paying off your debts. Like the shit we've talked about one-hundred times already."

"I am. I'm doing those things as fast as I can. I'm working on it."

"Yeah. Thanks to me."

"Yes, thanks to you. And even though I'm doing those things it's still not good enough. You're still always up my ass about something, picking me apart. I never pick at you. I never critique you."

"You know what they say in the army—break them down and build them back up."

"Jesus Christ," Daniel said and rolled his eyes.

"What?"

"Nothing. Except you never build me back up. And I don't want my relationship to feel like I'm in the army. Who the fuck would want that? I wanna feel loved, and supported. I want the occasional tough love when need be, but I don't want to be broken down every goddamn day."

"I knew it," Laura said, as if to herself. "I knew you were too sensitive for someone like me."

"No, I just think you're too much of a bitch for any sane, regular person."

"What'd you just call me?" Laura asked, even though, judging from the blue rage in her eyes, she clearly heard what Daniel just called her.

"I said you're a bitch," Daniel replied, calmly, as if hoping the calmness in his voice would help make the word sting even more. "But it's okay though, Laura. Because I'm trying to help you. I'm trying to help you realize you're a bitch so you can go about changing it. I'm breaking you down to build you back up. Just like you do to me."

Laura jumped up so fast that her chair skidded across the floor.

"Fuck you, you asshole! I don't need you! You need me! I make 90K a year! And you? You don't make shit! You're just a burden!

You're a burden on me, your father, on everyone! And I'll be damned if I'm gonna spend the rest of my life having to take care of you because you don't fuckin' know how to take care of yourself!"

Daniel's hand, as if moving of its own volition, lurched out in front of him, grabbed the empty energy drink can on the table leftover from the night before and crushed it. The volume of the aluminum crushing in his grip was surprisingly loud and made Laura jump. It even startled Daniel himself. Daniel held the can in place, squeezing it tighter and tighter, directing all of his anger into the can rather than doing something stupid, like punching a hole in the wall.

"I never once asked you to do anything for me. Or take care of me," Daniel said quietly, suddenly feeling drained, as if he'd transferred almost all of the energy from his body into the crushed energy drink can.

"And yet I have to," Laura said.

Daniel stood up and walked out of Laura's house. It was cold out and the sky still seemed to be mending itself from the storm. Even though the rain had stopped, his car was submerged in water, as was the rest of the street.

Daniel sat on the damp, concrete steps. He didn't have shoes on, and only when he looked at his hand did he realize he was still holding onto the crushed can. Daniel placed the can down beside him. It was completely mangled with a small hole torn in its side. Kind of like his palm, which had a small cut in it, seeping blood. Daniel licked the cut clean and the metallic taste of his own blood repulsed his taste buds.

Daniel and Laura fought a lot, but this time was different. And as he watched his cold breath funnel from his mouth, Daniel felt as if he was watching the last of his will and desire to do this anymore leave his body for good.

The front door opened and Daniel's entire body tensed, a clear fight or flight response as if he were about to be attacked by some random bear coming out of the house, which, at this point, seemed preferable to another encounter with Laura. A sad-looking blue whale stepped onto the front porch, holding Daniel's car keys, wallet and phone. Daniel couldn't believe it, the relief he felt seeing a sad-looking blue whale instead of Laura.

"Ooooh, oooh, ooooooooooooooooooooooooooooooooooooooohhhhhhhhhhhhhh!" the sad-looking blue whale cried, and then held Daniel's car keys in front of his face.

Daniel took the keys from the sad-looking blue whale and stood up. Following some strange and morbidly sentimental impulse, he picked up the crushed energy drink can, his jagged, recyclable souvenir from the end of his relationship, and took it with him as he walked down the front steps and into the water. He could come back for the rest of his things, or Laura could junk them. Daniel didn't give a flying fuck. All of them had flown away right then and there as he waded through the water almost halfway up to his knees.

When Daniel got in his car, four sad-looking blue whales were already waiting for him, one sitting shotgun, three crammed in the backseat, all buckled up and ready to go. To his surprise, he didn't mind them being there. The packed occupancy reminded him of college, when he and his friends would pile into his car for a late-night drive to Wendy's or Taco Bell, making him yearn for that period of his life, when he was still young and naive enough to believe he could turn out to be the person he thought he was capable of becoming.

Daniel stuck the key in the ignition. He hesitated, making the decision then and there to leave it up to fate. If his car started, if the engine hadn't flooded and he could drive home, it was over between him and Laura. If his car was dead, however, he'd take it as a sign to go back inside and talk to her, to try harder from now on, to not give up so easily.

Daniel rested his freezing bare foot on the brake. His hand holding the keys trembled both from nerves and the cold. He closed his eyes, held his breath.

"Oooooh, ooh, ooh, oooooooooh!" a sad-looking blue whale cried from the backseat.

Daniel pressed down on the brake pedal and turned the key.

His car coughed to life.

Unsure whether he was relieved or upset, Daniel shifted into drive and eased his way toward the other side of the road where the water wasn't as deep. Slowly, cautiously, and with little waves spurting up from his tires, he crept down the sheening street.

A large part of Daniel couldn't believe it was this easy, that just getting in a car and simply driving away was all the effort it took to leave behind someone you were in love with, someone you were *still* in love with, someone who you just talked about moving in with. Daniel thought it would be harder somehow, more difficult, like some epic jailbreak involving barbed wire fences, roaming spotlights, blaring sirens and a barrage of gunfire constantly trailing his running footsteps à la James Bond.

But all it took was driving away from Laura's house as if it were nothing more than some gas station he briefly stopped at to top off his tank. Even though he could feel her house getting smaller behind him, which burned like a pinching in his chest, one that only increased the further he drove, Daniel didn't look back. He couldn't help but notice, however, out of the corner of his eye, the sad-looking blue whale beside him undo its seat belt, turn around and stare back, as if doing it for him.

"Ooh, ooh, ooooooh, ooooooh!" the sad-looking blue whale cried.

And even though Daniel didn't know what the sad-looking blue whale was saying exactly, he agreed with it.

He understood the misery mired in its tone.

BEAUTIFUL GARBAGE

WHEN DANIEL WAKES up the next morning, the sky is the color of cold, lumpy, flavorless prison gruel, and the sun, as if exhausted from relentlessly berating Daniel the day before, hides behind a curtain of gray clouds like a diva refusing to go on stage. Something Daniel is more than okay with. Even though he's still chilly from the night before, he's also so sore and red from the sun's lengthy performance yesterday that he has no interest in catching an encore anytime soon.

Daniel's weary eyes eventually refocus on the empty Big Mac container nestled close to his face. The empty Big Mac container is so misshapen, its lid is so sunken-in, the container looks like it suffered a stroke, like even if it wanted to end the silent treatment it's been giving Daniel, it wouldn't be able to.

"Hey…" Daniel says to the empty Big Mac container. "Hey? You there?"

Daniel nudges the empty Big Mac container like a child post-nightmare trying to wake up their parents, but the empty Big Mac container, whether it be ailment or indignation, stays quiet, and correspondingly, as well rightfully so, Daniel feels the strongest sense of isolation he's ever felt in his entire life. His weakened mind mud wrestles with the staggering She-Hulk of a thought that he is, in fact, going to die out here on the ocean, alone, with no one to comfort him and no one to say a final world to. Daniel even finds himself missing the company of the sad-looking blue whale. He wishes he was still alive and floating beside him with that all too familiar look on his face, like he just finished watching *Titanic*. This isn't the end Daniel wanted, the end he imagined. He feels robbed even though, Daniel knows, he was already, ultimately, robbing himself.

Daniel wants to cry but his body is too dehydrated and worn down to produce tears. So he does all he can do. He lies there staring at the empty Big Mac container, occasionally blinking, although, now, no longer simultaneously, first his left eye and then his right a second later—some new kind of nervous tic.

Just as Daniel feels himself drifting off into another round of sleep, or, perhaps, the final round of sleep, a sound, loud and cascadingly abrupt, like a waterfall getting a vasectomy, jerks him awake.

Twenty-some feet away, a submarine bobs on the ocean's surface with water rushing down its sides. Daniel clenches onto the sides of the wooden paneling as it rides up and over the submarine's mild-mannered waves, and once the ocean settles, he feels this lone wriggling sperm of thought penetrate into his barren egg-mind.

I'm saved…

Daniel lifts one arm into the air and waves it back and forth, trying to signal the submarine. He doesn't stop until he sees a hatch pop open that a sad-looking blue whale with a mop climbs out of.

"Hey…" Daniel's parched voice tries to scream.

The sad-looking blue whale with the mop glances down at Daniel. Then, as if Daniel's nothing more than some piece of human driftwood, he begins swabbing the deck. A moment later, another sad-looking blue whale wearing a naval hat climbs out of the hatch and spits a wad of chewing tobacco onto the deck.

"Get that," the sad-looking captain blue whale instructs the sad-looking blue whale with the mop.

The sad-looking blue whale swabbing the deck stops what he's doing, then walks over to the stain and begins mopping it up. The sad-looking captain blue whale puts his fins on his hips and looks out at Daniel stranded on the wooden paneling.

"You the guy we're supposed to pick up?" he asks.

Daniel nods. The sad-looking captain blue whale's eyes dart around

"Where's the whale that called this in?" he asks.

Daniel's mute in thought for a moment, wondering how to answer, before just eventually blurting out, "He didn't make it."

The sad-looking captain blue whale hangs his head a little and nods.

"Froze to death," Daniel adds unnecessarily.

"Whatever. Let's just get going," the sad-looking captain blue whale says. And then, heading back toward the hatch, muttering to himself but still loud enough for Daniel to hear, the captain adds, "We've already wasted enough time out here looking for you…"

"How'd you find me?" Daniel asks as he begins paddling the wooden paneling over toward the submarine.

The sad-looking captain blue whale turns back around and spits again.

"Get that," he tells the sad-looking blue whale with the mop.

The sad-looking blue whale stops and, begrudgingly, cleans up the disrespectful glob of chewing tobacco.

"We followed your signal until we lost it. It got us in the general area. The rest was blind searching until we got a hit on our sonar. You're lucky," the sad-looking captain blue whale says.

The wooden paneling gently plunks into the hull of the blue submarine, and just before Daniel can begin dragging himself up its vivaciously curved hull, a voice, slurred and fish-hooked, speaks out.

One single word.

A warning.

"Don't…" the voice says.

"Don't do it," the empty Big Mac container barely manages to say as its haggard lid flops up and down like a soggy, broken jaw.

"Now?" Daniel says. "You start talking to me again *now*?"

"Uh, are you speaking to me?" the sad-looking captain blue whale asks.

"You can't do this," the empty Big Mac container pleads. "You don't *want* to do this."

"One sec," Daniel says to the sad-looking captain blue whale. Then, to the empty Big Mac container, he whispers, "What are you talking about? Why not?"

"Because you don't want to do this. I know you don't want to. And I know so because you can hear me again. Because you've been ignoring me this whole time but you're not any longer."

"What? I haven't been ignoring you. You've been ignoring me."

"Uh, kid?" the sad-looking captain blue whale interjects.

Daniel holds up a pointer finger in the sad-looking captain blue whale's direction, then directs his attention back at the empty Big Mac container.

"He probably thinks I'm fucking crazy thanks to you," Daniel says in a whisper.

"You are crazy if you go through with this."

"Why? After all I've been through, not only today but the past thirty-one years, why would going through with this be so crazy?"

"Because you don't want to die. You don't hate life, Daniel. You *love* life. You love it so much that it feels like you're wasting it by feeling sad all the time. To know that each and every precious moment you'll never get back is passing by and that you're not actually living it because you're unable to appreciate it. And so the acknowledgement of that waste becomes unbearable. It becomes a pain you feel like you can't suffer through. You've never hated life. You've only hated yourself for not being able to give every moment the respect and appreciation it deserves. That's what I've been trying to tell you this whole time. You just weren't listening. You didn't want to listen."

"Are we doing this or what?" the sad-looking captain blue whale asks.

"I don't know what you want me to do," Daniel says, ignoring the sad-looking captain blue whale. "It's too late."

"It's not too late. You're listening to me again, aren't you? Which means you're having doubts. Emptiness *IS*, Daniel. I know you don't want to admit it, but the sad-looking blue whale was right. Why do you think I'm so okay with life? Because I'm okay with the emptiness inside of me. Because I've learned to accept it, to live with it. Emptiness is the natural state of being, and you're starting to see that."

Daniel feels a catch in his throat.

"It's not enough," he says softly.

"Emptiness is more than enough because it's the only thing that will ever fill you. If you allow it to. If you stop trying to fill yourself with everything else you were made to believe is important. Emptiness is enough because existence is enough."

Daniel stares down at the wooden paneling. A bead of sweat drips off the tip of his nose. He's not sure if it's because he's been out to sea for too long, but this talking fast-food container almost seems to be making sense. The sad-looking blue whales emptied Daniel, which, as a human being, was an unacceptable "feeling" (for a lack of a better word) to have, consequently turning his life into nothing more than some unending struggle to feel, and stay, "full" at all times, to keep the spiritual gas tank inside of him—the old, rusted one with a dime-sized hole in it—with at least a little bit of gas in it at the risk of Daniel breaking down. The problem was the hole was too large, and so

Daniel, desperate for anything that could provide him with enough energy to keep him rolling forward on all four flats, had to constantly keep filling himself up with whatever was around. He had to consume, consume, consume. Not to mention as fast as possible, all just to replace what had recently leaked out of him. And why not relentlessly consume? It was the way of the entire world. But never once did Daniel contemplate doing the exact opposite, of letting the gas tank inside him go empty, as if, maybe, it had a hole in it for a reason, which, now that Daniel's thinking of it, was possibly to leak everything unhealthy he'd been consuming his entire life and prevent him from going anywhere because, really, there was no place to go. There wasn't, and there never had been.

"Are you coming or what?" the sad-looking captain blue whale asks Daniel with his fins on his waist. "Last chance."

The sad-looking captain blue whale spits again.

"Get that," he re-orders to the sad-looking blue whale with the mop.

The sad-looking blue whale with the mop stares at the sad-looking captain blue whale. Then he walks over to the spit stain on the deck, and instead of using the mop to swab up yet another small but unnecessary and disgusting mess, he cracks the handle of the mop over the sad-looking captain blue whale's head and the sad-looking captain blue whale drops to the deck. The sad-looking blue whale with the mop raises the mop up over his head and brings it down on the back of the sad-looking captain blue whale's head. He does this repeatedly, over and over, harder and harder each time, until the mop handle eventually snaps over the captain's head. Then the sad-looking blue whale with the broken mop uses his bottom fins to nudge the sad-looking captain blue whale over the side of the submarine and into the water. The semi-conscious sad-looking captain blue whale hardly makes any effort to stay afloat. He flails a little bit here and there but eventually sinks out of sight. The sad-looking blue whale with the broken mop tosses the mop overboard. He picks up the former captain's naval hat that had fallen off during the assault, puts it on his head and adjusts it until it's perfectly square on his perfectly round head. The new sad-looking captain blue whale puts his fins on his hips and looks down at Daniel.

"So are you coming or what?" the new sad-looking captain blue whale says in a tone alarmingly casual for someone who just committed murder.

Flustered over the unanticipated, random act of violence, Daniel watches bubbles surface from where the former sad-looking captain blue whale sank into the ocean.

"No..." Daniel says. "I'm not coming."

The new sad-looking captain blue whale sighs and looks up into the sun as if officially turning Daniel over to it and its mercy.

"Well, this was a waste of time," he says.

"Could you maybe tow us somewhere?" Daniel asks, as if momentarily spaced out and forgetting he's floating on a random piece of wooden paneling instead of some small, rundown dinghy.

"Us?" the new sad-looking captain blue whale says.

"Yeah. Me and him."

Daniel motions to the empty Big Mac container with his head. The new sad-looking captain blue whale gives Daniel a funny look.

"No," he answers, simply. "It doesn't work like that."

"Oh... Okay."

"We're not The Coast Guard or something."

"It's alright..."

"So, you're sure you want us to leave you out here?" the new sad-looking captain blue whale asks.

Daniel hesitates even though his mind is already made up.

"We're sure," he says.

"Even though you're going to die?"

The empty Big Mac container's lid flops up and down, a nudging nod prompting Daniel to do the right thing.

"Yeah..." Daniel answers.

"Suit yourself," the new sad-looking captain blue whale says with a shrug.

The new sad-looking captain blue whale walks over to the open hatch. Without looking back or saying goodbye, he climbs inside. As soon as the hatch closes, the submarine submerges and disappears out of sight so silently it was as if it'd never been there to begin with.

Daniel and the empty Big Mac container bob up and down on the wooden paneling like a forlorn turd in the world's biggest public toilet. He looks up at the sun trying to rip its heated talons through the billowing grayness above.

"This is going to suck," Daniel says.

A very fitting morgue-like silence has fallen over the ocean, and the sun, still veiled by gray clouds, looks, and shines, like an enormous tumor that only listens to Morrissey.

With his brow anxiously furrowed, and with the wrinkles in his forehead lined with sweat, Daniel clears his throat as if he's going to speak but doesn't say a word. His head has become an over-heated aquarium and his thoughts are the dead fish floating at its surface. Daniel can't make sense of anything right now, let alone the choice he just made, the very same one that sealed his fate of being abraded, inside and out, by three-hundred million-plus watts of authentic Atlantic sunshine.

"What'd I just do?" Daniel asks the empty Big Mac container in a voice dryer than the Roadrunner's talons. "However the sad-looking blue whales were going to do it, however they were going to extract my heart from my chest, was going to be a million times faster and less painful than being grilled by the sun."

"Yes, suffering is pain, but suffering is also grace," the empty Big Mac container says.

"Oh my god. Stop it."

"Stop what?"

"You're a fucking burger container. Stop talking like some card-boarded guru or some shit."

"Daniel..."

"And stop contradicting yourself."

"Life contradicts itself, Daniel. Remember? The only constant is change. If something scares you then you should probably be doing it. The more you learn the more you realize how little you actually know—and so on and so on... Suffering is grace. And suffering *is* grace because it brings you wisdom. You will always learn so much more from pain than you ever will from happiness. You shouldn't seek suffering out, but you need to allow it to happen naturally. You need to work with it and transform it if you ever wish to grow."

Daniel bangs his head into the wooden paneling.

"I'm sorry... I know you're going through a lot right now, and that you don't want to hear this, so I'll stop, but it is the truth."

Daniel turns his head away from the empty Big Mac container. As he holds back tears, his brain quickly compiles an enormous collage of all the sad-looking blue whales he's encountered since childhood. But as his mental eye floats back to take in and stare at the whole blue picture in all of its maudlin, seismic glory, Daniel can't pinpoint one single thing he's learned from the entirety of it, as if instead of learning and growing over the years he remained the same fledgling person, the same oafish lump, the same incapable man-child. Everything Laura ever said about him, whether it'd been spoken with malice or loving honesty, was true.

Daniel presses his hand against his pocket to feel Laura's picture tucked inside.

"It wasn't all bad," he says after a moment of muddled reflection.

"What wasn't?" the empty Big Mac container asks.

"My time with her. I know it wasn't supposed to last, and I know a lot of it was difficult, but it wasn't all bad. In fact, there was a lot of good. And when it was good, and when we weren't trying to hurt each other, I'd even say I—"

Daniel's tired eyes widen a little as he stops mid-sentence. Something inside his brain clicks, and deep in his gut something glimmers, something microscopic but still brilliant and warm, a flicker of radiance, a lingering lightning bug of infinite wattage. He reaches into his pocket, pulls out the wrinkled, ruined picture of Laura and stares at it differently than he ever has.

Daniel slowly and carefully rolls onto his back. Still holding Laura's picture, he folds his hands over his stomach and allows his thoughts to churn, beginning to think that the empty Big Mac container and the sad-looking blue whale were both wrong, that there's one thing—and one thing only—that can fill you at all times. One thing that can possibly be strong enough to propel you through shit day after shit day.

Laura's greasy hair smudging your glasses…

Laura sneaking vegetables into your Sunday morning omelet…

Laura screaming BAYBEEEEE!

Holding hands and walking down the beach with Laura…

Dollar store shopping with Laura…

Doing cocaine with Laura…

Dancing while high on cocaine with Laura…

Drinking champagne and eating chocolate while bathing with Laura…

These memories that once hurt Daniel to reflect upon suddenly have the opposite effect on him. Because of what little time he most likely has left, Daniel's forced to appreciate them.

Appreciation... Daniel's brain echoes.

It's always been there and readily available, he realizes. An untapped well of fulfillment, a miraculous virgin giving you her virginity every time. Although, in the past, whenever Daniel did feel an ounce of appreciation, it was usually accidental, a fleeting moment of gratitude that popped into his head only when he saw something upsetting or tragic, like a homeless person living on the street, asleep on a large, non-floating storm cloud of puffed out black garbage bags. But in that brief moment, however—unfortunately inspired by the hardship of a homeless person—Daniel felt okay, or even good. Although, Daniel realizes further, he always felt good when appreciating something. Whether it was a new book arriving in the mail or pizza delivery or returning to an air-conditioned room after a heated walk out on the summer streets, appreciation caused Daniel not to take life for granted. It made him view both things and moments as gifts, as little stocking stuffers that somehow managed to pack in enormous wads of peace. Even as he floats all alone in the middle of the ocean on some decorative hunk of wood like a piece of beautiful garbage, Daniel can finally begin to relate to the world without a sense of entitlement. He'd always known he wasn't owed or guaranteed a tomorrow, but now, staving off death, he finally understands that wholly and fully, and he only wishes it hadn't taken something as drastic as wanting to bury his heart in an empty Big Mac container beneath the ocean floor for him to see the glow of appreciative lighting.

Daniel crumples Laura's photo and tosses it over his shoulder into the ocean.

"So, what do we do now?" Daniel asks.

Daniel glances at the empty Big Mac container, but whether it doesn't know the answer to Daniel's question or whether it's giving him the silent treatment again, the former greasy, cardboard-heart coffin doesn't respond.

Daniel looks up at the sky. He can't say whether his deliriously sun-drunken eyes are playing tricks on him or not, but the clouds appear to be moving again. Especially one cloud in particular. One that looks like a sad-looking blue whale who's just finished watching *Titanic*.

But unlike all other sad-looking blue whales Daniel's ever known, this sad-looking blue whale, uncertainly wobbling across the sky like a toddler taking its first steps, doesn't find *Titanic* to be the saddest movie of all time. He even finds parts of it beautiful, uplifting.

Daniel takes a deep breath and closes his eyes. The sun, despite Daniel's abusive relationship with it as of late, feels good on his skin.

It reminds him he's still alive.

Somewhere, off in the distance, a lonely seagull makes a lonely sound.

ACKNOWLEDGMENTS

Homeless is greatly indebted to Lexi, Dad, Leza, Christoph, Alan ten-Hoeve, his ex-girlfriend, Ralph, Sam Pink (for the accidental alley-oop), the lovely crew members from the McDonald's at 1021 W Main Street, Bridgeport, CT, Hard Mtn Dew, Green Day, and all the sad-looking blue whales.

ABOUT THE AUTHOR

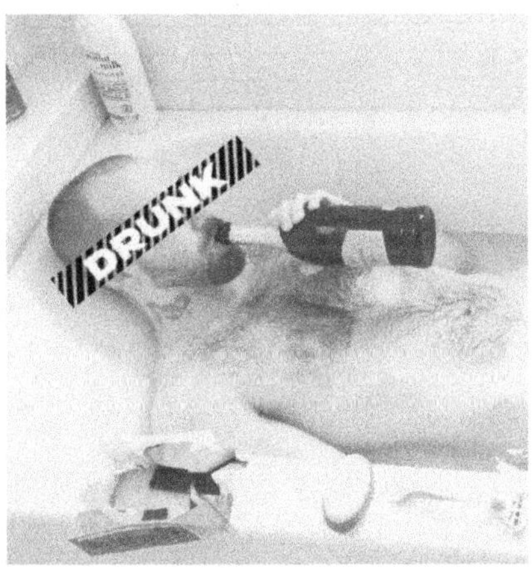

Homeless is the author of four other books, including the novel, *This Hasn't Been a Very Magical Journey So Far* and *Shithead Laureate*. He's been published by Hobart, House of Vlad and ExPat Press. He putters around NYC wondering whatever happened to predictability, the milkman, the paperboy, evening TV.

ALSO BY CLASH BOOKS

SHITHEAD LAUREATE

Homeless

THE KING OF VIDEO POKER

Paolo Iacovelli

BAD FOUNDATIONS

Brian Allen Carr

EARTH ANGEL

Madeline Cash

GAG REFLEX

Elle Nash

HOW TO GET ALONG WITHOUT ME

Kate Axelrod

ALL OUR TOMORROWS

Amy DeBellis

AMERICAN THIGHS

Elizabeth Ellen

VAGUE PREDICTIONS & PROPHECIES

Daisuke Shen

DARRYL

Jackie Ess

I MADE AN ACCIDENT

Kevin Sampsell

THE RACHEL CONDITION

Nicholas Rombes

WE PUT THE LIT IN LITERARY

CLASHBOOKS.COM

FOLLOW US

FB

X

IG

@clashbooks

EMAIL

clashmediabooks@gmail.com

Printed in the USA
CPSIA information can be obtained
at www.ICGtesting.com
JSHW021902171024
71843JS00002B/2